THE LAST OF THE WINE

Mary Renault was educated at Clifton High School, Bristol and St Hugh's College, Oxford. Having completed nursing training in 1937, she then wrote her first novel *Promise of Love*. Her next three novels were written during off-duty time while serving in the war. In 1948 she went to live in South Africa but travelled widely. It was her trip to Greece and her visits to Corinth, Samos, Crete, Delos, Aegina and other islands, as well as to Athens, Sounion and Marathon, that resulted in her brilliant historical reconstructions of Ancient Greece. Mary Renault died in 1983.

BOOKS BY MARY RENAULT

FICTION

The Alexander Trilogy
Fire from Heaven
The Persian Boy
Funeral Games

The Bull from the Sea
The King Must Die
The Praise Singer
The Last of the Wine
Promise of Love
Kind Are Her Answers
The Middle Mist
Return to Night
North Face
The Charioteer
The Mask of Apollo
The Lion in the Gateway

NONFICTION

The Nature of Alexander

THE LAST OF THE WINE

Mary Renault

arrow books

Published by Arrow Books in 2004

1 3 5 7 9 10 8 6 4 2

Copyright © Mary Renault, 1995

Mary Renault has asserted her right under the Copyright, Designs and Patents Act, 1988 to
be identified as the author of this work

First published in the United Kingdom in 1956 by Longmans, Green and Co.
First paperback edition published in 1967 by New English Library

Arrow Books
The Random House Group Limited
20 Vauxhall Bridge Road, London, SW1V 2SA

Random House Australia (Pty) Limited
20 Alfred Street, Milsons Point, Sydney,
New South Wales 2061, Australia

Random House New Zealand Limited
18 Poland Road, Glenfield
Auckland 10, New Zealand

Random House (Pty) Limited
Endulini, 5a Jubilee Road,
Parktown 2193, South Africa

Random House Group Limited Reg. No. 954009

www.randomhouse.co.uk

A CIP catalogue record for this book
is available from the British Library

Papers used by Random House
are natural, recyclable products made from wood grown in
sustainable forests. The manufacturing processes conform to
the environmental regulations of the country of origin

ISBN 0 09 946355 5

Typeset by Palimpsest Book Production Limited,
Polmont, Stirlingshire
Printed and bound by
Cox & Wyman Ltd, Reading, Berkshire

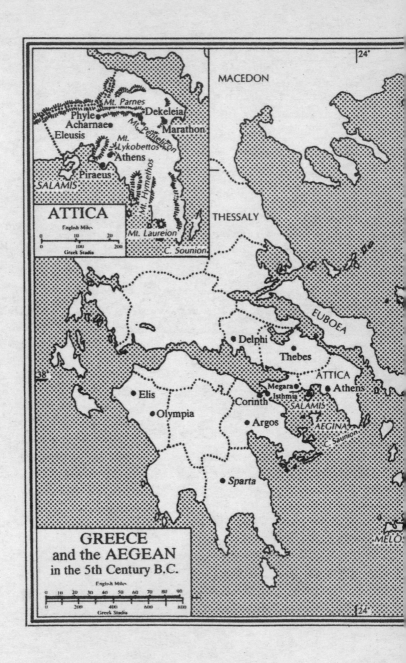

MACEDON

Mt. Parnes
Phyle
Acharnae
Eleusis
Dekeleia
Mt. Pentelikon
Marathon
Mt. Lykobettos
Athens
Piraeus
SALAMIS
Mt. Hymettos

ATTICA

English Miles
0   10   20
0   100   200
Greek Stadia

Mt. Laureion
C. Sounion

THESSALY

EUBOEA

Delphi
Thebes
ATTICA
Megara
Isthmia
Athens
Corinth
SALAMIS
Elis
AEGINA
Olympia
Argos
C. Sounion

Sparta

GREECE
and the AEGEAN
in the 5th Century B.C.

English Miles
0   10   20   30   40   50   60   70   80   90
0   200   400   600   800
Greek Stadia

MELO

THRACE

Selymbria

Byzanium

PROPONTIS

Aegospomi
(Goat's Creek)

Lampaacus

Sestos

LESBOS

Arginsae
(The White Isles)

CHIOS

Sardis

Notium
(Cape Rain)

SAMOS

Ephesus

Miletus

DELOS

ROS

RHODES

1

When I was a young boy, if I was sick or in trouble, or had been beaten at school, I used to remember that on the day I was born my father had wanted to kill me.

You will say there is nothing out of the way in this. Yet I daresay it is less common than you might suppose; for as a rule, when a father decides to expose an infant, it is done and there the matter ends. And it is seldom a man can say, either of the Spartans or the plague, that he owes them life instead of death.

It was at the beginning of the Great War, when the Spartans were in Attica, burning the farms. There was a notion in those days that no other army could meet them on land and live; so we were holding only the City, and Piraeus, and the Long Walls between. This was the advice of Perikles. It is true that when I was born he was still alive, though already sick; which is no reason for foolish youths to ask me, as one did lately, whether I remember him.

The country people, whose farms were being burned, poured into the City, and lived like beasts wherever they could put up a few boards, or a roof of hide. They were even sleeping and cooking in the shrines, and in the colonnades of the wrestling schools. The Long Walls were lined with stinking huts all the way to the harbour. Somewhere thereabouts the plague began, and spread like fire in old heather. Some said the Spartans had called on Far-Shooting Apollo, some that they had contrived to poison the springs. Some of the women, I believe, blamed the country people for bringing in a curse; as if anyone could reasonably suppose that the gods would punish a state for treating its own citizens justly. But women, being ignorant of philosophy and logic, and fearing dream-diviners more than immortal Zeus, will always suppose that whatever causes them trouble must be wicked.

The plague thinned my family as it did every other. My mother's father, Damiskos, the Olympic runner, was buried with his old trophies and his olive crown. My father was among those who got the disease and survived; it left him for some time with a bloody flux, too sick for war; and when I was born he had only just recovered his strength.

On the day of my birth, my father's younger brother, Alexias, died in his twenty-fourth year. He, hearing that a youth called Philon, with whom he was in love, had been taken sick, went at once to him; meeting, I have been told, not only the slaves but the boy's own sister, running the other way. His father and mother had already perished; Alexias found the lad alone, lying in the basin of the courtyard fountain, where he had crawled to cool his fever. He had not called out to anyone to fetch his friend, not wishing to endanger him; but some passers-by, who had not cared to go very near, reported that they had seen Alexias carrying him indoors.

This reached my father after some time, while my mother was in labour with me. He sent over a reliable servant who had had the plague already; who, however, found both the young men dead. From the way they were lying, it seems that in the hour of Philon's death, Alexias had felt himself sicken; and, knowing the end, had taken hemlock, so that they should make the journey together. The cup was standing on the floor beside him; he had tipped out the dregs, and written PHILON with his finger, as one does after supper in the last of the wine.

Getting this news at night, my father set out with torches to fetch the bodies, so that he could mix their ashes in one urn, and have a fit memorial made. They were gone, having been thrown already on a common pyre in the street; but later, my grandfather had a stone set up for Alexias in the Street of Tombs, with a relief showing the friends clasping hands in farewell, and a cup beside them on a pedestal. Every year at the Feast of Families, we sacrificed for Alexias at the household altar, and the story is one of the first that I remember. My father used to say that all over the City, those who died in the plague were the beautiful and the good.

Alexias having died before the time of his marriage, my father now decided to name after him the child that was being born, if it should be a boy. My elder brother Philokles, who was two years old, had been a particularly fine strong child at his birth: but I, when held up by the midwife, was seen to be small, wizened and ugly; my mother having brought me forth nearly a month too soon, either through a weakness of her body or the foreknowledge of a god. My father decided at once that it would be unworthy of Alexias to name me after him; that I was the child of an unlucky time, marked with the gods' anger, and that it would be better not to rear me.

As it happened, however, I had been born while he was out searching for the bodies; and the midwife had handed me over to my mother to nurse. This annoyed my father; for she had taken a fancy to me after this, as women will, and being rather sick and feverish begged for my life with tears. He was still reasoning with her – for he was reluctant to snatch me from her by force – when the herald blew for the horsemen, because the Spartans had been sighted making for the City.

We were a fairly rich family in those days; my father kept two or three horses; he had therefore to arm, and muster with his squadron. He took leave of my mother, not withdrawing his orders; but, whether through haste or pity, he charged no one with carrying them out. There is never much rivalry for such work; so there the matter rested till some days later, when the Spartans withdrew and my father rode home.

He found the household in distraction. My brother Philokles was dead, and my mother breathing her last. From the first she had ordered me to be kept away from her; I had been left with a wet-nurse found by one of the slaves.

Returning with shorn hair from the funeral, he had me brought to him, and, finding the wet-nurse a decent woman, left me in her charge. He had been, I believe, fond of my mother; I daresay too he called to mind the uncertainty of life, and thought it less disgraceful to leave even me behind him, than to perish without offspring as if he had never been. In the end, finding I put on flesh and seemed stronger and better-looking, he named me Alexias, as he had first meant to do.

2

Our house stood in the Inner Kerameikos, not far from the Dipylon Gate. The courtyard had a little colonnade of painted columns, a fig-tree and a vine. At the back were the stables, where my father kept his two horses and a mule; it was easy to climb on the stable roof, and thence to the roof of the house.

The roof had a border of acanthus tiles, and was not very steep. If one straddled the ridge, one could see right over the City wall, past the gate-towers of the Dipylon to the Sacred Way, where it curves towards Eleusis between its gardens and its tombs. In summer-time, I could pick out the funeral stele of my uncle Alexias and his friend, by a white oleander that grew there. Then I would turn south, to where the High City stands like a great stone altar against the sky, and search between the winged roofs of the temples for the point of gold, where tall Athene of the Vanguard lifts her spear to the ships at sea.

But I liked best to look north at the range of Parnes, snow-toppped, or scorched brown in summer, or grey and green in spring, and watch for the Spartans coming over. Until I was six, they came nearly every year. They came over the pass at Dekeleia, and as a rule some horseman brought word of their coming; but sometimes the first thing we knew in the City was the smoke on the hills, where they were burning a farm.

Our own place is in the foothills, beyond Acharnai. Our family has been there, as they say, since the grasshoppers came. The slope above the valley is terraced for vines, but the best crop is the olives, and the barley from the olive-fields. There was one grove nearly as old, I think, as the earth itself. The trunks were as thick as three men's bodies, and all knotted and gnarled. Athene herself was reputed to have planted them, when she gave the olive as a gift to the land. Two or three of them are standing still. We sacrificed there at every harvest-time; that is, when there was a harvest.

I used to be sent to the farm early each spring, to get the country air, and fetched back when it was time for the Spartans to come. But once, when I was four or five, they came early, and we had a great scramble to get away. I remember sitting in the cart, with the women slaves and the household gear, my father riding beside us and the slave pricking the oxen on; the cart-wheels jolting, and all of us coughing with the smoke of the burning fields. Everything was burned that year, all but the house walls, and the sacred olive grove, which they piously spared.

Being too young to understand serious things, I used to look forward, when they had gone, to seeing what they had been up to. One year a troop of them had been quartered in the farmhouse; and those who could write had inscribed the names of their friends, with various tributes to their beauty and virtue, all over the walls. I recall my father rubbing angrily at the charcoal and saying, 'Get this ignorant scrawl whited over. The boy will never learn to spell, or to make his letters properly, with this in front of him.' One of the Spartans had left his comb behind. I thought it a treasure; but my father said in disgust that it was filthy, and threw it away.

For my own part, I don't think I knew what trouble meant till I was turned six. My grandmother, who had taken charge of me whenever my father was at war, died then. My grandfather Philokles (a tall old man with a beautiful beard, always just combed, and white almost to blueness, in whose image I see the god Poseidon to this day) was growing infirm and could not do with me; so my father engaged a nurse, a free woman from Rhodes.

She was slim and swarthy, with a strain of Egypt in her. Presently I grew to know, without quite knowing what it meant, that she was my father's concubine. Not that he ever failed in propriety before me; but sometimes I used to hear things said by the slaves, who had their own reasons to hate her.

If I had been a little older, I might have consoled myself, when her hand lay heavy on me, with the thought that my father would soon be weary of her. She had no such graces as he could have found in a hetaira of very moderate accomplishment, and in those days he could afford the best. But to me she seemed as lasting a part of my house as the porch or the well. She herself began to guess, I think, that when I was old enough to go to school with a pedagogue he would take the occasion to be rid of her; so any progress I made was a signal for her anger.

Seeking some company, I had got a stray kitten from a slave; which presently finding, she wrung its neck before me. While trying to get it from her, I bit her arm; and it was then she told me, after her own fashion, the tale of my birth, which she had heard from the slaves. So, when she beat me, I never thought of telling my father, or asking his help. While he, seeing me grow daily more sly and sullen in my ways, paler and duller in the face, must I daresay have wondered, sometimes, if first thoughts would not have been best.

In the evenings, when he came in dressed for supper, I used to look at him and wonder how it felt to be beautiful. He was more than six feet tall, grey-eyed, brown-skinned, and golden-haired; made like those big Apollos Pheidias' workshop used to turn out, in the days before the statuaries began carving their Apollos soft. As for me, I was one of those who grow late, and still small for my age; it was clear already that I should favour the men of my mother's family, who are dark-haired, with blue eyes, and who tend to be runners and jumpers, rather than wrestlers and pankratiasts. The Rhodian had left me in no doubt that I was the runt of a good kennel; and no one else had told me otherwise.

It pleased me, however, to see him in his best blue mantle with the gold border, his brown chest and left shoulder bare, bathed and combed and rubbed down with sweet oil, his hair dressed into a garland and his beard short-pointed. It meant a supper-party; going by myself unwashed to bed while the Rhodian was busy in the kitchen. I would lie listening to the flutes and laughter, to the ring of the bronze bowl when they played kottabos, the rise and fall of voices in talk, or someone singing to the lyre. Sometimes, if a dancer or a juggler had been hired, I used to climb the roof, and look in across the courtyard.

Once he gave a party to which the god Hermes came. So at least

I first believed; not only because the young man seemed too tall and beautiful not to be a god, and had the air of one accustomed to worship, but because he was so exactly like a Herm outside one of the rich new houses, that his head looked to have been the model, as in fact it had. I was only shaken from my awe when he walked out and made water in the courtyard, which made me almost sure he was a man. Then someone inside called out, 'Alkibiades! Where are you?' and he went back into the supper-room.

My father, having at this time concerns of his own, seldom brought me into remembrance. But sometimes he would call to mind that he had a son, and set himself to do his duty by me. There was, for example, the day when our steward caught me stealing corn to throw to the doves, and took it away from me, for corn was scarce that year. With the kind of manners I had learned from my nurse, I stamped my foot at him, and said he had no right to forbid me, being only a slave. At this my father, who had overheard, stepped into the room. He sent out the man with a civil word, and called me to him. 'Alexias,' he said, 'my shield is over there in the corner. Pick it up, and bring it to me.'

I went over to where the shield was leaning on the wall; and, getting hold of it by the rim, began to roll it along, finding it too heavy for me to lift. 'That is not the way,' he said. 'Put your arm through the bands, and carry it as I do.'

I put my arm through one of the bands, and managed to stand it upright, but I could not lift it; it was nearly as tall as I. He said, 'Surely you can hold it up? Do you know that when I fight on foot I have not only that to carry, but a spear too?' – 'But,' I said, 'Father, I am not a man.'

'Put it back in the corner, then,' he said, 'and come here.' I obeyed him.

'And now,' he said, 'pay attention to me. When you are man enough to carry a shield, you will learn how it happens that men are sold into slavery, and their children born in it. Till then, it is enough for you to know that Amasis and the rest are slaves, not through any merit of yours, but by the destiny of heaven. You will refrain from hubris, which the gods hate, and behave yourself like a gentleman. And if you forget this, I myself will beat you.'

Such signs of interest in my father were hateful to the Rhodian; she began to see both buck and kid slipping through her broken net. As soon as she could she found occasion to turn a small fault of mine into a great one, and made me look a liar when I denied it. But she over-reached herself a little. My father said it was high time I went to school, and sent me forthwith.

He went on campaign soon after, so she did not go for a couple of months. I have lived in hard days and taken my share of them, but those are nearly the worst that I remember. How I should have borne it, I do not know, if it had not been for a friend I made at school, at a time when I had grown silent and furtive, and had no friends at all.

I arrived one morning to find the music-class laughing and nudging each other, and giving the master a new name, the Old Man's Teacher. And, in fact, there in the classroom on one of the benches sat a man who, being about forty-five with a grizzled beard, looked certainly rather old to be studying the first thing children learn. I could see at once that I, who was always alone, was the one who would be made a fool of by having to share his bench; so I pretended not to mind, and sat there of my own accord. He nodded to me, and I stared at him in wonder. At first, this was simply because he was the ugliest man I had seen; and then it was because I thought I recognised him, for he was the image of the Silenos painted on the big wine-mixer at home, with his snub nose, wide thick mouth, bulging eyes, strong shoulders and big head. He had seemed friendly, so sidling up the bench to him, I asked softly if Silenos was his name. He turned to answer me; and I felt a kind of shock, as if a bright light had been shone upon my heart; for he did not look as most people do at children, half thinking of something else. After telling me what his name was, he asked me how he ought to tune his lyre.

I was pleased to show off my little knowledge; and, feeling already at home with him, asked why an old man like him wanted to come to school. He replied, not at all put out, that it was much more disgraceful for an old man not to learn what could make him better, than for boys, since he had had time to know the worth of it; 'and besides,' he said, 'a god came to me lately in a dream, and told me to make music. But whether with the hands or in the soul, he did not say; so you can see I ought not to neglect either.' I wanted to hear more of his dream, and tell him one of my own; but he said, 'The master is coming.'

I was so curious that next day, instead of creeping to school, I ran, so as to be early and talk with him. He was only just in time for the lesson; but he must have noticed me looking out for him, and next day came a little earlier. I was at an age when children are full of questions; at home my father had seldom time to answer them, the Rhodian would not and the slaves could not. I brought them all to my neighbour at the music-class, and he never failed to give me answers that made sense, so that some of the other boys, who had mocked our friendship, began craning to listen. Sometimes, when I asked what makes the sun warm, or why the stars do not fall down on the earth, he would say he did not know, and that no one knew except the gods. But if anything frightened one, he had always a good reason not to be afraid.

One day I noticed a bird's nest in a tall tree near the school. When my friend arrived, I told him I was going to climb up after lessons, to see if there were any eggs. I did not think he was listening, for that morning he had seemed occupied with his thoughts while I ran on; when suddenly he stared at me intently, so that I was startled, and said, 'No, child; I forbid you to do it.' – 'Why?' I asked; for with him it came naturally to ask a reason. He told me that since he was a child as young as I, whenever he or his friends were about to do what would come to no good, something had made a sign to him, and had never told him wrong. And again he forbade me. I was overawed, feeling for the first time the force of his nature, and never dreamed of disobeying him. Not long afterwards, the branch with the nest on it fell to the ground, being rotten all through.

Though he never played as well as I did, his fingers not being so supple, he learned his notes more quickly, and the master had no more to teach him. I missed him greatly when he left. It may be that I had thought, 'Here is a father who would not think me a disgrace to him (for he is ugly himself) but would love me, and would not want to throw me away on the mountain.' I do not know. Whoever came to Sokrates, no matter by what absurd chance, felt afterwards that he had been directed by a god.

Not long after this my father married his second wife, Arete, the daughter of Archagoras.

3

When I and the other boys of my age became ephebes, it was sometimes said of us that we lacked respect for age and custom, took nothing on trust, and set up as judges of things on our own account. A man can only speak for himself. My recollection is that I believed most grown men to be wise, until a day when I was fifteen years old.

My father was expecting his club to supper, and needed crowns for the guests. I had told him the day before that I should get the best flowers by going early, before school. He laughed, knowing that I wanted an excuse to run about without my tutor; but he gave me leave, knowing too that at such an hour I should not meet many temptations. It is well known that he in his young day was called Myron the Beautiful, just as one might say, Myron son of Philokles. But he thought, like all other fathers, that I was younger and sillier than himself at the same age.

He was right that day in supposing that all I wanted was to look at the fleet assembling for the war. 'The war' we boys called it, as if there had not been war from our birth; for this was a new venture of the City, and this great armament really looked to us like war. In the palaestra, all round the edges of the wrestling-ground, you could see men drawing little maps for each other in the dust: of Sicily which the army was going to conquer, the friendly and the Dorian cities, and the great harbour of Syracuse.

My father was not going, which surprised me. Not that the horsemen had been called up; but many of the knights, not to be left behind, had volunteered as hoplites. It was true that he was not long back from campaign, having sailed with Philokrates to the island of Melos, which had refused us tribute. The Athenians had triumphed, and the Melians been utterly put down. I had waited for the story, to say to the boys at school, 'My father says so, who was there.' But he grew short-tempered when I questioned him.

Now, rising at the second cock, while the stars were still bright, I took care not to wake the household, which I knew would anger him, for we had been disturbed in the night. The dogs had made a great noise, and we had got up to make sure of the bolts and bars; but after all no one had tried to break in.

I waked the porter to lock up after me, and went out. In my youth I always went barefoot, as every runner ought. Coming from the forecourt into the street, I trod on something sharp; but my soles being as tough as oxhide, it drew no blood, and I did not pause to look at it. That year I had entered for the boys' long-race at the Panathenaic Games; so as I ran I kept my mind on my trainer's precepts. My steps felt light on the thin dust of the street, after the heavy sand of the practice track.

Early as it was, in the Street of the Armourers the lamps were burning, and the smoke was red in the mouths of the stumpy chimneys beside the shops. All along the way the hammers were clattering; the big ones flattening the plates, the lesser closing the rivets, and the little ones tapping at the gold ornaments which had been ordered by those who liked them. My father was against them; he said they often held a spear-point instead of glancing it off. I should have liked to go in and watch the work, but had only just time to climb to the High City and look for the ships.

I had never been there quite so early. From below, the walls looked huge, like black cliffs, with the great cyclops stones at the bottom still stained with the fires of the Medes. I passed the watchtower and the bastion, and climbed the steps to the Porch. Being for the first time alone there, I felt awed by its height and breadth, and the great spaces lost in darkness; I seemed really to be treading the threshold of the gods. The night was thinning, like a dark wine when clear water is mixed in; I could just see the colours painted under the roof, changed and deepened in the dust before dawn.

So I came into the open, beside the Altar of Health, and saw the wings and tripods upon the temple roofs, looking black against a sky like grey pearl. Here and there a little smoke was rising, where someone was offering or a priest taking the omens; but no one was in sight. High above me, great Athene of the Vanguard looked out from her triple-crested helm. There was a smell of frankincense on the air, and a smell of dew. I walked to the south wall and looked towards the sea.

The distance was dim as mist; yet I saw the ships, for all their lights were burning. Those at moorings had lit them for the watchmen, and those at anchor for safety, so many they were. You might have thought that Poseidon had won his old contest with Athene, and set the City upon the sea. I began to count them: those clustered about Piraeus, those on the curved shore of Phaleron, those out at anchor in the bay; but I soon lost count.

I had never sailed further than to Delos, where I had gone with a boys' chorus to dance for Apollo. I felt full of envy for the men of the Army, going out to drain the cup of glory and leave none for me. So must my great-grandfather have seen the fleet gather at Salamis, where the bronze beak of his trireme swooped like Zeus' eagle on the ships of the long-haired Medes.

There was a change in the sky; I turned and saw dawn smoulder behind Hymettos. The lights went out one after another, and the ships themselves appeared, sitting the water like grey birds. When the spearhead of Athene flashed a spark of fire, I knew I must go or be late for school. The painting of the statues and friezes was brightening, and there was warmth in the marble. It was as if order had that moment been sung up out of chaos and night. I felt my heart lift within me. Seeing the ships so thick on the waters, I had said to myself that these had made us what we were, the leaders of all the Hellenes. Now I paused, and looking about me, thought, 'No, not so; but we alone have given godlike things to the gods.'

Now dawn unfolded a wing of flame, but Helios was still beneath the sea. All things looked light and incorporeal and the world was still. I thought I would pray before going, but did not know which altar to turn to; for the gods seemed everywhere, all saying the same word to me, as if they had been not twelve but one. I felt I had seen a mystery, yet knew not what. I was happy. Wishing to praise all gods alike, I stood where I was and lifted my hands to the sky.

Going down the steps I came to myself and knew I should be

late. I ran for all I was worth to the market, and spending my father's money quickly, bought violets made up already into garlands, and some stephanotis; the woman gave me a rush basket for nothing. At another stall they had dark-blue hyacinths, for which I had kept something by. A man who was there choosing myrtle smiled at me and said, 'You should have bought those first. Hyakinthos.' But I raised my eyebrows and went on without speaking.

The market was crowded and people were full of talk. I am as glad as anyone to hear of something new; but I could see the man with the myrtle beginning to follow me, and besides, I did not want my father's temper to give out. So I hurried as fast as I could without breaking the flowers, and thus concerned, scarcely looked right or left till I reached home.

I had bought a myrtle-wreath for our guardian Herm, to dress him for the feast. He was a very old Herm, who had stood at the gate even before the invasion of the Medes; he had the face of the oldest images, with a closed smiling mouth like a new moon, a traveller's hat on his head, and a beard. Yet having known him from my infancy I had a fondness for him, and thought no worse of him for his rustic looks. I walked, then, towards him, searching in my basket for the garland, and looked up with it in my hand. The clear sun of morning shone full upon him. I started back in fear, and made the sign against evil.

Someone had come in the night and hammered his face to pieces. His beard and his nose were gone, and the brim of his hat, and the phallus on the column; half his mouth was knocked away, so that he looked eaten with leprosy. Only his blue painted eyes were left, staring out fiercely as if they wanted to speak. Chips were scattered everywhere; it must have been on one of them that, as I set out in the dark, I had hurt my foot.

In my first horror I thought the god himself must have done it, to curse our house for some frightful sin. But it seemed to me that a god would have split the image in two with one stroke of thunder; this was the work of men doing as much as they could. Then I remembered the dogs barking in the night.

I found my father dressed, going over some accounts-rolls. He began to rebuke me, for the sun was up; but when he heard my news he ran outside. First he made the evil-eye sign; then he was silent some time. At last he said, 'The house will have to be purified. A madman must have done it.'

Just then we heard voices approaching. Our neighbour Phalinos, with his steward and two or three passers-by, all speaking at once, poured out the news that every Herm in the street had been profaned and in other streets too.

When the clamour lessened, my father said, 'This must be a conspiracy against the City through her gods. The enemy is behind it' – 'Which enemy?' said Phalinos. 'You mean that impiety has conspired with strong wine. What man but one defies the law from insolence, and the gods for sport? But this is beyond everything, on the eve of war. The gods send that only the guilty suffer.' – 'I can guess whom you mean,' my father said. 'But you will find you are mistaken. We have seen wine make him extravagant, but not foolish; I have faith in the oracles of Dionysos.' – 'That may be your opinion.' Phalinos never liked even the civillest disagreement. 'We know that everything is forgiven to Alkibiades by those who have enjoyed his good graces, briefly though it might be.' I don't know what my father eventually replied to this; for he noticed me standing by, and, turning angrily, asked if I meant to let the whole day pass while I loitered in the streets.

I got myself breakfast, called my tutor, and set off for school. You can imagine we had enough to talk about on the way. He was a Lydian called Midas, who could read and write; an expensive slave to use for a pedagogue, but my father did not hold with putting children in the charge of slaves who are good for nothing else. Midas had been saving some time to buy himself out, by copying speeches for the courts in his spare time; but he had cost a good deal, I believe as much as ten minas, so he had not got half yet. My father had lately promised him, however, that if he looked after me well till I was seventeen, he should have his freedom as a gift to the gods.

There were broken Herms in every street. Some people were saying an army must have been hired for the work. Others said no, it was a band of drunks rioting home after a party; and we heard Alkibiades' name again.

Outside the school a crowd of boys stood gazing at the Herm

there. It had been a good one, presented by Perikles. Some of
the little boys, pointing, began to giggle and squeak; on which
one of the seniors went up and told them to behave themselves.
Recognising a friend of mine, Xenophon son of Gryllos, I called
to him. He came over, looking serious. He was a handsome boy,
big for his age, with dark red hair and grey eyes; his tutor stuck
close to him, for he already attracted attention.

'It must have been the Corinthians,' he said to me, 'trying to
make the gods fight against us in the war.' – 'They must be
simple then,' I said. 'Don't they think the gods can see in the
dark?' – 'Some of the country people near our farm hardly know
the god from the image he lives in. Now a thing like this could
never happen in Sparta.' – 'I should say not. All they have outside
their dirty huts is a heap of stones for a Herm. Let your Spartans
alone for once.' This was an old quarrel between us, so I could
not keep from adding, 'Or perhaps they did it; they are allies of
Syracuse after all.' – 'The Spartans!' he said staring at me. 'The
most godfearing people in Hellas? You know quite well that they
never touch anything sacred, even in open war, and now we're at
truce with them. Are you mad?'

Remembering that we had once drawn each other's blood over
the Spartans, I let it rest. He was only repeating what he heard from
his father, whom he was very fond of, and whose views were the
same as those my grandfather had held till his death. All the ruling
houses of former days, who hated the intrusion of the commons
into public affairs, wanted peace, and a Spartan alliance. This was
true not only in Athens, but all over Hellas. The Spartans had not
changed their laws in three centuries, and their Helots kept the
station the gods had ordained for them. I had had enough of that
myself, in the time of the Rhodian. But you could never be angry
long with Xenophon. He was a good-hearted boy, who would
share anything he had, and was never at a loss in a tight place.

'I daresay you're right,' I said, 'if their King is an example. Have
you heard about King Agis' wedding? The bride was in bed and
he was just crossing the threshold, when the earth happened to
shake. So, obedient to the omen, he turned round, went straight
out again, and vowed not to go back for a year. If that's not piety,

what is?' I had hoped to make him laugh, for he liked a joke; but he saw nothing comic in it.

Just then the headmaster, Mikkos, came out angrily to call us in. He was taking us for Homer. What with the public disorder, and ours, he was in a fine temper and soon got out his thong.

After the music-lesson which came next, we could hardly wait to hang up our lyres and run out to the gymnasium. While we were stripping we saw the colonnade full of people; now we should hear the latest news. Our trainer had commanded a company at Delion, but today he could hardly make himself heard, and the flute for the exercises was quite drowned; so taking some of the best wrestlers to coach, he set the rest of us to practise. Our tutors bustled up, seeing us listening to the men in the colonnade; but they were all talking politics. One could always tell this some way off; when they were quarrelling over one of the boys, they kept their voices down.

Everyone seemed to know for certain who was guilty, and no two agreed. One said the Corinthians wanted to delay the war; 'Nonsense,' said another; 'this was done by people who knew the City like their own courtyards.' – 'How not? Some of our foreign metics would sell their old fathers for five obols.' – 'They work hard and make money. Crime enough for the unjust.' And so people who were rivals in love or politics, but had kept it quiet, were all at once openly reviling each other. It had never happened to me before to be surrounded by frightened men, and I was too young not to be shaken by it. I had not thought till then that such great impiety might bring a curse on the whole City, if it had been done by someone within.

Beside me some young men were blaming the oligarchs. 'Only wait; they will try to fix this on the democrats, and then ask to carry arms for protection. Pisistratos the Tyrant's trick. But at least he wounded his own head, not a god's.' Naturally the oligarchs called this a piece of filthy demagogy, and voices rose, till a new one said, 'Don't blame the oligarchs nor the democrats, but one man alone. I know a witness who has taken sanctuary, fearing for his life. He swears that Alkibiades . . .'

Upon the name, there was a greater hubbub than ever. People began telling tales of his erotic feats, not very edifying to us boys,

who listened attentively; others spoke of his extravagance, his seven
chariots at Olympia, his race-horses, flute-girls, and hetairas; of how
when he promoted a play or a chorus, he outdid everyone else in
elegance and splendour by three to one. 'It was for gold and loot
that he began the Sicilian war.' – 'Then why should he do this to
hinder it?' – 'He would do better still out of a tyranny.' The City
never tired of gossip about Alkibiades. Tales twenty years old came
up, about his insolence to his suitors when he was a boy.

'He has kept the war going for his own glory,' someone said.
'If he had not fooled the Spartan envoys when they came to make
peace, we should have it now.' But an angry voice, which had
been trying a long time to be heard, cried out, 'Shall I tell you
the sin of Alkibiades? He was born too late into a City of little
men. Why did the mob banish Aristides the Just? Because they
were sick of hearing his virtue praised. They admitted it. It shamed
them. Now they hate to see beauty and wit, valour and birth and
wealth, united in one man. What keeps the democracy alive at all
but the hatred of excellence; the desire of the base to see no head
higher than their own?'

'Not so, by the gods. It is justice, the gift of Zeus to men.' –
'Justice? If the gods give a man wisdom, or forethought, or skill,
must he be brought down as if he had got them by theft? We shall
be laming the best athletes soon, at the demand of the worst, in the
name of justice. Or some citizen with pockmarks and a squint will
lay a complaint against such a boy as this' (here he pointed suddenly
at me) 'and his nose will be broken, I suppose, for justice's sake.'

At this laughter broke up the argument. The better-bred of them,
seeing me confused, looked away, but one or two kept on staring. I
saw Midas pursing his mouth, and walked away from them.

Of the few boys who had made some attempt to exercise,
Xenophon was one. He had finished his bout, and came over to
me. I thought he would say there would be less noise in Sparta.
But he said, 'Have you been listening? I'll tell you an odd thing.
Those who blame the Corinthians or the oligarchs all say it stands
to reason, or that everything points to it. But those who blame
Alkibiades all say that someone told them in the street.' – 'So they
do. Then perhaps there is something in it?' – 'Yes; unless someone

is putting it about.' He had an open face and quiet manners; you had to know him well to learn he had a head on his shoulders. He stood looking about the colonnade, then laughed to himself. 'By the way, if you want to study with a Sophist when you leave, now's the time to choose one.'

One could not blame him for laughing. I had forgotten, till he reminded me, that the Sophists were there. On any other day, each would have stood forth among his pupils like a flower among bees; now, seated on the benches or pacing the colonnade, they were questioning like the rest anyone who professed to know something; some with more seemliness than those around them, some not. Zenon was expressing fiercely his democratic opinions; Hippias, who was accustomed to treat his young men much as if they were still at school, had let them start a quarrel among themselves and was red in the face from calling them to order; Dionysodoros and his brother, cheapjack Sophists who would teach anything from virtue to rope-dancing at cut rates, were screaming like market-women, denouncing Alkibiades, and flying in a rage when people laughed, for he was well known to have taken them on together and refuted them both in half a dozen responses. Only Gorgias, with his long white beard and golden voice, though a Sicilian himself, looked as calm as Saturn; he sat with his hands folded in his lap, surrounded by grave young men whose grace of posture announced their breeding; when a word or two came over, you could hear that they were wholly engaged with philosophy.

'My father told me,' Xenophon said, 'that I could choose between Hippias and Gorgias. It had better be Gorgias, I think.' I looked round the palaestra and said, 'They are not all here yet.'

I had not confided my own ambitions to him. He shared my father's view that philosophers should dress and behave in a respectable way, suited to their calling. But Midas had found me out. He took his work seriously; and my father had ordered him, besides repelling suitors, to keep me away from all Sophists and rhetoricians. I was too young, my father said, to get anything solid from philosophy, which would only teach me to quibble with my elders and be wise in my own conceit.

Just then the trainer bawled out that we were there to wrestle, not to gabble like girls at a wedding, and that we should be sorry if he had to speak again. While we were all scrambling to find partners, I heard a loud commotion at the end of the colonnade. In the midst was a voice I knew. Why I did not stay where I was, I hardly know. A boy, like a dog, feels happier with the pack behind him. When his gods are mocked, down go his ears and tail. Yet I had to run to that end of the palaestra, pretending to look for a partner and avoiding anyone who was free.

Sokratès was arguing at the top of his voice with a big man who was trying to shout him down. As I got there he was saying, 'Very well, so you respect the gods of the City. And the laws too?' – 'How not?' shouted the man. 'Ask your friend Alkibiades that, not me.' – 'The law of evidence for instance?' The man shouted out, 'Don't you try to confuse the issue.' At this the bystanders exclaimed, 'No, no, that's fair, you ought to answer that.' – 'Very well, any law you like, and there ought to be one against people like you.' – 'Good. Then if what you've been telling us seems to you to be evidence, why don't you take it to the archons? If it's worth anything, they would even pay you. You trust the laws; do you trust the evidence? Well, speak up.'

The man did so, calling Sokratès a cunning snake who would argue black white and was in Corinthian pay. I could not hear Sokratès' reply; but the man suddenly hit him a swinging blow on the side of the head, rocking him over against Kriton, who was standing beside him. Everyone shouted. Kriton, who was very much put out, said, 'You'll regret this, sir. Striking a free citizen; you'll pay damages for this.' Sokratès had by now recovered his balance. He nodded to the man and said, 'Thank you. Now we can all see the force of your argument.' The man swore and raised his fist and I thought, 'This time he will kill him.'

Hardly knowing what I did, I started to run forward. Then I saw that one of the young men who had been walking behind Sokratès had stepped out, and caught the brawler by the wrist. I knew who it was, not only from seeing him with Sokratès or about the City, but because there was a bronze statuette of him in Mikkos' hallway, done when he was about sixteen. He was a former pupil, who had won a crown for wrestling, while still at school, at the Panathenaic

Games. He was said too to have been among the notable beauties of his year, which one could still believe without trouble. I saw his name every day, since it was written on the base of the statue: Lysis, son of Demokrates of Œxone.

Sokrates' enemy was a great hulking man. Lysis was taller, but not so thick. I had seen him on the wrestling-ground however. He bent back the man's arm, looking rather grave and careful, as if he were sacrificing. The man's fist opened and writhed; when he had leaned off balance, Lysis gave him a quick jerk which tumbled him neatly down the steps into the dust of the palaestra. He got a mouthful of it and all the boys laughed, a sweet sound to me. Lysis looked at Sokrates as if with apology for his intrusion, and drew back among the young men again. He had not spoken all this time. Indeed, I had seldom heard his voice, except at the mounted torch-race, when he was urging on his team. Then it carried over the cheers, the noise of the horses, and everything else.

There was a red mark on Sokrates' face. Kriton was urging him to bring an action, and offering to cover the speechwriter's fee. 'Old friend,' said Sokrates, 'last year an ass bolted in the street and kicked you; but I don't recall your suing him. As for you, my dear Lysis, thanks for your kind intentions. Just when he was starting to doubt the force of his argument, you re-stated it for him with eloquence and conviction. And now, gentlemen, shall we return to what we were saying about the functions of music?'

Their reasoning became too hard for me; but I lingered, standing in the dust, and looking at them on the pavement above me. Lysis was the nearest, being a little behind the rest. I set him in my mind beside his statue in the hallway; the comparison was easy because his face was shaved; a new fashion then, which the athletes had lately begun setting. It seemed to me a pity that someone should not do another bronze of him, now he was a man. His hair, which he wore short, lay half-curled against his head, and being mingled fair and brown, gleamed like a bronze helmet inlaid with gold. Just as I was thinking about him, he looked round. It was evident he did not recollect having ever seen me before; he smiled at me however, as if to say, 'Come nearer, then, if you like; no one will eat you.'

I took courage at this, and a step forward. But Midas, who never idled for long, saw me and came bustling over. He even seized me by the arm; so to save myself from more indignity, I went with him quietly. Sokrates, who was talking to Kriton, took no notice. I saw Lysis looking after me as I went; but whether approving my obedience, or despising my weakness, I could not tell.

On the way home Midas said to me, 'Son of Myron, a boy of your age should not need watching every moment. What do you mean by running after Sokrates after all I have told you? Especially today.' – 'Why today?' I said – 'Have you forgotten that he taught Alkibiades?' – 'Well, what of it?' – 'Sokrates has always refused to be initiated into the holy Mysteries; so who else, do you suppose, taught Alkibiades to mock at them?' – 'Mock at them?' I said. 'Does he?' – 'You have heard what all the citizens are saying.' It was the first I had heard of it; but I knew that slaves tell things to one another. 'Well, if he does, it's absurd to blame Sokrates for it. I've not seen Alkibiades go near him for years, or speak to him beyond greeting on the street.' – 'A teacher has to answer for his pupil. If Alkibiades left Sokrates justly, then Sokrates gave him cause and is to blame; or if unjustly, then Sokrates did not teach him justice, so how can he claim to make his pupils better?'

I suppose he had picked up this argument from someone like Dionysodoros. Though still untrained in logic I could smell a fallacy. 'If Alkibiades broke the Herms, everyone agrees it's the worst thing he has done. So when he was with Sokrates he must have been better than he is now, mustn't he? You don't even know yet if he did it at all. And,' I said, becoming angry again, 'as for Lysis, he only wanted out of kindness to put me at ease.' Midas sucked in his cheeks. 'Certainly. Why should anyone doubt it? However, we know your father's orders.'

I could think of no answer to this, so I said, 'Father told you I wasn't to hear the Sophists: Sokrates is a philosopher.' – 'Any Sophist,' said Midas sniffing, 'is a philosopher to his friends.'

I walked on in silence, thinking, 'Why do I argue with a man who thinks whatever will earn him his freedom in two years? He can think what he likes then. It seems I can be more just than Midas, not because I am good, but because I am free.' He walked a foot behind my elbow, carrying my tablets and lyre. I thought,

'When he is free he will grow his beard and look, I should think, rather like Hippias. And if he chooses, he can strip for exercise then, with other free men; but he is getting old for that, and might not care to show his body, soft and white as it must be.' I had not seen him naked in all these years; he might as well have been a woman. Even when he was free he would still be no more than a metic, an immigrant, never a citizen.

Once long before, I had asked my father why Zeus made some men to be Hellenes living in cities with laws, some barbarians under tyrants, and others slaves. He said, 'You might as well ask, my dear boy, why he made some beasts lions, some horses, and others swine. Zeus the All-Knowing has placed all sorts of men in a state conformable with their natures; we cannot suppose anything else. Don't forget, however, that a bad horse is worse than a good ass. And wait till you are older before you question the purposes of the gods.'

He met me in the courtyard when I got home, with a myrtle wreath on his head. He had got together what was needed for the purification of the house, water from the Nine Springs, frankincense and the rest, and was waiting for me to serve at the rites with him. It was a long time since we had needed to perform them, and then it was only because a slave had died. I bound the myrtle round my head and helped him with the lustrations, and when the incense was burning on the household altar, made the responses to the prayers. I was glad to finish, for I was hungry, and the smell from inside told me that my mother had cooked something good.

I ought to write of my stepmother for clearness' sake; but I not only called her Mother, but so thought of her, having known no other. Her coming had, as I have explained, saved me from much misery; so it seemed that such and not otherwise a mother ought to be. It made no difference in my mind that she was only about eight years older than I was, my father having married her when she was not quite sixteen. I daresay it might have seemed to other people, when she came, that she behaved to me more like an elder sister who had been given the keys; I remember that often at first, being uncertain about the ways of the house and not wanting to lose authority with the slaves, she would ask me. Yet because when unhappy I had dreamed of a kind mother, and she was kind, she seemed to me the pattern of all mothers. Perhaps this was why at my initiation into the Mysteries, having been shown certain things of which it is unlawful to speak, I could not be as much moved by them as the candidates I saw around me. The Goddesses pardon me, if I have said amiss.

Even in looks she might have been my sister; for my father had chosen a second wife not unlike the first, being, it appears, fond of dark women. Her father had fallen at Amphipolis with a good deal of glory; she kept his armour, in an olive-wood chest, for he had no sons. I think for this reason he must have been in the habit of talking to her with rather improper freedom; for when she first came to us, she used often to ask my father questions about the war, and events in the Assembly. About the first he would sometimes speak; but if she became persistent about business or politics, as a kindly reproof he would walk to the loom, and praise her work. So now, when I smelt the good food cooking, I smiled to myself, thinking, 'Dear Mother, you have no need to coax me, who for a bowl of bean soup would tell you all they are saying in the City.'

After the meal, then, I went up to the women's rooms. She had been weaving for some time a big hanging for the supper-room; scarlet, with a white ship in the centre on a blue sea, and a border of Persian work. She had just finished the centrepiece. At a smaller loom one of the maids whom she had taught was weaving plain cloth; the sound went smoothly on, while the noise of the big loom would change its pace with the pattern.

She asked me first how I had done at school. To tease her I said, 'Not very well. Mikkos beat me, for forgetting my lines.' I thought she would at least ask what made me forget them, but she only said, 'For shame.' Seeing her look round, however, I laughed, and she laughed too. The tilt of her head made one think of a slender bird with bright eyes. As I stood beside her I saw I had been growing again; for whereas our eyes had been level, now mine looked upon her brows.

I told her all the rumours that were going about. When she was in thought, her eyebrows lifted at the inner ends, making a hollow between them in her forehead, which was very white. 'Who do you think did it, Mother?' I asked. She said, 'The gods will reveal it, perhaps. But, Alexias, who will command the Army now, instead of Alkibiades?'

'Instead?' I said, staring. 'But he must command. It's his own war.' – 'A man charged with sacrilege? How can they put the Army under a curse?' – 'I suppose not. Perhaps they won't go to Sicily, then, at all.' My face fell, thinking of the ships, and all the great victories we had looked forward to. My mother looked at me and, nodding her head, said, 'Oh, yes, they will go. Men are like children who must wear their new clothes today.' She wove a couple of lines and said, 'Your father says Lamachos is a good general.' – 'He has been laughed at rather too much,' I said. 'He can't help being so poor; but when he indented for his own shoe-leather last time, Aristophanes got hold of it, you know, and started all these jokes about him. But Nikias will consult him, I suppose.'

She stopped weaving and turned round, the shuttle in her hand. 'Nikias?' she said. – 'Of course, Mother. It stands to reason. He has been one of the first of the Athenians ever since I remember.' And indeed, a citizen of my father's age could still have said this.

'But he is an old sick man,' she said. 'He ought to be taking soup in bed, not crossing the sea. And he had no stomach for the war from the very first.' I saw she knew something of events already; no doubt every woman who had the use of her legs had been running from house to house, under excuse of borrowing a little flour or a measure of oil. 'Still,' I said, 'he would be a good man if the gods are angry. They've never lost him a battle all his life. No one has paid them more attention than he has. Why, he has even given them whole shrines and temples.' She looked up. 'What is it worth to the gods,' she said, 'to be feared by a man who fears everything? How should he lose battles? He never took a risk.'

I looked round anxiously. Luckily my father was out.

'I myself have seen him in the street,' she said, 'when a cat crossed his path, waiting for someone else to pass to take off the bad luck. What kind of man is that for a soldier?' – 'No one doubts, Mother,' I said laughing, 'that you'd make a better one.' She blushed, and turning to the loom said, 'I can't waste any more time in talking. Your father's club is coming tonight.'

The club was called the Sunhorses. It was, in those days, moderate in politics, but though it served the usual purposes of that kind, good talk was its chief function, and they never let the number get above eight, to keep the conversation general. All the foundation members, of whom my father was one, had been knights of moderate wealth; but the war had brought a good many changes of fortune. They tried nowadays, as between gentlemen, to overlook the fact that they had become a mixture of rich and poor; the dinner subscriptions had always been moderate, with no costly additions expected from the host. But lately things had reached a point where some men could not afford the extra lamp-oil and condiments for a cold supper, and, ashamed to charge them to the common account, had dropped out on some excuse. One man, who was easy in matters of pride but well liked, had more than once had his share paid by a whip-round among the rest.

'Where are you off to?' my mother asked me. – 'Only to see Xenophon. His father's given him a colt to train for himself, to ride when he joins the Guard. I want to see how it's coming on. He says you must never train a horse with a whip; it's like beating a dancer and expecting grace, and a horse ought to move well out of pride in itself. Mother, isn't it time that Father got a new horse? Korax is too old for anything but hacking: what am I going to ride, when I'm ready for the Guard?' – 'You?' she cried, 'silly child, that's a world away.' – 'Only three years, Mother.' – 'It depends on next year's harvest. Don't stay late at Xenophon's. Your father wants you in tonight.' – 'Not tonight, Mother; it's club night.' – 'I'm aware of it, Alexias. And your father's order is that you are to go after supper, and serve the wine.' – 'Who, I?' I was much affronted; I had never been asked to serve tables, except at public dinners where lads of good family do it by custom. 'Are the slaves sick; or what?' – 'Don't show your father that sulky face; you ought to feel complimented. Run away, I have work to do.'

When I went to the bath that evening I found my father just finishing, with old Sostias rinsing him down. I looked at his fine shoulders, flat and wide without being too heavy, and resolved to spend more time with the disk and javelin. Even now, though the rising generation seems to think nothing of it, I cannot bear to see a runner gone all to legs, looking as if he would be fit for nothing, when off the track, except to get away from a battlefield faster than anyone else.

When Sostias had gone my father said, 'You will serve us the wine tonight, Alexias.' – 'Yes, Father.' – 'Whatever you may hear in the guest-room, nothing goes out. You understand?' – 'Yes, Father.' This put another colour on it. I went off to make myself a garland; I chose hyacinths, I believe.

They finished their business concerns early; while they were still eating my father commanded me to fetch my lyre and sing. I gave them the ballad of Harmodios and Aristogeiton. Afterwards my father said, 'You must forgive the boy's hackneyed choice; but it is while these old songs come fresh to them, that they can learn some thing from them.' – 'Don't beg our pardon, Myron,' Kritias said. 'I fancy I am not the only one here who felt, on hearing it tonight, that he understood it for the first time.' The slaves were clearing the tables, which gave me an excuse to pretend I had not heard.

After mixing the wine, I went round the couches, quietly as I had been taught, without drawing attention to myself; but one or two of my father's old friends held me back for a few words. Theramenes, who had given me my first set of knucklebones, remarked how I was growing, and told me that if I did not idle my time in the bath-house or scent-shop, but remembered the Choice of Herakles, I might be as handsome as my father. One or two other guests had a word for me, but when I got to Kritias, I took care to be as brief as if it were a mess-table in Sparta.

He was not much above thirty then, but already affected the philosopher in mantle and beard. He had a hungry-looking face, with the skin stretched tight on the cheekbones, but was not bad looking apart from his thinness, except that his eyes were too light, the skin being dark around them. He had not belonged to the club very long, and was considered something of a prize to it for he was extremely well-born, wealthy, and a wit. No one, as you may suppose, had asked for my opinion. As it happened, I had met him rather earlier than my father had. I had noticed him first in

Sokrates' company; which had disposed me so well to him, that when he came up afterwards while Midas' back was turned, I let him speak to me.

I was old enough to have received some attentions from men, while still young enough to think them rather absurd; as, for that matter, the kind of person who chases young boys usually is. But I had never been inclined to laugh at Kritias.

When I reached him with the wine, he was all graciousness, and remarked, as if we had never spoken before, that he had watched me on the running-track and noticed my style improving; and he named one or two victors my trainer had taught. On my replying as shortly as I knew how, he praised my modesty, saying I had the manners of a better age, and quoting Theognis. I could see my father listening with approval. But as soon as he turned his head away, Kritias moved his cup a little, so that the wine spilled down my clothes. On this he apologised, said he hoped it would leave no stain, and put his hand under the hem of my tunic in such a way that, to everyone but me, he would have seemed to be feeling the cloth.

I don't know how I refrained from bringing the pitcher down upon his head. He knew I should be ashamed to call attention to him, before my father and his friends. I withdrew at once, though without saying anything, and went over to the mixing-bowl to fill the jug. I thought no one had noticed; but when I got round to Tellis, the man who had been too poor to pay his own subscription, he spoke to me with a certain gentleness which told me that he knew. Looking up, I saw Kritias watching us together.

When the garlands had been brought in and the slaves had shut the door and gone, one or two people invited me to sit beside them; but I sat on the foot of my father's couch. They had been capping verses, a diversion in which Kritias had shone; but now being alone they glanced round at each other, and there was a pause. Then Theramenes said, 'Well, every dog has his day, and today is the demagogues'.'

To this several voices assented. He went on, 'They think with their ears, their eyes, their bellies or what you like, except their minds. If Alkibiades had been insolent to them, he must be guilty.

If he has spent money at the shop, and remembered to smile, he could walk the City with a smashed Herm under his arm and still be as innocent as the boy here. But remind them a little of expediency, point out to them that he is a strategist of genius such as Ares sends once in a century; their eyes glaze over; what do they care? They've not set foot on a battlefield in three generations; they have no armour, no, but they can give us our marching orders, and choose of the generals.' Kritias said, 'And we, who carry the burden of the City, are like parents with spoiled children: they break the roof-tiles, we pay.'

'As for justice,' Theramenes said, 'they have as much notion of it as the guts of a mullet. I tell you, my dear Myron, this very night I could raise a drunken brawl here, strike you before all these witnesses, wound your slaves; and if you would only come to court looking and behaving like a gentleman, I undertake you would lose your case. I, you see, should put on the old tunic I wear on my farm, and have a speech written for an honest poor fellow, which I should con till it came like nature to me. I should bring my children along, borrowing some little ones as the youngest is ten; and we should all rub our eyes with onion. I assure you, in the end it would be you who would pay the fine, for plying your simple friend with stronger stuff than he could afford at home, and trying to profit by it. They would spit on you as you left.'

My father said, 'Well I agree, they are often like children. But children can be taught. Perikles did it. Who does it now? Now their folly is tended and farmed for gain.' – 'Whoever complains of them,' said someone, 'it shouldn't be Alkibiades. He invented demagogy. Just because he practises it with a certain grace, don't let us close our eyes to that.' – 'Let us credit him with the invention, if you wish,' said Kritias, 'but not with perfecting the art. He should have known better than to insult his strongest ally. He will pay for it.'

'I must be slow tonight,' Tellis said. 'What ally do you mean?' Kritias smiled at him, not without contempt. 'Long ago,' he said, 'there lived a wise old tyrant. We do not know his name or city, but we can infer him. His guards were sufficient, perhaps, to protect his person, but not to rule with. So out of the stuff of mind he created twelve great guardians and servants of his will: all-knowing, far-shooting, earth-shaking, givers of corn and wine and love. He did not make them all terrible, because he was a poet, and because he was wise; but even to the beautiful ones he gave terrible angers. "You may think yourselves alone," he said to the people, "when I am closed in my castle. But they see you and are not deceived." So he sent out the Twelve, with a thunderbolt in one hand and a cup of poppy-juice in the other; and they have been excellent servants ever since, to whoever knew how to employ them. Perikles, for instance, had them all running his errands. You would have thought it might have taught Alkibiades something.'

It was the first time in my life that I had heard talk of this kind. My mind went back to the dawn of this same day, when I had stood in the High City; it seemed a small thing to have kept my body to myself, when this had no defence from his filthy hands.

My father, who clearly thought that my presence might have been better remembered, sent me round with the wine as a reminder. Then he said, 'For that matter, nothing is proven yet. Reason asks a motive, no less than the law. Nothing could profit him so much as to conquer Sicily; the difficulty, I imagine, would be to stop the people crowning him king. If any Athenian broke the Herms, look for one who has his own eyes on a tyranny, and fears a rival.'

Kritias said, 'I doubt whether anyone will look so far, when the story of the Eleusis party gets about.'

At this, there was a sound all round the room, of men filling their lungs to speak, and emptying them in silence. My father said, 'The boy is an initiate.' But they had thought again, and no one spoke.

It was my father in the end who broke the pause. 'Surely,' he said, 'even our heavy-handed friends of the Agora will hardly be solemn over that, after so long. Any good speech-writer . . . One knows what young men are who begin to reason, and think themselves emancipated. A procession with torches round the garden; new words to a hymn-tune; a surprise in the dark and some laughter; and the end nothing worse than a little love-making, perhaps. It was the year we . . . He had scarcely grown his beard.'

Kritias raised his brow. 'Why no. I don't imagine that would raise much dust today. Did he get the notion so long ago? I was speaking of this winter's party. He will hardly pass that off as a boyish romp, I am afraid. They raided the store, you know, for the ritual objects. It will take a very good speech-writer to explain *that* away. They did everything. The prayer, the washings, the Words; everything. Did you know, Myron?' My father put his wine-cup from him and said, 'No.'

'Well, those who were there will have taken care to forget it by this time, no doubt. Unluckily, as it was late and some confusion prevailed, the slaves were overlooked and remained till the end. Some were uninitiate.'

At this I heard, all around the couches, an indrawn breath. Kritias said, 'They did the Showing, too. They brought in a woman.' He added something, which it is unlawful to write.

There was a long silence. Then a man in the far corner said, 'That is not only blasphemy. It is hubris.'

'It is more dangerous than that,' Kritias said. 'It is frivolity.' He picked up his cup and set it down again, to remind me it was empty. 'He will destroy himself because he cannot keep his mind on serious things. His capacity is excellent; he begins a business of some gravity, knowing himself capable of success, and discounting the results of failure. Then something crosses his path: a quarrel, a love-affair, a practical joke, that he can't resist. He enjoys dangerous improvisations. He has the soul of an acrobat. Recall his public debut, to contribute to the war fund. No one knows better the value of an entrance. But he won't leave his fighting quail at home; and this when the ban is on. It gets out of his mantle; in the event, people are tickled, and tumble about the Theatre trying to catch it for him. Ignoring all who might be useful later, he receives it from a nobody, the pilot's mate of a warship; they go home together, and the man is about him to this day. Another time, entering on affairs, he will take a course in debate. He goes to Sokrates; not a discreet choice, but far from a foolish one, for the man, though mad, is a most accomplished logician; I have profited from him myself and don't care who knows it. His processes, of course, all lead towards a rationalism which he himself refuses to accept; one knows these eccentrics. But Alkibiades, who by this time has tasted everything beautiful in the City, of all three sexes, is taken by the man's extraordinary ugliness, and suffers him to extend the lesson in all directions. Before very long, he has caught his lover's vagary for reforming the gods, and, by a simple syllogism, infers that unreformed gods are fair game. Hence the dangerous little mummery you spoke of, Myron. Nowadays he has given up improving the Olympians, though in matters of love he could probably instruct them. And danger, like wine, has to be strong now to quicken his blood.'

I stood beside the wine-mixer, the jug in my hand, looking at Kritias. I was wishing him dead. I remember thinking that if I could make him meet my eye, my curse would be more effectual; but he did not look.

Then Tellis, who had not spoken for some time, said in his quiet voice, 'Well, we began by discussing the Herm-breaking. If we can be sure of anything, I should say, we can rule improvisation out. A couple of hundred men could scarcely have done it, all round the City in a night. Were they knocked up here and there by drunks, and no one remembers? None of these chance people refused, and denounced them? No, Myron is right; it was planned to a hair, and not by Alkibiades.'

Kritias said smoothly, 'No one, I am sure, will think worse of Tellis for supporting his host.'

The men had been drinking, and were full of their affairs. But I, who was watching, saw Tellis' face stiffen, as at the first bite of a sword-thrust. When you have thought yourself among good friends, who have given the best proof of their liking for your company, it strikes hard to be called a sycophant for the first time. I knew he would never sup with the club again. I went over to him and filled his cup, knowing no other way to show what I felt; and he smiled at me, trying to greet me as he always did. Our eyes met above the wine-cup, like men's who have picked up the sound of a lost battle before the trumpet blows the retreat.

4

Adonis was dead. My mother put on her mourning veil and went out to weep for him, with a basket of anemones to strew about his bier. Soon one met a procession at every corner, the dead god carried in his garden, the women with hair unbound wailing against the flutes.

I have never met a man yet who liked this festival. That year it was a cold grey day, with heavy cloud. The citizens crowded into the palaestra and the baths and any place where women cannot go, and muttered gossip about omens and prodigies. Word came from the Agora that a man had just gone raving mad there; he had leaped on the Altar of the Twelve, drawn a knife, and hacked off his genitals with it. The altar was defiled and would have to be consecrated again.

In the High City, the temples were so thronged that those who came to sacrifice stood in lines to take their turn. They came away like men who having touched the plague have just washed themselves, and doubt if they have washed enough. In the midst of the temple, great Athene gazed down upon us all. Her gold robes gleamed, her cloak worked with victories hung behind her; the soft light, creeping through the thin marble of the roof-tiles, glowed on her face, so that the warm ivory seemed alive; one waited only for her to raise her mighty arm and, pointing, say in a voice of clashing gold, 'There is the man.' But she kept her counsel.

Men were busier. A public award had now been offered to informers, and a board appointed to hear them. Soon information was coming in not about the Herm-breaking, but about anyone who might be supposed to have done, or said, or thought, something sacrilegious. My father said to anyone who would listen that this was bribing scum to come to the top, and that Perikles would have sickened at it.

Xenophon and I, to escape all this gloom in the City, spent our spare time at Piraeus. Here there was always something new; a rich metic from Phrygia or Egypt might be building himself a house in the style of his former city, or putting up a shrine to one of the gods whom one hardly knew in his foreign dress, with even a dog's head perhaps or a fish's tail; or there would be a new shipment in the Emporion of carpets from Babylon, Persian lapis, Scythian turquoises, or tin and amber from the wild Hyperborean places that only Phoenicians know. Our silver owls were the only coinage, then, that was good all over the world. You saw in the wide streets Nubians with plugs of ivory pulling their ears down to their shoulders; long-haired Medes, in trousers and sequin bonnets; Egyptians with painted eyes, wearing only skirts of stiff linen and collars of gems and beads. The air was heavy with the smells of foreign bodies, of spices and hemp and pitch; strange tongues chattered like beast speaking to bird; one guessed at the meaning, and watched the talking hands.

Alkibiades was denounced on the day when he stood up before the Assembly, to declare the fleet ready for sailing.

The accuser, who had a slave at hand, asked for an immunity, and for all who were not initiates to depart. This being done, the slave recited aloud the central Words, which, he said, Alkibiades had profaned before him.

It was the day after this that I missed Sokrates in the palaestra.

His absence in itself I should have thought nothing of; for he used to talk with all kinds of people, all about the City. I was not disturbed till I went out on the running-track, and saw among the onlookers a group of his friends, talking together like troubled men. At once it sprang into my mind that someone had denounced him, because he had taught Alkibiades, and refused to be initiated. Eryximachos the doctor had now joined the others. I could not endure my ignorance any longer. I leaned on one foot as I ran, stopped as if hurt, and went halting off the track. The trainer was too busy to come after me: I sat down near them to listen.

Eryximachos must have just asked whether Sokrates was ill;

for Kriton was saying that nothing ever ailed him. He went on, 'No, Sokrates is at home, sacrificing and praying for the army of the Athenians.' And Chairophon said, 'His daimon has spoken to him.'

They exchanged looks. I was too silent, nursing my foot in my hand, and remembering the nest in the tree.

As I sat lost in thought, scarcely hearing the noises of the track, I became aware of someone's shadow falling on me, and a voice. Looking up I saw Lysis son of Demokrates. He had been with Sokrates' friends when I first sat down, but almost at once he had gone away. 'I saw you twist you foot,' he said. 'Does it hurt much? You ought to bind it with cold water, before it swells up.'

I thanked him stammeringly, being taken by surprise, and overwhelmed that such a person should speak to me. Seeing I had a long way to look up, he came down on one knee; I saw that he had a wet cloth in his hand, which he must just have got from the bath. He paused a moment and then said, 'Shall I do it?'

At this I remembered that nothing was wrong with me. I was so ashamed at the thought of his finding out, and thinking I had sat down out of weakness, or the fear of being outrun, that I felt my face and my whole body grow burning hot, and sat unable to answer anything. I thought he would be disgusted by my boorishness; but holding out the cloth he said gently, 'If you would rather, then, do it yourself.'

All this while Midas, thinking me safe in the trainer's care, had been taking his ease. Now for the first time he saw where I was. He came up breathless, almost snatched the cloth from Lysis' hands, and said he would attend to it. He was doing no more than his duty: but, at the time, it seemed to me barbarous; I looked up at Lysis at a loss for words to excuse it. But he, without showing any offence, bade me goodbye smiling, and went away.

I was so angry and confused that I pushed Midas away from me, saying that my foot was better and I was now able to run. The impression this made on him, he is hardly to be blamed for. Going home he asked me whether I would take a beating from him, or would rather he told my father. I could imagine the kind of story he would make of it, and chose the first. Though he laid it well on, I bore it in silence; I was still wondering whether Lysis had thought me soft.

Meanwhile the City was on tiptoe waiting to see Alkibiades brought to trial. The Argives and Mantineans demonstrated: it was Alkibiades they had come to fight under they said and threatened to march home. The seamen looked so ugly that the trierarchs feared a mutiny. Those who had been pressing hardest for the trial, grew suddenly less loud; and other speakers came forth, by whom inspired nobody knew. Claiming to be friends of the accused, they did not doubt that he could produce a good defence when called upon, and moved he be allowed to set forth upon the war he had prepared so ably. People waited to see him jump at this opportunity; but he sprang up before the Assembly, demanding with passion and eloquence to be tried. No one knew what to make of it. In the end, the second motion was carried.

The fleet sailed a few days later.

A friend of my father had a warehouse at Piraeus, and let us boys climb on the roof. We felt like gods looking down upon a voyage of the heroes. All the storeships had gone on to the assembly at Korkyra; only the bright, slim triremes were left in the bay. The breeze of early summer lifted their stern-pennants; eagles and dragons, dolphins and boars and lions, tossed their heads as the beaks met the swell.

The cheering began in the City, like the sound of a distant land-slide, and crept towards us between the Long Walls. Then it roared through Piraeus; one could hear the music coming, and shield clashing on corselet to the beat. Now you could see between the Walls the helmet-crests moving, a river of them, a long snake bright with his new scales in springtime, bronze and gold, purple and red. Sparks of light seemed to dance above it, the early sun catching the points of many thousand spears; the dust-cloud shone like powdered gold.

On the roofs about us the foreigners were chattering together, marvelling at the beauty and might of the army, which the City could still send forth after so many years of war. Two Nubian slaves were making their eyes white and saying 'Auh! Auh!' We cheered till our throats ached. Xenophon's voice sounded already almost like a man's.

The troops deployed upon the water-front and on the quays; they filed along gang-planks, or were loaded into boats with their gunwales dipping, and ferried to the ships. Kinsmen and friends ran up for last farewells. An old man would bless his son, a lad run to his father with some gift the mother had sent after him; or two lovers might be parting, the youth being too young to go with his friend. That day not all the tears had been left at home with the women. But to me it seemed the greatest of all festivals, better than the Panathenaia in the Great Year. As the proverb tells us, war is sweet to the untried.

Noise sounded again between the walls. Someone shouted 'Long life to the Generals!' We began to hear horses and to see their dust.

Presently there passed below us Lamachos on his borrowed hack; tall and saturnine, greeting old soldiers when they cheered him, indifferent to the rest. Then Nikias, gravely splendid, his white hair garlanded, fresh from the sacrifice, his soothsayer riding by him with the sacred tripod, knives and bowl. The leaden tinge of skin that he always had only added dignity to him. People reminded each other as he passed of the ancient oracle, that in Sicily the Athenians should win lasting fame.

There was a restless pause then, like the quiet before the sea gets up. And the many-voice muttering that came nearer was like the sound of a great wave, sucking a stony beach, and drawing the pebbles resistless in its wake. Then a youth with a clear voice shouted, like a battle-paean, 'Alkibiades!'

He burst on us like the sun. His armour was worked with golden stars; his purple cloak hung as if a sculptor had set the folds. His groom rode behind him with his famous shield, the City's scandal and delight, blazoned with Eros wielding a thunderbolt.

His opened helmet showed his face, the profile of Hermes, and the short curled beard. His chin was up; his blue eyes, wide and clear, seemed open on an emptiness demanding to be filled. It seems to me now that they were saying, 'You wished for me, Athenians; I am here. Do not question me, do not hurt me; I am the wish sprung from your heart, and if you wound me your heart will bleed for it. Your love made me. Do not take it away; for without love I am a temple forsaken by its god, where dark Alastor will enter. It was you, Athenians, who conjured me, a daimon whose food is love. Feed me, then, and I will clothe you with glory, and show you to yourselves in the image of your desire. I am hungry: feed me. It is too late to repent.'

The crowd murmured and swayed, like a moving shoal drawn by the tide. Then from some doorway a hetaira leaned out, and blew him a kiss. He waved, his clouded eyes warming like the sea in spring; and the cheering broke forth, and roared about him. His smile appeared, like the smile of a boy crowned at his first Games, young and enchanted, embracing all the world; and they cheered him out of sight. Adonis had passed through the street before him; mashed by the horse-hoofs, the strewn anemones stained the dust like blood.

The Generals joined their ships, the bustle grew less and ended. A trumpet blew a long call. Then one heard only a dying mutter, the slap of the sea on the jetties, the cry of gulls, and the bark of some dog uneasy in the hush. The small clear voice of a distant herald cried the Invocation. It was taken up in the ships and on the shore; the sound flowed and rolled like surf; on each poop gold or silver flashed, as the trierarch lifted his cup to pour the offering. Then ringing across the water came the paean, and the shouts of the pilots, bidding the ships away. The chantymen began to give the time to the rowers; up went the great sails painted with suns and stars and birds. So they put out to sea, the crews answering song for song, and the pilots calling out to each other challenges to race. I saw Nikias' white beard flutter as he prayed with raised hands; and on the poop of Alkibiades' trireme, which already was standing away, a little shining figure like a golden image, no bigger than the Adonis dolls the women had carried in the streets.

The sails filled; the oar-blades all together beat up and down, bright-feathered wings; like swans the ships flew singing towards the island. Tears stung my eyes. I wept for the beauty of it, like many more. Happy for the Athenians, if the tears that followed afterwards had been like mine.

5

Quite soon after this, I got the news that Kritias was in prison.

An informer swore to seeing him, on the night when the Herms were broken, helping to assemble and instruct the gang, in the portico of the Theatre. The moon had been bright, the man said, and he could name most of the leaders.

I could not imagine, when I heard this, why I had not known it must be Kritias from the very first; for, being young, I supposed he was the only person of his kind in the world. When I walked past the prison there was a knot of women outside, some of them with children, sobbing and wailing. But I could not believe that Kritias had anyone to weep for him.

My triumph was brief, however, for his cousin Andokides, who was one of the accused, offered a full confession in return for immunity. The substance of it was that he knew about the plot, but had an alibi; Kritias was innocent too. Then he named the guilty ones, including some of his kinsmen. These were put to death at once; so was the first informer, for perjury. Some people said Andokides had made up the whole statement for the sake of the immunity, rather than risk his trial. No one knows the truth to this very day.

The dead were scarcely cold, when news came that the Thebans were on the frontier, making ready to invade.

We had just sat down in school when this was shouted outside. Armour began to sound in the street, as the citizens turned out to the mustering-places. Our trainer looked in, calling out to the master that he was off. Then the herald's trumpet blew from the temple roof of the Twins, calling the horsemen. At this Mikkos, knowing he could do no more with us, said we should be wanted at home, and dismissed the class.

I found my father standing in his armour, slinging on his sword, while Sostias brought him his spears to choose from. He said, 'Since you are here, Alexias, go to the stable and look over Phoenix for me. See that his frogs are clear, and the big saddle-cloth is strapped on to cover his belly.'

When I got back he had his helmet on. He looked very tall.

'Father,' I said, 'can I ride Korax and come too?' – 'Certainly not. If things go badly and they call for boys of your age, go where you are told, and obey your orders.' Then he put his hand on my shoulder and said, 'Though we may be here or there, defending the City we shall be side by side.' I replied that I hoped he would have no cause to be ashamed of me. When he had embraced my mother, she gave him his knapsack with three days' food in it. He stooped under the lintel, then vaulting on his spear leaped upon Phoenix, and rode away.

The City seethed all day. Everyone thought the Thebans had had a signal from the conspirators, and that the plot had come out in the nick of time. Some said it was the Spartans who were coming, and the plan had been to open the gates to them. The Senate marched up to the High City and sat all night.

My mother and I worked about the house, making everything fast. She talked cheerfully to the slaves, and said she remembered her own mother doing all this when she was a child. I went with our old slave Sostias to buy food in case of siege. But when dark fell and the troops were still standing by, I got tired of sitting indoors; so I said, 'Father would be glad of some wine, I expect, since everything is quiet.'

She gave me leave. I said she must keep Midas at hand, so, lighting a torch, I went up alone to the Anakeion. The temple precinct was full of the smell of horses, and the sound of their treading and snorting. High above the picket lines I could see the Great Twin Brethren, the friends of the horsemen, leading their bronze chargers against the stars. I put out my torch, for one could see by the light of the watch-fires; and I asked for my father by his name, and his father's name, and the name of his deme.

Someone said he was standing guard at the north-east corner of the precinct; and going that way I saw him on the wall, leaning upon his spear with firelight on his armour, like a warrior done in red on a black vase. I went up and said, 'Sir, Mother has sent you some wine.' He said he would be glad of it later; I put it down, and was going to bid him goodnight, when he said, 'You may stay for a while, and watch with me.'

I climbed up and stood beside him. One could not see far, for the night was moonless. No one was very near; as it got cooler, they were drawing round the fires, or into the temple. I felt I should say something to him; but we had never talked much together. At last I asked him if he expected an attack in the morning. 'We shall see,' he said. 'Confusion in a city breeds false alarms. Still they may be coming, in the hope we have not enough men left to man the walls.' He did not look round as he talked, keeping his eyes on the dark, as men do on watch, lest the firelight dull them. Presently I asked, 'How long will it take the Army, sir, to conquer Sicily?' He answered, 'Only the gods know.'

I was surprised and fell silent. After a moment he said, 'The Syracusans had not injured us, nor threatened us. The war was with the Spartans.' – 'But,' I said, 'when we have beaten the Syracusans, and have got their ships and harbour and the gold, shan't we finish the Spartans easily?' – 'Maybe. But time was when we fought only to hold off the barbarian, or to defend the City, or for justice's sake.'

In most men I should have thought such words poor-spirited; for I was used to hearing that we fought to make the City great, and leader of the Hellenes. But when I saw him standing in his armour I knew not what to think.

He said, 'In the third year of the war, when you were still at nurse, the Lesbians, our subject allies, rose against us. They were reduced without much trouble; and the Assembly voting on their fate thought it wise to make an example of them. The men of fighting age should be put to the sword, and the rest of the people sold as slaves. So the galley set out for Lesbos with this decree. But that night we lay sleepless, or started up from sleep, hearing the cries of the dying, the shrieks of women, and children's weeping, still in our ears. In the morning we all returned to the Assembly; and when we had rescinded the decree, we offered rewards to the rowers of the second galley to overtake the first. They did it; for the first had laboured along as if sick men pulled the oars, so much their errand oppressed them. When they were overhauled at Mytilene, the Athenians felt reprieved as much as the Lesbians; they rejoiced together and shared their wine. But last year, the Melians, who owed us nothing, being Doric, chose to pay tribute to their mother-city rather than to us. What we did, you know.'

I took courage to say he had never related it to me. He answered, 'When you sacrifice, pray the gods that it may never fall to your lot, either to suffer it, or to do it.'

I had never guessed that such things were in his mind. It was Alkibiades who had moved the Melians' punishment. 'The gods punish hubris in men,' he said. 'So why should we think they praise it in cities?'

Just then someone relieved his watch. We went to one of the fires, where he shared his wine with some friends, and presented me to them. 'You can see,' he said, 'that he has not done growing yet, from the size of his hands and feet.' Then I felt that he was apologising for me, because anyone could see I should never be as big as he was; I remembered how he had wanted to expose me at my birth; so as soon as it was civil I took my leave.

I was kindling my torch at a fire that was burning near the statue of the Twins, when a man, who had just come down from the temple, walked up to me. He had his helmet off, and turning with my torch alight I saw that it was Lysis. I had seen him before in armour, exercising with the horsemen; he looked very well in it. He said, 'Did you find your father, son of Myron?' I thanked him and said yes. He stood for a moment, so that I almost thought he had come out on purpose to speak to me; but he only said 'Good,' and went back up the steps again.

Next day no more had been heard of the enemy, and the troops went home. The next storm to shake the City concerned Alkibiades.

His sail had scarcely dropped under the horizon before the informers crept out. The tale of the Eleusis party was told in full. Even the woman, whose role it would be unholy to hint at (let the Twice-Born guess; they will be right) was found and induced to testify. Now that his face was out of sight, and his voice out of hearing, everyone saw the madness of trusting the army to such a man. So the state galley, the *Salaminia*, was sent to fetch him and his friend Antiochos the pilot, who had been denounced too. He was not to be seized, however, lest trouble with the seamen and the Argives should break out again. The trierarch of the *Salaminia* was to offer him civilly the trial he had asked for, and convoy him back in his own ship.

I remember, on the day of the decree, coming in to find my father standing by the big press with a painted winecup in his hands. It was one he rarely used, for it was valuable, one of the finest pieces of the master Bacchios. In the bowl was a picture, red on black, of Eros coursing a hare; it was inscribed on the one side MYRON and on the other ALKIBIADES. My father was turning it in his hands, like a man in two minds; when he saw me, however, he put it back in the press.

Nothing but Alkibiades was talked of in the City. In the street, the palaestra and the markets, old tales were told of his insolence and riot. Those who had once spoken for him would only debate, now, how he came to what he was, after being brought up by so good a man as Perikles. The answer was always the same: the sophists had corrupted him. They had taken him up as a lad, caught by his beauty and quick mind; they had puffed him up with vanity, taught him impious free-thinking (here someone usually quoted *The Clouds*) until he dared to chop logic with Perikles himself. After which he, having got from them what served his turn, laughed at their talk of wisdom and virtue, and went away.

I listened sick at heart, waiting for the name that always came up before long. It was common knowledge, people said, that Sokrates had been in love with the youth, and wanted to make a greater Perikles of him; would follow him to his loose revels, rebuke him in front of his friends, and drag him off like a slave, out of jealousy, unwilling to have the boy an hour out of his sight. I felt the disgrace as if it were my own. Since I could not silence the men, I spoke to Xenophon. We were scraping each other's backs after wrestling; as I worked on him with the strigil, I said I could not see any crime in trying to make a bad man good. He laughed at me over his shoulder. 'Scrape harder; you never scrape hard enough. I will say for you, Alexias, you stick to your side. Well, let's be fair to him; all these people were taken in by Alkibiades themselves and want a scapegoat. But a man like Sokrates, who goes about all day tripping people up and setting them right, can't afford to make a fool of himself. Do you know that when Alkibiades was a youth he once used his teeth in a wrestling-bout when he was losing? If that had happened in Sparta, they would have beaten not only him, but his lover as well, for not teaching him to be a man.'

I had not spirit enough even to rise to the Spartans. 'Look into the scent-shop,' he said, 'and you will see Sokrates' young men lolling about by the hour, word-splitting and discussing their souls; like Agathon who, if you mistook him for a girl, I should think would be delighted.' – 'He is a crowned tragedian,' I said. 'Why laugh at a man who will be immortal, when no one remembers you or me? Have you seen Sokrates in the scent-shop? I never have.' – 'It will be some time, I should say, before we see him anywhere. Ten knucklebones to one I'll lay you, that he doesn't show himself in the colonnade for a week at least. Do you take me?' – 'Yes.' He noticed then that I had stopped scraping, and looked round. 'Pax,' he said smiling, 'or we shall be having to clean-off all over again.'

Someone had said that Autolykos the athlete was wrestling in Taureas' palaestra, so we asked our tutors if we could watch. They agreed to pass through but not to stop. We found that Autolykos had finished his bout and was taking a rest; the place was full of people admiring his looks and waiting for him to wrestle again. A statuary, or a painter, was sitting and making a sketch of him. He was used to all this and took no notice of it. We were edging our way through the press, when from the other end came a hush, and then the muttering of an angry crowd. My hands felt cold. I knew who had come in.

He was alone. It did not occur to me that he had not sought for company; I thought they had all deserted him. Kriton, who had been watching the wrestling, came over at once to walk with him; and to everyone's surprise, Autolykos himself saluted him, but being naked and covered with dust did not leave the wrestling-ground.

Everyone else drew away as he passed, or turned their backs; as he drew nearer, I heard someone laugh.

As for me, I was neither brave enough to go forward, nor coward enough to go back. When others withdrawing left me in sight of him I could scarcely bring myself to look. The best I hoped for was to see him staring them all out, as they say he did the enemy at Delion in the retreat. But as he passed me he was saying as if conversing at home, 'But his contention is that the method can be taught, not the power of apprehending it. If it were a question of mathematics . . .'

I did not hear any more. As Midas was calling me, I turned to go: then I saw that Xenophon was standing just behind. At first he did not see me, for he was following Sokrates with his eyes. I waited for him to pay up his bet, for he was always a good loser. But still looking past me, he said, 'On the day when the gods send me trouble and danger, may they send me also that man's courage.'

On the way home, we climbed to the High City and looked out at the harbour. A ship was leaving: the day being clear, we saw a blue device upon the sail. 'That will be the *Salaminia*,' we said, 'with her blue owl.' She stood away quickly, making haste to Sicily.

6

That year at the Dionysia, my father took my mother and me to the theatre. The poet was one he was very fond of, because he laughed at the sophists and the democrats and at everyone who wanted to upset the City with anything new. Kydilla came to attend my mother, and Sostias to carry the cushions; my father gave him two obols to see the show. It was a clear bright day; a few little cloud-shadows swept across the sunny theatre, and blew away towards the sea. My mother with Kydilla went off to the women's seats. She had on a new pair of gold earrings my father had just given her, with little leaves hanging in them that trembled when she turned her head. The seats were already filling. The sheep-skins and undyed clothes of the working people at the top, and the bright colours on the lower benches, made the bowl of the theatre look like a great flower, lying against the flank of the High City in a calyx of dry leaves.

Nowadays I often wonder that I still attend the plays of Aristophanes, whose hands are stained, if words can stain the hand that wrote them, with the blood dearest to me on earth. That day I went unwillingly, because his mockery of Sokrates was quoted everywhere, as indeed it stuck to him all his life. Yet in this comedy was a song about birds, so beautiful that it made the hair prickle on one's neck. Indeed, while he is singing, he makes his own heaven and earth; the good is what he chooses, and where he sets their altars, there the gods alight. Plato says that no poet ought to be allowed to do this; and he is too distinguished now to be argued with any longer. I notice, however, that he goes himself. At all events, Aristophanes missed the prize that year. It went to a play called *The Drunken Revellers*, which roused the audience to great fury against Herm-breakers and blasphemers.

We were waiting outside for my mother, when a man came up and said, 'I stayed to tell you, Myron, that your wife has gone home. But don't be anxious; my own wife has gone with her, and says it is nothing of consequence. You can trust her; she has had four of her own.' He smiled, and my father thanked him with more warmth than he had shown at first. 'Well, Alexias,' he said, 'let us go home then.'

On the way he was in good spirits, and talked about the play. I don't know how I answered him. He went through to see my mother and I was left alone. Without giving a thought to what I was about, or looking for my tutor, or asking leave, I ran out of the house and through the streets. Near the Acharnian Gate someone called to me, 'Where are you going so fast, son of Myron?' I saw that it was Lysis, but I could not have spoken with anyone for my life; I turned my face to hide it from him, and ran on. I ran through fields and woods, and found myself at last on the slopes of Lykabettos.

Climbing the steep rocks above with my hands and feet, I came out on a level place, where a few small flowers clung to the stone. Even the High City looked flat below me; beyond the shoulder of Hymettos shone the sea. I lay down panting, and said to myself, 'What did I run for? One ought not to do things without a cause.' Then I turned my face and wept bitterly; yet I had not known when I ran that I wanted to weep.

I said to myself that my grief was absurd; yet it filled my heart and even hurt my body. It seemed to me that my mother had betrayed me; having taken me up when I was wanted by no one, now she had leagued herself with my father to put another in my place. I hated him for it, though I knew it was impiety towards the gods. Better, I thought, that Spartans had not come down on the day of my birth, and that long ago, in some such place as this, foxes had picked my bones and the wind scattered them.

In time my tears were spent; the little flowers threw long shadows and I felt the evening chill. It put me in mind of how I had climbed the roof on my father's wedding day, to see the bride brought home. I had supposed in my simplicity, being only seven years old, that I should be allowed to come to the feast. My father had said that he was bringing me a mother; and as if he had promised me a dog or bird of my own, I thought she belonged already to me.

It was not till the time of the lamp-lighting that I left my memories and came down from Lykabettos. I was hungry, for it was a sharp evening now the sun was down. I remembered that I had been gone some hours without my tutor, and wondered whether by good luck my father might be out. When I got in, however, he was in the living-room waiting for me.

He was alone; and instead of begging his pardon, I said before he had time to speak, 'Where is Mother?' for I was suddenly afraid that she was really sick. He got up from his chair saying, 'All in good time, Alexias. Where have you been?'

When he spoke as if I had no right to ask, anger rose in me. I stared him in the face with my mouth shut. I saw his face colour rise, as no doubt mine had risen. At length he said, 'Very well. If you have done what you are ashamed of, you have cause to be silent. But I warn you it will pay you better to tell me now, than to wait like a coward till I find it out.' At this a fire burned in my head, and I said, 'I have been in the men's palaestra, hearing the sophists, and meeting my friends.'

Being now very angry, he paused before he spoke; then without raising his voice he said, 'With whom, then, were you there?' – 'With no one more than another,' I said; 'though your friend Kritias asked me to go home with him.'

I tried to keep my anger between me and fear. He was a very big man. I set my teeth and resolved that if he killed me, he should not see me flinch. But he only said in a low voice, 'Go to your room, and wait for me there.'

The evening was cold and I was hungry. My little room was dark at evening, for it looked upon the fig-tree. I walked to and fro, trying to get warm. At last he came in, with his riding-whip in his hand. 'I have waited,' he said, 'because I would not lay my hand to you while I was in anger. Rather than please myself, I wanted to do what was just. If you grow up to be worth anything, you will have me to thank for correcting your insolence. Strip.'

I doubt if I gained as much as he did by his self-command, for that was the worst beating of my life. Towards the end I could not quite keep silent; but I kept from crying out aloud, or asking him to stop. After he had done I kept my back to him, waiting for him to go. 'Alexias,' he said. I turned then, lest he thought I dared not show my face. 'Well,' he said, 'I am glad to see you not so wanting in courage as in sense. But courage without conduct is the virtue of a robber, or a tyrant. Don't forget it.' I was feeling very sick, and if I was going to faint now in his presence I would as soon have died outright, so to get rid of him I said, 'I'm sorry, Father.' – 'Very well,' he said, 'that is the end of it then; goodnight.'

When I was alone I lay on my bed and felt, as one does when young, that my present misery would last without relief as long as my life. I determined that I would go to the shore, and throw myself from a rock into the sea. I lay resting, only waiting to get back enough of my strength to go, and seeing in my mind the streets I should pass through as I left the City. Then I remembered Lysis meeting me in the road and saying, 'Where are you going so fast, son of Myron?' I tried to imagine myself replying to him, 'I am going to leap in the sea, because my father beat me.' At this thought, I knew that I was being absurd. So I covered myself in bed, and at last fell asleep.

Later I learned that my father had sought me about the City, and must have known that I had not been to the palaestra, but had punished me for my disrespect, as any father would. I have never beaten my own boys so hard; but for all I know, they are the worse for it.

Next day I was slow to seek my mother at her loom; but she called me to her. 'When you were little, Alexias, were you angry at hearing you were to have a stepmother? I am sure you were; for in the tales they are always wicked creatures.' – 'Of course not. I have often told you how it was.' – 'But surely someone said to you that when a stepmother has a son of her own, she grows unkind to her husband's child? Slaves are full of tales like that.' I turned my face away and said 'No.'

She rattled her shuttle through the loom. 'Old women are much the same. With a young bride, they love to croak about the trials of a second wife; making sure she will be frightened not only of her husband, which will happen in any case, but of his slaves, and even his friends who will know no more of her than her cooking and weaving. More than anything, she is certain her stepson already hates her, and looks to her coming as the worst misfortune of his life. And when, expecting all this, she finds a good son with hands stretched out in welcome, nothing is so long remembered; no child can grow dearer than the first.' She ceased, but I could not answer her. 'You were a boy fond of your own way,' she said, 'yet when you saw that I was afraid of seeming ignorant, you told me the rules you had to keep yourself, and even how you were punished for breaking them.'

Her voice trembled and I saw she was going to cry. I knew I should have to run away without speaking; but as I went, I caught her arm in my hand to let her know we parted friends. Her bones felt small, like a hare's.

After this I grew used to the thought of the baby, and even told some of my friends at school. Xenophon gave me advice on how I ought to train it. At times it seemed he wanted me to bring it up as a Spartan; at others, as a horse.

I was now turned sixteen and had finished my schooling with Mikkos. Some of my friends were already studying with sophists. I was careful not to open this subject with my father, for after recent events I knew he would not let me go to Sokrates and might commit me to someone else. I meant to approach him when the scandal had faded somewhat from his mind. A good part of my spare time I spent at our farm, carrying out his orders and keeping an eye on things when he was busy; and sometimes Xenophon and I hunted hares together. He had his own leash of harriers, which he had bred from his father's dogs; he had trained them well to follow the line, and not be drawn off by the foxes and other vermin.

I had almost forgotten the *Salaminia* when she returned. Everyone flocked to the harbour, to see how Alkibiades would look, and if he would show any fear. Most people's anger had cooled by now; they were wondering what sort of defence he would make, and saying it would certainly be better than anything by a hired speechmaker.

The two ships came nearer; but he was not to be seen. Then

the trierarch of the *Salaminia* came ashore, looking like a man who has lost a bag of gold and found a rope. His news was overheard and flew from mouth to mouth. Alkibiades had agreed very civilly to come, and had sailed with them as far as Thurii in Italy. While they stopped for water, he and Antiochos had gone ashore to stretch their legs, and when it was time to start again, their ship lacked both trierarch and pilot. No one blamed the *Salaminia*'s trierarch much. Once the voyage began, Alkibiades had had as many men to defend him as the trierarch to make an arrest, which moreover he had been told not to do.

The dikastery sat in the absence of the accused, and the full indictment was presented. The verdict was confiscation of all his goods, and death. His house was cast down, and the site given to the gods. His young son was dispossessed. The auction of his goods lasted four full days. Almost everyone in the City bought something. Even my father came back with a gold-edged mantle; the hem was frayed, from Alkibiades' habit of trailing the end behind him, and I daresay my father thought it a bad bargain, for he never wore it.

Some time after, a ship came in from Italy, carrying letters from the colonists to their friends. Somebody had one from an Athenian called Thukydides, a former general who had bungled the relief of a town earlier in the war, and was living in exile. Having no occupation he travelled here and there, and wrote a good deal to pass the time. He told his friend he had been there when the death-sentence was brought to Alkibiades. Onlookers had waited to hear some high-spirited eloquence. But it seems he only said, 'I shall let them know I am alive.'

Before long we heard that he had crossed from Italy in a fishing-boat to Argos, and it was supposed he had settled there. But a few days later a trader docked in Piraeus and we learned the truth. I ran all the way to Xenophon's, to be the first with the news, for I longed to see his face. First he stared at me, then he threw back his head and laughed aloud. 'Is life really as dear to him as that? Alkibiades in Sparta? The gods must have crazed him, to make him work out their curse himself. What the Athenians would have done to him would have been nothing to this.'

All over the City, angry as people were, you could hear laughter. They painted the scene to one another: Alkibiades seated on a wooden bench in a barn, at the public mess (if any mess would have him) drinking filthy black broth from a wooden bowl, he who had kept Lydian cooks and lain on couches stuffed with down; his hair growing down uncombed, his body unbathed unless he cared for a swim in the cold Eurotas; no more scented oil for him, nor jewelled sandals; rushes for his bed, and no one to share it. 'It will kill him,' they said, 'and less gently than the hemlock.' Someone would add, 'No praise for his wit either; they like theirs short and dour.' No one quoted, it seems, his words when he heard his sentence.

The winter winds had dropped, the sea was blue, the gulls like kites on a string lay rocking with spread wings; it was sailing weather. One morning I saw a big trireme being loaded up at Munychia harbour and wondered where she was bound. When I got home I found our living-room all strewn with baggage and gear, and my father in the midst of it, his armour spread about him, oiling the straps.

I must have stared like a fool, for he called out impatiently to me either to go out or come in. I came over, asking if he was going to war. 'Oh, no,' he said, raising his brows at me. 'Don't I always wear armour to ride to the farm?' He sounded like a young man. I supposed when I came in his mind had been far away. 'What has happened, sir?' I asked. 'Are the Spartans coming?' He pulled an old thong from his corselet and threw it away. 'Not that I know of; if they do, my son, they will be your affair, so good luck to you. I am going to Sicily.'

I said foolishly that I had not known of it. 'Nor I until this morning,' he said. He chose a new thong and put it in, singing to himself a soldier's song which, recalling my presence, he stopped half-way. I had seldom seen him in such spirits. I supposed for a long time his nature had been pulling him two ways, and he was glad when his boats were burned for him.

He threw me over his greaves to polish and, as we worked, told me he had been drawn in place of another knight who was sick. 'Nikias wants cavalry, and should have foreseen it. The Syracusan horse are harrying his siege-works. When we get there, he may start to move; he needs a sting on the tail. At the Dionysia, Aristophanes had a fling at his sluggishness.' – 'Are you taking both horses?' I asked; thinking, I am afraid, of myself.

'Neither; he will mount us there. Don't leave Phoenix to the groom; exercise him yourself, as I have always done.' And he gave me a long talk on horse-doctoring. I promised to see to it all, and said I would consult Xenophon's father if in doubt. 'Gryllos is going with us,' he said. 'But you have chosen the right sort of friend in his boy.' He picked up his shield and began to polish it. Presently he said, 'When the Feast of Families comes round, don't forget your uncle Alexias, whom you were named after.' – 'No, Father.' – 'You must now be sixteen, or pretty near it.' I agreed to this. He put the shield down and looked at me. 'Well, then, you will be an ephebe in two years, and it would be stupid to treat you as a child. There are good looks on your mother's side of the family, as well as mine.' It was a moment before I saw it was my real mother he meant. 'I daresay we shall find they have come down to you, or so it seems at present. There is more sense in your hearing it first from me, than from someone who only tells you to make a fool of you.' I was astonished; not by his news, which he was wrong in supposing himself the first with, but that he should think it true.

'Even in youth,' he said, 'something has been written on the face by the man within. So of the suitors who are drawn by beauty there are a few, perhaps, who need not be distrusted; you must first deserve them. For the rest: those who would not care if you were a dolt, a coward, or a liar, I credit you with the wit to discern for yourself, but you will find others who, if they knew you to be so, would still let you tread on their pride and drag them about like slaves. Even though they may be distinguished in other ways, for this nevertheless despise them. To sell one's friendship for gifts is a thing not fit for discussion among gentlemen. But to sell it for flattery, or be weakened by mere importunity as one throws an obol to a noisy beggar, is not much better in my opinion. If you are in doubt, you might do worse than remember your uncle Alexias. Consider if what he did for Philon, this man would do for you; and, by the way, don't omit to ask yourself if you would do it for him.' He breathed on the shield and gave it another rub. 'I should hope at your age you have no need to be experimenting with women. Don't let anyone take you to such places as Milto's, where you will be robbed and poisoned. Koritto's girls, I am told, are clean.'

After this I suppose he was as glad as I was when my mother walked in. She was calm, though rather pale, and said the fuller would send back his cloak by nightfall.

He sailed a few days later. I went to the dock to see him off, with my great-uncle, Strymon. So much had our family been thinned, by the plague and then the war, that he would be my nearest kinsman when my father had gone. I wondered how this would turn out, for I did not know him well. My father had entertained him at festivals, sent him a present of meat when he sacrificed, and observed the usual civilities. He seldom asked him to supper with his friends. I think the only reason was that he found him dull.

Half the boys from my year at school seemed to be there, bidding their fathers goodbye. Xenophon did not see me; it was a mystery to me that a father and son should have so much to say to one another.

At last the ship cast off. I waved to my father a long while and he to me, both of us wishing, I suppose, to repair all omissions at the last. Afterwards I talked to some of my school friends; but Xenophon, though he kept a very good countenance, went off by himself. I don't think even his tutor was with him.

I had to walk back with my great-uncle Strymon. He was not much over sixty (having been a good deal younger than my grandfather) and healthy for his years. His views were always those of the majority of respectable men. I think if I could have laughed at him sometimes I might have liked him better.

At home my mother met me smiling, and gave me some sesame-cake. Her hair was wet at the edges, where she had been dashing cold water into her eyes. She was beginning to show her pregnancy a little, and to look pale and thin in the face. I told her not to grieve, that the war would soon be over now the cavalry had gone out; but she shook her head. I said, 'I expect you feel more easily frightened than at other times; but don't give way to it; I am here to look after you. And if you want anything special to eat' (for this was almost the only thing I knew about the matter) 'I will see you have it, no matter how scarce it is.' She looked at me, and started to laugh; but this brought on her weeping again, and she went away.

7

My father at departing had freed Midas ahead of his promise, as a dedication to Apollo. Old Sostias was now supposed to keep an eye on me; but I had grown a good deal lately, in height and in other ways. I soon saw that he was at a loss, and that I could do as I liked with him.

At first I had little time to please myself, there was so much to do on the farm. With my father to back me I had given his orders with some assurance; this I was now able to put into my own, without the slaves being much aware of the difference. Indeed it was not they who gave me trouble but the interference of my uncle Strymon. He had invested his whole patrimony in slaves, whom he leased to the silver-mines, with no more care than to collect their hire each month, and put something by for replacements: but he was a know-all, full of second-hand precepts, which he could not suit to the land. If I raised any objection, he would say, 'Well, well, I know the youth of today doesn't like to be told anything. I only do my duty by your father as well as I can.'

All this interrupted my training on the running-track; but going out to the farm I used to run across country while the groom took the horses, and there was plenty of exercise there to keep me from getting soft. In the last year I had been growing very fast, and had got rather lanky; now, up before dawn, out in all weathers, often sharing the work to set the slaves and hired hands a pace, I clothed my bones with muscle and grew firmly-knit, brown and hard. Soon I found that when I had time to visit the palaestra or the baths, people would turn as I passed who had never troubled themselves before. I even found it useful once or twice to have old raw-boned Sostias shambling after me.

The ship that had taken my father to Sicily brought back the news that Lamachos was dead. He had fallen storming a cross-wall which the Syracusans had built to command our siege-works. But, thanks to him, the town was almost invested, on completing which the war would be as good as over. The Syracusans had turned out to be raw soldiers, a rabble of little armies from here and there. They were fighting before the doors of their homes, which makes the worst troops tenacious, or they would long since have been swept away.

All Hellas was quiet, except that the Argives, having been raided by the Spartans, begged a loan of ships from us to defend their coast. Though we were at truce with the Spartans, to refuse seemed dishonourable, after the Argives had sent men to Sicily. When we heard that some of the ships had raided the coast of Lakonia, a few heads were shaken; but it was only a little action, like a pirate raid, and soon out of mind: out of my mind certainly, for this was the year when I first kept company with Sokrates.

I came at first like a thief in the night, lest he should notice me, and ask me some question which would show up my stupidity so that I should not dare to go again. When people asked him why he charged no fees, he used to say that he liked to be free to choose whom he conversed with, and he would not let anyone call himself his pupil, only his friend. So I was aware of my presumption. I used to wait till he had a knot of people round him, and hide behind them; if he seemed about to look my way I would step out of sight. I thought myself well concealed, till he said in the midst of some discussion, 'But now a fallacy will be evident, I expect, to the youngest of us; what do you think, Alexias?' I felt at once that we had been conversing all along; nothing new seemed to have happened, and I answered without fear. When he liked he could make any hard thing seem easy, and the natural thing to do; yet he could make something familiar look new and strange, so that one was surprised not to have seen its beauty, or not to have cast it away in disgust.

I think the world was made new for him every hour. Most of us see what other men tell us, who in turn were told by someone else. But to him, everything that is in the world was full of the gods, and it would have seemed to him the greatest impiety not to look upon it for himself. That, I suppose, is why he was hated both by the cowardly and the insolent of soul, and by all such men as dare to know neither themselves nor God.

Many things kept me away from him; a boy of my age could not go everywhere he went, and I had my work to do. There was also another cause that sometimes drove me away. As soon as my father had gone, Kritias had revealed himself; not as a suitor, who could be civilly refused, but as the kind of furtive pest who ought to be forbidden by law, in my opinion, to go near free men's sons at all. He had a disgusting way, as I have shown already, of trading on one's sense of decency, or respect for one's elders. In the last resort, I would sign to Sostias to fetch me away. Kritias never glanced after me; I would hear him as I left, making some apt syllogism.

At first I used to wonder how Sokrates could be so deceived. Later I understood that he knew, though not what I knew, much of the man that was beyond my grasp. It was clear that Kritias was going to make his mark in politics, so to teach him virtue was to benefit the City. For the rest, Sokrates was shrewder than most, but too great of soul to walk with his eyes down looking for dirt. So if I saw Kritias about him, I kept away. It was not too often; the man was full of affairs, and frequented other sophists, who taught the political arts.

A little after midsummer, my mother's time came to bear the child.

I was sleeping heavily after a day at the farm, when Kydilla came in with a lamp, and asked me to fetch the midwife. I jumped out of bed, forgetting to keep covered till the girl had gone; and her face told me pretty clearly that I was not a child any longer. But I had no time to care for that. I guessed that my mother had sent me, instead of a slave, because I was the swiftest and she was in pain. This happened long before dawn, and she was in labour all day.

When it was light, I went alone into the City, seeking some way to pass the time. First I went to the palaestra, where by taking on more than I could handle, I had no trouble in getting myself thrown till I was tired. While I was scraping-down and bathing afterwards, two or three people approached who had waited (they said) some time for the chance to meet me. I was scarcely aware of them, and did not know till much later how I first got a name for being cold and disdainful.

In the afternoon early I went home, but there was no news for me, and the midwife finding me near the door sent me sharply away. I snatched up a barley-cake and a handful of olives, then went down to Phaleron and swam till I could no more. I came to Piraeus at evening, feeling strange in myself, my sinews loosened from the water and from lying a long time naked in the sun. In a street behind Munychia harbour, I saw a woman walking ahead of me. Her dress of thin red stuff was pulled close to show her shape, which was slender and pleasing. When she had turned the corner, I saw her footprints in the dust. On the sole of her shoe some metal letters had been fastened, so that at each step her foot wrote, 'Follow me.'

I had guessed before what she was, from her being alone. The footprints led me to a low doorway, where I stood, making up my mind to knock; for I had never been with a woman before. I was afraid of finding a man there already, and that they would laugh at me. But I heard nothing, so I knocked. The woman came to the door, with her veil half drawn, showing her eyes, which were painted like an Egyptian's. I did not like her eyes, and wished to go, but she drew me in and I was ashamed to run away. The walls of the room were washed with blue; the one facing the bed had a lewd picture on it, done in red chalk. When I was in, she threw off not only her veil but her dress, and stood before me naked. It was the first such sight I had seen, and in the confusion of feelings natural to a lad of my age, I did not look clearly at her face. When she came up to embrace me, I saw nothing else. Though it was ten years since, though she had painted her lips and eyes and breasts, I knew her. It was the Rhodian. I drew back, as if I had turned a stone and found the mouth of hell. So she, thinking I was bashful, reached out for me, inviting me with the words such women use. With a cry of horror I thrust her off, remembering her voice. This made her angry, so that as I went to the door she screamed a curse at me, and once again I felt her hands striking my flesh.

I went down the street as if it were a race-track. When I came to myself, I had only one thought, that returning from all this I should find my mother dead. On reaching home, I found she had been delivered an hour before. The child was a girl.

I had not looked at the wooden billet upon the door, so sure I had been of seeing the olive-bough. Now it was as if some god had come down on a cloud to change my fate. I stood dumb, enjoying my felicity, till my uncle Strymon rose from his chair to point out that I had overlooked him. He said we must all rejoice at her safe delivery, and though no doubt my father would be disappointed, they were young and could afford to wait on the gods. 'Yet it is a pity; he had promised to call the child after her father Archagoras, that the name of a worthy man should not be lost.' Then I remembered that, whatever I liked to pretend to myself, this was her firstborn child.

When I came to the room, the women told me it had not been purified yet and I should incur uncleanness. I said, 'Be it so, then,' and went in. She was lying with her hair about her; it looked limp and damp, as after a long struggle; her face was drawn, and blue round the eyes. The child lay in her arm. I said, 'How is it, Mother?' and she looked up at me.

If a man has been beaten in the pankration, and knocked about till he can hardly stand; and as he drags himself off the ground, wiping the blood from his eyes, he meets in the way the man he knows will most rejoice at his defeat; then, however good his courage, something will show. So it was now, between my mother and me. When I understood this, then, I think, I first knew the grief of a man. But after the rain has fallen, you cannot put it back in the sky.

In this bitterness, each of us was sorry for the other. She smiled at me soon, and took my hand, and told me she was much better. I felt I should kiss her; but the room smelled of women and of blood, her flesh seemed like a stranger's and mine shrank from it. She said, 'Look, here is your sister.'

I had not thought about the child. She still had the bloom of birth on her, and her hair was like fine silver. I took her in my hands, being well used to puppies, which kept still in a firm grasp. As I had not kissed my mother, I thought it would please her if I kissed the child. I began to do it reluctantly but found she smelled sweeter when I brought her near. With my own children too I have noticed the same.

The next day I was buying food in the market, when a man said to me, 'Son of Myron, a seaman was asking for you with a letter. He is in Duris' wine-shop still.'

Sostias was there to carry for me. Prompted by I know not what, I said to him, 'Go to that stall and ask the price of the water-jars.' He went obediently; from my pedagogue he had easily become my servant. I went to the wine-shop and said, 'Who is asking for Myron's son?' A seaman got up and handed me a letter. I gave him a small present, such that he would not talk of me for praise or blame, then went round the corner and broke the thread. My father wrote that Syracuse was upon the point of surrender. He advised my mother to look after her health, to eat well and keep warm. Then he wrote 'Regarding the child, rear it, if it is a boy; if it is a girl, expose it.'

I stood with the paper in my hand. The child was less than a day old; it only remained to take home my father's command. It was clear that he had done prudently and with due regard for me. Since he had gone I knew something of our affairs; we could not afford a dower, and if he paid one it would come from my inheritance in the end. I had not liked to see my mother put the child to her breast, and should not have grieved much if it had died. But I had seen that it had already become pleasing to her, and a consolation in her defeat. Now that it was for me to take it from her, I thought of her pain and it tormented me. I remembered how when my bitch had whelped and Xenophon had said none of the litter was worth keeping, I had drowned them all; and she had come to me crying and pawing at my knees, believing I could give them back. It was this, I think, which drove me to the sin whose guilt clung to me for so long after. For as if I had planned from the first what I meant to do, I went to the yard behind the wine-shop, and tore my father's letter, and threw it away in the privy. Then I found Sostias and went home. When next my mother sent for me to write to my father for her, I wrote, 'By the gods' favour we hope to hear from you, having had no word since you went away.'

8

Without laughter, what man of sense could endure either politics or war? So we had pictured Alkibiades among the Spartans, weeping for his perfumer and his cook; while he, on the banks of the cold Eurotas, was out in all weathers, eating plain, sleeping hard and talking short. After a month, it is said, few who saw him could believe he was not Spartan born. I believe Xenophon was right in saying he once used his teeth in the palaestra. But it was before we were born, so we had missed the point of the story; not that he was weak or a coward, but that he would stick at nothing to win.

It was he who advised the Spartans that our loan of ships to the Argives was a breach of the truce. So they in turn made a loan. They lent the Syracusans a general. He came without troops, in a fishing-boat, served only by the Helots who carried his baggage and shield; so Nikias despised him, and let him get through.

After this news we had no more for some time. Xenophon, if one asked after his father, said he was well; he had been brought up in Spartan manners, not to talk of what he felt much. But he was livelier company than any Spartan, and we were still good friends. He was now a pupil of Gorgias, and could be seen among the well-bred youths who listened gravely and spoke in due turn. That he held his tongue about my own studies, I am sure was because he knew I had not Gorgias' fee. He had stopped making fun of Sokrates, but deplored most of his friends, who, as I was aware, would not have been received in Gryllos' house. He said as much to me one day on Hymettos, where we had been hunting. We had killed, and taken up our nets, and were eating our breakfast high on the stony upland, seated on a slab of rock which the grass sparkled with dew. The City lay spread below us, golden in the sun; out beyond Aegina, the hills of Argolis looked blue across the gulf, and behind them stood the high mountains of Lakedaimon. The dogs, who had been given their pickings, were licking their chops and hunting fleas. One speaks easily at such times, and he asked me without any ill-nature how I could spend my time with such people. 'Euripides, for instance. Is it true he shows Sokrates all his plays before he sends them in?' I said I had heard so. 'Then how can Sokrates pass anything so disrespectful to the gods?' – 'Define your terms,' I said. 'What *is* respect for the gods? Supposing Euripides thinks some of the old tales are disrespectful to them?' – 'Once you begin deciding for yourself what to believe about the gods, where do you leave off? Besides, he lets down women and makes them cheap.' – 'Not at all, he simply makes them of flesh and blood. I should have thought that would please you.' For he had lately begun to take some interest in them.

He whistled up the dogs, and worked the burrs out of their coats, while they shoved at each other to get near him. They were Kastorian harriers, red with white muzzles; their names, I remember, were Psyche and Augo. While he was searching the ear of the bitch for ticks, he said, 'Well, Alexias, a man has to be loyal to his teacher, we all know that. But from the way you go on about Sokrates, one might think he was your lover. If so, I'm sorry for what I've said.'

I saw he was perfectly serious, and only anxious to spare my feelings if such a thing should happen to be true. As I was beginning to understand, this kind of love was foreign ground to him. I may add that he never did, as far as I know, accept a suitor. He had always been impatient for manhood, and perhaps he feared, what is certainly true of inferior lovers, that they would want to keep a youth as long as they could. In this he was not swayed even by the example of Sparta. Sometimes indeed I asked myself whether he lacked the capacity for loving men at all; but I liked him too well to offend him by such a question.

For the sake of clearness, I had better mention at this point something concerning myself, that I had begun to attract a certain notice in the City. When I came nowadays into the palaestra, I could not fail to be aware of a general pause, with some manoeuvring and foolishness as various rivals tried to thrust themselves forward and others back. Nothing is more wearisome and ridiculous than to hear a man in the latter half of life running on about such youthful successes, as if in the meantime he had done nothing worthier of remark. All they generally amount to is this, that he was admired not by a hundred people taking notice for themselves, but by three or four who happened to lead the fashion. This is quite enough to set off a poet or two, to make the vase-painters letter some of their wares with BEAUTIFUL ALEXIAS, and so forth.

There was small danger of a youth's head being turned by all this while in the company of Sokrates; whose favourite joke it was that he was the helpless slave of beauty, just as a brave man will laugh after a battle and tell you he stood his ground because there was nowhere to run. No one was allowed to make fools of us with extravagant compliments in his hearing. He would take such people aside and say, 'Don't you see you are singing your own triumph-song before the victory? Moreover, you are making the game wild, and harder to catch; any huntsman would know better.' But this was not the only thing that kept me from getting proud.

One day I had arrived rather late, to find Sokrates already conversing in the colonnade, when young Theages remarked, 'But Sokrates, I don't think we have met what Lysis said just now. You objected, Lysis . . . Where is he? He was here a moment ago.'

It had puzzled me for some time that I never met Lysis now in Sokrates' company. It seemed to me that since he was not at all the kind of person to have made himself unwelcome, he must have some reason for staying away. These words of Theages stuck in my mind, and I asked him later whether Lysis was often there. 'Why, yes,' he said, 'nearly as often as you are. You must have missed him by chance.'

Not long after this, I learned that Sokrates had walked out to the Academy gardens. I made my way out there, and saw him sitting under the sacred olive, by the statue of the hero Akademos. The slope below was all open lawn then, so one had a long view. I saw Lysis at once, and felt, as one can at quite a distance, that he saw me. Just then my path bent round some oleanders; when I came out again, he had gone.

It is one thing when a man goes off in the palaestra into a crowd full of his friends; it is quite another, when the only new face is one's own. I had to go on, since they had all seen me; but I did not shine in the debate. Walking home I said to myself, 'What is this?' Not long ago, Lysis was not ashamed to speak to me before all the knights at the Anakeion. What has made me so repulsive to him? Perhaps someone has slandered me.' For I had naturally made a few enemies, some of them persons I had never set eyes on, whose friends, if they had lost them, I would very gladly have returned. 'But no, he is not one to be moved by chatter, it is I myself who offend him. I have not watched my manners as I ought, I have let myself be flattered by attentions not worth considering, so that men of good judgement are avoiding me in disgust.' When next I saw Lysis there before me, I walked off myself, not caring if he noticed it or not. At least I knew enough, I thought, not to let my elders make way for me.

A few days later came the feast of Olympian Zeus, when they hold the mounted torch-race. I went with Xenophon, whom I had no trouble in persuading to leave the music-contest early; so we got a good place, arriving even before the fig-sellers and the jugglers. The Hippodrome had been garlanded with oak-wreaths and flowers; there were two great flambeaux lit at the starting-line, and one at the turn. It was a clear night, with breeze enough to fan the torches but not to snuff them; the moon came up large and dusky, like a golden shield. The teams were now assembling under the flares. Seeing the naked men on the tall horses, one thought of centaurs gathering by moonlight for the chase. The team-leaders were ready; I heard a voice commanding a horse to be still, and saw Lysis reined at the line, his left hand grasping the bridle, his right with the torch in it held straight up. The trumpet sounded; hoofs drummed on the earth; the torch-flame leaned backward on the air, and the sound of the cheering followed it like smoke. When they rounded the turn, Lysis was leading; as he finished his lap, stretching forward to pass on the torch, the flame streaming from his hand, I saw him clearly, smiling at the next man and cheering him on. Xenophon said afterwards his team had won because they had trained their horses better to get off the mark. I replied that no doubt this was the cause.

A storeship returning from Sicily brought another letter from my father. My mother called me to read it to her; it said, 'The former letter I sent you by the Samian ship, the pilot's mate should have delivered to you. When this one reaches you the child will have been born. If he is a boy, call him Archagoras as we determined. To my son Alexias, who will be reading you this, my blessing. Let him not neglect to exercise nor to practise horsemanship, and let him find besides a good master-at-arms; I recommend Demeas of Mantinea, and I sanction the cost. In my opinion, the war will not be over as soon as the City supposes.'

I enrolled therefore for a course in armed combat, on horse and foot. Demeas lent one armour to practise in; my father had not told me to buy a suit, and it was a heavy outlay to make without his sanction. But by the time I was an ephebe, next year's harvest would be in. Meantime, the heavy drill strengthened my shoulders, and helped to balance them with my legs and loins, which were marked already with the Runner's Girdle. At about this time, a man took to following me in the palaestra so boldly that I took offence at it, and would not speak to him. He overtook me however when I was scraping-down, and turned out not to be a suitor but a statuary, who wanted a model. Feeling I owed him something for my incivility, I let him make some sketches, in spite of the annoyance of people standing to watch. But when he importuned me to come to his workshop, I had to refuse for want of time. I was now working every day with my trainer, for the Panathenaia was coming near; and this was the Great Year, when her new cloak is carried to Athene, and they hold the Games.

Thrice in my life I had seen the sacred procession; at four, at eight and at twelve years old: the ship-carriage of the Goddess, with the maidens holding out the robe to show the work; the gilt-horned oxen wreathed for sacrifice, the girls with the sacred baskets, the ephebes, picked for beauty, and the winners of the Games. Twice I had stood in the street, among the sweating crowds from the country, to see my father ride by with the knights, his purple-bordered cloak taken out from the chest of sweet herbs, his head crowned with myrtle, his horse groomed till it shone like bronze. This year he did not ride. Nor did I watch. For I won the long-race for boys, and marched with the winners.

More clearly than the race, I remember standing on the starting-stone, toeing the lines, afraid of getting off too soon and being thrashed by the umpires, or too late and losing. It was very hot; for many days Helios had parched the fields without rain. The dust of the track was scorching to the foot; it filled my throat and my nostrils, covered my tongue and burned my lungs; in the last lap I seemed to breathe knives, and to choke, and to be made of lead, and scarcely to move. My ears roared, with the shouting and with blood; I could hear my breath sobbing, yet as I toiled more the sound grew less; it was the runner-up I had heard and he was falling behind. And I had passed the mark before I knew it; of a sudden people were catching me in their arms and laughing, unbinding the sweat-rag from my head, wiping my face, and tying on my arm and thigh the ribbons of the victor.

I felt myself snatched as it were from hand to hand; my eyes dazzled, my body clothed with thick dust seemed to boil with heat; I felt smothered with the pressure of so many; my heart swelled and beat like a drum; I thrust my hands outward, feeling I must breathe or die. An umpire shouted 'Back there, back, make room for the boy.' Then the crowd grew less, and my great-uncle Strymon appeared in it, saying the proper things. My breath came easier, and looking round I saw all the people who used to crowd on me every day at the palaestra, the same faces again. While my eyes had been clouded, and all those hands were about me, I had fancied I know not what, some happiness, drawn by my victory as a moth flies to the torch. But the faces were all the same.

So I heard my name proclaimed by the herald, and in the Temple of the Maiden I was crowned with the olive crown; and seemed, as one does at such moments, to belong no more to myself but to the City and her gods, and to be clothed with gold. Outside, the sun beat white and scorching on the High City, and dazzled back from the rock, but it was cool in the Temple; we stood in our order, while they sang the Victors' Hymn. Before me, Autolykos, who once again had won the men's pankration, stood like marble, modest and calm. So it was over and I came down from the Temple, and saw on the steps Autolykos greeted by his father Lykon; laughing now and returning the embrace. I went home with my uncle Strymon, holding in my hands the oil-vase they had given me, with a picture of the race on one side and the Goddess on the other. The sacred oil I gave to my mother, for you can get nothing so good in the market. She was glad of my victory and had cooked a fine supper for me, tunny in cheesecake. So I called myself happy, and went to bed.

9

If so far I have mentioned none of my suitors by name, you will understand why. Only their numbers had been pleasing to me in some degree, as a mark of success, as if so many trophies had been awarded me for my looks; and even so, the crowns I had won for running had pleased me more, being a thing in which my father had not excelled before me. Yet I was civil to them, even to the most foolish, out of regard for my good name; so that people said I was not spoiled by admiration, which was as I wished.

I only once broke this rule. Kritias, after I became the fashion, decided to approach me seriously, with an epigram offering to drown himself in my unfathomed eyes and all the usual procedure. Him I turned my back on without speaking; and, as people were looking, he never came again.

Charmides had been courting me for some months. It was he indeed whose attentions had first launched me upon success. He was extremely handsome (except that he stood badly, for lack of exercise) and of the highest birth; influential, rich, and generally accomplished. I thought more than once that it would have been convenient if I could have taken to him; for if he had been my accepted suitor, the rest would immediately have retired. You may wonder why this had begun to seem so desirable to me; which brings me to Polymedes.

Polymedes was even richer than Charmides, but lacked both his breeding and his wit. Charmides, who had many love-affairs and could afford to wait, made himself always graceful and pleasant, thinking that after comparing him with the rest over some time, I would turn to him in the end. But Polymedes may, I suppose, have been in love with me as such people understand it. If you had wanted to typify the kind of lover my father had warned me to despise, you need have looked no further than Polymedes. I felt sure that if I had behaved in the most infamous manner, soliciting gifts from him in return for my favour, or if he had watched me insult in public some honourable old man, he would not only have gone on desiring me, but at my command would have lain down in the dust for me to walk on.

At all events, his antics had got beyond a joke. I could scarcely pass a wall near my home without finding 'Long life to the beautiful Alexias' flourished all over it. Our sleep was broken by his serenades; for in accordance with his nature, he hired twice as many musicians as anyone else. Whereas Charmides would bring a flute and lyre and sing quietly in a way which, I must admit, was pleasing, Polymedes made such a din that the neighbours started to shout, and I had to apologise to my mother in the morning. I did not care to discuss it with her; but I could not endure her to think I countenanced Polymedes. To my relief she took it lightly, only telling me not to let him come again because the noise woke the baby; and this message I gave him, hoping it would shame him into retreat. But he seemed delighted at my speaking to him, even for this. And as if my wishes were nothing at all to him, as if I were some image of gold or silver for which he was bidding against the rest, two days later he excelled even himself. For when I came back from exercise, quite early in the day, and was approaching the house, I saw him lying prone on the front steps, where he looked to have been already for some time.

I had heard of lovers pressing their suit in this fashion, but had really thought it only happened in comic plays. A number of little boys had stopped to look, and were wondering aloud where he had got drunk in the morning. Even as I paused, our neighbour Phalinos came up and, leaning over him officiously, asked if he had been taken ill. I saw Polymedes roll his eyes and guessed what kind of reply he must have made, for Phalinos went off muttering and shaking his head. I could picture the slaves inside chattering together and wondering what they had better do. Just then Polymedes heaved himself up on one arm like a wounded man, looking round, either for me or for someone to admire him. I drew back behind a porch and slipped away.

I ran round to the mews where the stables were, and took
Phoenix out, not calling the groom in case he knew what was
going on. It had come to something, I thought, when I could
not face our own slaves. I mounted, barefoot as I was, and rode
off, angry almost to tears. It was a matter where my uncle Strymon
might have helped me, if he had been a different man; but I could
not stomach the humiliation of asking him. It was bad enough that
he might easily come to call, and see it for himself.

But as I came into the Street of the Herm-makers, I saw in the
middle of it the only man in the world whom, that morning, it
could give me pleasure to meet. He was disputing with someone,
and, not wanting to interrupt him, I drew rein while still some
distance off.

The other man was no one I knew. Sokrates had got into
conversation with some ordinary citizen, as he often did; and I
could see at once that the man was getting warm. It was all very
well when Sokrates asked the people questions about their trade,
for he listened very humbly to all they told him; and if he showed
them in the end some wider application of their own knowledge,
it was by letting them think it was they who had taught it to him.
But sometimes they turned out the kind of man who dislikes being
made to think, and then there was trouble.

This man looked like the inferior sort of statuary who sets up
as a Herm-maker; a ham-handed fellow, covered with the white
dust of his trade; and the conversation had got to a point when
it sounded rather like the kind of row you can hear going on
in a stonemason's yard. It may be that Sokrates was reliving his
youth a little. As I looked, the man gave a bawl of rage and
set upon him. I saw that he had seized him by the hair, and
was shaking him about. I kicked Phoenix hard and he charged
forward, making everyone in the street scramble out of his way.
While I was coming up I could not see that Sokrates did much
to help himself; but he was still talking. Reaching them I called
out to the man to let go; on which Phoenix, hearing me shout,
reared up of his own accord and brandished his hoofs at the fellow's
head, as my father had taught him to do in battle. I was very
much surprised, but managed to keep my seat, and to pull him

aside from Sokrates. The man, whom I had had no time to think about, made off.

As soon as I had quieted Phoenix I jumped down. Sokrates moved out of the horse's way and I thought he had staggered. I threw my arms quickly round him, asking if he was hurt. His body was as firm as rock, and I felt a fool. 'My dear boy,' he said blinking at me, 'what are you trying to do to my reputation? It is one thing to have my hair torn out in the cause of reason; it will be quite another tomorrow, when everyone is saying, "Look at that old rascal, who outmarched all his rivals by hiring a bully to attack him, and is now the only man in the City who can claim that the beautiful Alexias embraced him in the street."'

'If that were true!' I said laughing. 'Cruel Sokrates, to mock me with such happiness!' The odd nature of our meeting had taken all my shyness away. I asked him what had caused the man to fall upon him. 'He was maintaining to a number of people that the Egyptians are barbarians because they worship beasts and birds as gods. I said we ought to enquire first whether they really did so. He had just led himself up to admitting that to worship a man-shaped image, really believing that the god resembles a man, is more impious than to worship divine wisdom in the shape of a hawk. At this point he became angry; you would have supposed he had something to gain by thinking every Egyptian more barbarous than himself.'

'Your head is bleeding,' I said, and wiped it with the corner of my cloak. Just then I saw a metic's son I knew by sight, and gave him something to take Phoenix home for me; for people were gathering to stare at him, as they do if you lead a good horse in the City. 'Now, Sokrates,' I said, 'I shall walk with you wherever you are going, for how will you shake me off? The whole town would denounce your inconstancy, after what has been between us.' And I gave him the side of my eye, as Agathon would have done.

He said nothing, but as we began walking, I saw he was laughing to himself. Presently he said, 'Don't imagine, dear Alexias, that I laugh out of foolhardiness, like a man reckless of his danger. But who would recognise in the accomplished beauty, who is drawing looks of hatred and envy upon me from every side, the shy lad who stood at the back, and ducked behind someone's shoulder whenever he felt in danger of being spoken to?' – 'With you, Sokrates,' I said, ceasing to laugh, 'I always feel the same.' He looked at me and said, 'Well, I believe you. For something is troubling you; yet when it comes to bringing it out, this charming boldness is only skin-deep after all. Or perhaps it is a matter of love? Naturally in that case a novice like me could scarcely help you.'

'You know if it were I should be at your door before daybreak with it, like all the rest. But it's only a matter of a suitor; and you would call me cold, as you did before, chasing me away without giving me any chance to prove to you whether I am cold or not.' I had heard Kallikles talk to him like this, and it had seemed to amuse him.

'Is this suitor,' he said, 'Polymedes by any chance? You and he have not fallen out, have you?' – 'Fallen out!' I cried. 'I have scarcely spoken to the man. You can't have been supposing Sokrates . . .' – 'Naturally in a case like this you will find foolish people saying that the suitor would never have gone so far without incitement, even if without reward. But I see they have been unjust to you.' I was so much hurt by this that, losing my head, I said I had had enough of it all, and was thinking of slipping off if I could to join the Army in Sicily. He said, 'Steady, my friend. Be what you would like to seem; that's a man's best shield against tongues. Calm yourself, and tell me what the particular trouble is.'

When I had done he said, 'I see I was wrong to let you send your horse home, for I imagine you were in a hurry to ask some friend for his advice and help; Charmides, for instance?' I denied this with indignation, indeed with too much. It was true that I had not been going to Charmides; but as I rode I had begun thinking, 'I won't seek his help, and be in debt to him; but, when I have shown I can take care of myself, it might do no harm to be seen in his company once or twice.' I said, however, 'Charmides is waiting for that very thing. If this is love and the behaviour of lovers, give me the enemy in battle.'

I spoke in anger, for my heart was sore. The truth is that I was getting to an age when one wishes for love, and has one's own ideas of what it ought to be; and I was ceasing to believe that what I sought was anywhere to be found.

'By the way,' Sokrates asked, 'what do you dislike so much about Polymedes? He looks undistinguished, of course, compared with a man like Charmides, and his father made his money in leather. Is it his vulgarity, or what?' – 'No, Sokrates. That too I daresay; but in himself he is base. He tried first to buy me with gifts; not flowers or a hare, but the kind of thing we can't afford at home. Then he sent word that he was dying, to make me take him out of pity; and now, what is surely as low as a man can go, he is willing I should do it simply to keep him quiet. If I were to lose my father and mother and all I have, if I were disgraced even before the City so that people turned from me in the street, he would be glad of it, if it put me within his reach. And this he calls love.' I had spoken too vehemently, but Sokrates still looked at me kindly; so coming at last to what had been behind the rest, I said, 'I shall always think worse of myself for having been his choice.'

He shook his head. 'You are wrong, my boy, if you think he is seeking a kindred spirit. He is looking for what he lacks, being limp of soul, and not wishing to know that the good must first be wrought with toil out of a man's own self, like the statue from the block. So now I think you need the advice of someone who understands these questions.'

I was about to say, 'Whose, Sokrates?' when a great noise of hammering reminded us that we were approaching the Street of the Armourers. Since the news from Sicily, they were busy again. We turned aside, to be heard without shouting. 'I suppose,' Sokrates said, 'you will be ordering armour for yourself before another year is up, so fast time flies. Where will you go for it?' – 'To Pistias, if I can afford his price. He's very dear; nine or ten minas for a horseman's suit.' – 'So much? I suppose you will get a gold device on the breastbone for that?' – 'From Pistias? Not if you gave him twelve; he won't touch them.' – 'Kephalos would make you something to catch the eye.' – 'Well, but Sokrates, I might need to fight in it.' He laughed, and paused. 'I see,' he said, 'that you are a judge of value, though so young. Perhaps you can tell me, then, who am getting too old to know much of such matters, what price one ought to pay for a true and honourable lover?' I wondered what he could take me for, and answered at once that one ought not to pay anything.

He looked at me searchingly, and nodded his head. 'An answer worthy, Alexias, of your father's son. Yet many things have their price which are not upon the market. Let us see if this is one of them. If we come into the company of such a lover, it seems to me that one of three things will happen. Either he will succeed in making us his equal in honour; or, if he fails both to do this and to free himself from love, seeking to please us he will become less good than he was; or, if he is of stronger mind, remembering what is due to the gods and to his own soul, he will be master of himself, and go away. Or can you see some other conclusion than these?'

'I don't think, Sokrates,' I said, 'that there can be another.'

'So, then, it now appears, does it not, that the price of an honourable lover is to be honourable ourselves, and that we shall neither get him nor keep him, if we offer anything less?' – 'It seems so, certainly,' said I, thinking it kind of him to be at so much pains to keep my mind from my troubles. 'And thus,' he said, 'we find what we thought was to be had for love turns out the costliest of all. You are fortunate, Alexias; for I think it is still within your means. But see, we are walking past our destination.'

We had just passed the portico of the Archon King, and were outside Taureas' palaestra. Not wishing to trouble him with my company out of season, I asked if he was meeting a friend. 'Yes, if I can find him. But don't go, Alexias. I am only looking for him to put your case before him. He happens to be much better qualified than I to help you.'

I knew his modesty; but having resolved to deal with Polymedes at once, I did not feel eager to spend the rest of the morning being improved by Protagoras or some other venerable Sophist; so I assured Sokrates that he himself had done me as much good as anyone could, except a god. 'Oh?' he said. 'Yet I believe you don't consider me infallible; I noticed just now that you thought more of Pistias' opinion than of mine.' – 'Only about armour, Sokrates. Pistias is an armourer, after all.' – 'Just so. Wait, then, while I fetch my friend. He is usually wrestling here about this time.' – 'Wrestling?' I said staring; Protagoras was reckoned to be at least eighty years old. 'Who is this friend, Sokrates? I thought . . .' – 'Wait in the garden,' he said; and then just as he was turning to go, 'We will try Lysis, son of Demokrates.

I believe that I gasped aloud, as if he had emptied a water-jar over me. Without regard for my manners, I caught him by the mantle, and held him back. 'Sokrates, I beg of you. What do you mean? Lysis hardly knows me. He will be exercising, or talking to his friends. Do not disturb him for such a trifle. He will be annoyed, and disgusted; he will simply think me a fool not to have managed for myself. I should never be able to look him in the face again.'

'Why, what is this?' he said, his eyes standing forth in his head so that I was half afraid he was really angry. 'If a man is too prejudiced to take an informed opinion, what can be done for him? We are wasting the day in trifling; I really must get on.' – 'Sokrates! Pray come back, I ask it in kindness. I ought to have told you before: Lysis dislikes me, and goes out of his way to avoid me. Haven't you noticed how . . .' But I had forgotten to keep hold of him, and found myself talking to the air.

I saw him go through to the inner court, and vanish under the colonnade. For a moment I was tempted to run away; but I knew I could not forgive myself after, if I treated him with disrespect. So I waited, in the little walled garden where the well is for drinking, standing under the plane-tree that grows just inside the gate. A few old men, athletes of Perikles' day, were sitting in the shelter of the eaves; nearer, around the stone benches in the centre which are usually left for them, some of the crowned victors were resting, sitting upon the seats if they were dressed, or stretched on the grass to sun themselves after the bath; for though late in autumn the day was quite warm. My own presence there was something of an impertinence; I wished Sokrates would make haste, and then again I wanted him to delay.

After quite a short time I saw him returning, speaking over his shoulder to someone behind. I knew Lysis while he was still in the dark shadow, by his height, and the way he held his head. Having been bathing or scraping-down he had come out as he was, with his towel hanging on his shoulder. Just inside the porch he stood still for some moments, as if in thought, looking before him. I said to myself, 'He has seen who it is that Sokrates has brought, and is displeased, as I expected.' But presently he walked forward. Autolykos, who was lying on the grass, called out something to him, and he turned to answer; but he did not pause, and came up to me leaving Sokrates outdistanced. I saw that his right shoulder, which one always leaves to the last in cleaning-off, still had dust and oil on it. He was at this time about twenty-five years old.

He stood looking down at me, without saying anything, and I looked up silently at him. I knew I ought to speak first, and apologise for troubling him; but an ox seemed to be treading down my tongue. Then Sokrates caught him up, saying cheerfully, 'Well, Alexias, I have told Lysis about your difficulty.' Just as I was going to speak Lysis said, 'Yes. Anything I can do . . .' He did not go on, and I sought for something to say before he lost patience with me. 'I am sorry, Lysis, for troubling you, when you were with your friends.' – 'Not at all,' he said. – 'If you would rather see me some other time . . . ?' – 'No,' he said, and smiled at me suddenly. 'Sokrates thinks this is the proper time. Come, let us sit down.'

He went over to the stone coping round the well, and threw his towel over it to sit on. When he invited me to be seated too, I looked round for Sokrates, expecting him to share our conversation. But I could not see him anywhere. So I sat down on the grass.

'Well,' Lysis said, 'so Polymedes is still giving trouble? He has staying-power at least.' I thought the talk in the City must have exceeded my fears, for even Lysis to have heard it. 'Indeed, Lysis,' I said, 'he never had anything to stay for. But now it seems that either I must speak to him, and give him the public scene he wants, or get him turned off by the slaves.' – 'No, by Herakles,' he said, 'that wouldn't do; it would get everyone on his side. Extremes people would think disgusting in a man mourning his father, or his only son, get tolerated in cases like this, as if . . .' He broke off frowning, then looked up and said, 'But if I insult the power of the god, he will make me suffer for it.' He smiled at me, looking into my eyes. I thought, 'He is trying to put me at ease, as he did once before; it could be nothing else.' I looked down, and pulled at a piece of grass, too shy to return his smile or to answer at all. His feet, which I found myself looking at, were big but very well-shaped, and as strongly arched as a runner's.

Becoming serious, he said, 'No, Alexias, this is a matter that a friend should take up for you. Have you someone in mind to ask?' And he looked attentively at my face. Raising my head I replied, 'Well, I did think of Xenophon. He usually has a plan of some sort. But he would never let me hear the last of it.' – 'Xenophon?' he said, frowning this time much more deeply; 'whose son is that?' When I told him, he said, 'I see,' and looked less severe, so that I almost thought he was going to laugh. 'I don't think we need trouble Xenophon for this. Polymedes is a man in years, if in nothing else. If you are willing, I will see to it for you, shall I? And to anything else of the kind that turns up, if you want me to. Now, or at any time.'

I could scarcely find words to thank him with, but managed to say something. He answered, 'Good; then if we go now, with luck we shall have him out of the way before your uncle calls. Wait while I get my clothes; I will be back directly.'

While I was waiting, one or two of the men who had been cooling-off came over to get a drink. I drew up the water for them, and they thanked me very civilly. No one made advances to me, or asked why I was there. I thought, 'Perhaps they suppose that Lysis invited me in.' Just then he came back bathed and dressed and said, 'Let us go.' I remembered he had been wrestling, and said, 'Shall I draw you some water first Lysis? I expect you are cool enough to drink now?'

He paused by the well and said laughing, 'Do you think I need to wash the dust out of my mouth? You should give water to Ephisthenes, whom I wrestled with.' Then seeing me look uncertain, he said, 'But you are right, I am rather thirsty. Thank you.' So I drew water, and filled with the dipper the bronze cup that stood there, and gave it to him, putting my hand under it and offering him the handles, as I had been taught in serving wine. He stood for a moment with the cup in his hands, then held it up and poured a libation before he drank. When he offered it me to drink from, wishing to omit nothing that was proper I did the same. He began to speak, but paused again. 'Come, then,' he said, and we went out into the streets.

As we walked he said to me. 'Don't have Polymedes too much

on your mind, even if one or two people do turn out to have seen you. It will all be forgotten in a week. Anything he has the wit to think of, you may be sure has been done before. I once heard of a man . . .' His tale was so comical that shy as I was of him, I could not help laughing. I almost asked the name of the youth, till I remembered how he himself must have been run after, even before he left school.

As soon as he turned the corner of our street, I saw Polymedes was still there. I advanced reluctantly; I felt sure that as soon as he saw he had an audience, he would fall to his sighing and groaning again, or sing one of his bad poems; for his lyre was beside him on the steps. 'I'm afraid, Lysis . . .' I began; but Polymedes must have heard my voice, for he turned his head. Instead of behaving as I had expected, he leaped to his feet as if a scorpion had bitten him, and without greeting me or even looking at me, shouted in a passion of anger. 'No, by the Mother, this is too much! You could teach a Cretan to cheat, Lysis, and a Spartan to steal! Do you think I shall lie down under your insolence?' Lysis looked him over, and without raising his voice answered that he had lain down long enough already, and had indeed obliged everyone by getting up.

But Polymedes called out louder than ever, 'A blind man could have seen what you were at! Oh, yes, I had my eye on you when you thought me far away. I have seen you looking, standing apart with that insufferable pride of yours, which the gods will take down, if there are any gods. You would not have deceived a child, let alone a lover. So this is what you were after, is it? Waiting like a horse-thief by the paddock while a better man breaks in the colt, then slipping through in the dark to steal him when the trainer sleeps.' Lysis made no answer to all this. I could not tell if he was angry. As for me, I was so overcome with shame at hearing such language used to him, that I should have liked to hide myself. He did not move, but stood gravely watching Polymedes; who, now that he was up, looked uncertainly about him. I thought, 'I suppose he is wondering whether it will look well to lie down immediately on the steps again. But if he stands, he must pick up his lyre.'

Turning my head, I saw the corner of Lysis' mouth move; and suddenly laughter clutched at my belly. Yet I hardened my body to smother it, though an hour ago I should have been glad to laugh. I suppose I knew already, though still not daring to presume on what I knew, that the gods had a precious gift for me, and that it would be base to insult a poorer man. Lysis too had quenched his laughter. But we could not keep from catching each other's eyes. Polymedes looked from one to the other of us, hitching his mantle at the shoulder as if it were his dignity he was trying to gather up; then suddenly turned his back and went off down the street, leaving his lyre where it was upon the steps.

Lysis and I looked after him with serious faces. The lyre seemed to both of us like the sword a dead man leaves on the field. Perhaps we should have known that open laughter would be less cruel to him than our pity. But we were young.

10

Next day we had great trouble in meeting; for Lysis had not asked me to fix any time or place, not wishing, as he told me later, to seem like a man who does a small service and asks at once for a return. So he and I spent half the morning wandering about in different places; and no one knew enough yet to say, 'Lysis was here just now, looking for you, and went that way.' But at last, when I had given up hope of him, and had gone to exercise, as I turned the post of the running-track I saw him watching at the other end. It was as if a great wind blew at my back and my heels grew wings. I scarcely knew that I touched the ground, and I finished so far ahead of the rest that everyone cheered me. I heard Lysis' voice; and being breathless already, from running and from suddenly seeing him, now I felt as if my heart would burst my breast, and saw black in the sky. But it passed and I was able to speak when he greeted me.

When I was dressed we walked into the streets together. He asked if it was true my grandfather had been a runner, and we talked about that, and about our parents, and such things. Presently I recognised across the street his brother-in-law Menexinos; who, when he saw us, lifted his brows, smiled broadly, and made to cross over. I saw Lysis shake his head at him; at which he raised his hand in greeting and passed on. Though Lysis quickly took up the conversation, I saw he had gone a little red. It had not come into my mind till then that he could possibly feel shyness too. We went walking from one street to another, pausing sometimes to watch, or seem to watch, a potter or a goldsmith working. At last he stopped and said, 'But where were you going, Alexias?' – 'I don't know, Lysis,' I said. 'I thought you were going somewhere.' At this we both laughed. He said, 'Shall we walk to the Academy, then?' So we went there, talking all the way, for we were not yet easy enough to be silent together.

On the grassy slope by the Kephissos, we sat down under a willow tree. The water smelled as it does in autumn, of black leaves. We had come to the end of our words, and waited for an omen, or I know not what. Just then I saw coming through the yellow poplars Charmides with a couple of friends. His salute we both returned; my heart sank when I saw him still approaching, for though he had always behaved like a gentleman, one cannot count on people at such times. Here I flattered myself absurdly; it must have been seldom he had less than two love-affairs on hand, to say nothing of women. At all events he came up smiling, and said in the pleasantest way, 'This is too bad of you, Lysis; you are like the horse they bring in from the country after the bets are laid. Have you held off so long just for the pleasure of seeing all the rest of us make fools of ourselves? I don't know how long it is now since I was doing my homage along with the other victims, and getting as usual only, "Thank you, Charmides, for your verses; I am sure they are excellent, if I were any judge of such things", when you passed along the colonnade without, it seemed, even looking over your shoulder. I don't think Alexias stood watching you for more than a moment; but I, being one not quite blind to the signals of Eros, said to myself at once, "There goes the winner, if he would only enter the race."'

This was worse than Polymedes; I went hot and cold; but Lysis answered smiling with hardly a pause, 'I see it's I, Charmides, who you want to watch making a fool of myself. Thanks for the invitation, but the tumbler begs to be excused. Tell me, while we are talking of horses, is your black going to win next week or not?'

Although Charmides had behaved better than I had thought was in him, he had left me dreading his departure more than I had his approach. He left with his friends almost immediately after. I picked up a handful of little stones, and began skimming them at the water. I can still remember their colours and shapes. 'They won't go far,' Lysis said. 'This bank is too high.' – 'I usually get them further.' – 'I expect,' he said, 'Menexinos is talking by this time, too.' I threw another stone, which went straight to the bottom. 'Well,' he said, 'we know now what they are saying. If it were displeasing to either of us, I think we should not be here together as we are. Or am I only speaking for myself?' I shook my head; then, taking courage from him, turned to him and said, 'No.' He was silent for a moment; then he said, 'As the gods hear me, Alexias, your good shall be mine, and your honour shall be like my own to me; and I will stand to it with my life.' I felt more than myself, and answered, 'Don't be afraid, Lysis, that while you are my friend I shall ever come to dishonour; for rather than to be a shame to you I will die.' He put his right hand on mine and his left about my shoulders and said, 'May it never be less than this with us.' With these words we kissed. The sun was sinking, and the shadows of the poplars were longer than the trees. After talking a little longer, we walked back to the City.

As we went, I asked him what I had done in the past that had so much offended him. He asked what could ever have made me suppose such a thing, 'for,' he said, 'I have only loved you too much for my peace.' – 'You were always avoiding me, yet I gave you no cause.' – 'Is it really true,' he said, 'that you noticed that for yourself; or did someone tell you to make mischief?' – 'What makes you think, Lysis, my sight is so thick?' – 'But when I spoke to you last spring, during the Dionysia, you ran from me in the street.' – 'I was in trouble at home; I ran all the way to the mountain. I never supposed you would think of it again.'

'The tale is still older than that,' he said. Then he told me that nearly two years before, on first seeing me in the palaestra, he had found himself possessed by the thought of me, and had planned to address me seriously as soon as he found a chance. But Sokrates had drawn it all out of him; and, instead of the sympathy he had hoped for, told him sharply that the love of young boys ought to be forbidden by law; the man, he said, was wasting his pains upon uncertainty, and ensuring they would be disappointed; for while the boy's nature was still malleable, he was being moulded to vanity and folly, called upon to play a part he was not ready to understand. 'If an athlete were to enter for a contest below his class, would he not be discredited in victory, and laughed at in defeat?' Relating it to me, Lysis added, 'To this I could find nothing to say.' Indeed, Sokrates had known well where to touch him.

He confessed that later, when he saw me so much courted, he had felt a good deal of bitterness. He had heard it said that I inclined to Charmides; and I was ashamed to ask him why he had not put it to proof. Remembering the silly extravagances of my following, I did not wonder he had thought such a scrimmage beneath him. Nor did I doubt he had heard them call me cold and disdainful; he who had been drawn to me before anyone had taken me up. 'My heart was sore at it,' he said. 'I could not forgive Sokrates for a time, and even avoided him; till looking about me, I saw some of the people who had refused to take his medicine before, and what kind of men they were. So next day I went back again.'

As he spoke he gave a great yawn. In apology, he said he had lain awake nearly all the night before, unable to sleep for happiness. I confessed that with me it had been the same.

Next day he took me to his home, which was outside the walls near the Sacred Way, and presented me to his father. Demokrates was a man of about fifty-five, but looked older, his health, Lysis said, having troubled him for some time. His beard was long, and already almost white. He received me very courteously, commending my father's courage in the field. Beyond this he showed a certain reserve; perhaps there had been some old difference between them, which he felt it would be petty to visit upon me.

The house, though it was getting shabby in the way I was used to at home, was a big one, with some fine marble and bronze in it. Demokrates was said to have lived with much splendour in his youth; it was to this house, as I recalled, that Alkibiades had run away from his guardians when he was a lad, the first proof of his wildness to reach the City, though Perikles tried to hush it up.

In the manner of men getting on in years whose circumstances have worsened, Demokrates ran on a good deal about the glories of the past. I saw Lysis listening patiently, like one who had resigned himself beforehand; but it was plain there was affection between them. 'I lost two other sons,' his father said, 'in childhood; but the gods relented with Lysis, making him a son as good to me as three. Now he is old enough not to have his head turned by it,

I can say his boyhood was all I wished; and as a man he has not disappointed me. I only need to see him married, and a son of his bearing my name; and I can go when the gods are ready.'

I don't know whether Demokrates said this simply because sick men tend to be wrapped up in themselves, or purposely, to see whether I was the kind of youth to stand in a friend's way out of petulance or jealousy. Thinking myself, as one does at that age, the centre of everything, I felt it became me not to fail in courage at the test; and answered so coolly as a Spartan that the son of Demokrates could choose a wife wherever he wished. When Lysis took me out to see the pleasure-garden, I felt as one does after a difficult sword-dance, when one has got out of the judge's sight. Lysis stretched himself like a man who has just taken off his armour, laughed and said, 'Father is in no such hurry to find me a wife as he pretends. One of my sisters was married last year, and there is still another who is fifteen already. By the time she is provided for, it will be a long while before I can afford to set up house, as he very well knows.'

He told me that the bulk of their wealth in former years had come from their estates in Thrace, where they had bred chariot-horses and mules for riding; but he himself had never seen these lands, for they had been seized and laid waste in the war, and the stock carried off, before he became a man.

Beyond the pleasure-garden were the fields of the flower-sellers, and even now in autumn the air was sweet. 'One ought to marry,' Lysis said, 'while one is still young enough to get strong sons; but there is time and to spare for that. When I want a woman's company I have a very good girl, a little Corinthian. She doesn't pretend to recite Anakreon and the lyric poets, like the fashionable companions; but she sings prettily, in a little clear voice like a bird's, a thing I like in a woman.' He smiled to himself and said, 'One has strange thoughts when one is lonely; there were times when I used to wish I were rich enough to keep Drosis entirely, as Perikles did Aspasia, so that she need never entertain anyone else. It wasn't that I minded much her going to bed with other men, seeing that if she had not been a hetaira I should never have met her, nor would she have any more conversation than the kind of girl one takes for a wife. No; although it sounds foolish, I didn't like to know that the behaviour she put on to please me, she would put off like a garment, and become a different being for another man. Well, she is good enough company in her way, but no Aspasia, poor little thing; and I don't think such notions will trouble me any more.' To all this I listened respectfully, and at the end nodded and looked solemn, like a man who is knowledgeable in such matters. Lysis smiled and took my arm and we went to look at the horses.

In the harness-room, where the yokes of old chariots gathered dust upon the walls, we played with a litter of boarhound pups, and exchanged old secrets, as people do at such times for the pleasure of saying, 'This I have told to no one but you.' He confided to me that though he had first known a woman when he was seventeen years old, he had never been in love with a youth at all, until he met me. He said it used to disturb him sometimes, when he read the poets, that he seemed incapable of that love which they praised as the noblest, and the inspirer of so many glorious deeds. 'I did not know,' he said, 'what I was waiting for. But the god knew.'

I wished my father would return, so that I could present Lysis to him. Here was something of mine with which he could have no fault to find. They knew each other by sight, from their cavalry exercises, being fellow-tribesmen; Lysis remarked that as I was not very like him, he supposed it was my mother from whom I got my looks. I told him I thought so, but that she had died at my birth. He looked at me puzzled. 'But,' he said, 'since we have been together, I have heard you speak of your mother a score of times. Is she only your stepmother, then?' – 'Yes, but it has never seemed so to me.' – 'She was a widow, I expect, when your father married her?' – 'No indeed, Lysis, she was not turned sixteen.' He heard me out smiling, and drawing his brows together. 'You are full of mysteries for me, Alexias. Not that I could imagine your ever failing in courtesy to your father's wife; but even to me you call her Mother, just as if she were really so. And now you tell me she is the same age as I am! You make me feel a hundred years old.' He spoke lightly; yet, I knew not why, his words distressed me. 'But she is my mother, Lysis. If she is not . . . if she is not, then I never had one.' He saw I was troubled, and embracing me kindly said, 'Why then, my dear, of course she is.'

I stayed to supper with him; Demokrates retired early because of his sickness, so we were alone. Summer flowers were done, but we had crowns of cyclamen and ivy. The wine was good, but we drank it well-tempered, having no need to believe ourselves happier than we were. After eating we played at kottabos with the wine-lees, ringing them in the bowl, or throwing them down hard and never failing to find in the spillings the letters of each other's name. There was an inlay in the floor of Athene fighting a Mede, and it began to look as if the blood had flowed pretty freely, which made us laugh, being in the mood to laugh at anything. Later, when the moon had come out, we walked in the garden, sharing a cloak.

In all this time, Lysis never asked anything from me beyond a kiss. I understood him, that he wanted me to know he was in love from the soul, and not, as they say, with the love of the Agora. As for me, it seemed to me that nothing could have added to the joy I felt in his company; and I wished for nothing, except to possess whatever would increase his happiness, that I might give it him. I felt that another time would come, as one feels an air of summer while still in spring. We had no need of words to say such things. We talked of I know not what; of our childhood, and of times when we had happened to see each other at festivals, or in the palaestra, or at the Games. When it grew late he threw the last of his wine into the bowl, saying, 'This for my Alexias,' and the bowl rang true. Then we drank to the Good Goddess in clear water; and he called for a torch and took me home.

At the door he said, 'All this happiness we owe to Sokrates. We ought not to stay away from him any longer. We will go tomorrow.'

Next day we met early, and went together to find him. At his house, his son Lamprokles told us he was already gone out. I had met this boy before, and had never borne him any grudge for looking at me with resentment, as he always did. It was not to be expected that Sokrates should have bequeathed him much beauty; and in him his father's ugliness had lost its strength, without gaining anything else. He had been apprenticed to a mason, but having wit enough, it seems, to learn the trade of sculptor which Sokrates had abandoned. The house was one of those poor ones so clean that the very threshold seems to curse your foot. As we spoke to the lad, we heard his mother, whose eyes we had seen at the window, shout out to him not to stand gossiping, as if one do-nothing in the house were not enough. This was nothing fresh to us, for she could often be heard railing at Sokrates before one got near the door. We called her vixen and shrew among ourselves; yet one can see she might find it bitter that he taught for nothing, hearing him asked for by so many young men who could have paid. He had kept at his work till Kriton, learning what his savings were, offered to invest them so that for his plain life they would bring in enough. I spoke gently to the boy, being sorry for him; not only because of his mother, but because he seemed much less Sokrates' son than Lysis was, or, I thought, even I.

The Herm at the door was the work of Sokrates. At the time of the sacrilege, he had got out his old tools as an act of piety, to make a new head for the god. The work was what we call sincere, when we mean that an artist we like is not exactly a master; being in the austere style of Pheidias' day, it already looked a little out of date.

We found Sokrates in the Lykeion gardens, already in conversation with five or six people all as it happened old friends of his. Kriton was there, and Eryximachos, Agathon with his friend Pausanias, and one or two more. Sokrates saw us first, and gave a smiling nod without pausing in his talk. The others made room with the kind of easiness people have ready beforehand; only Agathon widened his blue eyes at us and gave us openly one of his sweet smiles.

They had been conversing about the nature of truth. I don't know in what form this subject had first arisen. Soon after we came, Sokrates said that truth could not be served as a slave serves a master, who gives no reason for his commands; we should seek her rather, he said, as a true lover seeks knowledge of the beloved, to learn entirely what he is and what he needs, not like base lovers seeking only to know what they can turn to gain. And so, from this, he began to speak of love.

Love, he said, is not a god, for a god cannot want anything; but one of those great spirits who are messengers between gods and men. He does not visit fools, who are content with their low condition, but those who aware of their own need desire, by embracing the beautiful and good, to beget goodness and beauty; for creation is man's immortality and brings him nearest to the gods. All creatures, he said, cherish the children of their flesh; yet the noblest progeny of love are wisdom and glorious deeds, for mortal children die, but these live forever; and these are begotten not of the body but the soul. Mortal passion sinks us in mortal pleasure, so that the wings of the soul grow weak; and such lovers may rise to the good indeed, but not to the very best. But the winged soul rises from love to love, from the beautiful that is born and dies, to beauty in itself eternal; the life itself, of which mortal beauty is only a moving shadow flung upon a wall.

As his deep voice talked on, my soul grew impatient with my body, and reached beyond it, seeking a god above the gods. I remembered nothing of my life, except the moments this god had touched: when in the High City I had watched dawn break upon the ships; or in the mountains sometimes, when Xenophon had gone off with the dogs and left me watching the nets alone; or with Lysis on the banks of the Kephissos. Sokrates did not stay as usual to invite our objections to his argument, but got up at once, and bade us good day.

The others sat down on the grass to talk, and we sat too. No one spoke to us. Long after, Agathon told me he would as soon have spoken to the Pythia while she was in the trance of the god. But I don't think we were a trouble to them. We were so deep in our thoughts, not even looking at one another, that they talked round and over us, as if we had been statues or trees. After what I suppose was not so very long, I began to hear what they were saying. Pausanias said, 'It is a long time since Sokrates last gave us what we heard today. It was at your house, Agathon, do you remember? When we drank to your first crown.' – 'I shall be dead, my dear, when I forget that.' – 'And as he ended, Alkibiades came in drunk through the garden door.' – 'His looks can't stand wine as they did,' said Kriton. 'When he was a boy, he looked like a flushed god.' Someone asked, 'What happened then?' – 'Hearing us all praising Sokrates, he said, "Oh, I can tell you something more remarkable than that." And he described how he had tried, without success, to seduce Sokrates one night after supper. Drunk as he was, I must say he told the story well; but you could see that years later he was still puzzling it over. I really think he offered the highest praise he knew. Sokrates made a joke of it, which indeed it was, in its own way. I should have laughed myself with the best, if I had not remembered when he loved the boy.'

At this my thoughts, which had been nowhere and everywhere, settled and grew clear. I remembered the dull youth at Sokrates' house. And Alkibiades had received his love as a cracked jar holds wine. Yet being in love with the good, he could not, I thought, have ceased desiring to beget her offspring. It was for Lysis and me, not to be chosen (for no man can lay such a thing upon another) but to choose ourselves his sons.

I felt Lysis look at me, and turned towards him. Understanding each other, we got up and walked out through the gardens into the streets. We did not speak, having no need of it, but made for the High City, and climbed the stairway side by side. Leaning on the northern wall we looked out to the mountains. On the tops of Parnes the first snow had fallen; the day was bright and blue, with a few small clouds, white and violet-dark. The wind from the north blew our hair from our brows, and streamed our garments behind us. The air was clear, keen, and filled with light. It seemed to us that at our command the wind would have lifted us like eagles, that our home was the sky. We joined our hands; they were cold, so that in clasping them we felt the bone within the flesh. Still we had not spoken; or not with words. Turning from the wall we saw people offering at the altars or going in and out of the temples; it had seemed to us that the place was empty, but for ourselves. When we came to the great altar of Athene I stopped and said, 'Shall we swear it?' He thought for a moment and answered, 'No. When a man needs an oath, he has repented that he swore it, and is compelled by fear. This must come from our own souls, and from love.'

When we reached the porch I said, 'I must make an offering

to Hermes, before I go. He has answered a prayer of mine.' –
'What prayer is that?' – 'I prayed he would tell me if Sokrates
wanted anything.' He looked at me a moment under his brows,
then laughed. 'Make your offering; we will talk later.' I went to
get some myrrh, and Lysis went away into the Temple of the
Maiden. He was gone longer than I, so I waited for him beside
the little Temple of Victory on the bastion, which that year was
almost finished. When he came, I asked him why he had laughed.
'To tell you the truth,' he said, 'I was wondering whether it was
Sokrates you were in love with, or me. Am I only the sacrifice you
have killed on the altar, so that you can ask your friend to sup with
you on the meat?'

I turned to protest, but he was smiling. 'I forgive you,' he said.
'I must; I've been his captive myself since I was fifteen. It was
Hermes' Day at school when some visitor brought him in. My
tutor and Menexinos' had slipped off together for a drink, so we
started listening. He saw us stretching our ears behind the men,
called us to talk to him, and asked us what friendship was. In the
end, we never clinched a definition; Menexinos and I wrangled it
over for the rest of the day. My poor father got no peace till he
let me go to him, after that.'

Before we went down, we paused to look once more at the
mountains. The air was so clear that we could see northward as
far as Dekeleia, where the Spartans used to come down before the
truce. A little trail of smoke came up from it, where some guard,
or a shepherd, was lighting his mid-day fire.

11

The weeks passed by, bringing winter to the fields and spring to me. As, when great Helios shines upon a frost-bound pool, the birds begin alighting, and at evening the beasts come down to drink, so I, being happy, instead of suitors began to have friends. But my head was too full of Lysis to notice the change, and, when he was busy, I scarcely knew how my time was spent.

One day a despatch came in from Sicily, and was read to the Assembly. We boys who were not of age hung about at the foot of the hill, waiting for news. The men trooped down, long-faced and loud-mouthed, from the Pnyx.

Nikias wrote that Gylippos, the Spartan general, had raised a force on the far side of the island, had trained it, taught it discipline, and marched it to the relief of Syracuse. He had dug in on high ground penning our Army between him and the town. He had united Sicily against us, and troops were expected from the Spartan confederacy as well. In the upshot, Nikias asked for a second army not less than the first, and a second load of treasure to maintain it, and for a general to relieve him. He was sick in the kidneys, he said, and could not do his work as he would wish. He could hold out over winter, but help must not be delayed beyond the spring; and so he ended.

Lysis told me all this while the crowd still surged around us. Everyone sounded angry; but I don't remember any foreboding. They were more like people come to a festival, who have been told nothing will be ready for a week, and they must all go home.

Before long the muster-rolls came out, and ended fears which I had kept to myself. Lysis was not going: too few cavalry were left as it were to guard the frontier. When the knights sailed, he had been taken out of his tribal squadron, and made a Phylarch of the Guard in place of an officer who had gone. Though he was young for it, they were glad to find someone who could get himself respected by the youths, and keep them in order. It took him much away from me, and I thought it long till I should be an ephebe myself; for he had promised to ask that I should be enrolled under his command. Finding me eager to improve, though there were many things he enjoyed more than soldiering, he often gave up his leisure to take me practising across country, which Demeas never did.

We used to ride out with buttoned javelins, and he would teach me how one steadies himself to throw from a gallop; or we would close in and try to drag each other off. I thought he would be afraid of hurting me, but he was often rougher than Demeas. Once when he had unhorsed me in a place full of stones, so that I was grazed and bruised all over, he was really sorry, but said he would rather hurt me himself than see me killed in battle by someone else.

It was seldom now that we could spend many hours at a time with Sokrates; who, however, certainly never wished to keep young men from useful work. But as someone was always falling under his spell, one would find new faces about him, which had come while one was away. Some went, some stayed; but none struck me with such surprise as one I found in Phokas the Silversmith's, where I overtook the company one morning. On the opposite wall a polished silver mirror was hanging. As I came up behind, it showed me first Sokrates' face, then the one beside it. I did not believe my eyes at first. The face was Xenophon's.

Afterwards, when I got him alone, he laughed at my surprise, and said he had been about Sokrates for some weeks, and wondered we had not met before: 'but I suppose it's one man's work to conduct the most celebrated love-affair in the City, and you'll be looking up your friends in a few years.' I saw that he was really a little hurt; and it was as difficult to put things right with him, as to tell a deaf man why you went to the theatre.

'But,' I said, 'what brought you to Sokrates?' – 'He did.' – 'How? Through your overhearing his talk?' – 'No, he asked me to come.' More than ever surprised, I demanded the story. He said he had been walking down a narrow alley-way, when Sokrates had met him in it. 'I had never been so near him, and at the risk of my manners could not keep from looking at his face. "Yes," I thought, "people can laugh; but still, that is a man." I dropped my eyes, and was going to pass him; but he put his staff across the way, and stopped me dead. "Can you tell me," he said, "where one can buy good oil?" I thought it odd he should need telling, but I directed him. Then he asked about flour and cloth. I told him the best places I knew; he said, "And where can one get the good and beautiful?" I must have looked pretty blank; at last I said, "I'm sorry, sir, I can't tell you that." – "No?" he said smiling. "Come with me, then, and let us find out." So I turned and walked with him, and stayed with him all day. Why, Alexias, didn't you tell me more about him?'

'What!' I said.

'I thought the sophists spent their lives measuring the moon and stars, and arguing whether matter was one or manifold. You yourself, if you'll forgive my saying so, are inclined to have your head in the clouds, so I thought that would be just the kind of sophist you would take up with. But now I find he's the most practical person one could possibly go to for advice. I heard him say myself that no one should presume to read the universe till he has first read and mastered his own soul, else there is nothing to prevent his turning all other knowledge to evil. He says the soul sickens without exercise just like the body, but one can only know the gods by training as hard in goodness as one trains for the Games.' – 'Did he say that? I see now why he would never be initiated.' – 'But it's quite untrue, Alexias, that he lacks reverence; I assure you, he is a most religious man.' – 'Are you now, Xenophon, defending Sokrates to me?' – 'I'm sorry,' he said. 'But people's injustice makes me angry. What do they mean by their accusations? My own father, the best of men, believes this legend of Aristophanes' that Sokrates teaches young men to despise their parents and deny the gods. Surely among all his friends who write and compose, somebody could put him into a play as he really is? If they would do no more than jot down a few notes of his daily task, it might get justice done him.' – 'You should do it yourself,' I said. He blushed. 'Now you're laughing at me; I only mean that sooner or later someone must.'

There was another who came to Sokrates about this time; I think in the early spring.

I noticed him first one day when we had all walked in from the Agora to talk in the Stoa of Zeus. The youth I am speaking of came up quietly, and stood half hidden by a column. Sokrates, however, as soon as he saw him turned in welcome. 'Good morning, Phaedo; I hoped we might meet today. Come and sit where we can hear each other.' Then the boy came forward, and sat at his feet. Lysis murmured in my ear, 'Silenos with a leopard.'

He could scarcely have put it better. The youth had what one often hears of from the lyric poets, but seldom sees; very dark eyes, with hair of the clearest blond. It swung like heavy silk, cut straight across his brows, which were strongly drawn and lifted outward. His mouth was nobly carved, but strange, brooding and secret; his beauty was not of Apollo but of Dionysos. His eyes never left Sokrates' face. They were deep and subtle; you could see the thoughts running in them like fish in dark water. So it struck me as odd in every way that he should sit without opening his mouth, and that Sokrates seemed to expect nothing better. Just once he said, 'This may interest you, Phaedo, if, as I think, it bears on our enquiry of yesterday,' and the lad said something in assent, so that I no longer wondered whether he was dumb. As we were going away I said to Lysis, 'Who is he, do you know?' – 'No; but he came one day when you were at Demeas'. He walked up quietly, looked the company over, and went away. It was much like today's, except that Kritias was there.' Nowadays Kritias never came within a spear's-length of me. I was sorry for the boy. But then all the world, not being the beloved of Lysis, seemed pitiable to me.

Soon after, when he was absent on manoeuvre, I was in one of the public gardens, the small one by the Theatre, where Sokrates was disputing with Aristippos, whether the good is identical with pleasure, or not. They stood in debate, looking each like the image of his cause. Aristippos was about thirty, a good-looking man, but sagging in the face a little, and wearing the price, I should say, of a good riding-mule on his back. Sokrates in his old drab mantle was as brown and firm as a nut. You could believe the story that when he was on campaign in Thrace he stood all a winter's night in meditation, while the troops were shivering under heaps of skins.

A man's strength, he was saying, depends on toil to maintain it; his freedom depends on strength to protect it; and without freedom, what pleasure is secure? I don't think Aristippos found any way of meeting this; but just then I saw Phaedo again, loitering, half hidden by some trees. He drew back when Sokrates glanced his way; but as soon as Aristippos had gone, came forward of his own accord. Sokrates greeted him, and he sat down on the grass close by. I forget the conversation, which I suppose related to what had passed; Phaedo sat silent and attentive, his head close to Sokrates' knees. Those slopes round the Theatre catch the late sunlight, which shone on the boy's fair hair, showing its lucid beauty; Sokrates, as he sat talking, put out a hand half absently to touch it, and ran a strand of it through his fingers. It was as a man might touch a flower. But I saw the boy start away, and his face change. His dark eyes looked quick and ugly; he made you think of a half-tamed animal that is going to bite. Sokrates, feeling the movement, glanced down at him; for a moment their eyes met. Suddenly the boy was quiet again. His face grew still, as before; he sat listening, hands clasping knees, and Sokrates stroked his hair.

It had increased my curiosity, which I was determined to satisfy this time. When Sokrates had gone, I began making my way over. But, what was hardly surprising, some man who had been waiting his chance got there before me. One could see he was a stranger, making the usual kind of civil approach. The youth smiled coldly at him, and gave him some answer. I did not hear it; but the man looked shocked, and retired as if struck.

You may be surprised that after this I did not change my mind. But those were days when I thought well of mankind, and had confidence enough for two. At all events, I overtook Phaedo, greeted him, and said something about the debate. At first he barely answered, closed his beautiful sullen mouth, and left everything to me. Yet I had the feeling he was more confused than angry; so I persisted, and at last he began to to talk. At once I perceived that in the comparison of our minds I was a child to him. He asked me about a discussion he had heard of, but missed. I retailed it as best I could; once he stopped me, to make a rebuttal which even Kritias had not seen. I could find no way past it; but he, after considering, answered it himself.

I said he was too modest, and ought to let his voice be heard more often. We had been talking without any constraint; but now he shook his head, and grew silent again. At the next corner he said, 'Thanks for your company, but I go this way now. Goodbye.' It was clear he did not want me to see where he lived. I thought, 'His family has fallen into poverty; perhaps he has even to work at a trade.' He was quite well dressed, and I caught from his hair the scent of camomile-flowers; but people will keep up appearances when they can. In any event, he seemed to me now an excellent person; and he had not appeared to dislike my company; so seeing we were near the palaestra where I usually exercised, I said, 'It's early yet; come and give me a match.' But he drew back from me, saying quickly, 'No thank you, I must go.'

I could not believe he was afraid of my seeing his style, for he stood and moved like a gentleman. Just then I noticed a deep wound in his leg, as if a spear had gone clean through. I apologised, and asked if it gave him much trouble. He looked at me strangely, 'It's nothing. I never feel it now.' Then he said slowly, 'I got it in battle. But we lost.'

The scar was almost white, yet he seemed no older than I. He spoke a Doric Greek, with the accent of the islands. I asked him what battle it was he had fought in. But he stared in silence, his eyes like a winter midnight under his shining hair. I felt troubled and constrained; at last I said, 'Where do you come from, Phaedo?' – 'You should have asked before, Athenian. I come from Melos.'

I was about to hold out my hand to him, and say the war was over. But the words died upon my tongue. I knew why he could not go into the palaestra. Till now, it had only been a tale to me. It is the victor who can say 'The war is over,' and go home. Only death ends it, for a slave.

He was withdrawing already; I put out my hand to keep him, as bewildered as if I had seen the sun shining in the west. In everything I had found him my superior. I had not believed such things could be in the world. There was no time to think more, for I saw in his face that he suffered. I said, 'Can we both be friends of Sokrates, and not of one another? And they say, "Fate is the master of all men."'

His dark eyes paused, dwelling on mine. Young as he was, I felt not pleased by his gratitude, but honoured by his approval. 'I am sorry, Alexias,' he said, 'that we can't wrestle; we might have matched up well. They used to say of me too that I was not bad for a runner.' He smiled at me; there is a beauty of the soul that works up through bitterness like a vein of marble through earth. 'Be sure,' I exclaimed, 'the gods will not suffer this forever.' He looked at me as an old man looks at a child. 'I come to Sokrates not in the hope of understanding the gods, but that he may lend me, perhaps, his belief that they are good.'

'Tell me if you will,' I said, 'what master do you work for?' His face grew dark. It grieved me to have offended him. I begged his pardon and said it was no matter. He looked up from the ground and said, 'It wasn't there that I met Sokrates.' – 'No matter,' I said. 'We shall meet tomorrow, or very soon?' He said, 'I come when I can.'

I wondered how he got away, and if they would beat him. He was hardly out of my mind all evening. Next day I was setting out to tell Lysis the story, when I met my uncle Strymon in the court. He told me in his weightiest manner that he had something to say to me; adding, when I would have led him to the living-room, that it was no fit matter for my mother's ears. Now fairly mystified, I took him to the guest-room. After coughing, stroking his beard, and saying he felt responsible to my father, he began. 'What do you do behind closed doors, Alexias, I cannot control. Yet I am sorry to see debauchery in one so young, who lacks even the excuse of ugliness or deformity which might have kept you from enjoying the pleasures of love in an honourable way.'

'Debauchery?' I said, staring at him as if he were mad. My last party had been a fortnight ago; Lysis had been there, and wishing to avoid anything that might disgust him, I had gone home nearly sober. 'I assure you, sir, you haved been misled.' – 'Not unless my eyes mislead me; and I may say I have always been noted for excellent sight. To walk the public streets with a boy from Gurgos' bath-house! Alkibiades himself was rarely so shameless.

I assure you, at your age I hardly knew such people existed.' – 'What boy?' I asked. But he saw my face change and said, 'I see you understand me.'

'A slave does not choose his master,' I said, 'and war is war.' I felt angry with the whole world, with Necessity and Fate. He was stroking his beard again, getting something ready. 'And what shall we say of a man setting himself up to instruct the youth, who not only resorts to such creatures himself, but admits them among his pupils?' Anger almost choked me; but I mastered it, the better to deal with him. 'I am to blame, sir, that as I have only talked philosophy with the youth. I forgot to ask him what he did. But I thank you for the information. How, sir, did you find it out?'

In the street, I daresay; but it did me good to see his face. At least he could see my teacher had sharpened my wits. But Lysis looked serious when I told him, and said that if my uncle thought ill of Sokrates, a pert answer would not make him think better. This was the first time he had ever reproved me. When he saw how I felt it, he soon relented.

He went out of his way after this to greet Phaedo kindly; but the boy grew silent in company, as Sokrates had found. He would talk, when we were alone, but always across an invisible shield. He was waiting for me to find out what he was and turn against him, and I saw it. You may wonder indeed why I did not feel a distaste in spite of myself. But first love, like the light of dawn, sheds a kind of beauty wherever you look. Besides, though I knew what his life was, I knew it without understanding, as one knows of a country where one has not been. It only gave him a strangeness for me.

One day I met him early in the morning, walking out to the Academy. As we went up the Street of Tombs, we fell to talking of death; and Phaedo said he did not believe the soul survives it, whether in the underworld, or in a new body, or in the air. I replied that since I had loved Lysis, it seemed impossible to me that the soul should be extingushed. 'The soul is a surfeit-dream,' he said, 'of a man with food and drink in him and his lust fed. Let the body be hungry, or thirsty, or in desire, and what is his soul but the dog's nose that leads it to flesh? The dog dies, and rots, and its nose smells nothing.' He spoke as if he hated me, and wished to leave me nothing that could give me joy. Yet I remembered I had failed Sokrates once, and Lysis had reproved me; and I paused to think. I said, 'If you put a fat old man into the long-race, he will fall down dead. Does that prove it can't be run? This, Phaedo, is why I think the soul outlives the body: I have seen how the body can be bought and sold, and not only that, but forced to what it hates and would never consent to; yet the soul can be free, and keep its courage, and defy its fate. So I believe in the soul.'

He was silent some time, walking so fast that the limp from his wound appeared. At last he said, 'It seemed incredible that you could know.' I said I would never have intruded in the matter, except that the silence was putting a distance between us. 'I can't keep much from Lysis,' I said. 'But you can rely on him not to talk, as you can on me.' He laughed shortly and said, 'Don't make a trouble of it. Kritias knows.'

A little later, finding he had never been out of the City, I took him walking in the pine-woods at the foot of Lykabettos. It was there he told me how he had been enslaved. After his city had been some months besieged, his father, who was a strategos, had raised a troop of volunteers to storm the Athenian siege-wall, a desperate enterprise which had almost succeeded. Phaedo, fighting at his father's side, got a wound there, which did not heal well, because by then they were almost starving. The Athenians sent for more troops, and closed the gap; no food came in at all, and they could only throw themselves on the mercy of the enemy. Phaedo, who could not walk alone, lay on his bed, listening to the clamour as the gates were opened and the Athenians marched in. Presently he heard a great shrieking of women, and the death-cries of men. Soldiers ran in, dragged him from his bed to the Agora, and threw him down among a crowd of young lads and children, who had been herded into the sheep-pound. Just across the square was a pile of corpses newly killed, and still being added to; sticking out of the midst of it was his father's head. There was an auctioneers' rostrum in the Agora; here, where he could see well and be out of the dirt and mess, stood Philokrates the Athenian commander, directing the slaughter of the fighting men which the Athenians had ordered. It went on for some time. Phaedo did not come too late to see his lover brought in with bound hands, and run through the throat before his eyes. When it was time to lead off the women to the ships, Philokrates came down from the rostrum to choose a couple for himself. The rest were taken away to be sold. Thus Phaedo saw the last of his mother, a woman not long past thirty, and handsome still.

He had been brought to the Piraeus slave-market very sick with his wound; but Gurgos had taken a risk on him for the sake of his looks, and nursed him well. At first he had not understood what the place was, and thought he was to work as a bathman. When he knew, he refused food and drink, intending to die. 'Then,' he said, 'in the evening old Gurgos came and left a cup of wine beside me. The wine-jar had just been drawn up from the well, and the cup sweated with coolness. I was faint and thirsty; and I said to myself, "For whom an I doing this? I who have neither father nor friend to be dishonoured, who believed neither in men nor in any god? The birds and beasts live from hour to hour, and they live very well."' He had learned the arts of his calling, and commanded a high price. But on a certain day, feeling his soul sickened and his mind in turmoil, he had locked the door as though someone was with him, and getting out by the window, had wandered about the City. There he had passed Sokrates talking, and had stayed to listen. 'Is it true, Alexias, that there is an Athenian who lives in a cave and hates men?' – 'Yes: Timon.' – 'When I came to Sokrates I was much the same, I mean in my soul. I had taught myself to withdraw my mind from them, as the herdsman sits apart on a rock, to windward of the goats. I did not wish to share my rock with anyone; if one of my beasts aspired towards manhood, I had learned how to keep him in his place.'

I was eager he should meet Lysis; but at first Phaedo always found some reason to be gone. Presently, however, I got them acquainted, and it was plain each thought well of the other. Shortly after, Lysis being about to give a supper for Sokrates and his particular friends, I said, 'It's a pity Phaedo can't come; Sokrates would like to see him.' – 'Why not?' said Lysis at once. 'A good thought of yours. I'll go down beforehand and buy an evening of his time.' I asked to come too, but he said, 'Are you serious? Your reputation would never recover from it. When boys of your age go to Gurgos', they don't go to buy but to sell.'

The party went well, and Phaedo seemed to enjoy it. When everyone had gone, and Lysis and I were yawning in the first light but still unwilling to part, I asked him what Gurgos' place was like.

'Very fashionable. You are received first by Gurgos, who is a fat Phrygian with a dyed beard. He enquires your tastes, rubbing his hands; when you ask for Phaedo he bows himself in two, like a cloth-seller when you order purple. You are directed through the bath, where you find all those bodies that are never seen in the palaestra, and the boys who are free, making themselves useful till they are needed elsewhere. They are mostly slaves, so I supposed they could be worse off, but when a child of nine years or so came up ogling me, the pleasure I would have paid highest for would have been that of throwing Gurgos head first into the cauldron, to rinse his beard for him. The rooms are behind the baths. Phaedo has the apartment of honour; his name is over the door, together with his price. He had a customer when I got there. Phaedo's clients are treated like gentlemen and not hurried; Gurgos' strong man is at hand, lest some impatient person should try to break down the door. In due course I knocked, and Phaedo opened. All he had on was the paint on his face. I knew then I shouldn't have come. The next moment, he slammed-to the door. He was almost too quick for me; but being rather stronger I managed to hold it. "Next room," he said through the crack, "I'm engaged." – "Wait, Phaedo," I began. Suddenly he flung open the door, so that I nearly fell inside. He stood there laughing. He looked like something you might come upon in a dark wood. "Come in, Lysis," he said. "Honour the threshold. Who am I to turn away trade? Ever since Alexias sang me the hymn of your virtues, I've been expecting you here. What can I do for you?" He added one or two remarks, compared with which Gurgos had talked like a schoolmaster. All the same, you can tell he was brought up a gentleman; he knows how to apologise and keep his dignity. It was my fault for going to his room. But I've never set foot inside a boys' house before. I told him anyone who was ready to be angry for your sake was a friend of mine. I only wish I could afford to buy him out; it would be as good a dedication to the gods as one could make in a lifetime. But I had to pay two gold staters for one evening of him. To sell outright, Gurgos would want the price of a racehorse.'

They were good friends after this; but Lysis never spent long alone with Phaedo, who never seemed offended at it. I daresay he felt a compliment to himself, which he was too well-bred to hint at to me; and I daresay he was right. Even I myself felt something of his attraction; for Eros had certainly smiled upon his birth. But to him it had all become such a weariness and disgust as the oar is to the rower. I was as safe with him as with my father.

All his life was in his mind which Sokrates had awakened. I, who had followed the man for love of his nature, seemed to Phaedo only half a friend; he had no mercy on my softness. He would force me to the logic of the negative elenchos, attacking my dearest beliefs till, driven from my last ditch, I would say, 'But Phaedo, we *know* it's true.' – 'Oh, no. We may have a true opinion, perhaps. Do you call that knowledge? We know what we have proved.' Once I lost my temper with him, and trying to hide it walked on in silence. Presently he said, 'You look rather the worse for wear today, Alexias; has someone been knocking you about?' – 'Of course not,' I said. 'Lysis threw me at practice, and I got a few bruises, that's all.' – 'Does he call himself a friend, and treat you like that?' I drew breath for an angry answer; then I understood, and begged his pardon. 'No harm done,' he said. 'But I daresay I know as well as Lysis what a good guard is worth.'

I never heard him pity himself, or complain of what he was going back to. But in the meantime, a better friend than I had his cause in hand. Sokrates had told his story to Kriton; the man who, in their own youth, had urged him forth from his workshop to take his place among the philosophers. Kriton was rich; he offered at once to buy Phaedo out.

The bargaining took some time. Phaedo's fame had spread and his price gone up again; Gurgos treated Kriton at first like one who had lost his head over the boy and would pay anything. But he soon found out he was dealing with a business man; Kriton asked if his boys had drunk of the fountain of youth, offering to come back in a year or two and ask the price again. Gurgos was scared, and closed the deal.

Happy enough at such a change of masters, Phaedo could scarcely be got to understand that he was free. Kriton finding he wrote a good hand, employed him in his library, copying books, and recommended him to other men of learning, so that he could be studying as he worked. Soon none of us could remember what our circle had been like without him. There was that in his bearing which even the shameless had to respect; you did not find his former customers being familiar in the street. He on his side was strict in not giving them away, saying that every trade has its ethic. But sometimes, when a self-important citizen was holding forth in the Agora, condemning foreign luxury or wondering what young men were coming to, I saw Phaedo watching with irony in his dark eye.

12

The earth quickened to spring; on the great Academy training-ground, the army exercised every day under Demosthenes' eye. He was a man as solid as a rock, but not as cold; red-faced, from weather more than wine in spite of the jokes at the theatre; loud-voiced and hearty, but confident, not blustering. I thought my father would be glad of his coming.

All this while, the child at home was thriving. My mother had called her Charis, after my father's mother, since he had not named her himself. She could crawl, and would try to stand by clinging to my fingers. One day I had thought, 'If he who gives life is the father, then I am he.' In this I had felt some sweetness; but soon it seemed impious and I put it away. Then I thought, 'She shall never know it. No one shall suffer through me what I myself remember.' So I went out to the household altar, and burned some saffron, and vowed it to Zeus the Merciful. The guilt of my impiety sometimes rode my pillow; yet even with Lysis I had kept my oath. Perhaps I might have broken it some dark night; but at this time each bore himself before the other like the player chosen to wear the mask of the god.

One morning, when even the City was scented with spring, I woke happy; I was to ride to the farm, and Lysis had promised to come too. The first sunlight was green in the new leaves of the fig tree; the doves were calling, and Kydilla sang at her work an old country song about a bride. From the courtyard I could hear the child piping and chattering indoors like a young bird. I took up the song and sang the verse for the bridegroom; Kydilla giggled and broke off, and started singing again. Suddenly there was a great clatter of hoofs under the entry. I sprang to see my father's image in my mind. But it was Lysis, full-armed and helmed, his javelins standing in the holster. When he saw me, he said without dismounting, 'Alexias, have you got your armour?'

'Armour?' I was still two minas short of Pistias' price, and had not even been measured yet; I was not sure I had done growing. 'When shall I need it, Lysis?' He said, 'Now.'

The doves were still making love, and the child singing. He said, 'The Spartans have broken the truce, and come down into Attica. Dekeleia fell last night. They are nearly at Acharnai. From the High City you can see the fires. What armour have you? My troop's three men short.'

I looked up at his tall crest of blue enamel, his breastplate and greaves bordered with studs of gold. 'Wait for me, Lysis. I'll be ready in a moment.' I was running in when he shouted after me. It brought me standing. I might have been one of his troopers. 'But so I am now,' I thought. I came back and said, 'Yes, Lysis?' – 'Have you armour,' he said, 'or not?' – 'My hunting-leathers are just as strong.' – 'This is war, not a torch-race.' Then he saw my face, and leaned down to pat my shoulder. 'Don't take it so hard; we've all been caught napping. How should you have armour, a year under age? But I must get on now; I came to you first.'

I thought, 'Some god will help me'; and then help came. I caught him by the foot and said, 'No, wait, Lysis, I know where to get it. Don't go. Wait.'

I shouted to the groom to get Phoenix ready, and ran in. My mother was up; she still fed the child herself sometimes, and had just put her to the breast. She drew her dress across, and got to her feet, holding the child and staring at me. 'Mother, the Spartans are coming. They have reached Acharnai. Don't be frightened; we'll soon turn them back. But I must go at once, and I've no armour, only a sword. Give me the armour of your father Archagoras.'

She drew the child from her and laid it in the cradle and stood up, pressing her mantle with her hand over her breast. 'You, Alexias? Oh, no, you are still a boy.' – 'If I am not a man today, it will be too late tomorrow. Lysis has come for me, to join his troop.' She still looked at me without speaking. I said, 'You promised me, Mother, I should be truly your son.'

She said, still gazing, 'You are, Alexias,' and with the words, the trumpet blew from the Anakeion the horsemen's call. 'You must have it then. But it is too soon.' She took the keys from her casket and opened the chest. She had kept the armour perfectly, polished and oiled, all but the straps which had perished. But my father had left some of his. I said, 'I will come back when I have it on. I shall need food; tell Kydilla.'

Lysis had dismounted and was waiting in the guest-room. I spread the armour on a couch. I had not seen it for years, and its appearance dismayed me. In old Archagoras' day, if a man was someone he saw no reason not to make it known. The gold studs were well enough; but the Gorgon's head, with snakes raying over the nipples, went beyond moderation. I said, 'This is too fine, I shall be laughed at.' – 'Today? One of my boys has a Mede's tunic with fish-scales, that's hung sixty years on the wall.' He helped to arm me. It was not such a fit as Pistias would have given me, being a little big, but better than Demeas' practice suit, so I thought myself well off. Lysis held me out at arm's length and said, 'Now it is on, it is not too fine, and no one will laugh. Kiss your mother and get your food; we must be going.'

Archagoras' sword was better than mine. I slung it on and went through to the living-room. My father's old kit-bag was on the table. 'I'm ready, Mother. Let me try the helmet.' It was in her hands; she had been burnishing it. The crest was a triple one, of sea-horses whose tails fell together behind. She set it on my head, and it fitted well. There was a silver mirror on the wall behind her; as I moved, I saw a man reflected in it. I turned round startled, to see what man had come into the women's rooms. Then I saw that the man was I.

'You must take a cloak,' she said, 'the nights are still cold.' She had my thick one ready. 'I will offer for you every day, dear son, to Athene Nike and to the Mother.' She did not come forward. I pushed the cheek-plates back from my face: a thing one does like breathing, yet there is a first time for everything. It was long since I had embraced her; when I drew her near, I found I had grown tall enough to lean my chin upon her head. I thought of her goodness to me in childhood, when I was small and weak; it was strange to feel her so little in my arms, and trembling like a bird when you shut your hand on it. In gladness that I could now go out to defend her as a man, I began lifting her face to kiss her. But I must have hurt her on the armour, never having worn it before, for she put me away from her. She took the cloak and hung it on my arm and said again, 'I will pray for you.' I laid my hand on hers. 'When you pray for me, Mother, pray for Lysis too.' She looked up, and as she withdrew from me, 'Yes,' she said, 'I will pray for him indeed.'

So that day Lysis and I rode out after all to the farmlands. As the City gate swung open for us, I saw the back of his helmet-crest, leading out the troop; and his voice carried over to me above the noise of the horses, when he gave an order. We formed in column of three, and I rode in the midst of the column. At the rear came Lysis' Second, who was a veteran of the troop, being nineteen and a half years old. Lysis was the only one of us who had ever fought in battle. We trotted along the Acharnian Way, trying to talk like soldiers. Behind us sounded the noise of the City calling to arms; the hoplites were turning out, the dust of horsemen was white before us and behind.

As we rode, the boy on my left said he had heard the troop on patrol had met the Spartans and been badly cut up. I replied that Lysis had told me so on the way. 'Lysis?' he said. 'You mean the Phylarch? Do you know him?' I said yes, but did not like to say that I knew him well. So the youth, who had lately joined, began to ask what kind of officer he was: 'Does he drive one like a Spartan, or is he easy; does he see to things himself or leave it all to the Second; is he fond of women, or will he want one of us to sleep with him?' The boy on my right said, 'You fool, it's his friend you're talking to. Alexias, Myron's son. What else would you like to know about the Phylarch? Ask him anything, don't be shy.' The first youth looked rather confused; the other said, 'Frontier manners; you'll get used to it.' He added that he had been in the Guard a year, or nearly, and Lysis was the best officer he had served under. This was enough to make me his friend. His name was Gorgion.

We rode and led our horses by turns, to save their feet. It was quiet; the Spartans were still in the hills. At noon Lysis took us off the road to water our horses and to eat. When we had sat down, he said, 'Before we ride on, I'll tell you what we are doing.

Demosthenes will see to Dekeleia; we are not looking for King Agis today. Hit and run is our work, and to save the farms. Where they are straggled to loot, we shall meet with parties we can handle. This is the signal for silence. Give it me, all of you, to show that you know it. Good. Those who have done the exercises, keep an eye on the new men. If we charge, you all know the paean. Take the note from me, and give it as loud as you can, to honour the City. It won't frighten the Spartans; it takes their women at home to do that. However, if they'd rather die than hear a troop of naked girls singing a dirty song about them at the next festival, it's for us to oblige them. I hope we Athenians can do a man's part for honour's sake, without being beaten and starved to make us brave. We fight for our City, where the mark of a citizen is to have a mind and speak it, and people live their daily lives as they choose, with none to put them in fear. Let us be worthy of our fathers, and a source of pride to our lovers and friends.' And he made the offering, commending us to the gods.

When he came with his food to sit among us, I felt nearly as shy of him as when we walked out to the Academy the first day. Then he looked at me sideways, and I knew he wanted me to tell him he had spoken well, only that the others were too near. So we smiled, understanding one another.

The wind had changed. We began to smell smoke on the air, the heavy smoke of war, with little draughts of foulness in it, from things burning that ought not to burn. As we went up between the hills, I saw the first farm we should come to would be my father's, and the smoke was coming from there.

It smelt as I remembered in my childhood, and I thought, 'The olives have gone.' Then we came round the side of the hill and saw that they were not only fired but felled. The raw stumps stood up among the burning boughs. They had not had time to finish cutting them down, so had fired them afterwards. I fancy they had meant to spare the sacred grove again; but with the changing wind the fire had caught it. We rode on towards the house. The straw was smouldering under the roof-tiles; the smoke came out in puffs under the eaves, and trickled out of the cracks between the tiles. Just as we got there, the beams gave and the roof fell in.

The household stuff had been piled up in the farmyard and set alight. At the top was my bed, burning brightly still. I could see the letters of my name, that I had carved on the frame as a boy. On the far side of the fire, a dog was eating something. The bailiff was there, with his head knocked in and his brains spilled on the cobbles. Nothing else human was in sight. Wherever the slaves had run to, it was a certainty we should never see them again.

It was a good bit of land, the best in the valley. We had been there as long as the grasshoppers, father and son, throwing stones out of the fields and building terraces with them. I myself had made a new one on the hillside, and planted vines. They had ridden their horses over them, across and across; the young green was all mashed down into the earth. I might as well have pleased my uncle Strymon by training them his way. Of all the livestock, not a hair or a feather was left.

I could hear a murmur running along the troop, as they told each other whose place it was. They looked at me with solemn respect, as people do at a man in calamity. Lysis rode up to me and put his hand on mine. 'They are thieves from their birth,' he said, 'but this, by Herakles, they shall buy.' I answered as cheerfully as an actor in a play, 'Never mind, Lysis, it's not the only one.' They all thought I showed great fortitude; the truth is that I did not feel it yet. When a supper-table is overturned there is a great mess; then the wine is wiped up, a clean cloth set with fresh cups and plates, and all is as before. So, it seemed, I should find it here when I came again.

There was nothing to stay for. At last from high ground we saw a whole roof, from which the smoke came up while we looked. Lysis said, 'Good,' and gave the word to ride on.

We passed two more burned farms. It was rare to see as much as a pullet that had got away. As Lysis had said, Spartans are the best thieves in the world. They keep their boys always half-fed, so that they can never have a belly-full without stealing; this is so that they will learn to live off the country. They get a thrashing if anyone sees them at it. There is a well-known story about this, not the least remarkable part of which, to my mind, is that the boy was hungry enough to have intended eating a fox.

We overtook the Spartans in a little valley between Thria and

Phyle. They had not burned the farm yet, for it was now evening, and they had camped there for the night. The scout reported that they had lit a fire in the farmyard and were having supper. They had no infantry with them, only a few Helots who were unarmed. One of our troop came from this part of the country, and showed Lysis a narrow ride above the olives, where we could avoid the scout they had posted by the stream.

We came out into the farm and rode in among the pens, shouting the paean. The Spartans scattered from their fire, calling to arms and running for their horses. Some we rode down between the fire and their picket-lines. But the rest of the troop, who had got to their mounts, spurred up and met us hand to hand.

I had wondered to myself whether, when it came to the moment, I should believe it was really war, and not another bout at Demeas'. I need not have been in doubt. As you may know, the Spartan knights' class is not made up of those who can buy horse and armour, but is a privilege given for merit. Xenophon (who was certainly safe of his entry either way) had often said to me how excellent this custom was. I daresay it is, except that any commoner who wants to get in is urged to watch the knights, and report any fault he sees; if he can prove it he may get the other man's place. You may suppose that a few years of this leave some mark on a man. I will not say they looked as if they never laughed; but they had certainly taken good care what they laughed at. They had on their plain round helmets and the scarlet tunic that does not show blood; their long hair (which they had oiled and combed and dressed, because they were at war) reached to their shoulders. I saw one of them coming for me and needed no prompting to think. 'This man will kill me, if he lives to do it.'

But, as often happens in war, something swerved his horse aside, and I found myself facing a different man who seemed to have sprung out of the earth, but who glared at me as if I had done him some injury. Throwing as Lysis had taught me, I got him with my javelin, deep in the neck. He fell with it in him. As I reached for another, I saw Lysis fighting some way off. He looked round for a moment; I thought, 'He doesn't know where I am.' So I yelled out the paean, and dashed into the mêlée where he could see what I was up to.

How it all ended I don't well remember. It was like a score of skirmishes I fought in, that year and other years. But I remember we killed four or five of them, and they only got a couple of ours, because they were outnumbered and surprised. We also killed one of their Helots, who took up arms to fight for them. He was a brave man; so if he had stayed in Lakonia, the Krypteia (which is a corps of youths trained to attend to such people) would probably have killed him in any case.

After the remnant made off (for they were only raiders, and had no orders to stand and die) Lysis told us to take up their weapons and armour to make our trophy. So I came to the man I had struck with my javelin, lying on his back with the shaft sticking in him. I put my hand on it, and then saw he was still alive.

I recognised his face by his beard, which was quite soft and young; I suppose he was not much over twenty years old. Both his hands were clutching the ground beside him, digging down into the dirt; his teeth were clenched, and his lips drawn backward; the whites of his eyes showed and his back was lifted in an arch. He was trying to breathe, or not to breathe because of the pain, and a bubbling came from his throat. As I looked he put up one of his hands, which was covered with ordure from the earth, and felt at the javelin where it stood in his neck. I had sent it downward within the collar-bone, as Demeas had recommended. No one had told me what happened afterwards.

As I stood gazing in the dusk, his eyes moved and looked me in the face. I thought, as one can in a short time, of many things; of the pains he had suffered in Sparta, first to be a man and then to be a knight, and now so soon to end. His hand fell back and scraped at the ground and he stared at me grinning; whether defying me, or braving out his death, or in the convulsion of his pain, I could not tell. Someone had come up beside me; I turned and saw Lysis looking down. He said, 'Pull out the javelin; then he will die.'

I put out my hand, and saw the man's eyes still on mine. I wondered if he had heard Lysis' words. My hand touched the shaft, and drew back again. Lysis said 'Pull it out.' His voice had changed; it was the Phylarch giving an order. I had thought that he would help me; but he stood there waiting.

So I put my foot on the Spartan's breastplate, and pulled. I could feel the javelin-head tearing out through the sinews and grating on the bone, and heard the breath hissing in the man's throat, either of itself or as he tried not to scream. He gave a great cough, and blood splashed out of his mouth on my arms and on my knees; then he died, as Lysis had told me he would. Lysis said nothing; he nodded at me and went away. I stripped the arms from the body and threw them down on the pile; then I went off and vomited behind a wall. It was getting dark, and when I came back I don't think anyone noticed I was pale. Someone said to me, 'How many did we get?' I looked at the bodies, and the man I had killed was one body among them, and I said, 'Five.'

Soon after, the Spartan heralds came to take them away under truce; and we put up our trophy of arms, being left masters of the field. Afterwards we made a pyre to burn our dead: for there was no knowing when we could have brought them home. This is another thing not easy to watch the first time; indeed, to this very day when the fire feeds upon a man I broke bread with at noon, I would look elsewhere, except that one must keep one's men in heart.

But when all was done, our arms stacked and our sentries posted, and we sat round the fire to eat the food we had snatched from the Spartans, then we got the feel of victory, and the joy of tasting life when the enemy is slain. The sentries were relieved to eat; then we came back and stripped off our armour and clothes, and oiled and scraped ourselves in the warmth of the fire, and talked of the fight. Now for the first time Lysis called me over to sit beside him; we pooled our food and shared it as we used to do. I knew what it meant, that for the sake of the squadron he had not wanted to single me out before I was proved. When I had stood at the feet of Athene after the race, to be crowned with the sacred olive, I had been proud, but now it seemed little, compared with this.

I looked into the bright fire, and saw it shine on the faces and bodies of my comrades, and Lysis beside me, and thought, 'If strangers came now, naked as he is they would not ask, "Which of you is the leader?"' Then a dead log fell from the fire, and I remembered our farm lay in ruins, the crops destroyed, the cattle and sheep gone and the slaves fled, and I thought, 'We are become poor; we shall be poor for years and perhaps always.' Yet being young, and filled with the present, I remembered it like a tale; and I could not understand that I should ever feel it more than I did then.

We gathered hay and straw for our beds, and while Lysis made a round of the sentries I gathered his too. Then we rolled ourselves in our cloaks and lay down side by side. We talked for a little while, and he said that if his father's farm was spared, he would lend us slaves, and stock for breeding, when the Spartans had gone home, and the place would soon be bringing something in again. 'They never stay more than two months,' he said, 'and often not so long.' Then he fell asleep like a lamp going out. I was stiff from riding, and had never made my bed on the ground before; one moment, it seemed, I was thinking I should never close my eyes, and the next it was morning.

This day, or something like it, we lived over many times in the weeks that followed. Sometimes we saved all the stock from a farm, by holding the Spartans off till it could be got away; sometimes they beat us and kept what they had. Some of the cattle were sent over to Euboea for safe keeping, according to the custom of the Athenians in war. What our troop did was a small matter, for the army of Demosthenes was now in the field, and the Spartans began to be contained in the fort at Dekeleia. King Agis was leading them in person; having two kings they are always freer with them than other folk. This was the same Agis who, on the omen of an earthquake, had avoided his new wife's bed for a year, as I have related. He prosecuted the war with great bitterness, as if he had some reason to hate the Athenians; of which more in good time. But Demosthenes kept a curb upon his wishes. He could not be got out of Dekeleia itself, it is too strong a hold, and he had only taken it because in the truce it was lightly manned. He had done, however, as much as a raider usually expects to do in a season; it could not be long, we thought, before he went home, and left Demosthenes free to sail for Sicily. Meanwhile, the work of the Frontier Guard got easier, and days might pass without our seeing action.

As for Lysis and me, anyone who has gone campaigning with a lover will know what I mean, when I say we had never been together so much, and never so little. We seldom spent an hour out of each other's sight; for after the first day I always rode with Lysis, and fought at his side, and no one, I believe, ever questioned my place. We got a new way of talking to each other from being always overheard; sometimes, if we were alone for a while, we were almost tongue-tied, and would look at each other smiling, not knowing how to begin. The best times were when I was standing the midnight watch; Lysis would leave visiting my post till late, and stay with me talking quietly before he slept. But as we rode with the troop, we tried sometimes to examine a question and determine the truth by logic; for, we said, what use to chase the Spartans from Attic soil if we grow Doric wits ourselves? Then we remembered Sokrates, and other things we did not speak of.

The troop, as soon as they saw I took my share of hard work and night watches, were kind to our friendship. The usual jokes were made, but without any malice. Now the country was quiet, we used sometimes when the evening fire was lit to go for a walk together in the night. Once, coming back quietly over the grass, we heard young Gorgion, who had a salty tongue, accounting for our absence. Just afterwards, they saw us in the firelight. Of course we joined in the laughter. But next time we went we were a little constrained, knowing what they thought, but not quite willing to speak of it, out of modesty or for another cause. For I was not so young in war as not to have felt already how death touches love's shoulder and says, 'Make haste.'

Our patrol ended at last, and another troop relieved us. The country was all quiet just then; we made our last camp near Cape Sounion. I doubt what the garrison at the fort there told us afterwards, that they could hear us round our fire half a mile away; but we were certainly cheerful. I remember that everyone was picked up in turn, head and heels, and slung on top of the others; at the end half the troop fell upon Lysis and, when we had overpowered him, slung him too. The next night we were to be quartered at Sounion, and that day was our own.

Lysis and I rode off together along the coast, the blue sea beside us and the red rocky shore all broken into little bays. At one of these, after a long gallop, we drew rein; and looking at the clear blue water, threw our clothes off with one accord. The water was brisk at first and warm after, and we swam far out to sea, till we could see Poseidon's temple at Sounion standing against the sky. Lysis was the faster, his wrestling having strengthened his shoulders and arms; but waited for me, as I did in running for him. We rested on the water, then swam shoreward, and in shallow rock-pools tried laughing to catch fish in our hands. But as we walked out of the water afterwards, I felt a sharp pain in the side of my foot, and found it bleeding. I must have trodden on a broken shell or a potsherd, for the cut was deep. Lysis knelt and looked at it while I leaned on his shoulder. 'This will give you trouble,' he said, 'if you fill it with grit as you cross the beach. It might cost you a crown. Wash it well in the sea, and I will carry you over to a place where a horse can go.' For the beach was stony.

I sat on a flat-topped rock, and trailed my foot in the sea. The water was clear, and the blood unrolled in it like smoke in a blue sky. I sat watching it till Lysis touched me on the shoulder and said, 'Come'. I leaned back for him to take hold of me, and fastened my arms round his neck. But he did not carry me; nor did I let him go. We spoke without sound each other's names. A gull screamed over us, an empty sound, to tell us we two were alone upon the shore.

I said to my heart, 'What mighty power hast thou been defying?' Truly love may be likened to the Sphinx of the Egyptians, with the face of a smiling god and a lion's claws. When he had wounded me, all my longing was to leap into his darkness, and be consumed. I called on my soul, but it bled away from me like salt washed back into the ocean. My soul melted and fled; the wound in my foot, which the water had opened, streamed out scarlet over the wet rock.

I lay between sea and sky, stricken by the Hunter; the fiery immortal hounds of Eros, slipped from the leash, dragged at my throat and at my vitals, to bring the quarry in. It seemed to me now that my soul was here, if it was anywhere; nothing remained to me of what I was, save this, that I remembered I had promised

Sokrates a gift. He whom I loved knew my mind; perhaps it was his own. We were still, understanding each other.

He let me go, and kneeling beside the rock, covered the wound with his mouth till the bleeding stopped. We were silent, he kneeling in the water, and I lying like the sacrifice on the altar-stone, the blue sky burning my eyes. After a while he bent and rinsed his face and got up smiling. 'The Thracians when they swear friendship mingle their blood, or drink it, I forget. Now we are really one.' He carried me over the shore to the horses, and tore his tunic and bound my foot. It healed cleanly, and I was running again in a couple of weeks.

A little time after, when we were back in the City, I saw him for the first time with the Corinthian, Drosis, bidding her goodbye as he left her house. Several times, before the fighting began, he had invited me to supper with her to hear her sing. I had refused laughing, and telling him that as long as we did not meet, we could never doubt how all three of us would love each other. One does not need much knowledge of the world, to have heard that a man's mistress usually likes his friend too little, or too much. I had never been troubled by the thought of her at all. Yet now that I saw her, looking just what I had imagined, a small downy girl, holding his hands, I felt grief and anger, and drew back into a porch so that he should not see me as he went.

So I went off to find Sokrates; and though I listened only and did not speak, in a little while I mastered these thoughts and put them from me: for I saw that if I let them possess me, Lysis and I had exchanged the good not for the best, but for the worst.

13

My mother, when returning I rode into the courtyard, stood looking at me in silence. I was too young and thoughtless to consider what she might feel, at the sudden sight of a man wearing her father's armour, upon her husband's horse. I jumped down and embraced her laughing, and asking if she had mistaken me for a stranger. 'I took you for a soldier,' she said, 'and now I look at you it is true.' This pleased me, for I would not have had her think the armour was fallen on evil days. There was no use now in my ever thinking again of a suit by Pistias.

Going out to the stables I found Korax, my father's second horse, disgracefully neglected, with a thrush in one of his feet. I was calling indignantly for the groom, intending to give him the thrashing he would have had from my father (for the horse, which was old, looked finished now to me), when my mother told me he had run away. This was an old story now in the country, but that it had been happening in the City was news to me. She said that thousands of slaves had gone, and half the crafts and trades in the City had been crippled. The Spartans always let a slave through their lines, to encourage more to run, knowing how it damaged us. This was war, and we did the same by their Helots when we could.

Meantime, thanks to them, our fortunes were half ruined. We had a little estate in Euboea, good cornland, which would bring in something still, and a small property of rents in the City itself. We should have to sell old Korax, as soon as his foot was healed. My uncle Strymon came round to warn me against extravagance, with a face as long as his account-rolls. He had had a great fright when half a dozen of his slaves ran off, and had no peace till he had sold all the others.

'It can't be long now,' I said to Lysis, 'before King Agis goes home again. He's already stayed on the frontier longer than ever before.' Lysis shook his head. 'The scouts have been up to Dekeleia again. Now, when as you say he is due to be going, he is strengthening the walls and digging-in.'

At first I could hardly understand him. 'What? How shall we grow anything, or get any harvest in?' – 'Why grow what the Spartans will gather? We must beat our ploughshares into swords.' – 'But why, Lysis? The Spartans never changed their customs. They never did this before.' – 'Do you think a Spartan had the wit to think of it? It took an Athenian for that. No one can ever say of Alkibiades that he doesn't earn his keep.'

I was slow to see beyond all this; then I said, 'But Lysis, if Demosthenes has to stay here holding the Spartans, how will he get to Sicily?' Lysis laughed. We were walking through the City; he had a clean mantle, and sandals on his feet; but I felt for a moment we were back in the field. 'How? How do you think? We will get there, my dear, by our holding them instead.'

I had never thought it possible that Demosthenes would sail while the Spartans were in Attica. Nor had Demosthenes perhaps. We had begun the war in Sicily as a man who is doing well may begin a new house beyond his means. If all goes well, the show will raise his credit. We had grown into a habit of victory; glory was our capital, as much as ships and silver; and we had drawn pretty heavily on all three.

We had a week or two in the Munychia fort at Piraeus, on garrison duty. To most young men, who go there in peacetime after enrolling as ephebes, it comes as the first taste of soldiering; to us it was a rest-camp. Even so it has a feeling of its own, as you march past the galley-ships and in through the old arsenal, and see the scribbles your fathers left on the walls when they were ephebes themselves. We got plenty of leave, for by then we had earned it.

One day we were in the Argive's palaestra, watching the boys at exercise, when Lysis pointed and asked, 'That boy there is going to be something remarkable. I have noticed him before.' – 'Do you think so?' I said. 'He looks rather thickset to me.' Lysis laughed and said, 'No, I mean as a wrestler.' I watched the boy, who had been matched with, or chosen for himself, someone much bigger. He looked about fifteen, but was powerful beyond his years. As he was getting a thigh-hold, he made a slip and nearly got thrown. In spite of this he won the bout; but Lysis said, 'He has made that fault before and I can't think how the trainer has missed it. The boy can't at his age wrestle with men, so he never gets a proper match. Do me a favour, Alexias. Go after the boy and tell him with my compliments what he did wrong and how to correct it. If I speak to him myself, his tutor will faint with fright.' We made some joke or other about this, and laughed. Then he told me what to say.

I followed the lad into the dressing-room, and found him scraping-down. He was certainly too square for beauty; by the time he was a man, if he went on wrestling, he would have no proportion at all. His brows were heavy and overhung, making his eyes very deep-set; but when he looked at me I was struck with them, for they were brilliant and fearless. I greeted him, and gave him Lysis' advice. He listened most attentively, and at the end said, 'Please thank Lysis for me. Tell him I am honoured by his taking this trouble, and assure him I shan't forget what he says.' His voice was rather light for his build, but pleasant and well-trained. He went on, 'And thank you too, Alexias, for bringing his message. I had begun to wonder whether all was well with you in the war, it is so long since we had the pleasure of seeing you.'

He delivered this, though quite modestly, with a polish I had never seen in one so young. But what struck me much more was that as he spoke he raised his eyes to my face, admiring it, not at all impertinently, but with as much composure as if he had been thirty years old.

It was certainly the first such compliment I had ever received from a boy a good two years younger; yet one could not take offence, much less laugh, for he was clearly a serious person. I noticed just then that his ears were bored, and guessed from this that he came from one of the very old noble families, some of whom at that time still wore the ancient adornments handed down since the Wars of Troy. The rings had been taken out, no doubt because they interfered with his wrestling. Putting down part of his self-possession to his birth, it was still rather remarkable. I confessed he had the advantage of me and asked his name. He said, 'Aristakles, son of Ariston.'

All this I related to Lysis, who was much tickled, and said he had thought he could safely send me among schoolboys without a rival trying to cut him out. But when I told him the name of the boy's father, he frowned and said, 'Well, in the matter of birth you could scarcely go higher. His father is descended from King Kodros and his mother from Solon; the divine seed of Poseidon on either hand. Indeed, if Attica were still a kingdom, I think his elder brother might be the heir. But his family thinks of its past too often for the City's good; in fact they're a nest of oligarchs, and this boy must be a nephew of our accomplished Kritias, who I daresay instructs him already in speech-making and the political arts. Ah, well, he can wrestle at least.'

We said no more, for Kritias had become harder than usual to stomach. A young lad called Euthydemos had lately attached himself to Sokrates. He was only about sixteen, but of an aspiring mind, and prone to the absurdities it often runs into at that age; full of the things he meant to do, with no idea of how to set about them. I doubt if I could have had patience with him myself; but Sokrates had divined that under all his nonsense the lad was really in love with excellence, and took endless trouble with him, teasing him out of his pomposities, drawing him forth when he was shy, and putting something solid in the place of his airy notions. By the time I met him he was beginning to show some quality; but that was of no concern to Kritias.

As he valued excellence less and less, he began to lose his skill in assuming it. This time he had scarcely stayed to go through any decent ceremony, or pretence of honourable attachment, before making his demands; and his crudeness had clearly shocked the lad, who, as I have said, was shy. Having made a bad start with him, Kritias was now resorting by turns to flattery, a disgusting importunity, and – what was much more dangerous to this kind of youth – the promise of distinguished introductions. I had the whole story from Phaedo, who loathed Kritias more than anyone, for reasons it had always seemed better not to ask.

After Phaedo was free, he did not let Kritias drive him away from Sokrates. He stayed; but he used to stand looking as if his face were something he had dressed in. Dionysos wears such a pleasant mask in the play where he sends out King Pentheus to be torn by maenads. I said, 'Sokrates ought to be told. I can see why no one has done it. It is bound to hurt him that someone who has been about him so long can turn out like this. But it's better than his being deceived.' – 'Yes,' said Phaedo, 'I thought so too.' – 'You told him? What did he say?' – 'He said he had spoken to Kritias already. He asked him, it seems, why he chose to come like a beggar before one in whose eyes he wished to seem precious; and a beggar not for something noble, but for something base.'

It amazed me after this that Kritias could so much as look at Euthydemos in Sokrates' presence. And, in fact, he seldom did. But having suffered myself, I did not take long to perceive what was going on. The boy's father had confidence in Sokrates, and used to send him without a tutor; and he was ashamed to say anything, as I had been before.

It happened, soon after this, that the chance of war had released more of our circle than usual. Xenophon had just got back with his troop, looking as if he had been years in the field. Some of them had been cut off not long before and the Second killed. Xenophon had taken over, and done so well that the Hipparch had confirmed him in the rank. He must have been the youngest Second in the Guard. Phaedo was there. Agathon (who had been in action somewhere with the hoplites, and arrived drenched in scent to take off, he said, the smell of the camp) had come with Pausanias; Lysis with me; and Kritias had followed Euthydemos. At the time I am speaking of, Sokrates was talking to Xenophon about his promotion; but in the midst of it Euthydemos, whom Kritias had edged up to, flinched aside. And Sokrates broke off what he was saying, in the middle of a word.

There was an extraordinary pause, made up of suspense on the part of those who knew the cause, and surprise among the rest. I saw Phaedo's mask dissolve and his face appear through it, with slightly parted lips. Euthydemos, poor lad, who I suppose had long dreaded something like this, looked ready to die of shame; but we all had something else to attend to. An empty space had opened through the company, along which Sokrates and Kritias were staring at one another. I had often seen Sokrates pretend to be angry: he looked very droll, half comic and half terrifying. I had never seen him really angry before, and it was nothing to laugh at. Yet for all the force of mind in it, there was something too of a stocky old stone-mason cursing in the yard. If he had picked up a mallet and hurled it at Kritias' head, I should not have been surprised until later. But he said, 'Have you got swine-fever or what, Kritias, that you come scraping yourself on Euthydemos like a pig on a stone?'

The silence that followed you may imagine, seeing that Sokrates had never rebuked the very youngest of us before others. Kritias was by a long way the eldest man there, the most influential, the richest and best born. If Zeus himself had thundered, and blasted him at our feet, I don't think we young men would have gazed on his body with more solemn awe than now we did upon his face.

He had grown yellow about the mouth, and looked suddenly thinner; but it was his eyes that held me. He was sick with rage; yet he was using it, as an instrument of his will. I said to myself, 'He is trying to put Sokrates in fear.' The man in me was shocked and the boy stood gaping, as if at a house afire.

I looked at Sokrates. His face was still red with anger but his anger had died. He stood like rock, and I felt a creeping in my hair. It was not what fear gives one, and I did not understand it for a long time afterwards, till one day I felt it in the theatre; there too it was a case of a brave man standing up to the logic of fate.

Someone, I think, felt this more keenly than I did, for suddenly Agathon gave a little cracked laugh, and clapped his hand over his mouth. Kritias' eyes opened out and narrowed again; then he turned on his heel, and walked away.

'Tell me, Xenophon, now you are an officer yourself. . .' I think Sokrates alone of all the company remembered what we had been talking about before; even Xenophon stammered a little before he picked up the thread. But he steadied at once, and went on with the conversation as coolly as if it had been a march through enemy country, till the rest were ready to join in.

Afterwards Lysis and I walked off rather silently. At last I said,

'Lysis, Kritias would have killed him if he could. I saw his eyes.' –
'It wasn't pleasant,' he said. It was a way of his to talk things down
when they disturbed him. 'However, keep it in proportion; this is a
civilised City. Sokrates takes no part in politics and doesn't teach for
fees. That's as far as Kritias' writ runs. I call it a good riddance.'

I had just got in that evening, and was going to change, when
Phaedo called, a thing he had never done unasked before. He stood
in the courtyard and said, 'Come walking with me.' I was going to
ask him in to supper; then I looked again, and went out beside him
into the evening. He led me very fast to the Pnyx, and climbed
in. No one was about on the hill, but a few lovers, and children
playing. We sat on the slab of the public rostrum, and looked across
to the High City. The columns looked black against a thin green
sky, and the lamps shone yellow in the shrines. There was a smell
of dew on dust and on crushed leaves; the bats came out, and the
grasshoppers. Phaedo, who had gone up the hill like a leopard on
a leash, sat chin on hand. He would be old, I thought, before he
would be pitied when he suffered as other men are pitied. One
seemed to be looking at such a masterpiece as is only carved in the
after-calm. At last I said, 'Beasts must bleed in silence; but the gods
gave men speech.'

He smiled at me, as one does at a child who tugs one's clothes.
Then he said, 'Have you ever wondered why I hate Kritias?' –
'No, Phaedo; I can't say I have.' He nodded. 'You are half right.
I was a beginner at Gurgos', the first time, and green enough to
show I didn't like him. I even expected he would complain of
it.' He smiled slightly. I wrapped my arms across me; I was feeling
cold. 'Most people charge fees for teaching, but Kritias paid for the
privilege of instructing me. I got to know his knock . . . As Sokrates
was saying the other day, the gift of knowledge can never be taken
from us.'

I remembered in time that if one touched him, he would always
move away. I waited. In the dead light he seemed to wear a cap
of silver; his dark eyes were old and brilliant, like the eyes of
Apollo's snake.

'I came to Sokrates first,' he said, 'for his negative method. It
pleased me to watch him undermine the security of fools. There,

I thought, is a man who will not tame the truth, but will follow it into the dry places. So in my turn I followed him; and he led me where I had not thought to go. It doesn't frighten me when he tears down the definitions, and leaves nothing in place. Justice, holiness, truth . . . if one hasn't defined, one has had the demonstration. Well, from today I can say, I think, that I'm his prize student of the negative elenchos. I've outstayed my rivals . . . Kritias, and Alkibiades.'

I was silent, trying not to be angry with him for having drawn me too within the circle of his pain. Presently he turned to me. 'Still thinking with your belly, Alexias. Don't let Lysis make you soft. He's in love with you, and too simple to know what he is doing. If you turned your back on a battle he would die of shame. Think with your head even if it hurts you. When a man is freed from the bonds of dogma and custom, where will he run? To what he hates, or what he loves? Tell me, do you think many people hate Lysis?' – 'Lysis? I don't think it would be possible to hate him.' – 'So Sokrates feels about what he is in love with, wisdom, and God. So he turned the key of the cage, and set Alkibiades free. And now Kritias too is running on the mountains, with no more between him and his will than a wolf has. For a long time now I have watched Kritias getting loose, from the soul, if you like the word, or from whatever keeps a man on two feet instead of four. I have gone step by step with him, for his reason is a mirror held up to mine, till I stood at the very edge of his conclusions. It is the true teacher's gift, they say, to discover a man to himself . . . At Gurgos' once I lay awake considering how to kill him. But already it was too late.'

14

We went back to war soon after. King Agis was at Dekeleia in command, and saw to it that if the Thebans relieved his Spartans they should not sit idle. We found them easier, however, partly because they are inclined to be a little slow (though not as slow as the comic writers pretend) and partly because we had been coming and going in the truce till we knew each other better as neighbours than as enemies. I remember particularly two whom we picked up badly wounded. One could have got away, but had rushed back when he saw the other fall. Next day we handed them over through the heralds; for it would be long before they fought again, and to despatch helpless men is always disagreeable, particularly if they have shown courage first. I brought them some food and drink at night, and asked them if they were lovers. They said they were, and that it was a custom of their city for friends to take a vow at the tomb of Iolaos, whom Herakles loved. After this they always served together in battle, and were put in front to stiffen the line, as being more likely than anyone else to prefer death before dishonour. 'Some day,' the younger one said, 'they will make one regiment of us, and then we will conquer the world.' And he turned to his friend, who though weak with his wound looked round and smiled. I would have liked to talk longer to them, but they were in pain so I let them be.

Demosthenes sailed for Sicily in early summer. The fleet went soberly, with no ceremony beyond the sacrifices, and libations to the gods. Lysis and I sat our horses on a hill, with the troop about us, and saw the sails grow little on the sea. He and I caught each other's eyes and smiled; then he turned and called, 'A cheer for our fathers, and good luck to Demosthenes!' We all gave it, and felt proud that when the army came back with victory, no one could say we had sat idle among the women.

We had need of pride in the months that followed. I was strong and in the flower of youth, yet I knew weariness then as since I have seldom known it. The remnant of the harvest was ripening in the farms. There was only the cavalry to save it. All the infantry that was left was manning the City walls, so near were the invaders. By day the citizens watched in shifts; you could see men plying their trades in armour, or shopping in the market. By night every fit man slept in the mustering-places about the temples, lest Agis should surprise us.

The horsemen were based on the Anakeion; we in turn saw the Twins' bridles against the stars, and more than once I stood watch on that same wall where I had stood with my father when I was fifteen. Dawn would grow red in the sky and we would wait for the sound of the trumpet, which was never long delayed; we would take out our weary horses, rub their legs still lame and stiff with yesterday's riding, and set out again. But often we slept the night in the hills, with what shelter we could find.

Sometimes when the night was chilly, or there was rain, and we ached all over from riding or from wounds, Lysis and I would draw together, seeking a little warmth; but we never shared a cloak, because when you do that in winter you will do it in spring. Remembering those days, I hardly know what kept us to our resolve; we had no time to pursue philosophy, or be quiet, or consider the gods except when the squadron made the morning or evening prayer; and I think it was weariness more than anything that made it easy to us. Yet sometimes in the night watch, when the Galaxy unrolled its book across a moonless sky, I knew what we were about, and where Sokrates was sending us. When Lysis had left me and gone to sleep, I would feel my soul climb love as a mountain, which at the foot has wide slopes with rocks and streams and woods, and fields of every kind, but at the top one peak, to which if you go upward all paths lead; and beyond it, the blue ether where the world swims like a fish in its ocean, and the winged soul flies free. And thence returning, for a while I found nothing created that I could not love; the comrade I had been angry with in the day, the Spartans sitting in Dekeleia; even Kritias I was sorry for, and knew why Sokrates had not sooner cast him out. Yet I was not drowsy, nor lost in dreams, but saw the night sparkle like a crystal, and every coney stirring, or the silent owl.

Towards the end of summer we got a despatch from Sicily; but I quote my father's letter which came with it, for brevity's sake. I had written to him, by one of Demosthenes' ships. After some instructions about reclaiming the farm, he said, 'Your choice of a friend I approve, a young man of good reputation, whose father also I know. Do not neglect his instruction, whether in virtue or in the field, that your fellowship may be held in honour by gods and men. With regard to the war, since I cannot amend your news with better, receive mine like a man. Nikias by infirmity of purpose has paltered victory away. Demosthenes, a good man out of luck, threw for double or quits and lost. He knows the game is up, and means to bring us home again with what he can save. Nikias lingers, waiting on omens, or for a democrat to open the gates of Syracuse, or for the intervention of a god; but Syracuse is not Troy. In my opinion he fears to face the Athenians with a defeat. Demosthenes, however, is a man and will do what is needful. Endure till we come; we will sweep Attica clean together.'

I was half ready for the news, for it came after long delay, and the sound of victory flies fast. I don't think there was great astonishment anywhere. People looked rather sullen, but everywhere one heard 'When the Army is home again . . .' We thought of our farms; we had had enough of King Agis sitting on our skyline.

It was he, however, who lightened for us a weary evening at the Anakeion. I had been polishing my armour beside the fire; we had eaten, but were only half-full, for now the food had to come round by sea, rations were short. Xenophon had left his own fire and come to sit at ours; I shared my oil-flask with him, and we compared our wounds. One could always tell a cavalryman in the palaestra, by the way he was scarred about the arms and thighs and wherever the armour stops. Xenophon was trying to expound to me an invention of his, a long leather guard for the left arm and hand, which would not impede the reins like a shield. Suddenly a tremendous burst of laughter came from one of the other watch-fires. Then it spread to the next, as if a flaming stick were being passed round to kindle it. We were getting up to satisfy our curiosity, when Gorgion arrived with the news. He was laughing so much that he nearly fell in the fire.

When he could speak, he said, 'Do you want to know the true story of King Agis? Perhaps you thought he has been staying here because he hates us, and wants to do us harm. You were wrong, my friends. King Agis stays here out of family feeling, being united to us, you might say, by the most sacred ties. How proud he must be that he obeyed the omen, and left his new wife untumbled. If he hadn't, he would just have fathered one Spartan more, instead of an Athenian.'

'An Athenian?' I said, not daring to believe what I saw coming, till I remembered the laughter. 'Don't tell me Alkibiades has been keeping King Agis' bed warm all this time?' – 'No one was using it. I daresay he used to feel chilly, after swimming in the Eurotas twice a day. Now we know why he never caught cold.'

A few years ago, when I was Xenophon's guest at his place near Olympia, I happened in our talk to recall this occasion. He said he had always reckoned it a most shocking thing, a virtuous man's piety being abused, and he could not conceive of anyone finding humour in it. People's recollections differ after so long; but my own is that he laughed as loud as I did.

'Well,' I said, 'he's warmed the Eurotas for himself now, at all events. It must be blazing.' – 'Yes, indeed. For the Spartan ladies, whose privilege it is to tell the City if a man drops his shield, aren't as shy as ours; it's no glory in *them* not to be talked about. When he gave her a boy, she boasted of it everywhere.' – 'Tell us,' said Lysis, 'how he proved his innocence.' – 'The child's his picture in little, they say. But he carried it off with his usual grace, and taught her to make a fool of him. He told all enquirers that he, for his part, had never been the helpless prey of Aphrodite. Noble ambition alone had moved him. He had wished to found a line of kings.' We gasped, and wiped our eyes. Someone said, 'Say what you like, there will never be another like him.'

So we laughed, and shared the last of our wine, and fell to telling bawdy tales and then to sleep. I daresay I remember the night so well, because soon afterwards there came an end of laughter in the City.

15

We were driving the Spartans off a farm near Marathon, when Phoenix stumbled and threw me. But for Lysis, I should have been speared on the ground; as it was I broke my collar-bone, and had to lie up at the farm. But I was in such fear for Phoenix, who had gone very lame, that I used to get up every day to see to him; moreover the farmer was old, but his wife not. Like Sokrates, she made no charge for instructing the youth; but she undid the bandage Lysis had braced back my shoulder with, because it made me awkward. He rode over a few days later to see how I was mending, or I should be crooked to this day. I had to be carted back to the City, and the bone set again.

He was disabled himself, with a thrust in the arm he had got in beating the Spartans away from me. He had made light of it at the time, but now it had an angry humour in it, and had to be dressed every day. Most of us found that we did not heal so quickly as at first; the food was bad, and we were tired. This was the first time Lysis and I had been wounded together; so we thought it a holiday.

One day we were walking in the Agora, both feeling a little weak and sick; Lysis was feverish from his wound, and I had not long got on my feet again. We heard a great clamour from the other side, and went to see, not hurrying much, because it hurt to be jostled in crowds. As it happened, however, the man who had caused the commotion was coming our way, and bringing it with him. He was a metic, a Phrygian, with a barber's apron on. He was spreading his hands, calling on the gods to witness his truth, and demanding to be taken before the archons.

I remember the look of him well: short, smooth and paunchy, with a ruby in his ear, and a black beard crimped to display his art. Having come some way in a hurry, he was sweating like a pig from his hair down into his beard; he looked the kind of little man who gets a roar in a comedy by pretending to have dirtied himself with fright. But no one was laughing, unless the gods were, as they sat above the clouds. They, it may be, were saying, 'We sent you Perikles to counsel you, and was not that dignity enough for your City? We sent you omens and prodigies, and writing in the stars, and the gods in your streets were wounded for a sign; but you know better, you Athenians. You would tread upon purple; you would be greater than Necessity and Fate. Very well; take this in your face.'

He came towards us, out of breath, with a brawl about him, as if he might have cut a customer he was shaving, or overcharged. Seeing us, he outran the men who were shouting at him, and panted, 'Oh, sir, I can see you're a gentleman, sir, and a soldier; speak to them, sir; the City's given me a living these seven years, and what call would I have to leave my shop on a busy morning with a ship just in, and make up such a tale? I swear, sir, the man left me not an hour ago, and I came straight here, the gods be my witness. Stand by me, sir, you and the noble youth your friend, and take me to the archons, for people take liberties, sir, with a foreigner, though seven years I've . . .'

So Lysis turned to the people, and said they ought to leave the man to the law, whatever he had said, and anyone was welcome to come and see justice. Then they grew quieter, till an old man in leather, an armourer, said, 'And how many more will he tell on the road? Stop his mouth with pitch, I say. It's well enough for you, son of Demokrates, to keep your temper, but I've three sons with the Army, three sons, and how many more like me won't close their eyes tonight for the liar's tale? All to make himself somebody for a day, the foreign bastard, and cry up his stinking shop.' Then the noise broke out again worse than before; the little man ran in between Lysis and me, like a chicken under a hen's wing, and we were forced to walk with him where he was going. He chattered in our ears, and the crowd shouted behind us, and called to others who shouted in their turn and joined the press. And the barber wheezed and panted out his tale, between the names of patrons who would put in a word for him, or sometimes broke it off to promise us a hair-trim or a shave for nothing.

Such was the messenger the gods sent to the Athenians, to tell us that our Army in Sicily had perished from the earth.

He had a shop in Piraeus by the wharf where the traders come in from Italy. The colonists used to go there when they landed, to get polished up after the voyage. A ship was in, and one of the passengers sat down on the bench to wait his turn. And getting into talk with the men beside him, he said, 'Last time I came to your City it was a time of festival; garlands in the streets, torches at night, and the wine flowing. Now I dread to see the friends I made then, for what can one say to people in such calamity? I thought the war a mistake myself, for living at Rhegium I know something of Sicily; I doubted if the Athenians would come off with much to show; but, by Herakles, if anyone had told me that all would be lost, two great armies, two fleets of ships, the good Nikias and the brave Demosthenes both dying as wretchedly as thieves; yet what are they after all beside so many brave men, all butchered, or what is worse, enslaved . . .' At this all the people in the shop stopped him with an outcry, asking what he meant; and he looking about him in amazement, said, 'But has it not reached you here? Has no one heard? All Italy talks of nothing else.' So the barber had flung down his razor, and run all the way from Piraeus, and here he was. And Lysis and I believed him no more than the rest.

We saw him safe to the Prytaneion, for it is not good that Hellenes living under law should deal out punishment on hearsay in the street. We left him there and went away. I saw that Lysis' cheeks were flushed along the bone, and his eyes bright with fever. 'You have walked too long,' I said. – 'It's nothing, only that my wound is hot.' I made him come home, and bathed it with the infusion the doctor had ordered, and wrung out warm cloths and bound them on; while I worked my shoulder ached again, more than it had for days. All this time we were saying how the barber ought to be made an example of, for upsetting the City with false news. Yet it was as if our bodies knew the truth.

The archons were severe with the barber. Rumour was running like yeast, and he could not name his informant nor say where the man had gone. He was racked in the end, not being a citizen; this getting no sense out of him, they thought him punished enough, and let him go. About nine days later, another ship came from Italy; and the men she brought did not sit down at the barber's first, although they needed it. They were fugitives from the Army in Sicily, who throwing away their shields had saved themselves in the woods. Then we knew that the barber had let us down lightly, compared with the truth.

When Demosthenes came out to the Army, he had been like a man after long absence visiting a friend. The family says, 'He has been ailing this last year'; but the fresh eye sees death behind the chair. The Syracusans held both horns of the harbour, and the heights above; he had taken the bold line, and attacked the heights. For a while it had been anyone's battle; but darkness fights for the man who knows the land. Even then, Nikias would have delayed, seeing a lifetime of honour about to close in disgrace; but Demosthenes, being sounder in body and nobler in mind, shamed him into decision. He agreed to go. With prudence and secrecy, everything was made ready; the Syracusans had no word of it; only a dark night was needed for the ships to flit away. It was the great moon of Athene's feast-day. Here in Athens we had a cloudy night, but there she shone clear upon the sea and the rocky headlands; till at her zenith, her face was seen to grow less, and to be cut away, and at last all darkened, as if a great sheild had been held before her.

You might have thought Nikias would have raised both hands to heaven, and vowed a hekatomb of oxen to Athene, who had cared for her people so well. For it happened on the night of her feast, when the prayers of all the Athenians were lifted up to her; and it has always seemed to me that to reject her gift, the shelter of her shield, was as great an impiety in its own way as that of Anaxagoras, who pretended that Helios is only a glowing stone. Yet Nikias would see nothing in the omen but calamity, and he carried so many with him that Demosthenes was over-ruled. They decided to wait another full course of the moon, before they sailed.

So they waited; and the Syracusans attacked the ships again, and sank many more than they could still afford to lose. While they were debating what to do, the enemy strung his own ships across the harbour mouth and linked them with a boom. Then they needed no divination to know they must break out, or die. They prepared for battle.

As if just wakened from a drugged sleep, Nikias worked like two men, seeing the ships made ready, exhorting the trierarchs and the soldiers. He recalled to them the famous words of Perikles, that they belonged to the freest people in the world; as if the Syracusans had been subjects of a tyrant, and not Hellenes themselves, resolved to be free or die. For two years they had seen the fate of Melos hanging over them. They manned their ships along the shore, and waited.

It was Demosthenes who led out our ships to break the boom. They fell on it with such courage that they stormed the boom-ships, and were even casting off the ropes and chains; but then the Syracusan fleet fell on them from behind.

They say two hundred ships fought that day in the Great Harbour. The water was choked with them, ramming and boarding, and drifting while grappled into ships already engaged, so that battles merged and joined in unutterable confusion; hoplites springing from deck to deck and, as they fought, being struck by javelins from their own ships; rudders crushed in the press, the lame ships fouling friend as well as foe; the din so great, and quarters so close, that men hardly knew if the orders they heard came from their own trierarch, or the enemy's.

Meanwhile on shore the Athenians watched the battle, as helpless as if it were a game of dice, with their lives at stake. They swayed this way and that, crying out in triumph or gasping in despair as their own glimpse of the fight looked well or ill. But the Syracusans held four-fifths of the beaches; they could put in anywhere, if they were pressed; the Athenians had only the tiny ship Gylippos and his men had left them. They were trapped on all sides; the ships that were not sunk were driven back to land. At the sight of them returning, the waiting army gave one great groan of anguish, and stared from the sea strewn with wreckage and with dead, to the hostile land.

To the land they turned their faces at last, leaving the dead unburied; and as if the reproaches of the homeless shades were not enough, they had to abandon the wounded and the sick. It was that, or stay and die with them. They dragged themselves on the flanks, clung to their friends till they could neither walk nor crawl; and then lay pleading, or cursing, or calling out last messages; their voices hung above the Army along with the ravens and the kites. The walking remnant marched on over the stony land, empty, thirsty, harried by the enemy on either side, until the end. At the last they came to a steep-banked river. They poured down into it, to cross over and to drink; and the Syracusans closed in, before and behind. As the Athenians struggled in the water, stones and darts and arrows rained on them. The river was churned to mud and ran with the blood of the dying. But such was their thirst that those who could reach it lay in it and drank, till others trampled them and they drowned.

Demosthenes fell on his sword, but was taken alive to give the enemy the pleasure of killing him. Nikias too they put to death, no one knows how. Of the rank and file, many thousands perished on the spot; many were dragged off by Syracusan soldiers, to sell for gain. The rest were the common spoil of the State. The fugitives, hiding in the woods, saw them driven away like starved cattle, and knew no more.

They had gone out from the City with women wailing, and flowers strewn in the streets. But one may weep when Adonis dies; for crying eases the heart, and the gods return.

In the silent streets, a man who saw his friends approaching would cross to the other side, lest speech be asked of him. Sometimes as you passed a house you could hear a woman weeping alone, a dull sound, moving as she dragged herself about her work. I had heard it at home, and fled at last into the City. Lysis and I drew together like animals in winter; for hours at a time we hardly spoke.

A night or two later, I walked to the Anakeion. The horses shifted and snorted, made uneasy by the quiet. Here and there by a watch-fire one or two men would be playing dice, to make the time pass. I came up behind the man I was looking for. He had thrown two sixes, but did not notice it till someone pushed his winnings at him. I touched his shoulder and said, 'Xenophon.'

He looked round, and got up from the fire and came aside with me. I saw his eyes searching mine; but he said calmly, as if we had met by chance, 'I'm glad to see you Alexias. Are you able to ride now?' – 'No; but I have news for you. Your father is dead.' I saw him give a long noiseless sigh, like a man from whom a burden has fallen. 'Is it certain?' he said. – 'I have talked to a man who saw him die. He fell at the storming of the heights, a month before the end. All those dead were buried, by the shore of the harbour, in a common grave.' He took my hand, which he had never done before. 'Thank you, Alexias. Don't go yet; I have some wine here.'

Often I had wondered what I could ever say to Xenophon by way of comfort if his father should fall. Thus the event makes fools of our expectations. He divided his wine with me, insisting as one does with the bringer of good tidings; as I was leaving he said, 'And for yourself, Alexias? No news yet?' – 'Not yet,' I said. – 'I am sorry. But there is still time.' I heard nothing, however, though I questioned every survivor I could hear of.

So the Assembly was called, and the men went up the Pnyx. They did not stay very long. I waited for Lysis at the place we had appointed, a saddler's shop in a street near by. The place smelt of old leather and horse-sweat. Hardly anything in the place was new, so few of the knights could afford it; it was all repair-work. The saddler was at the Assembly; I talked to the foreman, who was a metic, about horse-embrocation and swollen hocks. Our horses were lame half their time for lack of rest; my broken shoulder had been good for Phoenix at least. Then Lysis came in, looking better than he had since he was hurt. The saddler was with him; they were laughing together. He said to me, 'All's well. No surrender.' The saddler slapped the foreman on the shoulder and said, 'Cheer up, Brygos. They won't make a Helot of you yet.'

'Don't rub your arm, Lysis,' I said. 'You know that makes it worse.' – 'It itches. It will mend now. I feel in myself that the poison is gone.'

Autumn drew on. The courtyard vines bore their few grapes, and on the hills of Attica the wasted vineyards bore weeds. The war slowed down again, as wars do when winter comes. We made our patrols; the Thebans came out sometimes and made little raids, lest we should feel at ease. Half the cavalry strength kept watch at the Anakeion; the rest, turn and turn about, went home. Sharp mornings began, when, as one pulls off one's clothes and runs out to the palaestra, one sees steam coming up from the wrestlers. But most of my leave I was running. For the people of Corinth had sent us a herald, announcing the sacred truce of Poseidon, and inviting us to send competitors to the Isthmian Games. I did not tell Lysis my hopes, in case they came to nothing. The City, which would have to send all the entrants round by sea, would not choose many.

We went on patrol again in a fine spell of weather; frosty nights, silver mornings, and noons of gold. One evening we passed the farm where I had lain with my broken shoulder. While we were buying some cheese, the farmer's wife beckoned me round a corner. With all that had happened, I had remembered her mostly for her bad nursing; but meeting again, it was another matter, and she lost no time in persuading me that what had been good with a sore shoulder would be better with a sound one. She was a fair-haired young woman, slim and firm; her face was tanned, but her body very white. The end of our conversation was that I should come back that night, if we made camp near enough, and meet her in the barn.

Being unable to keep anything long from Lysis, I had confessed my former adventure long ago. If he was ill pleased, he had not the pettiness to show it; but he said I ought not to go after married women, as if a husband had no rights. 'It can happen to anyone,' he said, 'in a case like that; but the fact remains that it is stealing. You would be ashamed to go off with another man's horse, after all, so why make free with his other property? Next time you want a woman, you ought to pay for one.' I said, 'But Lysis, he cares nothing for such things; he is long past it, and only wants a housekeeper; she told me so.' Seeing me bring out this old tale with such a serious face, he could not keep from laughing. But I did not care now, as you may suppose, to tell him where I was going. I had no watch that night, and slipped off as soon as he was asleep.

I knew, or thought I knew, a short way over the mountain; so I left my horse and my armour; but took a sword, which was sillier than taking nothing, as I should have known. Starting before moonrise I lost my way, and wandered some time before I found a landmark, a shoulder of broken rock. At the same time I heard voices and the sound of armour. The rock threw off echoes and confused the sound. Coming round it, I ran straight into a Theban hoplite. I had drawn my sword when two more seized me from behind. So I could not pass myself off as anything but what I was.

I thought they would kill me out of hand, but they took me round to their camp on the hillside. One does not understand, until one feels it, the difference between struggling with a friend in the palaestra, and being handled by an enemy. They were a small troop, twenty or thirty. Coming to the watch-fire, where their officer sat, they pushed me forward roughly, so that I stumbled; having my hands bound I could not save myself, and fell hard. They all laughed at this. I got to my knees, then to my feet. My hair was singed, and my face bleeding. The officer was a stocky man, with a thick black beard and a bald head. They told him I was a spy they had found looking for the camp. He walked up to me, turned me round, and looked at my arms. My left was scarred in one or two places, which you do not find in a hoplite who carried a shield. 'Frontier Guard?' he said. I made no answer. 'Where's you squadron?' – 'I don't know. My horse fell; I have been lost all day.' I hoped he would believe me, for I was afraid. He said, 'Where's your armour, then?' The man who caught me said, 'He carries a sword.'

The officer said, 'I don't take prisoners, Athenian. But tell me where your squadron is, and you can go free. See how few we are; we only want to save ourselves.' Two of the men looked at each other. I heard a sound from behind some rocks, where the rest were; there was a glow too from their fire. 'Tell me,' he said, 'and you can have your life.' I thought, 'If I invent something, it only means being dragged along as a hostage, and a worse death at the end.' So I said nothing. Someone said, 'Try sitting him on the fire.' The captain said, 'We are Hellenes here. Will you speak, Athenian?' – 'I know nothing.' – 'Very well. Who caught this man?' The hoplite came forward. 'Finish your work.'

Two of them grasped my shoulders, and another hit me across the back of the knees with a spear-shaft, to bring me down. They held me kneeling. It was a bright cold night; the fire crackled and spurted, and in the sky the stars were like sparks from an anvil, white and blue. You never learn how much your courage owes to the wish for a good name among men, to the eyes of lover and friends upon you, till you are alone among enemies. If I had thought that to beg for my life would move them, I would have begged for it; but I would not be their mock. I thought of my mother, left alone with the child. My tongue felt dry and bitter mouth. I wondered how long it takes to die, when the sword is in. Then I thought of Lysis.

The captain beckoned the man who had caught me, and motioned with his hand. The man nodded and moved out of sight. I heard his armour creak behind me. My heart leaped in my throat and I said, 'Wait.'

Someone laughed. One of the men holding my shoulders spat, and said, 'Are you frightened, Athenian? My son was at Mykalessos, which your City sacked with the Thracians. Are you too young, ephebe, to be brave? He was eight years old.' – 'May the child's shade rest; blood for blood pays all. That man behind me, bring him in front.' The man at my back said, 'Will you be better for that?' – 'I think so,' I said. 'I was told you Thebans understood these matters. Is it all one to you, then, whether your friend finds you wounded before or behind?'

They paused, murmuring to one another. Then a man who had come over from the other fire said, 'I know that voice. Let me see him.' He picked up a burning stick and looked at my face. His I could not see, the flame blinding me; yet there was something I remembered. He said, 'Yes, I know him. I have a score to settle with this one. Let no one trouble himself further; give him to me.' The officer said, 'Take him and welcome, if it's any pleasure to you. But do as he asked.' The man pulled me to my feet and showed me his sword and said, 'Come.'

I wondered what it was he meant to do to me, that he was ashamed for the rest to see. He took me some way off, past rocks and some trees. The stars glittered and flashed. It was cold away from the fire. He stopped at last. I said, 'Your friends are not here, Theban; but the gods are.' – 'Let them judge between us. Do you know me?' – 'No. What wrong have I done you?' – 'Last summer I was taken by the Frontier Guard, I and my friend. There was a lad called Alexias; they said the captain was his lover.' – 'They said well. If your quarrel is with Lysis, I stand here for him. But he will kill you.' – 'He sent us food at night; you brought it. My friend could not sit up to drink, so you raised his head.' I remembered then. 'His name was Tolmides,' I said. 'He wanted to raise a regiment of lovers and conquer the world. Is he here too?' – 'He died the evening after. If you had been rough with him, I would have cut out your heart tonight.' He slid his sword under my bonds and cut them with a couple of jerks of the edge; his sword was sharp, and he was strong. 'Are you that Alexias who was crowned for the long-race?' – 'I am the runner.' – 'All Athenians boast,' he said. 'Prove it.'

When I got back go the camp, it was within an hour of dawn. The outpost, when I gave the countersign, would hardly speak to me. He said that Lysis had watched all night. I found him lying in his place beside the stacked arms, his armour by him, wrapped in his cloak. When I came near he did not open his eyes. I knew he was not asleep but angry. All the way back I had been thinking of him. I said to myself, 'If I speak, we shall fall out. Let me be near him now, and he can be angry in the morning.' I got my cloak, and lay down beside him. I was tired, but could not sleep, and did not know whether he slept or not. I must have dozed in the end, for I woke to a cold dusk of dawn, and Lysis leaning over me.

Presently he said softly, for the rest were still asleep, 'Are you much hurt?' – 'Hurt?' I said. 'No.' – 'You are bruised all over, and covered with blood.' I had forgotten how roughly the Thebans had handled me. We got up, and went down to the stream to wash. A grey mist filled the valley and hung on the water. I was stiff all over, and cold. It was the hour when life burns low, and the sick die. His face looked grey with weariness; I understood his wish had been to let the troop look after itself, and to come seeking me. He said, 'There is blood in your hair too,' and found the cut and washed it. I thought, 'The love one feels at a time like this, must be truly the love of the soul.'

'If the man had killed you,' he said, 'finding you with his wife, the law would have upheld him. Are you cold?' – 'The water was cold.' He put his arm with his cloak about my shoulders.

'Was it for this,' he said, 'that we made our offering to the god?'

I said, 'Yes, Lysis.' We stood by the stream, for it was too cold and wet to sit, and I told him. The first birds woke, and the face of the opposite mountain showed grey through the haze; the dark thorn-tree wept with dew. At last the sun shone red on the peak, and we heard the others waking; so we went back to rub down our horses, and make ready for the day.

16

In the spring, King Agis came back to Dekeleia, and marched straight down into Attica again. Nearly all the farms which had been saved or missed before were burned this time, and Demokrates' went among the first. Lysis got the news while we were in the City, and came to tell me.

'Rather than complain,' he said, 'we ought to thank the gods we saved what we did. For that matter, Father can thank me for some of it. We picked the place bare a month ago, but he wouldn't strip off the roof-tiles till I had been at him for days. There is the horse-farm in Euboea, which will bring something in as long as we can ship the horses. We shan't starve; but it's hard for a man of his age to take a change of fortune, and now he is sick again. Come home with me, I've something to show you.'

I went, and he unlocked one of the stables. The door creaked with rust. Inside was a chariot, covered with dusty cobwebs. The work was very grand in the old style, painted with figures from Homer, the carvings gilded. A bleached and withered garland hung on it, with faded ribbons; Lysis pulled if off, and spiders ran out. 'That must be from the Pythian Games,' he said. 'It's ten years or more since we kept up the stud to race it; it ought to have gone long since. When I was a boy, our charioteer used to take me up at practice sometimes, and let me put my hands on the reins and believe I was driving. I had great notions of winning one day with myself up, as my grandfather Lysis did. I don't want Father to see this before it has been cleaned. We're selling it tomorrow.'

Not very long after this, I was brought at last the news of my father's death.

It was Sokrates who prepared me for what I was going to hear, and led me to Euripides' house. For he had one, like anyone else, in the City, not far from ours, though one hears everywhere lately a silly tale that he lived in a cave. This has grown, I suppose, from his having had a little stone hut built on the shore, where he went to work and be quiet. As to his being a misanthrope, I think the truth is that he grieved for men as much as Timon hated them, and had to escape from them sometimes in order to write at all.

He greeted me with gentleness but few words, looking at me with apology, as if I might reproach him for having no more to say. Then he led me to a man whom, if I had not been forewarned, I should have taken for some beggar he had washed and clothed. The man's bones were staring from his skin, the nails of his hands and feet broken and filled with grime; his eyes were sunk into pits, and he was covered with festering scratches and with sores. In the midst of his forehead was a slave-brand done in the shape of a horse, still red and scabby. But Euripides presented me to him not him to me. He was Lysikles, who had commanded my father's squadron.

He began to tell me his tale quite clearly; then he lost the thread of it, and became confused among things of no purpose till Euripides reminded him who I was, and who my father was. A little later again he forgot I was there, and sat looking before him. So I will not relate the story as he told it then.

My father, as I learned, had been working in the quarries at the time of his death. That was where the Syracusans took the public prisoners after the battle, and where most of them ended their lives. The quarries at Syracuse are deep. They lived there without shelter from the scorching sun or the frosts of the autumn nights. Those who could work quarried the stone. They all grew grey with the stone-dust, which only the rain that sometimes fell on them ever washed away. The dust filled their hair, and the wounds of the dying, and the mouths of the dead whom the Syracusans left rotting where they lay. There was nowhere in the rock to dig them graves, if anyone had had the strength to do it; but because a fallen man takes up more room than one on his feet, they piled them into stacks; for the living had scarcely space to lie down and sleep, and in this one place they lived and did everything. After a time not much work was demanded of them, for no overseer could be got to endure the stench. For food they were given a pint of meal a day, and for drink half a pint of water. The guards would not stay to give it out, but put down the bulk and let them scramble for it. At first the people of Syracuse used to come out in numbers to look into the quarry and see the sight; but in time they grew weary of it and of the smells, all but the boys who still came to throw stones. If any citizen was seen from below, those who were not already resigned to death would call out to him, begging to be bought into slavery and taken anywhere. They had nothing worse to fear than what they suffered.

After about two months the Syracusans took away the allied troops from among them, branded these on the forehead, and sold them off. They kept the Athenians in the quarry; but at this time they removed the dead, among whom was my father. His body had then been lying there some weeks: but Lysikles had recognised it while it was still fresh.

On this he paused and drew his brows together, as if trying to recall what it was he had omitted. When his forehead wrinkled, the legs of the horse, which was branded on it, seemed to move. Then he remembered and offered me a condolence on the loss of my father, such as a man of breeding makes to a friend's son. You might have thought it was I who had given the news to him. I thanked him, and we sat looking at one another. I had made his memory live for him, and he had made it live for me. So we stared, both of us, with an inward eye, seeking blindness again.

His own story he did not tell me, but I heard it later. He had passed himself off as an Argive, having picked up some of their Doric, and having been branded with them was sold. He had been bought for a small price by a rough master; and at last, preferring to starve in the woods, he had run away. When too weak to go further, he had been found by a Syracusan riding out to his farm. This man guessed he was an Athenian, yet gave him food and drink and a place to sleep; then, when he was somewhat recovered, asked him whether any new play by Euripides had lately been shown in Athens. For of all the modern poets, it is he whom the Sicilians value most. And living so much out of the way, they are the last to hear of anything new.

Lysikles replied that the year before they sailed, Euripides had been crowned for a new tragedy upon the sack of Troy, and the fate of the captive women. Whereon the Syracusan asked him if he could repeat any of it.

This is the play Euripides wrote just after the fall of Melos. I did not hear it myself, for my father, having thought his former work unorthodox, did not take me. Phaedo once told me that he heard it. He said that from the moment when he was struck down in battle, through all he saw on the island, and while he was a slave at Gurgos', that was the only time he wept. And no one noticed him, for the Athenians were weeping on either side. Lysikles had both heard the play and read it; so as much as he knew, he taught the Syracusan, who in payment gave him a bag of food and a garment and set him on his way. This was not the only case of the kind; Euripides had several visits from Athenians who came to tell him that one of his choruses had been worth a meal or a drink to them. Some, who had been sold as house slaves at the beginning, were promoted to tutors if they knew the plays, and at last saw their City again.

But for my father, who had liked to laugh with Aristophanes, there was no returning. I did not even know if a handful of earth had been sprinkled over him at last, to put his shade at rest. We performed the sacrifice for the dead at the household altar, my uncle Strymon and I; and I cut off my hair for him. In only a little while, when I became a man, I should have been offering it to Apollo. This was the god my father had always honoured most. As I laid the wreath on the altar, with the dark locks of my hair tied into it, I remembered how his had shone in the sunlight like fine gold. Though he had turned forty when he sailed for Sicily, the colour had scarcely begun to fade; and his body was as firm as an athlete's of thirty years.

I told Strymon that my father had died of a wound in the first days of his captivity; for I could not trust his tongue, and this was the story I had given my mother.

Soon I was back in the field again; and this, I found, was as good a consolation as any. For however little sense there may be in it, while risking one's life one feels that one makes an offering, and that the gods who afflict men with remorse are appeased.

Now that spring was here, the shipyards worked all day; ribbed keels stood everywhere on the slipways; here and there you could see a vessel ready, with torches burning half the night to light the fitters. It was a fine sight and put heart into you, till you saw what was ready to take the sea. Only one piece of news was dreaded now whenever a ship came in, that the island allies were in revolt.

All this while, I was waiting to go before the gymnasiarchs when they picked the entrants for the Isthmian Games. If I could have entered as a boy, I could have been fairly sure of it; but I should have turned eighteen by then so must enter as an ephebe. Yet, at the trial runs, the gods gave me in swiftness what I lacked in art, and I found myself among the chosen.

I stood transported with joy, till the public trainer came up and said to me, 'Your body is now dedicated to the god; report to your officer that you are freed from military service till after the Games, and be here tomorrow morning.' I walked with dragging feet through the porch into the street; I had not thought ahead, nor known that separation would come so hard. It troubled me; there seemed something excessive in it; I should have been ashamed to confess it, even to Lysis himself. I was walking to his house, resolved to put a sensible face on it, when Xenophon met me in the street and said laughing, 'Well, when you and Lysis celebrate tonight, don't forget to take plenty of water with it; you're both in training now.'

I was getting to an age when people stare if you run in the street; but I did not pause till I found him. It was true; he had been chosen along with Autolykos to fight the pankration. He had not even told me he was going before the selectors, for fear of its coming to nothing. We embraced each other laughing like children.

Next day our training began in earnest: practising all morning, a walk after supper, two parts of water always to one of wine, and to bed with the dark. Another knight had taken over the troop from Lysis; till after the Games, we should only take up arms if the enemy attacked the walls.

One day when we met after exercise, Lysis said, 'Do you remember that young cousin of Kritias', Aristokles, the wrestler?

You gave him a message from me once, in the Argive's palaestra.'
– 'Oh, yes; Ariston's son, the lad who talks like a prince. I've
not see him since.' – 'You'll be seeing him soon; he's going to
the Games with us, to wrestle in the boys' class.' – 'You were
right, then, when you said he would be heard of again.' – 'Yes,
and I fancy his chances too, unless another city puts up someone
outstanding. He was born for a wrestler; it's stamped all over him,
too clearly indeed for grace. They have a nickname for him now
in the palaestra; they all call him Plato.' – 'How does he like that?'
I asked. I remembered the boy gazing at my face, as if he were
putting it up against some notion of beauty in his mind which for
a moment I satisfied. 'If his proportions are bad,' I said, 'he looked
the kind of lad who wouldn't need reminding of it.' – 'Probably
not; he practises running in armour, to keep himself in balance. I
daresay a little teasing won't hurt him; he is inclined to be solemn.
He takes it very well; at least they learn manners in that family, and
it's a pleasant change to see one of them in the palaestra instead of
on the rostrum.'

I meant to go and watch the boy at practice if I could find time;
but just then something happened which drove trifles from my
head. I came home, and met in the court my little sister Charis
weeping. She was always tumbling about and bruising herself, for
she was just learning to run. I picked her up; being only two years
old, she went bare unless it was cold, and her body was as sweet as
fresh apples. When I had made her laugh I looked for her hurt but
could find none; so I carried her in. There I saw my mother, seated
in talk with my uncle Strymon. She had pulled her veil across her
face. I thought it modest of her to take this trouble with so old a
man; yet something in it disturbed me. I set down the child and
went in. On this my mother dropped her veil, and turned to me,
as a woman to the man under whose protection the gods have
placed her. I went over and stood at her side. Then looking up
I met the eyes of Strymon and thought, 'This man is an enemy.'

I greeted him, however, in the usual way. He said, 'I have
been pointing out to your stepmother, Alexias, and not for the
first time, the unfitness of her staying here alone, now that your
worthy father is gone, in a household without a man at its head. The

gods have given me means enough to take care of such obligations: kindly assure her of it, since she seems to fear being a burden in my house.'

I considered this. Being almost eighteen, I should soon be of age and her legal guardian. Still he was, in the meantime, head of the family; his proposal was correct, if rather officious. At first I was chiefly concerned lest he might want me to go too. Then I saw her eyes flinch before his; and I understood.

He was a man of only five-and-sixty, in good health. Without doubt he would have offered her marriage, and many women in her place would have thought themselves well off. The extreme of horror I felt, was no doubt the effect of my youth. Like one deprived of sense, I put forward none of the reasonable objections I might have made to her going, but cried out, 'She will stay here, by Zeus, and let me see who will take her away!'

He rose from his chair. We stood eyeing one another; I have met kinder looks across the top of a shield. Never destroy without thought your enemy's pretences; they are usually your best weapon against him. We were both drawing breath to speak again, when my mother said, 'Alexias, be silent. You forget yourself.'

I felt as if she had stabbed me in the back while I defended her. Turning round, however, and seeing her face, I understood that she was afraid. This was natural enough; for an open breach with him would have made our lives very unpleasant. Her sharpness recalled me partly to myself. I begged his pardon, and began to say some of the things I should have said at first. He replied, 'Pray don't trouble yourself, Alexias, to apologise. I imagine that in your own circle of friends, what we have heard is nothing out of the way. Where the teacher does not even worship the immortal gods, but sets them aside for new divinities, one can hardly expect in the pupil much reverence for age and kinship in mere men.'

It had been a way of mine since childhood to throw back my head when I was angry. I did this now, and felt a strangeness; I was used to the weight of my hair, and it had gone. It was as if a hand had been laid on me to say, 'Remember you are a man.'

'The blame is mine, sir,' I said. 'He would have rebuked me sooner than you. Thank you for your offer; but I don't wish my mother to leave this house, where I shall be master shortly.' – 'In a few years,' he said, 'when you bring home a bride, your stepmother will have little cause to thank you.' – 'Sir, when I choose a bride, it won't be one who does not honour my mother.' He said, 'You have no mother, and this woman is your father's wife.'

I had to fix my eyes on his white beard, or I could not have answered for myself. I have seldom been so roused in battle. When my mother spoke I seemed at first scarcely to hear. She said, as a woman speaks to a slapped child, 'That is enough, Alexias. Bid your uncle goodbye, and go.'

I had not even answered him. Her injustice stung me; but it sobered me too. After that moment I said, 'Well, sir, I am sure neither of us cares to parade family business in a lawsuit. I should be of age too by the time it was heard, and your case would fall away. We have kept you long enough from your affairs; may we offer you something before you go?'

When he had left, I was reluctant to go in again. I suppose I felt I had mishandled the matter, and feared my mother's reproaches. I went out into the street instead; and now I found only one thought in my mind. Whenever I met with an acquaintance, I asked if he had seen Lysis anywhere. Someone told me he was still at the gymnasium. He was not on the wrestling-ground; but I found him on the sand-track, throwing the disk. He had just got it poised, and was starting the swingback, when he saw me, and checked his arm, and made a bad cast. The others laughed at him, seeing the cause; then he took up the disk again, and made a good one. Soon afterwards he finished, and came out to clean-off. It seemed to me that I had never beheld him with such joy; I could scarcely greet him. When he had dressed and we were walking away, he said, 'What is it? You don't look like yourself, is anything wrong?' – 'No, Lysis. But sometimes I wonder how I got along before I knew you; for it seems now that if I clung to life at all, it was only through ignorance of what I lacked. And if you were not going to Corinth too, I would withdraw my name, rather than we should be parted so long.'

He stared at me half laughing. 'Withdraw? What, from the Games? That wouldn't earn me much credit in the City. I see now what it is; you've been training too hard, and getting nervous. Take my advice, and don't waste time fretting in case another city sends a faster man. You can't know, nor help it if you did. As Sokrates said to me years ago, you can only make your body as acceptable to the gods as you can. If we didn't know they give the crown to the best man, we might as well save ourselves the hard work, and sit drinking at home. So be at peace with yourself, my dear, for there is measure in everything. Shall we go swimming? Or watch the horse-race? Or talk in the colonnade?' He gazed at me, his brows drawn in thought. 'Autolykos says he generally has a girl halfway through his training. It's not what the trainers say, I know, but he recommends it.'

'I think I'll stick to the training,' I said, 'and wait till I get to Corinth.' I knew what that city is famous for, and thought this sounded manly enough. In the end we went to the horse-race. Whatever had been in my mind when I sought him out, I went home in the evening feeling like someone who has shaken off a fever.

A few weeks later I turned eighteen, and went up for the scrutiny. My uncle Strymon went with me, for decency's sake. When I had verified my age and parentage, the strategos swore me in. He said with a straight face that he supposed I was eager to start my military service; then he held up one of my arms, and looked at my scars, and laughed.

At home I found laid out on my bed my man's mantle, which my mother had woven ready a long time back; it smelt of the sweet herbs she kept her dresses in. Lysis had taught me already how to drape it. I put it on, and went in to show myself. 'Now, Mother,' I said, 'let me see you smile; from this time on you have nothing to fear.' She smiled at me and tried to speak; then suddenly the tears stood in her eyes. It is natural in women to give way like this upon joyful occasions. I came forward with open arms to comfort her; but she cried out that it would be unlucky to sprinkle my mantle with tears at its first wearing; and so avoiding me went away.

17

On the day appointed, we assembled at Piraeus: the priests and important citizens who were to lead the procession; two trainers; and the athletes, men and boys. The lad Aristokles greeted me on the dock with his old-fashioned courtliness. His nickname had stuck; boys, trainers and everyone called him Plato now. He took it cheerfully, and I soon got in the way of it like the rest.

The City sent us to Corinth in the State galley *Paralos*. This was my first acquaintance with men I was to know much better afterwards; but it is remarkable how quickly you notice the difference in a ship where the whole crew are free citizens, rowers and all. A place on the *Paralos* was the most honourable open to any man who could not afford the panoply of a hoplite, which is the reason in many cases why a man takes to the sea. But their necessity had become their choice. They were great democrats and stood no nonsense from anyone; and one or two of the passengers, who were oligarch-minded, complained of their insolence. For myself, after weeks of palaestra small-talk I could have listened to them by the hour. I confess I cannot see why a sailor should not take as much pride in himself as a soldier or even an athlete. No one can say it is a base employment, like that of a man cramped indoors at a work-bench, which spoils the body and confines the soul.

Autolykos was a favourite with them, as with everyone else. I have heard superior people say he had no more mind than a fine bull, and I don't pretend he would have shone in a disputation; but he was modest in success, a good fellow and a thorough gentleman. Once when Lysis was praising him to me, I said, 'I can't think how you pankratiasts manage in the contest. A runner only needs to leave his rivals behind; but in a day or two, if you and Autolykos are drawn in the same heat, you will be buffeting each other about the ears, flinging each other down, kicking and twisting and throttling; doing each other as much harm, short of biting and gouging, as two men can without weapons in their hands. Don't you mind it?' He laughed and said, 'One doesn't go out to do a man harm, only to make him give in. I can tell you, Autolykos in action is no object for tenderness.'

We were having supper at the time at a tavern in Salamis, where the wind being contrary we had put in for the night. Autolykos was there too, treating the pilot. I said to Lysis, 'He's grown very heavy this last year. It has almost spoiled his looks. I've never seen a man eat as much as he does.' – 'He's only following his training-diet; in fact, according to that he ought to eat even more, two pounds of meat a day.' – 'Meat every day! I should think it would make one slower than an ox.' – 'Well, there is something in weight too, and the City trainers are rather divided on it, so they let us go on as we did with our trainers before. I agree with mine that the pankration was founded to be the test of a man, and the right weight for a man is the weight for a pankratiast.'

The inn lamp had been lit; and all Salamis, it seemed, had gathered outside on the harbour front to watch us eating, word having got round of who we were. Seeing them stare, I looked at Lysis with a stranger's eyes, which I had almost forgotten how to do. I thought that Theseus, setting forth in his flower of strength to wrestle at the Isthmus, could have looked no better. His mantle being open, the lamplight showed the beautiful hard sheen of his body, like oiled beechwood, and the smooth curve of muscle and sinew. His neck and shoulders, though firm as rock, had not thickened; he moved them as lightly as a racehorse. It was plain that the people outside were betting on his victory, and envying my place beside him. Yet he thought in his modesty that they were looking at me.

Next day we sighed the port of Isthmia, and, standing against the sky, the round-topped mountain where the Corinthian citadel is. As the haze lifted, one could see the walls twined like a fillet about its brows. On the very summit I saw a small temple shining, and asked Lysis if he knew what it was. He said, 'That must be the shrine of Aphrodite, to whom the Girls of the Goddess belong.'

'Do they live there?' I asked him. It seemed beautiful to me that Aphrodite should keep her girls like doves in a tall pine-tree, not lightly to be won; I pictured them walking in the dawn, and clothing their rosy limbs against the brisk air of morning, and going down to the mountain spring; girls like milk, like honey or like dark wine, presents to the Cyprian from every land under the sun. 'No,' he said, smiling as he watched my face, 'the shrine's for people like you, who like love on top of a mountain. The girls are in the City precinct, of the Goddess wouldn't grow very rich. But never mind; after the Games we'll go to both. The girls at night; daybreak for the mountain. We'll watch them make the morning sacrifice to Helios as he rises from the sea.'

I agreed, thinking all this very fitting for men who have been contending for glory before a god. In my mind I saw the girl of my choice, opening her arms by the light of a little lamp, her shining hair heavy on the pillow.

Round about us people were watching the coast grow nearer, and talking, as men in strict training will, of the pleasures of Corinth, exchanging the names of bath-houses and brothels, and of the famous hetairas from Laîs down. Seeing the lad Plato near by, looking as usual rather serious, I clapped him on the shoulder and said, 'Well, my friend, what do *you* want to do in Corinth?' He looked round at me and answered, without so much as a pause for thought, 'To drink from the Fountain of Peirene.'

'From Peirene?' I said staring. 'The spring of Pegasos? You're not intending to set up as a poet, are you?' He gave me a straight look, to see if I was laughing at him (I had remarked already that he was no fool) and having satisfied himself, said, 'Yes, I hope so.' I looked at his heavy brows and solid frame. His face had a distinction which just kept one from calling him ugly; it occurred to me that as a man he might even become impressive. So I asked him with proper gravity whether he composed already. He said he had written a number of epigrams and elegies, and had almost completed a tragedy, upon Hippolytos. Then he dropped his voice, partly with a boy's shyness, but partly it seemed, with the discretion of a man. 'I was thinking, Alexias, if you and Lysis should both be crowned at the Games, what a subject for an ode!' — 'You young fool!' I said, half laughing and half angry with him. 'It's a proverb for bad luck, to make the triumph-song before the contest. No more of your odes, in Apollo's name!'

But now nearing the port we saw between the pines the great temple of Poseidon, and around it the gymnasiums and palaestras, the stadium and the hippodrome. The Council of the Games met us very courteously when we landed, read us the rules, and saw we were shown our lodgings and the athlete's mess. All the dressing-places and the baths were much finer than at home; marble everywhere, and every water-spout made of wrought bronze. The place was full already of competitors who had arrived before us. When I got out on the practice-track, I found youths from every city in the Aegean, and as far as Ephesos.

The practice itself was quite properly conducted. But I did not care for the way that all kinds of idlers were allowed to crowd in: hucksters selling luck-charms and unguents, touts from the brothels, and gamblers who laid their odds on us as noisily as if we had been horses. It was hard to keep one's mind on what one was about; but when I was used to it all, and had time to study the form of the other youths, I did not think there were more than two or three from whom I had much to fear. One of these was a Spartan, called Eumastas, to whom I spoke out of curiosity; I had never conversed with one, unless it is conversation to shout the paean at one another. His behaviour on the track was excellent, but his manners were rather uncouth; having never been outside Lakonia before even for war, he felt unsure of himself in this large concourse, and thought to cover it by standing on his dignity. I fancy he envied me my battle-scars; for he showed me the stripes on his back, where he had been flogged before Artemis Orthia, according to their custom. He had been the victor, he told me, in the contest, having held out the longest; the runner-up, he said, had died. I was at a loss for a proper reply, but congratulated him. There seemed no harm in him, beyond some dullness of wit.

I liked much less a youth from Corinth, one Tisander. His chances were a good deal fancied, by himself even more than the rest; and finding a newcomer talked of as a threat to him, he showed his pique with an openness as laughable as unseemly. I made a sprint or two, and left him to his conjectures.

Lysis, when we met, told me the crowds had been worse in the palaestra than at the stadium; for the Corinthians are devoted to wrestling and the pankration. I did not ask after his rivals' form; for naturally no pankratiast practises the all-in-fight just before the Games, for fear of getting an injury. He was rather quiet; but before I could ask him why, it was put out of my mind by the din about us. We had intended to walk over the Isthmus to Corinth. It seemed, however, that not only Corinth had come to us, but most of Hellas and all of Ionia. The throngs at the Panathenaia were nothing to this. Every shop-keeper in Corinth had set up a stall here; there were whole streets of them, selling not only oil-flasks and ribbons and strigils, and such things as you find at any Games, but all the costly luxuries of the City: bronze images and mirrors, helmets studded with silver and gold, silks you could see through, jewels and toys. The rich hetairas in clouds of perfume were walking with their slaves, pricing others' merchandise and showing their own. Mountebanks were swallowing swords and serpents, tossing torches in the air, or leaping into circles of knives; dancers and mimes and musicians were quarrelling for pitches. I thought I should never be tired of walking up and down; every moment there was something new. We visited the temple, in whose porch a crowd of sophists was debating, and saw, within, the great gold and ivory Poseidon, who almost touched the roof. Then we walked back through the shops again. My eye began to be caught by things: a silver-mounted sword, a gold necklace which seemed made for my mother, and a beautiful painted wine-cup with the exploits of Theseus, which was just the kind of keepsake I had always wished to offer Lysis. I found I was thinking for the first time about the hundred drachmas the City gives to an Isthmian victor, and of what they would buy.

Next morning I went seriously to work; for we were within three days of the Games. In any strange gymnasium one will drift into someone's company more than the rest, scraping each other's backs or sluicing each other in the wash-room, and this happened with me and Eumastas; from curiosity at first, and from our both disliking Tisander; and thereafter I can't tell why. I had never known anyone so dour, nor he, it was plain, anyone so talkative; yet when I got tired of talking for two, in his curt way he would contrive to start me off again. Once when we were resting he asked me if all Athenians had smooth legs like mine; he thought it was natural, and I had to explain to him the uses of a barber. He was a lank youth, with the leather look all Spartans have from rough living, and a shock head; he was just starting to grow his hair long, at the age when we cut it off. I even made one attempt to tell him about Sokrates; but he said anyone would soon be run out of Sparta who taught the boys to answer back.

I feared Eumastas as my greatest rival in staying-power; Tisander in a sprint; and Nikomedes of Kos because he was variable, the kind who may take sudden fire during the race. My mind was running on all this towards the end of the second morning, when the flute-player came in to time the jumping. As I was waiting in line to take my turn, I saw a man beckoning me from the side. One might have taken him for an ill-bred suitor; but, knowing those, I saw that this was some other thing. So I went over, and asked him what he wanted.

He said he was a trainer, and was studying the Athenian methods, having been out of the way of it because of the war; and he asked me a few questions. I thought them not much to the purpose, and soon began doubting that he was what he claimed. When he asked me what I thought of my own chances, I put him down as a common gamester, and answering with some trite proverb would have gone away. But he detained me, and began running on about young Tisander, his birth and wealth, and his family's devotion to him, till I made sure I was listening to some besotted lover. Suddenly he dropped his voice, and fixed his eyes on mine. 'The lad's father told me, only today, that it would be worth five hundred drachmas to him to watch his son win.'

It may be that we are born remembering evil, as well as good; or I don't know how I understood him so quickly. I had been practising the long jump with the hand-weights, and had them still in my hands. I felt my right begin to come up of itself, and saw the man flinch backward. Yet even in his fright there was some calculation. It came to my mind that if I struck him down, I should be taken up for brawling in the sacred precinct, and could not run. I said, 'You ditch-born son of a slave and a whore, tell your master to meet me after the truce. I will show him then what is the price of an Athenian.'

He was a man nearly as old as my father would have been; yet he took this from me, with a silly smile. 'Don't be a foolish boy. Nikomedes has agreed, and Eumastas: but if you won't come in, then the deal is off; you may be beaten by any of them, without being an obol to the good. I shall be in this same place at noon. Think it over.'

I threw at him a filthy phrase that boys were using just then, and left him. The flute was still piping away. You must have seen in battle a hurt man get up, not yet feeling it and thinking he can go on; so I went straight back into the line and took my turn, and was surprised when I made the worst leap ever seen, I should think, upon that ground. Once was enough of that, and I withdrew. I could see neither what to do, nor indeed, the use of doing anything. All the world I knew seemed to give, like rotten fruit, under my hand.

In the line of jumpers I could pick out the tall back of Eumastas, by the pink shiny scars on his brown skin. If anyone had told me I considered him a friend, I should have stared and laughed; yet now a bitter sickness filled me. I remembered what one always hears of the Spartans, that never being allowed to see money at home, when they meet it they are sooner corrupted than anyone. You may well ask why I should be tender for the honour of someone who next year might be killing me, or burning my farm. Yet I thought, 'I will go to him, and tell him of this. Then, if he has agreed to take the bribe, he will merely deny it. But if he has been offered it and refused, he will agree to come with me and report it to the Council of the Games. Thus I shall be sure of him; and Tisander will be whipped, and scratched from the race. But wait. In a place where men buy their rivals out, slander may be commoner still, being much cheaper. If we report and are disbelieved, the dirt will stick to us forever. And if Eumastas with this in mind refuses to go with me, I have no witness; nor shall I ever know whether he was bribed or not. No; let me run a good race, and keep my own hands clean; what is it to me how clean the others are?'

With this I felt quieter, and firmer in mind; till it seemed that the voice of the Corinthian whispered in my ear, 'Clever lad! You guessed I lied to you when I said the others would call off their deal if you refused. I told you that lest you should grasp the chance of an easy win. Well, you were too quick for me, Eumastas is bribed, and Nikomedes; now you have only Tisander to beat. Go in, and get your crown.'

I walked away from the gymnasium, not regarding where I went. It seemed there was no way I could turn with perfect honour, and that I should never be clean again. In my trouble, my feet had carried me of themselves to the gate of the men's palaestra. I thought, 'He will know what I should do,' and already my heart was lighter; till it paused, and said to me, 'Is that what you call friendship, Alexias? The Games are almost on us; for a man fighting the pankration, his own troubles are enough.'

He came out rather before the usual time. I did not ask how it had gone with him that day, in case he should return my question. He was quiet, which I was glad of, having little to say myself; but after we had walked a short way, he said, 'It's fine and clear, and the wind is cool. Shall we climb the mountain?'

I was rather surprised; for it was unlike him, having fixed a time for anything to change it at a whim. I was afraid he had noticed my low spirits; but indeed I was glad of this diversion. The noonday heat was over, and the tower-wreathed head of Acrocorinth looked golden against the tender sky of spring. As we climbed, the other hills grew tall around us, Corinth shone below, and the blue sea spread wide. When we were just below the walls, I said that perhaps the Corinthians would bar us from their citadel, being their enemies but for the sacred truce. But the man in the gatehouse spoke civilly, chatted about the Games and let us in.

There is still a good way to climb on Acrocorinth after you have passed the walls. Being so high, the place is not thronged like our own High City; it was quiet, so that one could hear the bees in the asphodel, the little clappers of the mountain goats, and a shepherd piping. Beyond the walls were great spaces of blue air;

for the citadel stands on high cliffs, like a roof on the columns of a temple.

The sacred way wound up between shrines, and holy springs. There was one sanctuary built of grey stone, which we entered. After the bright sunlight it seemed very dark; in the midst, where the god should stand, was a curtain of purple. A priest in a dark-red robe came out and said, 'Strangers, come no nearer. This is the temple of Necessity and Force; and the image of this god is not to be looked upon.' I would have gone at once, for the place disquieted me; but Lysis paused and said, 'Is it permitted to make an offering?' The priest answered, 'No. This god accepts only the appointed sacrifice.' Lysis said, 'Be it so, then,' and to me, 'Let us go.' After this he was silent so long that I asked if anything troubled him. He smiled, and shook his head, and pointed forward; for now we had reached the crown of Acrocorinth, and stepping on small heath and mountain flowers, saw before us the shrine.

The image of Aphrodite there is armed with shield and spear; yet I never knew a place so full of peace. The temple is delicate and small, with a terrace from which the slopes fall gently; the walls and towers seem far below; the mountains round about hang like veils of grey and purple, and the two seas stretch away, all silken in the light. I thought of the day when Lysis and I had heard Sokrates and gone up to the High City; it seemed that the memory had been already here awaiting us, as if the place were a dwelling of such things.

After a while Lysis pointed downward and said, 'Look how small it is.' I looked, and saw the precinct of the Games, the temple, and the fair-booths round it, smaller than children's toys of painted clay. My soul felt light and free, and washed from the taint of the morning. Lysis laid his hand on my shoulder; it seemed to me that doubt or trouble could never assail us again. We stood looking down; I traced the long wall of the Isthmus, cutting the south of Hellas from the north. Lysis drew in his breath; I think then he would have spoken; but something had caught my eye; and I called out, 'Lysis, look there! There are ships moving on the land!'

I pointed. There was a track drawn across the Isthmus, as thin to our eyes as the scratch of a child's stick. Along it the ships were creeping, with movement scarcely to be seen. Around each prow was a swarm as fine as dust, of seamen and hauliers dragging on the ropes, or going before with rollers. We counted four on the shipway, and eight in the Gulf of Corinth, waiting their turn. They were moving from the western to the eastern sea.

I turned to Lysis. He looked as he did before a battle, and did not see me. I caught at his arm, asking what it was. He said, 'I have heard of the shipway; that is nothing. But the ships are too many.' On this I understood. 'You mean they're Spartan ships, slipping through to the Aegean behind our backs?' – 'Revolt in the Islands somewhere, and the Spartans supporting it. I thought Alkibiades had been quiet too long.'

'We must go down,' I said, 'and tell the delegates.' The snake which had slept all winter was putting forth its head. Yet this seemed small, compared with the grief I felt that we must go down from the mountain. I said to Lysis, 'We will come here again together, after the Games.' He did not answer, but pointed eastward. The light came slanting from the west, and was very clear. I said, 'I can see even as far as Salamis; there is the ridge of her hills, with the dip in the middle.' – 'Yes,' he said. 'Can you see beyond?' I narrowed my eyes. Beyond the dip something shone like a chip of crystal in the sun. 'It is the High City, Lysis. It is the Temple of the Maiden.' He nodded, but did not speak, only stood looking, like a man sealing what he sees upon his mind.

It was dark when we got down into Isthmia, but we went straight to the harbour and hailed the *Paralos*. Most of the crew were enjoying themselves in Corinth; but Agios the pilot was there, a stocky man, red-faced and white-haired, who offered us wine beneath the cresset burning on the poop. When he had heard, he whistled between his teeth. 'So,' he said, 'that's what is coming into Kenchreai.' He told us that he and his mate, walking by the shore, had seen the harbour there filling with ships; but before they could get near, some guards had turned them away. 'Spartan guards,' he said, 'I've not seen the Corinthians taking trouble to keep this quiet.' – 'No,' said Lysis, 'or why are we Athenians here at all? It's their right to ask us and ours to come, both cities founded the

Games together; yet it's a strange time to offer us the sacred truce, with this work on hand.'

Agios said, 'They've always been our rivals in trade; to see us poor would suit them well; but never tell me they'd welcome a Spartan Hellas. Pretty toys; pleasure; luxury; it's more than their life, it's their living. It may well be that they're trimming now, with things as they are. I'll see the men go about Corinth with their ears open. One thing at a time; you lads should be going to bed, with the Games so soon.'

On the way back we met Autolykos, taking his training-walk after supper. He hailed Lysis, asking what he had been doing to miss it. 'I'm turning in,' Lysis said, 'we climbed Acrocorinth this afternoon.' Autolykos raised his brows at us; he looked quite shocked, but he only bade us goodnight and walked on.

Next morning I woke a little stiff from the climb; so I spent an hour with the masseur, and after that only the exercises to music, to loosen up and keep fresh for tomorrow; for the foot-race opens the Games. I was civil to Eumastas when we met. Once I caught him looking at me; but if I had grown more taciturn, it was not for a Spartan to notice it.

Besides all this, the Cretan athletes had arrived, the last of everyone, having been held up by a storm. Considering their fame as runners, I had more than Eumastas to think about. Sure enough, warming-up on the track I found a lithe swarthy youth who, I could tell at a glance, might well be the master of us all. The news flew through the Stadium that he had run at Olympia, and had come in second. Though anxious on my own account, I could not keep from laughing when I thought, 'Tisander won't sleep tonight.'

I woke to the sound that is like no other, the noise of the Stadium when the benches and the slopes are filling. People must have started arriving long before the first light. Already you could pick out the 'Houp!' of the jugglers and acrobats, the hawkers crying ribbons and cakes and myrtle, the call of the water-sellers, bookmakers giving the odds, the sudden shouts of people squabbling for a place; and through it all the buzz of talk, like bees in an old temple. It is the sound that tightens one's belly, and makes one shiver behind the neck.

I got up, and ran to the water-conduit outside. Someone overtook me; it was Eumastas; he picked up the pitcher and sluiced me down. He always threw the water hard in one great drench, trying to make one gasp. I rinsed him in turn, and watched it trickle down his scars. Suddenly I felt compelled, and said, 'I'm running to win, Eumastas.' He stared and said in his abrupt way, 'How not?' His face never showed surprise, nor anything he felt. I did not know if he spoke in innocence, or discretion, or deceit. Not from that day have I ever known.

At the march-in, the Athenians were cheered as much as the Spartans. The people were there to enjoy themselves, and forget the war. I sat with Lysis, watching the boys' races. The Athenians did quite well, but did not win anything. There was a break; the tumblers and flute-players came out; then suddenly all round the Stadium the ephebes were getting up. Lysis laid his hand on my knee and smiled. I made a little sign which was a secret between us, and got up with the rest. Next moment, as it seemed, I was standing beside the Cretan youth, feeling with my toes the grooves of the starting-stone, and hearing the umpire call for the second time, 'Runners! Feet to the lines!'

It was one of those fresh spring days that make one feel at first one could run forever, and tempt beginners to crowd on pace as they never would at a summer Games. I let these people pass me; but when Eumastas went ahead it was another thing. It was hard to look at his striped back and not spurt after it. 'Know yourself, Alexias,' I thought, 'and look to what you know.' Tisander too was using discretion. We were almost neck and neck.

After those of no account, the first runner to fail was Nikodemes. I had seen yesterday that he had lost his hopes beforehand to the Cretan. For him that was reason enough.

Tisander, gaining a little, moved sideways. I thought he was going across to foul me; it would have disqualified him, and I need have watched my thoughts no longer. But he changed his mind. Then there was a diversion, when some nobody put on a sprint and got in front. All this time I had known that Cretan was just behind me, because I never saw him when I turned the post. Now, smoothly as a wolf, he shot forward, and straight on into the lead. It was halfway up in the sixth lap. 'Alexias,' I thought, 'it is time to run.'

After that I thought with my breath and my legs. At the starting-turn I passed Eumastas. I was sure he would challenge my lead; but no, he was finished. He had gone ahead too soon, like the green boys. That left Tisander and the Cretan. At the start I had seen that Tisander was wearing a horse's tooth round his neck as a charm, and had despised him for it; but as a runner he was not at all to be despised. He knew himself, and would not be flurried. Before us was the Cretan, running smoothly, well in hand. We turned into the last lap. People who had been quiet before began to shout, and those who had been shouting to roar. Suddenly over it all I heard Lysis yell, 'Come on, Alexias!' It was the voice he used in battle, for the paean; it carried like a trumpet-call. Just as if something were lifting me, I felt my spirit overflow and fill my flesh. Soon after the turning-post I left Tisander behind me; and the Cretan I overtook halfway down. I glanced at his face; he looked surprised. We ran level for a while; but little by little he fell back out of my sight.

The crowd had pressed right up to the finishing-post, and I ran into the midst of it. It parted for me at first, then closed round. My head was ringing, and the noise made it spin; a great spear seemed to transfix my breast, so that I clutched at it with both my hands. While myrtle-sprays fell on my shoulders and struck me in the face, I fought for my next breath against the thrust of the spear. Then there was an arm stretched out to make space for me, and shelter me from the press. I leaned back against Lysis' shoulder, and the weight of the spear grew less. In a little while I could distinguish the people about me and even speak to them. To Lysis I had not spoken, nor he to me. I turned round for him to tie the ribbons on, and we looked at each other. His white mantle, which he had put on clean that morning for the sacrifice to Poseidon, was smothered all over the front with oil and dust. He looked so filthy that I laughed; but he said softly in my ear that he would put it away and keep it as it was. I thought, 'I could die now, for surely the gods can have no greater joy for me'; and then I said in my heart, 'Olympia next.'

When the Athenian delegates had congratulated me, Lysis took me away to get clean and to rest before watching the stade-race. He got me some cooled wine and water, and some honey-cakes, knowing I was always mad for sweet things after a race; and we lay down under a pine-tree just above the Stadium. One or two friends came up with ribbons they had bought for me, and tied them on, and stayed to chat. Somebody said, 'Young Tisander was lucky at the end, to get the second place.' – 'Tisander?' I said. 'He came in third; the Cretan was second.' Lysis said laughing, 'Well, no one sees less of a race than the winner.' The other man said, 'You took the heart out of the Cretan when you passed him; there was no fight left in him after that.' – 'I thought he was better-winded than Tisander,' I said. 'Careful,' said Lysis, taking hold of the wine-jar; 'you nearly spilt it; your hand's not steady yet.'

I bent and scooped a little pit in the pine-needles, to hold the jar. The ribbons they had tied round my head fell about my face, but I did not push them aside. I remembered seeing the Cretan sprint ahead, and thinking, 'There goes victory, the real victory of the gods.' He had looked so proud on the practice-track, as sure of himself as a man could be; and he had come so late. Yet after all, he had been at Isthmia overnight. I recalled the surprise in his face when I drew level. I had supposed he was astonished to find anyone there his match.

I find in the archives that the men's long-race was won by someone from Rhodes, and the stade by a Theban. All I remember of these events is that I shouted loudly; I would not have it said that I cared for no victory but my own.

Next day were the boxing and hurling events; then came the day of the wrestling. The weather held bright and clear. Quite early the Athenians had a victory; for young Plato won the contest for boys. He fought some very good scientific bouts, using his head as well as his broad shoulders, and was well cheered. Lysis praised him highly. I could see how this pleased the boy; when his eyes lit up under their heavy brows, he had even a kind of beauty. Before he went, he wished Lysis luck in his own event. 'Lysis,' I said after, 'how well do you and this Aristokles know each other? You smiled so seriously into each other's eyes, that I'm still wondering whether to be jealous.' – 'Don't be a fool,' he said laughing. 'You know that's always his way; what about yourself?' Yet I had really felt, for a moment, that they were sharing some thought unknown to me.

In the Frontier Guard the boys had a phrase, 'As cool as Lysis.' He played up to his legend, as any good officer will. He could deceive even me; but not every time. I always knew he was on edge when he was very still. The herald called the pankratiasts; he made our sign to me; I watched him out of sight into the dressing-room, and waited till the heats were drawn. He was in the third bout, matched against Autolykos. 'If he wins that,' I thought, 'then nothing can keep the crown from him.' I jumped up from my seat, for I had made my plan; and I ran up the sacred steps to the great temple. There I took from my bosom a gift I had bought for the god at one of the shops outside. It was a little horse made of fine bronze, with mane and tail silvered, and a bridle of gold. I bought incense, and went up to the altar. Always I am awed in the presence of Poseidon, so old a god, who holds the earthquake and the sea-storm in his hand. But horses are dear to him, and this was the best one I could find. I gave it to the priest for him, and saw it offered, and made my prayer.

Although they hold the contests just before the temple, when I got back to my place the first bout was over, and the athletes had gone in. The crowd seemed excited by the fight, and I was sorry to have missed it, in case Lysis should meet the winner later on. The second bout, however, was not very remarkable; a Mantinean won it, a lumbering fellow, who got a body-hold that Lysis would never have given him time for. Then the herald called, 'Autolykos son of Lykon; Lysis son of Demokrates; both of Athens.'

It was Autolykos after all who held my eye. 'What has become of his beauty?' I thought. When he was dressed one looked at his pleasant face, and did not see how much his body had coarsened. No sculptor would have looked at him for a model now. The crowd cheered them in; one could tell, as one commonly can, that they were cheering Autolykos for what they had heard of him, and Lysis for what they saw. He stood like a bronze of Polykleitos; you could not fault him anywhere; whereas Autolykos looked burly, like a village strong-man who lifts a bull-calf for a bet. But I was not fool enough to underrate him. He was still very fast for all his bulk, and knew every trick in the game. While they were exchanging the standing buffets, I could see the weight his had behind them; and I prayed that when they went down Lysis would fall on top.

Yet for all my fears, within the time it takes to run five stades I was cheering myself hoarse with joy. I fought my way through the crowd and ran to Lysis. He was not very much the worse for the bout. He had got a thick ear, and some bruises, and he was rubbing his left wrist where Autolykos had got a grip and nearly broken it, trying to twist him round for a flying mare. But on the whole he was in very good shape. I walked in with him and went to see Autolykos, whom Lysis had had to help to his feet after the decision. He had torn one of the big muscles in his back, and it was that which had finished him. He was in a good deal of pain, and it was years since he had yielded the crown to anyone; but he took Lysis' hand and congratulated him on a good win, like the gentleman he always was. 'I deserve this,' he said, 'for listening to too much advice in training. You had more sense, Lysis. Bring in the parsley and good luck to you.'

I had lost my place; but Plato made room for me by heaving everyone sideways. He was the strongest boy at his age that I remember. During the other heats I saw no one who seemed to me the match of Autolykos. Then it was time for the semi-finals. There were eight contestants, so no one had drawn a bye. The herald called out, 'Lysis son of Demokrates, of Athens. Sostratos son of Eupolos, of Argos.' The name was unknown to me. I guessed this must be the winner of the first bout, which I had missed while in the temple. Then they came out, and I saw the man.

At first I could not trust my eyes; the more because I recognised him. Two or three times, indeed, I had seen this monstrous creature, going about the fair. I had not doubted he was some travelling mountebank, whose act consisted of raising boulders or bending iron bars; so I had been struck by his air of absurd conceit. Once Lysis had been beside me, and I pointed out the man, laughing and saying, 'What a hideous fellow! What can he be, and who does he think he is?' Lysis had answered, 'He's no beauty, is he?' and spoken of something else. Now here he stood, a mountain of gross flesh, great muscles like twisted oakwood gnarling his body and arms; a neck like a bull's; his legs, though they were thick and knotty, seemed bowed by the weight of his ungainly trunk. Why do I go on describing a sight with which everyone has grown familiar? Today even at Olympia they appear without shame, and afterwards some sculptor has to turn out a portrait that people can see in the sacred Altis without disgust.

It must seem to you now that we were simple in those days. For at the sight of a man too heavy to leap or run, who would fall dead if he had to make a forced march in armour, and whom no horse could carry, we thought we were looking at someone worse than a slave, since he had chosen his own condition. We waited to see him run out of the company of free Hellenes, and cheered Lysis on to do it. He stood by this ugly hulk like the image of victory: hero against monster, Theseus with the Beast.

Then the fight began; the voices altered; and I woke from my dream.

I had not seen Sostratos' first bout; but the crowd had, and got used sooner than I did to seeing Lysis duck away from a buffet. No one booed him, and one or two people cheered him. When he landed one himself they went wild. But you could see it was like punching a rock. The man's great arms were like flying boulders; one caught Lysis' cheek, only glancing, and at once the blood began to flow. And now, as if the news had been brought to me for the first time, I thought, 'This creature too is a pankratiast.'

Lysis was the first to close. He grabbed Sostratos' arm as it was striking, and the hand grew limp in his strong grip. I knew what came next; a quick twist and then the heave, a cross-buttock. I saw him begin it; and could tell the very moment when he knew he could not get this ton of flesh high enough for a throw. Then Sostratos reached for a neck-hold; if Lysis had not been as quick as a cat, he would never have got away. The crowd cheered him for escaping, as if he had scored. By now he had measured the enemy's speed, and he began to take those risks that the faster man can take with the slower; except that here the risks were doubled. He ran in head first, I heard the monster grunt; before he could seize Lysis' head he had slid free and got a body-hold. Then he hooked his leg behind Sostratos' knee, and they went over together. The thud was like a block of stone falling.

The crowd cheered. But I saw that as they fell Sostratos had rolled over on Lysis' arm. He lay like a man trapped by a landslide. Sostratos was starting to come over on him; but Lysis got a knee up in time. He was still pinned by the arm. I got to my feet and shouted for him. I tried to make it carry, though I don't suppose he could hear me above the noise. He thrust his flat hand into Sostratos' great pig-face and pushed the head back and got his arm free. It was scraped and bloody, but he could still use it. He twisted round like a flash; they struggled together on the ground, hitting and grappling. Always it was Lysis who had the speed. But speed in the pankration is only a man's defence. It is strength that wins.

Someone was punching me on the knee. I found it was Eumastas the Spartan, attracting my notice. He never wasted words. When I glanced round he said, 'Is the man your lover?' – 'Which one?' I asked; I had no time for him just then. He said, 'The man.' I nodded, without turning again. I could feel him watching me; waiting to approve of me, if I could see Lysis mauled with a wooden face. I could have killed him where he sat.

Just then Lysis came uppermost for a moment. His hair was matted with dusty blood; blood covered his face like a mask, and streaked his body. He rose, then seemed to fall backward, and the crowd groaned. But as Sostratos rushed upon him, he threw up his foot and swung the man right over so that he crashed to the earth instead. The noise was so great I could hardly hear myself cheer. But there was something new in it. I had not noticed it at first, but it was growing. In those days, the pankration was a contest for fighting men. I suppose there had always been a few slave-minded ones who had got another sort of pleasure from it; but they had known enough to keep it to themselves. Now, like ghosts who get strength from drinking blood, they came out into the light and one heard their voice.

As Sostratos went over him, Lysis had gripped his ankle and held on. He was twisting the foot, trying to make Sostratos give in. Sostratos managed at last to kick him off with the other foot, and I saw the great mass coming down on him again. But Lysis slipped from under, grabbing an arm as he went; next moment he was on Sostratos' back, legs locked round his middle, and as fine a strangle-hold on his neck as I ever saw. Sostratos' free arm was all he had to hold up on; Lysis had pinned the other. All around people were on their feet; young Plato, whose very existence I had forgotten, was digging his fingers into my arm. The fight looked as good as won.

Then I saw Sostratos begin to rise. With the weight of a strong man on his back, and half-throttled, still the huge creature heaved up on his knees. I heard the blood-bay from the faces I had not seen. 'Let go, Lysis!' I shouted. 'Let go!' But I suppose his strength was nearly done, and he knew it was now or never. He set his teeth and squeezed his arm round Sostratos' bull-throat. And Sostratos upreared backward and fell on him like a tree. There was a great silence; then the blood-voices cheered.

All I could see of Lysis at first was his arm and hand. It lay, palm up, in the dust; then I saw it feel for a purchase. Sostratos turned over. I saw for the first time in his wide face his little eyes; not the eyes of a boar in rage, but cold, like a usurer's. Lysis began to struggle up on his arm. I waited to see him lift his hand to the umpire. It may be he was too angry to give in; but I think he was only too dazed to know where he was. At all events, Sostratos hurled him back on the ground so that you could hear the blow of his head meeting it. Even after that I thought I saw him move; but the umpire brought down his forked rod, and stopped the fight.

I jumped to my feet. Plato was holding me by the arm, saying something: I shook the boy off and climbed through the crowd, while people I had trodden on shouted and cursed me. I ran to the dressing-room, and got there while they were still carrying him in. They took him through to a little room at the back, where there was a pallet on the floor, and a water-tap shaped like a lion's mouth, running into a basin. Outside, the next bout had begun. I could hear the cheering.

The man in charge said to me, 'Are you a friend of his?' – 'Yes,' I said. 'Is he dead?' I could not see life or breath in him. 'No; he is stunned, and I daresay some of his ribs are broken. But he may die. Is his father here?' – 'We're Athenians,' I said. 'Are you a doctor?

Tell me what to do.' – 'Nothing,' said the man, 'but keep him quiet if he wakes with his wits astray. Give him water if he asks for it, but no wine.' Then he looked up from Lysis and seemed to see me for the first time, and said, 'He fought a fine pankration, but I wonder what made him enter at his weight.' He went then to watch the fight outside, and we were left alone.

He was breathing, but very slowly, and so lightly that I could hardly hear. One side of his face was bruised all over; his nose had been bleeding and his scalp was cut; his forehead was split over the eyebrow; I could see he would never lose the scar. I drew down the old blanket they had thrown over him; his body was so battered and grimed that I could not tell what might be broken. I took a towel that was hanging on the wall, and washed from him the black blood, the oil and dust, as far as I could reach; I was afraid to turn him over. I talked to him, and called his name aloud; but he did not stir. Then I saw I ought not to have washed him; for the water was cold from the spring, and the place was made of stone; his flesh under my hands grew as cold as marble, and his mouth looked blue. I thought he would die as I watched him. Someone else's clothes were lying in a corner; I heaped those on him, but he still felt cold, so I added my own, and came in beside him.

As I held him, trying to put some life in him, and cold myself with fear, I thought of the long patrols with the Guard, in the winter mountains, when even the wolves in their caves had been warm together, and he had lain alone. 'You gave me courage in battle,' I thought; 'when I was unhorsed, you saved me and took a wound. After so much toil, who would not have looked for honey from the rock? Yet you offered it to heaven; there was only blood for you, and the salt-tasting sea. What is justice, if the gods are not just? They have taken your crown away from you, and set it on a beast.'

His mouth felt cold to mine; he neither opened his eyes, nor spoke, nor moved. I said in my heart, 'Too late I am here within your cloak, I who never of my own will would have denied you anything. Time and death and change are unforgiving, and love lost in the time of youth never returns again.'

Someone was coming, so I got up. The light was darkened in

the doorway. I saw that what filled it was Sostratos. He said, 'How is he?' It was strange to hear human speech coming out of him, instead of a boar's grunt. I was glad to see Lysis' marks on him. 'He is alive,' I said. The man came near, stared, and went away. I lay down with Lysis again. Bitterness filled my heart. I remembered his statue at school, done before I knew him; and thought how from a boy he had run and jumped, thrown the disk and javelin, swum and wrestled, and ridden on manoeuvre; how I myself had toiled, swinging the pick and throwing the weight, to balance my shoulders with my legs; how young Plato had run in armour; how all of us had sacrificed in the gymnasium to Apollo, the lord of measure and harmony. This man had sold grace and swiftness, and the honour of a soldier in the field, not caring at all to be beautiful in the eyes of the gods, but only caring to be crowned. And yet to him the victory had been given.

The fight was over outside. The crowd was chattering, and someone was playing a double flute. Lysis moved, and groaned. He felt a little warmer. Presently he tried to sit up, and was sick. As I finished cleaning up, the doctor came in again. He pinched Lysis' arm and seeing him flinch a little said, 'Good. But keep him still, for men who have been stunned sometimes die if they exert themselves soon after.' When he had gone, Lysis started to toss about, and to talk nonsense. He thought he was on a battlefield with a spear in his side, and ordered me not to touch it, but to fetch Alexias, who would draw it out. I was at my wits' end, remembering the doctor's words. While I was trying to lay him down, Sostratos came in again, and asked how he was. I answered shortly, but thought a little better of the man for his concern.

Soon afterwards the shouting began again outside; the final was on. It seemed hardly to have begun before it was over. I thought Sostratos must have finished his antagonist with a buffet; what had really happened was that this man, having seen Lysis carried off, had gone down on the ground almost at once, and given the bout away. I heard the herald announce the victor. The cheers were rather half-hearted; there had been neither a good fight nor any blood, so no one was pleased.

The crowd dispersed; outside in the dressing-room people

chatted and laughed. Presently the man whose clothes I had put on Lysis came in to get them. It was getting cooler, but I dared not leave him to look for more, and hoped someone would come in. At last voices approached; Sostratos stood in the doorway, speaking to someone over his shoulder. The ribbons tied on him made him look like a bull going to sacrifice. As he paused, I heard the man who had been in for his clothes say, 'Come, be easy, Sostratos; I went in just now and heard him talking. He will do till after the Games, and it makes no difference then.' I had forgotten that, except in Sparta, to kill in the pankration disqualifies the victor.

I sat looking at Lysis; then I heard someone behind me. Sostratos had come in after all. He peered into Lysis' face, then asked me again how he was. I did not trust myself to answer. He began looking at me instead; suddenly he assumed fine manners, which sat on him like a violet-wreath upon a swine. 'Why so downcast, beautiful youth? Fortune rules the Games. Will you spend the time of your triumph moping here, like one in prison? Come away, and meet some of the other winners. It is time you and I knew each other better.'

There is a certain gesture of refusal which everyone knows, but no gentleman employs. I wished however to be explicit. 'You have got your crown,' I said to him. 'Go and play with that.'

As he was going, I heard Lysis say, 'Alexias.' He sounded angry with me. I don't know how much he had understood. I bent down and said, 'Here I am; what is it?' But the eyes grew dull again. He looked very weary. The cold of evening came on; but I was afraid that if I went for more clothes he would try to stand. It would soon be dark. Tears stirred in me like sickness; but I dared not weep, lest he should hear.

By now the dressing-room outside had emptied; a footstep sounded loud in it. Young Plato came in quietly, and stood looking down. While we were watching the fight he had been wearing his ribbons; but they were gone now. I said, 'Can you find me a cloak, Plato? Lysis is cold.' – 'You look cold yourself' he said. After a short time he came back with two shepherds' blankets; I laid them over Lysis, and put my clothes on. Plato watched in silence; then he said, 'They have given the crown to Sostratos.' –

'Yes?' said I. 'And the war's over in Troy; what else is new?' – 'This is new to me. What does Sostratos think he has got? What good? What pleasure? What did he want?' – 'I don't know, Plato. You might as well ask why the gods allow it.' – 'The gods?' he said; raising his heavy brows and drawing them down again, just as he does today. 'What use would it be for the gods to do anything, if it's not enough that they are? Have you had any supper? I brought you something to eat.' I felt warmer for the food. When he had gone, I saw that both the blankets were new; I think he must have bought them himself in the market.

At nightfall, they carried Lysis to the precinct of Asklepios; next day he could speak sensibly and take food, though because of his broken ribs it hurt him to move. He did not talk much, and I let him rest. I wanted to stay with him, but he said I must watch the chariot-races; it seemed to fret him, so I went. They were held with great splendour, to the glory of horse-loving Poseidon, who had not been moved by my horse of bronze. I understood that this was the great day of the Games, which every Corinthian came to see, and that no one was thinking about the long-race or the pankration.

When I got back, Lysis seemed stronger. He said he was going to get up next day, to see me crowned. This was too much for me, and I told him the story of the long-race. He listened quietly, frowning a little, rather in thought than in anger or surprise. 'Don't brood on it,' he said. 'You ran a fine race; and very likely no one was bribed at all. Any fool could have picked you out as the fastest, and would have made sure of you before throwing money away on the others. I was watching the Cretan, and he looked spent to me.' – 'Perhaps. But now I shall never know it.' – 'Why think of it then? We must take the world as we find it, Alexias.' Then he said again, 'But you ran a fine race. You had them all in your hand.'

Next morning was the procession to the temple; and the winners were crowned before Poseidon. There was a great deal of music and ceremony, much more than at home. The priests of the precinct would not let Lysis get up. I went back to him afterwards, and he made me show him my crown. I had had enough of their parsley garnishing; but when I threw it in a corner he told me sharply not to play the fool, but to go out and celebrate in Corinth with the others.

It was evening. The sun was shining on the mountain with its wreath of walls. He must have known that if he waited till after the Games, he would never climb it. 'What should I do in Corinth?' I said. But he became impatient, and then angry, and said I should be talked of if I stayed away. Then I knew what troubled him, that they might say he had kept me back from the revels out of envy; so I said I would go.

There is a great deal of coloured marble in Corinth, and much bronze, some of it gilded; they burn perfume in the shop doorways; the tavern where we drank had a talking bird in a cage outside, that whistled and said 'Come in'. I was with the runners and the boxers; then some of the wrestlers arrived. I got drunk as quickly as I could; and for a little while Corinth looked quite gay to me. We walked through the streets singing, and bought garlands to wear; then we went into a bath-house, but it turned out to be a respectable one, and we were asked to leave. Someone had got pushed in the plunge-bath, and walked dripping water; one or two flute-girls, who had been picked up on the way, played us along. We came to a tall porch of slender columns, ornamented with doves and garlands; someone said, 'Here's where we're going, to the Girls of Aphrodite. Come on.' When I would not go in, he tried to drag me, and I struck him in the face. Then someone else, whom the wine had made genial, stopped the fight, and said we would all go to Kallisto's house instead. It had a fountain in the courtyard, of a girl holding her breast, which spouted water. Kallisto made us welcome, and a boy and girl acted the mime of Dionysos and Ariadne, while we drank more wine. A little later five or six of the wrestlers calling for music jumped up to dance the kordax, and started throwing off their clothes. They called me to join them, but I was past dancing even if I would. One of the girls lay down with me, and presently took me away. When I awoke she made a great tale of my performance, as they do with young men to make them pay well. I can't even recall whether I did anything or not.

Two days later we went back to Athens. Lysis could not sit a horse, his bones not having knit, and had to be carried to the ship on a litter. The passage was rough, and he was in pain all the way. Agios the pilot came to see ous, and said it was Chios the Spartan ships were making for; he had employed his time in Corinth better than I. So we made haste back, to bring this news to the City.

That is all I have to relate of the Isthmian festival, the first of the ninety-second Olympiad. Since Theseus founded the Games to honour his father Poseidon, they had been held every second year in the same place, before the same god; and if you ask me why this year's Games should have brought forth something different from those before them, I cannot tell.

18

The ships we had espied making for Chios were met, defeated and driven aground: but Alkibiades, with his friend Antiochus the pilot, took it just the same. Tales of his craft and courage came back to us every day. You could hear people saying in the Agora that we had thrown away more than we knew, when we exiled him, and that before he went to Sicily he had asked for a trial, like an innocent man. A rumour was current also that he had taken to the sea at the right time; for King Agis' hatred was glowing red-hot, and in Sparta Alkibiades never slept without a guard.

But one day when I called on Lysis at home, he said, 'Come in and see Father, Alexias, and talk to him for a while. Talk about horses, or anything but the war. Today's news has hit him worse than I can understand myself, bad as it is.'

I had been in the City, and had met the same thing in other old men. I went in to do my best. Demokrates received me kindly; but he looked five years older, and would talk of nothing but the news. 'I feel today,' he said, 'as if I had seen Perseus sell Andromeda to the dragon for a bag of silver. Sparta and the Medes! That I should live to see the blood of Leonidas treat with the Great King, and sign away Ionia to him for money! Is there no honour left under the sun?' – 'It's to pay their rowers, sir,' I said, as if I were called on to defend them. 'They are too few to row themselves, even if they could sink their pride to it; and they can't trust themselves to Helots.'

'When my father was a boy,' he said, 'his father took him to Thermopylae after the battle, to learn from the fallen how men should die. He often described it to me; the friends lying where the living had stood to defend the body of the slain, as they did in Homer's day; and those who had fought till their weapons broke in their hands, locked to the dead barbarians with teeth and nails. And now it has come to this. How quietly you young men take it.'

I felt for him; but just then I was more concerned for his son. Lysis' bones had mended well; except for the scar on his brow, the fight with Sostratos had left no mark on his body. But he had ceased to practise the pankration. For some time he kept this from me; he took enough exercise to keep in condition; but often he would tell me he was going to the palaestra, and I would find him in the colonnade, or sometimes I could not find him at all. When I saw how things were, I don't think it came as any great surprise to me. I remembered how, when Polymedes and the rest had taken me up, he had withdrawn; he could never stoop to base antagonists. He had said nothing to me, lest he should seem to slight my crown. He was as honourable as always, but less open than he had been. He would fall into silences; and when I asked him his thoughts, he would be short with me.

We were less hard-pressed in the Guard, the war being fought so much at sea. I found a freeman who would do something on the farm for a small wage and a share of the crop; we only put in quick-growing things.

One fine summer morning in the City, I had just put the last touches on our house, which I had been fresh-whitening. I had been doing it each daybreak till people were about; for though everyone knew nowadays that his neighbour was putting his hand to slaves' work, no one cared to have it noticed. Still, now it was done I was well pleased with it; so was my mother, especially with the courtyard, where I had painted the tops of the columns red and blue. I had had a bath, dressed my hair, and put a clean mantle on; I was carrying the walking-staff I used in the City, a good blackwood one that had been my father's. After the dirty work, I felt the pleasure of trimness, as I paused in the porch to take a last look at my handiwork. When I turned my face to the street, I saw a stranger approaching the house.

He was a raw-boned old man, who had been tall when he was straight; he walked halting, and leaning on a stick cut from the thicket, one of his feet being hurt and wrapped in a dirty rag. His white hair was ragged, as if he had trimmed it himself with a knife, and he wore a short tunic of some drab stuff, such as poor workmen wear, or slaves. He was dirty enough for either of these, yet bore himself like neither. He was looking at our house, making straight for it; and seeing this, I felt the sinking of some unknown fear; he seemed to me like the messenger of bad news. I stepped forward from the porch, waiting for him to speak; but when he saw me, he only stared. His drawn and bony face with its month-old stubble was weathered nearly black; his eyes, being grey, showed in it piercingly. I had been about to hail him, and ask him whom he was looking for. At first I did not know what it was that kept me from asking. I only knew I must not ask.

His eyes moved past me to dwell on the courtyard. Then he looked again at me. I felt before his silent expectation a creeping in my flesh. He said, 'Alexias.' Then my feet carried me down into the street; and my voice said, 'Father.'

I don't know how long we stood there; I daresay not many moments. I said, 'Come in, sir,' scarcely knowing what I did; then collecting myself a little praised the gods for his preservation. On the threshold he stumbled with his lame foot; I reached out to help him, but he righted himself quickly.

He stood in the courtyard, looking about him. I remembered Lysikles, and it seemed strange to me now that I should have taken his word without any doubts, seeing how broken the man had been and how his tale had wandered. What had put me in mind of him was the sight of my father's hand, callused and knotted, with dirt sealed into the cracks and scars. My mind was at a stop. I groped for words to say to him. I have felt this painful dumbness in war, at the sight of a brave enemy flung down before me in the dust; but in youth one does not recognise such thoughts, nor indeed ought one to understand them. I made again, in different words, the speech about the gods I had made before. I said we had despaired of this happiness. Then, beginning to come to myself, I said, 'I will go before you, sir, and tell Mother.'

'I will tell her myself,' he said, and limped towards the door. He moved quite fast. In the doorway he turned and looked at me again. 'I did not think you would grow so tall.' I made him some answer.

I had grown a good deal; but it was the bowing of his back that had brought us eye to eye.

I reached the doorway behind him, and then paused. My heart was pounding, my knees felt like water and my bowels were loosened within me. I heard him go into the women's rooms, but I could not hear anyone speak. I went away; at last, after what I thought must be a proper time, I went through to the living-room. My father was sitting in the master's chair, with his foot in a bowl of water whose steam smelled of herbs and of a putrid wound. Before him knelt my mother, with a cloth in her hands, cleaning the place. She was weeping; the tears were running down, her hands not being free to dry them. It came into my mind for the first time that I ought to have embraced him.

The walking-stick was still in my hand. I remembered the corner where I had found it first and put it back there.

Drawing near them, I asked him how he had come. He said from Italy, in a Phoenician ship. His foot was puffed up to twice its size, and green matter came from it. When my mother asked if the shipmaster had trusted him for the fare, he said, 'They were short of a rower.'

'Alexias,' said my mother, 'see if your father's bath is ready, and that Sostias has not forgotten anything.' I was going, when I heard a sound come near, and the breath stopped in my throat; it was I who had forgotten something.

The child Charis came in, singing and chattering. She was holding a painted clay doll I had brought her from Corinth, which she was talking to; so she had come into the middle of the room before she looked up. Then she must have noticed the smell, for she stared with round eyes, like a bird. I thought, 'Now he sees how pretty she is, surely he will take pleasure in what he has made.' He leaned forward in his chair; my mother said, 'Here is our little Charis, who has heard so many tales of you.' My father drew down his brows; but he did not seem very angry or surprised, and my breath came easier. He held out his hand and said, 'Come here, Charis.' The child stood still; so I came forward, to lead her up to him. But as soon as I tried to move her, her face grew red, and her mouth turned downward; she hid herself in the skirt of my mantle, wailing with fright. When I tried to carry her to him, she clung to my neck and screamed. I dared not look at him. Then I heard my mother say the child was timid, and cried at any strange face; the first lie I had ever heard her tell.

I took my sister away, and went to look at the bathroom. Poor old Sostias, in his confusion, had made a bad job there; I found razors and comb and pumice, and carried in the clean towels and mantle my mother had laid out. She said, 'I will come with you, Myron; Sostias is too clumsy for today'; but he said he would manage for himself. I had seen already that his head was lousy. He went off, using the stick I had laid by. As my mother cleared away the cloths and bowl, she talked quickly to me of how sick he was and what he should eat, and which doctor to get for his foot. I thought of the miseries he had endured, and it seemed to me that my heart must be made of stone, that I had not wept for him as she had done. I said, 'At least he will let me trim his hair and beard for him. He won't want a barber to see them as they are.'

When I entered he looked ready to order me out again; but after all he thanked me, and told me to close-crop his head, for nothing else would get it clean. Taking the razor I went behind him; then I saw his back. Eumastas the Spartan would have been humbled before it, and owned himself a beginner. I don't know what they had used on him; it must have had lead or iron tied into it. The scars went right round his sides.

At this sight, I felt all the anger that a son ought. 'Father, if you know the name of the man who did this, tell me. One day I might meet him.' — 'No,' he said, 'I don't know his name.' I worked on him in silence. Presently he told me that he had been taken out of the quarries by a Syracusan overseer, to sell for himself. He had changed masters several times; 'But that,' he said, 'can wait.'

His head was so filthy and scabby that it made me feel sick; luckily I was out of his sight. When I had finished, I rubbed him down with some scented oil of my own. It was good stuff from Corinth, which Lysis had given me; I only used it for parties myself. He sniffed at it and said, 'What's this? I don't want to smell like a woman.' I apologised, and put it by. When he was dressed, and one no longer saw his hollow ribs and flanks, he looked nearly presentable, and not much above sixty.

My mother bound his foot with a dry bandage and set food before him. I could tell it was hard for him not to snatch at it like a wolf; but he soon had enough. He began to question me about the farm. I had pulled things together as well as one could expect to; but I found he knew little about the state of Attica; he seemed to suppose I could have given it all my time. I was going to explain that I had other duties; when, as if answering my thought, the blast of the trumpet swelled over the City. I sighed, and got to my feet. 'I'm sorry, sir; I had hoped they would leave me longer than this with you. It's some days now since we had a raid.'

I ran out shouting to Sostias to make my horse ready; then, coming back in my riding-kilt, reached down my armour from the wall. I could see him following me with his eyes, and hoped, after what he had said about the oil, that I now looked enough like a man to please him; but at the same time my mind was running on the raid, thinking of one way or another the Spartans might be coming, and where we could head them off. My mother, who was used to these alarms, had gone, without my asking her, to get my food ready. Now she came back and, seeing me fight with a twisted shoulder-buckle, went to help me. My father said, 'Where is Sostias? He ought to be here for that.' – 'In the stable, sir,' I said. 'We lost the groom.' It was too long a tale to begin on. Just then Sostias came to the door and said, 'Your horse is ready, Master.' I nodded and turned to take leave of my father. He said, 'How is Phoenix?'

Suddenly I remembered him, standing to arm himself on the spot where I stood now. It seemed like half a lifetime gone. 'Over-worked, sir, I'm afraid,' I said, 'but I've kept him for you as well as I could.' I should have liked to pause and think, and to say more; but the trumpet had blown, and the troop had never yet had to wait for me. I kissed my mother; then, seeing his eyes on me and glad this time not to have forgotten my duty, I embraced him before I left. He felt strange to the touch, bony and stiff. I don't think I had embraced him since my grandmother died, except on the dock when he went to Sicily.

We had a hard patrol, and were gone some days. It was scorching weather, the hills burned dry, flies round the camp and tormenting the horses. We saved a valley of two or three farms; but in the pursuit young Gorgion was killed. It was hard to see him, who had always been the joker of the troop, dying in pain, and in astonishment that here was something he could not laugh away. Lysis, whose lot it always was to bring such news to the dead youth's father, seemed more than commonly oppressed by it. We could not bring back the body, because of the heat, and had to burn it on the hillside. It was so hot that one could not see any flames, only rippling air, and the body smoking and crackling. As it burned, Lysis said to me, 'Had he a lover?' I said no, only a mistress, a little flute-girl. 'I'll take her some keepsake of his,' I said; 'I daresay she would like it.' – 'Why do that?' Lysis said. 'What they had, they had.'

When we got back, he came to pay his respects to my father, and they had some talk about the war. Presently my father said, 'And Alkibiades, I suppose, is still among the Spartans? Hard living must come easy to him by now.' – 'No longer, sir,' Lysis said. 'He sleeps on down; he's in Persia now.' We had had this news some months, but I had not mentioned it. My father said, staring, 'In Persia? How was he taken? What was he doing, to fall into the barbarians' hands?' – 'Why,' said Lysis smiling, 'he fell as a cat falls in the cream-bowl. Sparta got too hot for him; King Agis got out a warrant for his death. But they say Tissaphernes the satrap thinks the world of him, and that he makes the Persian princes look drab, like cocks beside a pheasant.' My father said, 'Is it so indeed?' and spoke of other things. That evening, as I passed the courtyard, he was there throwing some broken crocks into the well. Going there by chance soon after, I saw a small sherd lying beside the well-head. The painting looked so delicate that I picked it up; there was a running hare on it, and an outstretched hand. It was a piece from the bowl of Bacchios' wine-cup.

If I had guessed that things would not be easy now at home, I had tried not to think of it, shocked at the baseness of grudging anything to one who had suffered so much. But this could not be for long. The first trouble came from little Charis. If she had been only a year or two older, one could have reasoned with her. But she had been filled with stories of her father's fine looks and gallant deeds; I had often seen her point to some hero on vase or wall, or even to a god, and say 'Dada.' Now we offered her instead this ugly and stern old man; and I don't think her trust in people ever after was quite the same. I know that full fourteen years later, when I had arranged her betrothal to an excellent person, she listened unmoved to my accounts of him till she had seen him for herself; I was almost angry with her, till I remembered this time. My father, who seemed not to question that his letter had been lost, would I believe have acepted her with a good grace, if he had not been daily wounded by her aversion. This was bad enough; but worse was the way she had of running at these times to me. She could never be got to call him Dada: which was the more noticeable because she had called me Lala ever since learning to talk. I began at once to train her out of it, and heard my mother doing the same.

I knew myself happy, compared with her. You would have supposed that after so much want and toil, simple comforts would have been bliss to him; but he could not bear the least change from our former ways. She would explain the cause, and the reasons for the want of labour; he would assent, but still be unreconciled. She never complained to me, and only once touched on the matter at all. This was when she begged me not to say that while he was gone I had taught her to read. She had been a quick pupil; these lessons had been a happiness to me, and I think to her too. She could even read poetry now if it was easy, and I had begun teaching her to write. Now we could seldom talk together at all, for he hated to have her out of his sight, and would always call for her if she were gone for long.

I dwelt on it as little as I could; for it was pain to me, so that I was not always in command of my own thoughts. After a while I found I did not like to see her dress his foot, which she did last thing before they retired: I used to go out, and walk about the streets.

Even to Lysis I could not say much. It was not only that I felt how shabby my feelings would appear to him. There was another cause. Lately things had not been so happy with us as before. That he should have been out of spirits after the Games I could understand; but when I found him becoming jealous, I was bewildered. I was too young to have learned understanding of it; I only knew I had given him no reason even in my lightest thought. That he should suspect such baseness in me as to be changed by his reverse, injured me to the soul; yet to tax him with it seemed baser. In past times no one had been a better loser when outmatched by a better man; I could not see why it struck him so deeply to be beaten by a worse. I felt only my own wrongs; like a silly peasant who, when the roof is shaken from the temple, complains about his broken pot.

If I had brought this trouble to Sokrates, he would have helped not only me, but have been in the way to help Lysis too. But it was all entangled in my mind with things I could bring to no one.

It was while I was away on patrol that Strymon had first called upon my father. Since I was of age he had troubled us little, so that I had not kept him in mind. It was only by degrees that the mischief he was doing appeared. First my father brought out the rolls of the farm, and had nothing but fault to find with them. It was plain where he had got his misinformation, and I soon cleared it up; yet I still felt him resentful. Again I heard that Strymon had called while I was out in the City; and just afterwards my father charged me with keeping bad company. As soon as Phaedo's name came up, I knew whom to thank. 'Sir,' I said, 'Phaedo is a Melian. You know better than I what choice he had. His breeding is as good as ours, and he is living now as befits it. You surely won't judge a prisoner by the lot that falls to him in war?' This went too near the bone. He grew angry; and, naming Sokrates, used a phrase of him which out of respect to the dead I will not set down, even after these years.

A little while after, I found my mother crying at her loom. No one was there, and I begged her to tell me her trouble. She shook her head, and made no answer. I drew near to her, till our garments touched, and I felt against my face the outermost threads of her hair. I had meant to embrace her, but confusion fell on me; I held my breath hard, and was still. She kept her head turned away, trying to hide her tears. At last I said, 'Mother, what shall we do?'

She shook her head again, and turning to me a little, laid her hand on my breast. When I covered it with both of mine, I could feel through it the beating of my heart. She began to draw her hand gently away from me; suddenly, with a swift and violent force, she thrust me off. Then I too heard the sound of my father's stick outside. I stood as one dazed; I could neither bear to stay nor fly; till I heard her voice, sending me on some errand about the house. As I went, I heard him asking her sharply what ailed her.

After this, I used to see his eyes on me, following me as I moved about the room. It seemed clear that he thought we complained together against him. There was only wretchedness at home, and I spent all my time in the City. While walking in the colonnade, I fell in with Charmides. I was now so far from the green youth he had courted, that I could take a man's pleasure in his conversation; for his light manner hid an accomplished mind. We took two or three turns together, while he told me that Sokrates had taken him to task for wasting his wits on idle talk, when he might be applying them usefully to the City's business. Unhappily Lysis saw us together, and took it very ill. I defended myself with indignation. Yet I did myself more than justice, and him less; for it had been plain to me that Charmides had not grown indifferent to my person, and that it was not to talk politics he had sought me out.

I had enough of them at home. My father's foot had healed; he was beginning to get about the City again, and to pick up his old friendships, together with some new ones that dismayed me. All his moderation was gone; I heard him express himself against the democrats with such bitterness as I had scarcely heard within the walls of our house before.

I took my concern to Lysis, during a time of peace between us. He said, 'Let it pass. Can you wonder only the past seems good to him? A man getting on doesn't see that the sweet taste he remembers was the taste of his youth and strength.' – 'But Lysis, he isn't forty-five.' – 'Let it pass. He can't choose but be bitter, when you think of how the Army was lost. The commons let Alkibiades charm them into a venture which only he had any chance of succeeding in. Then they let his enemies frighten them into transferring the command. I still think the answer is to teach the people better; but I've not paid the price that your father has.' We were happy that day, and more than commonly tender with one another, as was apt to happen now between our quarrels.

But at home, the clouds always came back after the rain. I, who had slept soundly even the night before the Games, used to lie awake, afraid of I knew not what, knowing only that things did not stand still, and were not getting better. I did not understand myself. Once, after a quarrel with Lysis, I went to a brothel, which I had never done except that once in Corinth. But it sickened me beyond reason.

One day, a little after supper-time, I heard my father shouting for Sostias, and no reply. My heart sank; I slipped off to search, knowing where to look. Sure enough, Sostias lay drunk in the wine-store. I shook and cursed him, but could not bring him to himself. Since he had got older, this happened once in every month or two. Of course I had always beaten him, but perhaps not as hard as I ought. He was willing-hearted, and fond of us. I did not know then that he had done it quite lately, while I was at war. He was frightened of my father, which had brought back his clumsiness worse than ever; I suppose he drank to pluck his spirits up. Just as I was hauling him to his feet, my father found us, and said to him, 'I warned you what to expect if I found you drunk again. You have brought it on yourself.'

He thrashed Sostias with more strength than I had known was in him, and locked him in the empty store by the stable. When night came, I asked to let him out. 'No,' said my father. 'We should have him slipping off in the dark. I am selling him to the mines tomorrow, as I warned him last time.'

I was too much taken aback to answer. Sostias had been with us since I could remember. No one we knew had ever sold a house-slave to Laureion, except for some gross brutishness. At length I said, 'He's not young, sir. In a silvermine he won't live long.' – 'That depends on what he is made of,' my father said.

Later, in the quiet of the night, I heard my mother pleading with him. He answered her angrily, and she fell silent. The night was hot and close; I lay tossing on my bed, thinking of the old days not long gone, when our little make-shifts had been a joke in which old Sostias had shared. My childhood too I remembered, and how he had hidden me from the Rhodian woman when she wanted to beat me. At last I could bear it no longer. I got softly up, and fetched some food from the larder. As I stole up to the outhouse door, I heard a strange fumbling noise within. I opened. Moonlight shining in through a small barred window, showed me Sostias turning to stare. In his hands was a rope, which he had been throwing at the beam above.

There was a short painful scene, in which we both shed tears. I am not sure what I had intended at the outset; perhaps only to give him some supper, and say farewell to him. 'Sostias,' I said, 'if I forget to lock up after me, you know where to go. You may meet horsemen in the hills. Hide till you hear them talk. If they speak Doric, tell them what you're doing and they'll let you through. You can get work in Megara, or Thebes.' He knelt, and wept upon my hands. 'Master, what will he do to you for this?' – 'No matter; at least he can't sell me to Laureion. Keep off the drink, now; and good luck.'

Next morning I dressed with some care, to put a good face on it, and waited about the house. My father was out already; he came back bringing the mine agent with him, which I had not bargained for. He opened the door in the presence of this man, who, being disappointed (for the scarcity of slaves was increasing), grumbled at his vain journey, and spoke insolently to my father. He scarcely replied; it was as if he did not hear. As the man left, I felt a cold sweat break out upon my palms.

'Go in, Mother,' I said. 'I must speak with Father alone.' I think she had not guessed before what I had done. 'Oh, Alexias!' she said. Then the blood warmed my heart, and its courage returned. 'Go in, Mother,' I said; 'alone is better.' She looked once more at me, and went.

When my father came in, he hung the outhouse key on the nail again. Then, without speaking, he turned towards me. I faced him and said, 'Yes, sir, I am to blame. I went last night to bid Sostias goodbye, and I was careless, it seems.' The flesh of his face seemed to grow heavy and dull, and his eyes widened. 'Careless! You impudent dog, you shall pay for this.' I said, 'So I intend, sir,' and laid on the table the money I had ready. 'For a man of his age, whom but for me you would have found hanged this morning, I think thirty is enough.' He stared at the silver, then shouted, 'Do you dare to offer me my own? You have done now with playing the master here.' – 'The City gave it to me,' I said, 'for running at the Isthmus. Call it a gift to the gods.' He was still for a moment, then thrust at it with his hand, so that part of it fell, ringing and rolling on the floor-tiles. We stood unheeding it, looking in each other's eyes.

He drew in his breath; I thought from his eyes he was going to lift his hand to me, or even to curse me, for he seemed beside himself. But a stillness fell on him instead. In this pause it was as if fear put out a hand, and pulled me by the hair; yet the face of fear was hidden.

He said, 'Before you came of age, your uncle Strymon offered your stepmother the protection of his house. Why did you oppose it?' He had never called her my stepmother before. I felt a chill at it, beyond all reason, so that I must have grown pale; I saw his eyes fixed on my face. Then, remembering what a homecoming I had saved him from, I grew angry, and answered, 'Because I thought it too soon to presume your death.' I was about to go on; but before I could open my mouth again, he thrust forth his head at me like a madman, and spat out, 'Too soon! You had done that, both of you, soon enough!'

I stared at him, his meaning knocking at the doors of my mind, while my soul tried to close them. In the pause, there was a sound under the table. My father turned quickly and stooped down. There was a loud scream, as he dragged out little Charis. She must have been playing on the floor when he came in, and crept there out of the way. He shook her, and asked her what she meant by eavesdropping, as if she could have understood a word of what had passed. Terrified out of her senses, she struggled in his hands, and seeing me shrieked, 'Lala! Lala!' straining towards me. 'Don't Father,' I said. 'You frighten her, let her go.'

Of a sudden he thrust her away, so that she fell at my feet. I picked her up, trying to quiet her while she sobbed and wailed. 'Take her then,' he said, 'since you claim her.' The child was crying in my ear; I could not believe I had heard him rightly. He strode forward, and seized each of us by the hair, holding our faces side by side; his lips showed his closed teeth as a dog's do. 'She is small,' he said, 'for a child of three.'

I have seen evil in the world, and known horror, as any man must who has lived in times like these. But none of it has been to me what that moment was. Since then, the Gorgon's head has never been a children's tale to me. I felt the blood sink back upon my heart, and my limbs grow cold. It seemed that a voice of madness spoke in me, saying, 'Destroy him, and this will cease to be.' I cannot tell what wickedness I might have done but for the child. Prompted by a god, she did not let me forget her, but thrust her hot wet face into my neck, and clutched my hair. I moved my hand over her body to calm her, and came partly to myself. 'Sir,' I said, 'you have suffered much hardship; I think you are sick. You ought to rest, so I will leave you.'

I walked out into the courtyard with my sister in my arms. There I stood still, looking before me. It seemed that if I did not move, I could remain as stone, and know nothing. But this sleep was not permitted to me. The child broke it, speaking in my ear. She was saying that she wanted her mother.

I bent and set her on her feet. Calling the maid Kydilla, who was passing through, I told her to take the child in, and find her mother for her. For she had a right to what was hers. Then I walked out into the street.

At first, if I had any clear thought, it was only to find a place to be quiet in. But as I moved on through the City, seeking it in vain, the movement itself became needful to me: I walked faster and faster; I was like a man trying to leave his shadow behind. Presently passing through the Acharnian Gate I was out of the City. Then, the need pressing me more strongly, I girded my mantle up, and began to run.

I ran through the level plain between the City and Parnes. I did not go very fast; for I knew in myself I must run far, and my training worked in me though I did not regard it. The high wall of Parnes rose before me, pale with the summer drought; bleached grass and dark scrub and grey rock, standing against a hard dark sapphire sky. I reached the footslopes and ran between the olive fields, where poppies splashed the barley-stubble with blood. At last hearing a stream below me in a gulley, I felt thirst, and climbed down the rocks to drink. It was shady after the heat of the road, the water cool and fresh; I lingered there, when I should have hastened on. By this I learned that what I had been flying from was madness; for there it overtook me.

The form of my madness was this: that the sin I had been charged with, I was guilty of, at least in my soul. As in the terror of this thought I climbed up from the stream and began to run over the mountains, all sense fled from me, and it seemed I had committed it in my body also. Sometimes my mind would partly right itself, and I would throw off this last frenzy; yet I never really came into my wit. Who can doubt it was the judgement on my impiety, in destroying my father's letter, and disobeying his command? For I could not see, what any man in his senses must have seen, that being beside himself he had been carried to an absurdity which he must perceive already; that a dozen of our acquaintance could bear witness to the time of Charis' birth; that Strymon himself, who though mischievous was not a villain, would have testified for me in this at least. I only felt myself accursed by heaven and among men. So I hastened on, deeper into the hills and higher, into the wild country above the farms; climbing, and running where there was any place to run. My legs were torn by the heath and scrub, my feet bruised upon the stones. Once a troop of Spartans sighted me; but they took me for a runaway slave making for Megara, and rode past.

At last I came into the high places, where nothing is to be seen but dry stony tops and deep gorges, and far-off rock-shapes shuddering in the heat. I felt no hunger. Sometimes I felt thirst, but I was loth to stay and quench it, for I knew myself pursued; so that I began to look round for what hunted me, seeking to surprise it. The sunburnt mountain was the colour of a wolf's pelt, and once I thought I saw one move. But it was the wind playing with a bush; it was not wolves that trailed me.

The sun shone brightly; but after the noontide, the wind blew small dark clouds across the sky, whose shadows hovered, and swooped like ravens down the slopes of the mountains. At first when I saw what followed me, I seemed to see only such a cloud as this, coming up behind. I had now run far in the summer heat, and climbed high; my breath came loudly, my legs began to fail, and my tongue was as dry as a dusty shoe. I saw water before me flowing down from a spring, and flinging myself on the earth drank as a beast does. As I lay there, I felt the cold that ran before the cloud; and looking up I saw them.

They were not in the cloud, but in the shadow of the cloud, running over the brush and the little stones towards me. Their faces and their feet were blue like the night; their garments were without substance, sometimes showing their dark limbs, sometimes the ground behind them. With a shout of horror I leaped to my feet, and fled; and now I knew that what I had taken only for the noise of my labouring breath, had been the hiss of the snakes that twined and darted in their hair. As I ran I prayed; but my prayer fell back like a spent arrow; I knew I was given to them for my sin, as Orestes was given, and no god would save me. Yet I ran, like the hunted wolf who runs not in hope nor thought but because he is made so.

I do not know how long I ran. As they gained on me I began to hear their voices, like the cry of a mixed pack, some deep, some high; and the snakes hissing, back and forth. Then as I was running downhill, I heard one shout, 'Now!' and reach out towards me. I leaped forward, and missing my footing rolled down the mountain-side. I think my senses left me. But in time level ground checked my falling. I got up wondering that I could stand, for I had thought that all my bones were broken. I stood swaying on my feet; the hillside was dark behind me, and before me was something pale, on which the late sun was shining. Those, whom it is better always to call the Honoured Ones, I could not see any more. But I felt that I was dying; so perceiving that what stood before me was the shrine of a god, I went forward till I reached the steps before the precinct. Then my eyes blackened, and I fell.

I awoke to feel water on my face, and found an old man beside me. He wore on his white hair a garland of laurel; and, my senses coming back to me, I saw he was the priest of the shrine. At first I could not speak to him; but he gave me water to drink with wine in it; in a little I could sit up, and return his greeting. I looked over my shoulder the way I had come; but the Honoured Ones had withdrawn from me.

He saw me looking, and said, 'You have run far; your clothes are torn, you are bruised and bleeding and dabbed with mire. Have you shed blood, and do you come for sanctuary? If so, come into the holy place; for Apollo cannot protect you outside.' And he bent to raise me. His hands were old, but dry and warm, and there was healing in them. I said, 'I have shed no blood. Better I had shed my own; for my eyes have seen my heart, and its light is turned to darkness for ever.' – 'There is a labyrinth,' said he, 'in the heart of every man; and to each comes the day when he must reach the centre, and meet the Minotaur. But you have not profaned anything sacred to a god, or killed under a pledge of safety, or committed incest?' I shuddered, and said, 'No.' – 'Come then, poor boy,' he said, and set me on my feet.

If he had not been strong for his years, he could not have brought me the little way to his house; for my knees failed under me as we went, and but for his arms I should have fallen. His wife being an old woman appeared before me, and helped him to lay me on a bed. She gave me soup to drink, and took away my garment; they washed me, and cleaned my wounds with wine and oil, and covered me with a mantle. It was like being a child again in my grandmother's house. Last he gave me a hot spiced posset, with poppy in it; as soon as my wounds ceased smarting from the wine, I fell asleep.

I slept through the evening and the night, and on till almost noon-day. Then I put on the mantle they had laid over me, and went out. I felt tired and sore; my limbs moved heavily, but they were sound. The sanctuary stood beside a cleft in the mountains, with a steep hill above it on which pine-trees grew. One could see a great way down the gorge, to the plain and the sea. It was the kind of place Apollo loves. But the beauty of the morning was strange to me, and I saw that it was good only for other men.

The priest, seeing me up, came down from the shrine, which was a small one, made of a silver-coloured stone. He brought me back to the house, and put food before me, not questioning me at all, but telling me how the shrine had been founded, by one to whom the god had appeared in that spot. When I had eaten, he asked if I would like to see the sanctuary; 'for,' he said, 'the image of the god is very beautiful; though this place is hard to come at, people journey a long way to see it, having been told of it by others. It is not as old as the shrine; indeed, I was here myself at its dedication. Pheidias made it, the statuary of Athens.'

Out of civility I went with him, with my commendations ready made, because of his kindness; for I could not care for anything. But when I saw the statue, I found he had been too cold in its praise. The god was represented as in early manhood, a glorious youth, of nineteen or twenty years, his face most noble, mingled of grace and power. A blue chlamys hung on his shoulder, and his left hand held the lyre. As I looked, for a while I forgot even what brought me there.

The priest said to me, 'You are admiring the image as if astonished; and indeed, it is not as well known as it ought to be. But the same thing happens to those who come full of expectation. You have been told, I daresay, that after Pheidias had brought his art to full perfection, he worked no more from the living model. He waited on the inspiration of the gods. But while he was carving this, there was a certain young knight, of a beauty, he said, almost divine, whom he would ask sometimes to come as a service to the god, and strike the pose for him. Then letting the young man go, he would meditate, and pray to Apollo, and afterwards begin to work.'

I looked again, and thought both Pheidias and the youth must have been visited by some vision; for it seemed that this and no other was the very form and face of the god. I asked if he knew who had posed for the work. 'Certainly,' he said; 'it is common knowledge, and though you are young you will surely have heard of the man, for it is only a few years since his name was in everyone's mouth: Myron son of Philokles, whom they call The Beautiful.'

My mind was silent, like fallen snows in a still air. I stood, and gazed. Then, as winter's white comes crashing down the mountain-side and runs away in water, grief fell upon me for all mortal men, so great that my body would scarcely hold it. I had no care that the priest stood there beside me; but, remembering presently that I was in the presence also of the god,

I lifted my arm, and covered my face with my mantle as I wept.

After a while, the priest touched my shoulder, and asked me why I was weeping. But I could find nothing to say to him. 'You wept,' he said, 'when I told you the name of the youth. Perhaps he has died, or fallen in battle?' I shook my head, but could not speak. He paused, and said, 'My child, I am old, and time stands still for me! nor do I fear death as an evil, more than one fears sleep after a full day. Pray rightly, that at each time of your life your desires may be conformable, and do not fear; old age will come not to you, but to another whom the gods will make ready. And as for the youth you grieve over, he is fortunate, since his beauty having become the dwelling of a god lives on in this temple, as well as in his sons.'

I bowed my head, honouring his wisdom. Yet he had not reached my grief; and to this day, though I have read many books, I have found no words for it.

All that day I rested there, and the next, and the night following; for my strength was slow in returning. On the last evening, when the lamp was lit and the old woman was cooking supper, I told him what I had been accused of, and that I did not know where to go. He told me I must go home, and the god would protect my innocence. Then, seeing my eyes fall, he said, 'A certain man went a long journey, leaving his money in the charge of a friend. On returning, he got back all he had left in trust, and was satisfied. If it were found that the friend, while the money was in his house, had been in want, would he be honoured less among men, or more?' – 'It is not the same,' I said. – 'It is the same to the gods. Believe in your own honour, and men will do so too.'

So, early next day, I set off for the City. Though a good way, it was not so far as I had come, for I had wandered to and fro on the mountains. I returned at evening, a little before the lighting of the lamps. The priest's wife had mended the rents in my mantle and washed it, so that I looked more like myself, though somewhat bruised from the fall. As I came into the courtyard, I saw the lamp begin to shine from indoors. I waited outside for a while; but the dogs knew me, and ran up making a noise; so then I went in.

My father was seated at the table, reading. As he raised his eyes, my stepmother came in from the kitchen. She looked at him, not at me, and waited. He said, 'Come in, Alexias; supper is almost ready, but you have time for a bath first, I daresay.' Then, turning towards her, 'Has he time?' – 'Yes,' she said, 'if he is not too long.' – 'Hurry, then; but as you go, bid goodnight to your sister. She has been asking for you.'

So we sat down to eat, and talked of matters in the City; and what had passed was never spoken of again. What he had said to my stepmother while I was gone, or she to him, I never knew. But as time went by, I saw there had been a change. Sometimes I would hear her say to him, 'The evening will be cool; your cloak is not thick enough'; or 'Don't let them give you the spiced meat that kept you awake last time.' He would say, 'What's that?' or 'Well, well!' but he would obey her. I had not perceived that he always treated her as a girl, till now when I saw him treat her as a woman.

How this had come about, I never knew; nor, I think, did I wish to know. It was enough that nothing would be again as it was before.

19

During the time that followed this, I was much in the City, and little at home. There was a great emptiness within me; I was always glad to be in company, and did not always wait to find the best.

I could not speak of what had happened, even to Lysis. But some hint at least I would have given him, if he had not asked me in anger where I had been, and reproached me with leaving no word for him. Natural as this was, yet being still not myself I felt he had failed me at need, and only said shortly that I had been hunting. 'Alone?' he asked. I told him yes. Seeing I had lied, I need not have been injured by his disbelief; yet I felt it an injury.

After this, though needing him more now than ever before, from being thoughtless I grew to be unkind. I often tormented him, well knowing what I did; saying to myself that his baseless jealousy deserved to be punished. Then lonely and wretched, and full of shame, I would return to him, as if this were to undo the past, or as if I had treated lightly a man without pride. At his first coldness I would let fly, and it would all begin again. Sometimes out of longing for his company I would beg his pardon, or set out to get round him in spite of himself, and we would be reconciled. But it was like the clouded gaiety of fever. At parting he would ask me with forced carelessness what I meant to do next day and whom I was seeing. I would laugh, and give him some slight answer; later, alone at night, I would have given anything to have parted friends, and could not think what had possessed me. For often in company, or with the troop about us, I would look at him knowing the world held nothing so dear; if at that moment we could be alone, it seemed, there would be no cloud between us. And I even thought he felt the same.

While I was with Sokrates, I could always stand aside and see my folly. Yet I did not come to him for counsel. When one day I could bear myself no longer, it was to Phaedo that I turned.

By chance I found myself lying next to him at the hot-bathhouse. It was Kydon's place, an irreproachable establishment. When the bath-man had done with us, and we were waiting for the masseur, we drew up our couches and talked. It is a place, one finds, for loosening the tongue, and I found my troubles pouring out with my sweat. He listened, lying on his belly, his head on his folded arms, looking round at me through his fair hair. Once he seemed about to interrupt me, but was silent, and heard me out. At the end, he said, 'You're not serious, are you, Alexias, when you say you can't understand all this?' – 'Why, yes; for I don't think either of us really cares any less for the other. Indeed, I think . . .' He pushed the hair out of his eyes to look at me, then let it fall back. 'Well,' he said, 'if you can't understand it, it must be because you don't wish to; and for all I know you may be right. No, I can't tell you what to take for the pain, Alexias; I am not the doctor you are needing; you know I never pretended to know anything of love. Why don't you ask Sokrates?' I said I would think of it. I did not choose to ask him what he meant.

A short time after, I met Charmides in the palaestra. We watched the wrestling for a while, and fell into talk. Presently glancing through at the dressing-room, I saw Lysis. He had been about to strip for exercise, but seeing me he had paused. I looked away quickly, as if I had not noticed him. It was folly, not malice. I was afraid he would be too angry to return my greeting, and that people would see we were estranged. When I looked again, he was gone. Then too late it came to me what he must think: that I had meant to put an affront on him before Charmides, or even perhaps that Charmides had prompted it.

I was now more than sobered, I was afraid. I left at once, and sought Lysis about the City. At last I went to his home. There I found him sitting at his writing-table, his papers about him. When I came in he went on writing for a few moments, as if a servant were waiting; then he looked up and said, 'I am busy; come some other day.'

Never before had it come to this between us. I sank my pride, and excused myself to him. He listened coldly and said, 'All this is nothing to me. I am busy, as you see; and I have asked you to go.' He turned to his work again, leaving me to stand there. I began to be desperate; yet I could not abase myself any further, for his contempt would have been too much to bear. So ready to try anything that came into my head, I said, 'Very well. I called to ask if you'd come hunting tomorrow; but if you don't care to, I shall go alone.' — 'Yes?' he said. 'As you did before?' — 'If you choose to come, you can see for yourself. But be there at daybreak; I shan't wait longer.' And then, determined to make him notice me, 'If you come, bring your boar-spears. Or if you are busy, stay away.'

At this, as I had hoped, he sat up and stared at me. 'Are you joking,' he said, 'or out of your mind, to talk of hunting boar alone?' — 'It's your affair,' I said, 'whether I go alone or not. If you're not there, I shan't waste the morning looking for someone else.' With that I left him.

Next day I was up in the dark, to make my preparations, such as they were. You may guess how much forethought had gone to my proposal. I had not even boar-spears of my own, and had only been at two hunts in my life; once years before, in the care of Xenophon's father, who had sent us boys into a tree when he and his friends brought the beast to bay; and once with the Guard, when ten or twelve of us had gone out together. I had borrowed spears, however, from Xenophon; whom, when he assumed I was going with a party, I did not undeceive.

As the stars were fading, I heard horse-hoofs in the empty street. Then the sickle guards of Lysis' boar-spears stood up black against the sky. Running beside him were his three tall Spartan hounds; behind him on muleback a slave carried the stakes and nets, which I had not even remembered.

He looked down at me grimly, to see how I liked being taken at my word. Since that was the way of it, I greeted him briskly, thanking him for bringing the nets, as if I had counted on it. I thought then he would call it quits; but he asked what dogs I was taking. I whistled them up; one big Molossian and two Kastorians, an absurd pack for the work. He glanced at them, raising his brows. Then the Molossian started fighting one of his dogs, which had happened before. We jumped in to part them, and I thought this would thaw him. But he was still cool and sensible, and a mile away. So I said, 'Well, let's be going.'

We rode to Pentelikon, where there was plenty of boar that year, hunting having been much cut down by the war. It was now a fine fresh morning, with a breeze from the sea; from the top of the range, we could see Dekeleia clearly, and half a dozen places where we had fought side by side. I could not keep from pointing, and saying 'Do you remember?' It is my nature to flare up hotly, but not to hold it long. Lysis was a man slow to anger; but once being moved to it, he did not easily put it by. He answered me shortly, and pointing to a wooded fold of the mountain, said he would try there.

On the way we met a farm-boy with some goats, and I asked him if there were boar in the wood. 'Yes,' he said, 'there's a very big one. He drove out another boar who lived near here. Only yesterday I heard him rooting.' When he had gone, Lysis turned to me. I could see from his eyes that he thought things had gone far enough. But the words came hard to him; and now I was angry in my turn, because he had been cold to my signs of peace. So I said, 'Do you think I'll turn back now, so that you can throw it for ever in my face? If you came for that, you came for nothing.' On that he answered me coolly, 'Save your wit for your work, Alexias.'

We dismounted in silence, and sat down to eat, each with his own food and his dogs about him, not speaking. Presently looking up he said, 'Since we are doing men's work, shall we do it like men and not like children?' He told me what we should do, shortly and clearly, as if giving orders in the field. Then he leashed the bitch-hound he used for tracking, and leaving the other dogs and the horses with the slave, led towards the thicket.

After the bright day it seemed dark and tangled within. The sun came through the trees in round coins of gold; the black damp earth smelled of rotten oak-leaves. Soon we began to find boar-droppings and tracks. They looked very big. I stole a quick glance at Lysis' face, which told me nothing, for he now looked just as he did in war.

Presently we came to an oak-tree whose bark was all ploughed and torn with the tusks of the boar. The bitch tugged at Lysis' arm, and bristled along her back, and growled. Ahead was a dark covert, with tracks coming out. Lysis said, 'That is his run. We will net it here.'

We took back the bitch and tied her up with the others, and set up the nets in a bay before the lair, fixing them to strong stakes and to trees. A little way behind, there was a steep rock; on this, where he was safe, we posted the slave with a pile of stones, to keep the boar from breaking the wrong way. Then we got our spears. Lysis said, 'Stand at the ready, and don't take your eyes off the covert for a moment. Boar are fast.' So we fetched the dogs, which were in clamour already at the hated scent, and slipped them in the thicket. Lysis stood to the right of the nets, I to the left. In a proper hunt you will see four or five men in each of these places, with spears, and some further back with javelins to throw; to make up for numbers, we came closer in. At our signal the slave began shouting, and throwing stones. Then between two black bushes I saw the boar.

I thought, 'He's not so big after all.' He stood with the hounds in cry about him, his head low, his tusks yellow against his hairy black snout. His little eyes looked round, and I saw at once he was not going to rush blindly into the net. He was an old cunning one. Lysis and I stood in our places, our spears pointed forward and downward, gripped in the right hand, guided with the left. Then Phlegon, Lysis' biggest dog, ran in. The boar's head jerked once; Phlegon flew kicking in the air, fell and lay still. When I saw him die, and Lysis standing there, I came to myself at last. His dogs were better than mine; they would work the game his way, and he had known it. So I shouted at the boar to make it look, and stepped towards it. At once Lysis shouted too, louder than I. But the boar had seen me first. Before I could think 'Here he comes,' he was on my spear.

I never knew before what strength meant. With his red eyes flaming he thrust towards me, squealing and trampling, trying to run himself up the spear to reach me. His weight felt more than my own. I set my teeth and leaned on the shaft; for moments that seemed hours I looked along it at his tusks and his wrinkled snout. Then quick as lightning he gave, and twisted aside. The spear turned like a live thing, and left my hands.

I felt a great astonishment, in which all was still and it seemed I could easily take back my spear again. Just in time Lysis' voice reached me shouting 'Down! Lie down!' Used to obeying him in battle I flung myself down quite blindly; then I remembered why, and clutched the roots and small growth below me, to anchor me fast. A boar's tusks curve upward; he must get them under before he can gore.

My fingers dug into the ground, my teeth met on bitter stalks and leaves. I felt the snout of the boar thrust at my side, and smelt his hot stink. Close by me Lysis shouted; the boar was gone. I lay with my wits scattered, then looked round. Lysis with the boar on his spearhead was fighting for his life. It was thrashing about like a demon, bearing him here and there in the tangled ground, full of hazards for the foot. My mind seemed at leisure and very clear. I thought, 'If he falls, I have killed him. But I will not live to carry it in my heart.'

My spear still trailed from the boar's shoulder. I leaped to my feet and dragged it out and, as he turned toward me, thrust it in lower, at the base of the neck. There was a great surge against my arms; I could hear Lysis pant as we thrust together. Then the boar settled, like a boulder after hurtling down a hill. His mouth opened; he grunted and was dead.

Lysis set his foot on him, drew out his spear, and drove it upright into the earth. I did the same. We stood and looked at each other across the boar. In a while he came round and took me by the shoulders. What we first said is nothing to set down. Presently we went to look at the killed dog; he lay bravely, his teeth still bared for battle, the slash of the boar on his broken neck. 'Poor Phlegon,' said Lysis, 'he is the sacrifice of our pride. May the gods accept him and be appeased.' Then we called the slave down from his refuge. He was in great agitation, having thought, I believe, that when we were both dead the boar would sit down to besiege him. Being now rather light-headed, we laughed at his fears; then we broke the boar, and cut off the gods' portion, and sacrificed to Artemis and Apollo. Afterwards we sent home our spoils, with the mule and the slave.

All afternoon we sat on the hill-side, on a slope beside a spring. Below us the blue bay of Marathon washed its sea-wrack shore, with the ridges of Euboea wine-dark and clear beyond. When we had exchanged forgiveness and could scarcely believe in our former discord, I told him in part why I had gone to the mountains, saying my father had charged me with an impiety too shameful to name. He stared for a moment; then caught his breath quickly, and took my hand, and said no more. After that he was so good to me, you might have supposed I had done something wonderful, instead of hazarding his life.

The blue of the sea grew dark, the light deep and golden; shadows leaned down the eastward slopes. I said to Lysis, 'Today has not run away from us, like days that are filled with nothing. They are wrong who say that only misery lengthens time.' – 'Yes,' he said. 'Yet the day is ending, and still too soon.' – 'At the end of life do you think it is the same?' – 'I suppose the man does not live who has not said in his heart, "Give me this, or that, and I can go content."' – 'What would you ask for, Lysis?' – 'Some days one thing, and some another. When Sophokles grew old, he said the escape from love was like a slave's from a tyrannous master.' – 'How old is he?' – 'Eighty years or so. We ought to be calling the dogs in; they're over the hill.' – 'Lysis, must we go back to the City? We've enough meat left here; let's cook it, and stay in the hills. Then the day will last as long as we choose.' – 'See,' he said, 'how near Euboea looks. It will rain tonight.' Then, as I had hoped he would, he asked me to have supper with him at home.

On reaching the City, I went in to shed my hunting leathers, and get clean. I dressed my hair, and put on my best mantle, with my worked sandals; coming to his house I found he had done the same. Soon after we had begun supper, the summer rain came down upon the City. It pattered on the terrace vine, and drummed the roof. The air grew soft, with scents of slaked dust and freshened leaves, and of drenched flowers from the market-fields beyond. We said we could hear the scorched hills we had come from, drinking their fill, and raised our cups in company. When the slave who waited had gone, we set the bronze bowl for kottabos, and threw for each other, calling toasts as we threw. Lysis made a better score and laughed at me; so I declared I would not accept the omen, and re-filled my cup to challenge him. This time I won; but he would not yield the victory; and so on, till the more my effort the worse my aim, and Lysis reaching to take my cup away, said, 'My dear, you have had enough.'

'What?' I said, laughing and taking it back again. 'Is my speech thick, or have you heard me talking nonsense? Or am I one of those who lose their looks at the third cup?' – 'You deserve yes to that.' – 'Drink up yourself, you are taller and need more to fill you. All the earth is drinking and growing beautiful, so why not we? It is to feel as I do now, that men plant the vine and press the vintage. Not only you, Lysis, look beautiful to me as always, but the whole world is beautiful. For what else was wine given us by the god?'

'Leave it so, then,' he said, 'and don't spoil it with more.'

'One more, for us to pledge each other. Have you thought, Lysis, that now my life is yours? But for you, tonight I should be who knows where? A shadow, shivering out there in the rain, or flitting about on the shores of Styx, squeaking "Lysis! Lysis!" in a little bat-voice too high to hear.'

'Stop,' he said. 'No more, Alexias. Death comes soon enough to divide friends.'

'Here's to life, then. You gave it me. This lamplight; the scent of flowers and rain; the wine, the garlands; your company best of all. Don't you want me to praise your gift? I only need one thing to make me the happiest of all mankind; something to give you in return. But what would be enough?'

'I told you,' he said, 'that one more would be too many.'

'I was only fooling. See, I'm as sober as you are; soberer I daresay. Tell me this, Lysis; where do you think the soul goes, when we die?'

'Who has come back to tell us? Perhaps, as Pythagoras taught, into the womb again. Into a philosoper if we have deserved it, or a woman if we were weak; or a beast or bird if we failed altogether to be men. It would be pleasant to think so, because it would be just. But I think we sleep, and never awaken.'

His sadness reached me through the wine-fumes, and I reproached myself. 'Sokrates says not. He has always held the soul is immortal.' – 'His may be. One can't doubt it is made of harder and clearer stuff than other men's, less easy to disperse.' He roused himself and smiled. 'Or perhaps the gods mean to deify him, and set him in the heavens as a constellation.' – 'He'd laugh at that. And draw you in the dust the Constellation of Sokrates, with two little stars for the eyes, and five or six big ones for the mouth.' – 'Or reprove me for being disrespectful to the gods . . . One can't tell him everything; he doesn't understand the weakness of ordinary men.' – 'No,' I said. 'He has the heart of a lion; nothing frightens him, nothing tempts him aside. Seeing the good and doing it is all one to him.' And I was going on to add, 'But he says it comes by daily practice, like victory at the games.' Then I remembered, and instead of speaking lifted my cup to drink.

Presently I said, 'I daresay he knows he is one to himself, and doesn't look to others to be what he is.' – 'He isn't a man for compromise.' – 'Not with himself. But he is kindly. He has learned not to expect too much.' Lysis said, 'I should think Alkibiades taught him that.' He got up from his couch, and walking away stood looking out at the terrace.

I followed and stood beside him. 'Don't be angry with me tonight, Lysis. What is it?' – 'Nothing. I have been angry with you too often without a cause. Look, the rain is over.'

A white new moon had come out of the clouds, and there were one or two stars. The garden air was fresh in our faces; behind us the supper-room smelled of bruised flowers, lamp-smoke and spilled wine. 'I provoked you without cause too,' I said, 'or with the same cause. There is more rain to fall; don't you feel it, Lysis?' – 'It has been a long drought,' he said. 'Too long. If the earth doesn't drink deep, we shall have great storms, and fires upon the mountains.' – 'Well, if you had had your way, we should have been out on Pentelikon tonight.' – 'I suppose,' I said, 'we should have found some cave to creep into, wide enough for two.'

A laden leaf spilled its water, pattering in the vine. 'It is late,' he said. 'I will call a torch for you.' – 'Late? It must be an hour short of midnight still. Are you treating me like a child now, because I lost my spear?' – He cried out, 'Don't you understand?' and then after a moment, below his breath, 'I saw death reach out for you; and I had no philosophy.'

'You did well enough with a boar-spear,' I said, trying to make him smile. 'At war we have each seen the other brushed by death and at night have joined in the singing.' – 'Shall I sing now? Singing is easy. I saw you dead, and beyond it nothing. Only toil for a burned harvest, with spring and summer lost. And now I have told you, though I never let wine loosen my tongue before. Have you heard enough? You had better be going.'

He turned from me, and walked towards the doorway, to call the slave. But running I overtook him, and caught him back by the arm.

My garland slipped back on my hair as I ran; he put up his hand to it, and it fell behind me. I could hear the vine shedding its last heavy drops upon the terrace; the croak of a frog at the cistern beyond; and my own heart beating.

I said, 'I am here.'

20

It was the winter after this that Lysis and I took to the sea, and sailed to the island of Samos.

Each had his reasons to leave the City. Lysis' father died, carried off by a winter chill; and Lysis, who had sheltered him for years from the cares of a sinking estate, now could not bear to stint his tomb. He was laid among the trophies of his chariot-races; and when it was over, Lysis could afford to keep a horse no longer, unless he applied to the cavalry levy fund, which he was too proud to do.

My father grew stronger; he might yet want Phoenix back, and I did not care to wait for his asking. These days he and I walked softly, as men do in a house cracked by an earthquake.

He was now very thick with a set of oligarchs, who had the name of being rather more than homesick for the past. They came together without gaiety, like men with a common purpose; often I found the supper-room closed on them, and the slaves shut out; there was a feel in it all I did not like, over and above the presence of Kritias. If, as some said, there were men in the City who would let in the Spartans if they might hold office under them, it seemed to me they might be such as these. At my age, I might well have felt it within my rights to take it up with him; but we did not speak of serious matters any more. If he rebuked me, it was in passing for trivial things: for not growing my beard, or for sitting in the scent-shop, which indeed I only used if I found friends there already, and why does one walk in the City except to meet and talk? It was true, however, that when Lysis was not free, sometimes I would spend my time with unprofitable people, rather than go home.

Lysis was uneasy at it, yet had no heart to blame me. We had our own life to live, which was no one else's concern. But where both are restless, it will appear in this also; there was a certain wildness in us at this time, which broke out sometimes in violent joy, and sometimes in recklessness; in extravagant pranks at drinking-parties, or over-boldness in the field.

Sokrates never spoke of it. Indeed, I don't think the cause was a secret from him long. Love is a boaster at heart, who cannot hide the stolen horse without giving a glimpse of the bridle. No one could have been kinder in those days than he. Without a word spoken, simply from being with him, I understood this: that while we had supposed we were doing something for him, it was he who, out of affection for us, had thought to give us some of his riches; and now he was gentle to us, as to friends who have suffered a loss.

This we knew, but did not feel it, then, within ourselves. What had defeated us was something beyond; and this, which had come after, seemed to us now a consolation and a joy. We did our duties to the gods, and were faithful together, and held each other's honour dear. Only from this time on I found the visions of my youth grew fewer, and faded, and turned to memory. But I have been told that this is the necessary effect of years.

So things were drifting, when on a certain day I visited Asklepios, son of Apollo.

One could not go to Epidauros, because of the war; and indeed that would have been making too much of it. So I went to the little shrine in the cave, in the rocks of the High City, just below the walls. I went at evening. A fading sunlight fell on the pillars of the porch, but it was dark inside; the dripping of the holy spring sounded solemn and loud. The priest took the honey-cake I had brought, and gave it to the sacred snake in his little pit. He uncoiled himself, and accepted it; and the priest asked me why I had come. He was a dark man, thin, with long fingers; while I talked he felt my skin, and pulled my eyelids back from my eyes. I said, 'It is my desire, at the next Olympic Games, to enter for the men's long-race.' – 'Thank the god, then, for good health,' he said, 'and if you want a dietary, consult your trainer. This place is for the sick.' I was going away when he stopped me and said, 'Wait. What is it?'

'Nothing much,' I said. 'I ought not to have troubled Apollo.

A runner's wind is a small matter to him. But sometimes, running the last lap, or at the finish, when I am short of breath, I have felt a pain like a knife thrust into me. Sometimes it strikes me in the breast, and sometimes in the left arm; and sometimes with the pain the light of the sun turns black. But it passes, after the race.'

'When did this begin with you?' he said. – 'At the Isthmus a little. But lately I ran across country a good way, up in the mountains; and since then, even at practice the pain will come.' – 'I see. Go, then, to the Agora. Salute the Altar of the Twelve, and come back here quickly, not staying to speak with anyone.'

The run was nothing; but the climb at the end made me pant, and feel the pain a little. He put his hands on my neck and wrists, then laid the side of his head against my breast. His beard tickled me, but I knew it would be unseemly to laugh. He brought me a cup and said, 'Drink this, and sleep; and when you wake, remember what dream the god has sent you.'

I took the draught, which was bitter, and lay down on a pallet in the porch. There was a man sleeping on another pallet, and the rest were empty. I fell asleep at the time of lamp-lighting. On awaking I smelt myrrh, and found the priest at his morning prayer, for it was near sunrise. The man on the other bed was still sleeping. I felt drowsy, and heavy in the head, and strange. Soon the priest came from the altar, and asked me if the god had sent me a dream.

'Yes,' I said, 'and a lucky one. I dreamed that something cold touched my brow, and I opened my eyes upon this place; and the god appeared to me. He was as one sees him in the temple, but a little older; about thirty years old, shaved clean like an athlete. He had a white chlamys on his shoulder, and his bow at his back. He stood over there.' – 'Yes,' said the priest. 'What then?' – 'And then,' I said, 'the god himself held out to me the olive crown, with the ribbons of Olympia.' The priest nodded, and stroked his beard. 'In which hand was the god grasping it? In the left or the right?' Then I remembered, and said, 'In neither. He drew an arrow from his quiver, and on the point of the arrow he hung the crown; and so he held it out to me.'

'Wait,' he said, and threw incense on the altar, and looked at the smoke. The sacred water fell into the hollow of the rock with a heavy dripping, and the dry coils of the snake stirred in his pit of sand. The morning was misty, and rather cold. The priest came back to me, with the garland on his head. 'Thus says Apollo. "Son of Myron, I have been your friend till now. Even the olive of Olympia I will not refuse you, if you ask it with all your will. But do not ask; for with the crown comes the arrow, swiftly, out of the open sky."' And he looked at me, to see I had understood. I considered it a while in silence, then I asked him why this should be. He said, 'Your heart is too great for your body, Alexias. That is the message of the god.'

The sun was up. I walked round the rocks, and climbed to the High City, and looked towards the tall blue hills of Lakedaimon, beyond which Olympia lay. I thought how after the very last Games, when the long-race winner returned to his own city, they had thought the town gates too mean for him and breached the walls to bear him through. When I first heard the tale of Ladas the Spartan, who fell dead with the olive still fresh in his crown, I thought man could scarcely look for a happier end. But since then I had been at the Isthmus; and now it seemed to me more fit for a gentleman to spend himself as Harmodios and Aristogeiton did, for the City's freedom and the honour of one's friend. Yet, as I walked home, my mind felt bare, its familiar furnishing gone. So long I had dreamed of Olympia: the green by the pebbled river, Kronos' Hill with its solemn oak-woods, the stadium at its foot; and the statues of the victors lining the walks, from the time of the heroes till yesterday. When the sculptor in the palaestra had asked me to pose for him, I think I had said in my heart, 'There is time enough.'

This, then, is why I ceased to run the long-race. The time is coming, I daresay, when I shall pay the price of my old crowns; since I turned fifty, after a climb or a hard ride, I have felt again the arrow of Far-Shooting Apollo prick my breast. So I set things down while I remember them.

It was soon after this that we fell in with an Athenian of the Samos squadron, attached to one of the ships as a hoplite of marines. We were all easy with wine, so he asked us cheerfully why good fellows like us should starve ourselves to feed horses, when we could be living like gentlemen in the finest city of the islands, and seeing action worth a man's while against the ships of the Spartan league, which were based on Miletos just across the straits.

'There's no better station than Samos,' he said. 'The Samians will do anything for an Athenian, since they threw out their oligarchs, and our men that were in harbour fought on the democrat side. You can have what you like, or whom. And, by the way, they need every democrat they can get there, for there's trouble blowing up.'

This last we discounted; for only a fool, as Lysis said, will dash straight into politics in a strange city. But the rest seemed good to us. He told us of a new ship, the *Siren*, which was fitting at Piraeus, with her complement not made up. The trierarch, wanting a lieutenant of marines, was glad to get a man with Lysis' record; and as we were fellow-tribesmen, it was easy to get me posted aboard. I was still a little under age for foreign service; but in war one can generally get leave to do more than one need, particularly if it is a case of helping out lovers.

It was still winter when the *Siren* was fitted; but the trierarch, for reasons we were to learn, was eager to be gone. It was my father's turn to stand at the dockside and see me off. 'Well, Alexias,' he said, 'if you could have given some of your time to the City's business these last months, I could have done something for you; but let that pass. You have a decent record in the field and I have no fear that we shall be ashamed of you. Only keep your eyes open in Samos, and use your wits when you see how the land lies. Athens has been governed too long by the lot of the pebble, and counting fools' heads. It is time for people of quality to show it.'

I had no time to ask the meaning of this oracle. My thoughts were aboard already. I smelt the hemp and pitch, the bodies of the rowers, the casks sweating salt fish and oil, and the cold brine of the winter sea. The gulls hung waiting, to feed upon our wake.

The *Siren* was a war-trireme, not a transport, and carried only her own fighting unit of fifteen men. We lived on the foredeck, under an oxhide awning, just above the first bank of the rowers; our action-station was the catwalk running outside the hull. A crew of twenty-five worked the ship, and there were three tiers of rowers, the lowest being slaves. Free men will not work down there; the oarholes are valved with leather to keep out the spray, and a rower sees nothing all day but the back of the man in front, and the second-bench rower's feet on the rests either side. But when it rained and blew they were better off than we, huddled under our roof of skins. I had thought that even a winter voyage could not be harder than some of our hill bivouacks in the Guard. I had forgotten one is not sick on a horse. But the wind changed the second day out, and I was better.

Though we had kept it quiet, it had somehow got aboard that Lysis and I were lovers. After being in the cavalry, where there is a certain feeling in these matters, I found it hard to put up with some of the vulgar notions you can meet with in an infantry unit. It may be that in those days I was too quick to take offence. Most of them were good enough fellows, as I learned in time; their talk came from habit, and from never having been made to define their terms.

We were carrying pay for some ships stationed at Sestos, which, the wind being fair, we made within six days. But in Sestos harbour we were fouled by an unhandy grain-ship; two or three rowers were hurt, and some planks staved in; we had to kick our heels about the Hellespont while repairs were done, and then were held up by weather. So it was some weeks before we made Samos, during which we got no news at all.

After killing time in a small colonial town, it was good to see the great city of Samos glowing between hills and blue water, into which the town thrust outward like a spur, with the harbour in the curve of it. Westward on the strand was the Temple of Here, the biggest of all Hellas. Eastward, the barley-terraces fell like a broad stairway to the sea. Across the strait, quite near, stood up the lofty coast of Ionia, violet-coloured, just as it is named.

The harbour was packed with ships. For the first time we saw the new navy of Athens, for most were sent here as soon as they came off the stocks. They made a fine sight, with their burnished beaks and ramheads, their cheeks new-painted with vermilion, the trierarchs' pennants at their sterns. Some were stripped for action, with the masts ashore, in case of a raid on the harbour, the Spartans being so near. Some were up for scraping on the beach, the sails spread out beside them, having their devices brightened with fresh dye. The curved waterfront under the plane-trees was thronged with citizens and seamen and soldiers and merchants, sitting before the taverns, strolling up and down, or bargaining with the Phoenicians who had brought up their boats with the wares spread out in them.

The Athenian camp was by the shore where they beached the ships, between the town and the temple. It had been here so long that there were no tents; it was like a little town of wood, or daub and wattle, thatched with reed. We found our quarters, and set out to see the sights.

It would be tedious, in these days, to rehearse what we found. Any man about my age, or younger for that matter, knows some such picture. After weeks of intrigue, of move and counter-move, the city was on the brink of revolution. It was clear enough, after an hour or two, why my father had told me to use my wits. The Athenian army itself was split from top to bottom, the oligarchs intriguing with those of Samos, the democrats rallying to the citizens. But what gave to everything an extra stink of corruption was this, that the Samian oligarchs were not, for the most part, those who had been expelled before, but men who had been in the van of the democrat revolt. Some subtle nose had smelled out the rotten patch in the core, the men who had wanted, not freedom and justice, but only what some other man had.

What it meant to our own force, we got our first taste of next day, when the Spartan fleet was sighted making to pass the island. The trumpets sounded; the ships were stripped and hauled down the slipways; the benches manned; the weapons and shields stacked amidships; the cup stood ready on the poop for the libation. We only waited to sing the paean, and sail out. Lysis had not wasted our wait at the Hellespont, and already the marines had caught something of his spirit. We sang as we waited for the signal; the rowers caught it, and I even heard the slaves. But we waited till the singing died, and the men grew restless and weary; the Spartan fleet sailed on, past the temple and round the point, and we all went ashore to drink away our shame. It was not the enemy our generals were frightened of. It was one another. You heard it said openly, after, of this trierarch or that, that he might cover you in a fight, or he might sail across to the other side. Things hardly hinted at in Athens were taken for granted here.

Samos is an old and a noble city. Even its ancient tyrants hung gifts upon it, like jewels on a favourite slave. Now it was at the height of prosperity, the sculptors and masons and painters never idle, the streets growing like tendrils up the slopes of the hills, in flower with yellow marble, or pink, or green, carved and gilded in the light Ionic style. Yet one picked one's way about as if in a foul quagmire, trusting no one. Even our own trierarch we were uncertain of: a pale thin-lipped man who at the Hellespont had been biting his nails over the delay, yet, when impatience was natural enough, had tried to hide it.

Over all this murk, there flickered like a marsh-fire the name of Alkibiades. He had come down to the coast from Tissaphernes' palace, and was living just across the straits. The oligarchs were putting it about that if the democracy, which had unjustly exiled him, were put down in Athens, he would forgive us and would come back, with the Persians eating from his hand, to win the war for us. And this might well be true, for at Magnesia he feasted with a sword hung over him; if the Spartans got the mastery of Hellas, the Medes to keep in with them would certainly hand him over. He could be sure of his death in Sparta, as long as King Agis lived.

The oppression of the place was weighing on us, so that we were growing silent even with each other, when we had the good luck to meet with our old friend Agios, the pilot of the *Paralos*, which was stationed at the port. To him we knew we could speak freely; and he soon put a little solid ground under our feet, telling us that the seamen were sound democrats to a man. He could afford to speak for them, the *Paralos* being the crack galley, and he the senior pilot of the fleet.

Next day by arrangement we met him again. He took us to a certain tavern, with the sign of a golden tripod. It had a little whited courtyard behind it, shaded with a vine. Here at a table a tall lank man was sitting, dressed in a marine's seagoing kilt and leather jerkin. He was lean but broad-chested, with a big firm mouth, and brown eyes that looked straight into one. Agios said, 'Here are my friends, Thrasybulos.'

This man had come to Samos as a simple hoplite, but being a natural leader had found his level; by now all the democrats looked to him. He had a bigness not of his body alone; you knew he would remember your face and name, and be concerned in your trouble.

Agios having told him we could be trusted, he spoke to us very frankly; saying our trierarch was deep in the plot, and that if fighting broke out, Lysis must be ready to take command. It was now certain that this Samian business was only the spear-head of a greater one. The Athenian oligarchs were using it to seize control of the Navy and presently of Athens itself. Then they would treat with Sparta for terms; how disgraceful was no matter, if they could grow fat on the carrion of their City. Athens would be only one more, then, of the Spartan vassals, crushed under such a rule as no Spartan would bear at home, to make the leaders servile and the people weak. We were to be sold to the Spartans, as long ago the tyrant Hippias would have sold us to the Medes.

But just now, he said, the traitors had had a blow they were still reeling under. Alkibiades had slipped off their hook.

Either (which was what he claimed) he had never meant to support them, and had only been probing the plot, or for reasons of his own he had changed his mind. After all, he had always been a democrat. At all events he was working for us now, and had given proof of it; taking his chance of a pardon when he had saved the City's liberties. In Athens, he had been the biggest bait the oligarchs had had to fish with; only since his exile had his real genius in the field been fully known. 'So,' said Thrasybulos, 'don't leave Samos at present, even for an hour. Unless I'm a fool, they mean to strike before this news breaks at home.'

Afterwards, as we went, we were both rather quiet. I was thinking that if my father had gone into this with open eyes, I should never hold up my head again. Even Lysis, I thought, would be touched by the disgrace. I looked at him, as he walked beside me shut in his own trouble: he was not the kind of soldier who shakes off lightly his faith to his commander. His thoughts were on his honour, and mine on him.

It had seemed to me, since I was nineteen, that the common

exchanges of scent-shop and drinking party struck on my ear for the first time. 'How are you, friend, after so long? And how is the beautiful So-and-So, whose praises you filled our ears with?' – 'Why, time runs on, you know. He must be turned twenty by now, wherever he is.' When I laughed too loud, or drank too late, or took a foolish risk in battle, this was the spur that pricked me. Now on the threshold of manhood, when aspiration should have beckoned me onward, I thought only how I had put myself into the hand of time, and counted only the loss.

But time was busy in Samos with larger concerns than mine.

Next day, Lysis and I had walked out a little beyond the walls, to see the ruined castle of old Polykrates, the Samian tyrant: he who was so long fortunate that he dropped his great emerald in the sea, to break his luck lest the gods do it for him. But they sent it back in a fish's belly, to let him know there is no running from fate; and now his walls are as the Medes left them. There was a sheepfold within them, and a scatter of little flowers. Spring was here; on the terraced fields below us, new barley bloomed the earth with green, and the black vine-stocks were budding. We were sunning ourselves with the lizards on the great warm stones, when of a sudden Lysis said, 'How long have we been here? We ought to be going.'

'Why?' I said. 'Everything's quiet. It's not often now we can get away together.' – 'I feel a warning. Perhaps I saw some omen I did not regard.' – 'A warning that you have had enough of my company? The omen is for me.' – 'Be serious,' he said. 'Something is happening; I feel it. We must go.'

We found the Agora full, but no more uncomfortable than it usually was. I was about to reproach Lysis with it, when I myself began to feel uneasy. For something to do, we were watching a silversmith, who was beating out on a fish-platter a border of shells; when Lysis, who had been looking out at the door, said, 'By Herakles, I swear that's Hyperbolos.'

I craned to look, half expecting to see a serpent covered in scales. He had been banished when I was quite a little boy, and I had never heard my father refer to him except as a kind of monster. I had forgotten that he had made his home in Samos. Now I saw him, he looked just like any other disreputable old demagogue, one who lives by denouncing and exposing while he is in credit, and, when he is out, by sycophancy and informations, with a little perjury thrown in. He had a pale face with a loose mouth and thin sandy beard, and spluttered as he talked, slapping his hand with a scroll he carried, as such men do, for show. Some friend was with him, listening with half an ear. Even from afar, the old rogue was stamped with the marks of invincible boredom. Which made it doubly odd that, now in Samos, he should have an audience.

Five or six men were gathered behind him. Some seemed like lumpish apprentices, the kind who, when the craftsman curses their slovenliness, would rather smash the work than do it better. There were also two older men, who seemed of their company but did not speak.

I saw one or two citizens glance at Hyperbolos and his following, and pass swiftly on. There was a statue beside him of some athlete, with two or three steps at the base. On one of these, as if from habit, he set his foot; and, feeling at home there, he began to orate. What it was about, I do not know. He turned then, and saw the men behind him. He was a pale man, but he did not go paler. I saw him go red. He went straight up the steps till he stood on the highest, and started to address the people.

Lysis and I looked at each other. He threw his arm round me and patted my shoulder; then he said, 'Let us hear this.'

We left the shop and crossed over. Whenever I think I have summed up a man, I remind myself of Hyperbolos. He gave that day, I suppose, the performance of his life. He was the vilest speaker I ever heard: vulgar, ignorant, not seeking to teach his hearers, but rather to stir in men as vulgar as himself the irrational excesses to which such people are prone; a whore among orators. Yet, when he denounced the men who were putting the City in fear, there was a kind of flame in him. He was a man so ignoble that if he remembered anything of the nature of excellence, I should think it was only so that he could taunt someone with the lack of it. He lived in spite and hate. And now he only invoked the good in the name of hatred; yet for a moment nobility glanced back at him, and made him brave. It was like seeing some mangy cur, who for years has lived on scraps and filth about the market, raising his hackles at a pack of wolves.

He was leaning out, wagging his finger at the crowd, dragging out some phrase word by word before a peroration, when one of the young men jumped up the steps, grabbed him by the leg, and tumbled him over. There was a laugh, for he had looked absurd going down with his mouth still open.

At the natural sight of someone speaking in the Agora, a number of people had come up. While Lysis and I were trying to see over them, we heard a sound from the foot of the statue, between a cry and a grunt. Then there was a shout, and the feet of men running away. The crowd began to work and seethe about, some people trying to get out and others to press forward.

I law Lysis' hand feeling his belt. Even in Samos, one could not walk the streets wearing a sword like a barbarian. But we both had Spartan daggers, which had been approved ornaments in the Guard. Every Athenian carried something, even if only a hunting-knife.

Suddenly the crowd gave way before our shoulders, and we found ourselves at the statue. Here no one disputed our place; there was a little space quite empty of people, except for Hyperbolos, who lay with his thin beard pointing to heaven, and the food-stains on his mantle mixed with blood. His mouth was wide open, with a kind of grin on it, as if he had just exposed someone beyond shadow of doubt.

As we stepped forward, everyone else seemed to fall back in relief, like people saying, 'Pray help yourself, the affair is yours.' But just then the crowd parted on the other side.

Some of the men who pushed through I had seen following Hyperbolos before. One pointed at the body without speaking. His face and his thumb said, 'Take this dirt to the midden.' None of the crowd moved; but a little man said, 'It was murder. The magistrates ought to see him.' At this one of the youths turned quickly and spat in his face. They stepped towards the body.

I felt Lysis' fingers grip my arm, and he was gone from my side. Running after, I saw him bestriding the mean little corpse, his dagger in his hand. The youth who had spat, about whom was nothing Homeric, was looking at him, much put out. I drew my own dagger, and leaped in to cover his back. Then I could see him no longer; only the encircling faces: some frightened, some making themselves dull so as not to understand, some awaking to battle-joy and friendship; and the faces of the men who had come for the body, as they dragged out the long knives from under their arms.

I never doubted we were in as much danger as ever in war, and of an uglier death. Yet, strangely, I had not to force up my courage; I was in such spirits that I could have cheered aloud, or sung. The truth is, I think, that I felt myself enacting the kind of scene every schoolboy dreams of, when he first hears the ballad of Aristogeiton and Harmodios. My head was full of great words; like a boy, I saw our bodies lying together on a hero's bier, but did not imagine myself dying. I stood there feeling Lysis' shoulder and looking, I don't doubt, as if I had been requested to strike the pose of a Liberator. I was so carried away that I shouted 'Death to the tyrants!' at the top of my voice.

Next moment, I felt Lysis take the shock of someone springing at him, and saw two of the youths making for me. Then I forgot heroics; it was war again, and standing to it unhorsed when your spear is gone. In the confusion around, I heard some voice shout 'Death to the tyrants!' but I could only see the two men I was fighting, till one of them was pulled off me from behind. The press closed in again; I felt a limb of the corpse tangle my feet and cursed it as I fought. I heard Lysis' voice; we put our shoulders side by side and backed up the steps till we felt the statue-base behind us. Now we could see there was fighting all round. Lysis threw back his head and shouted, 'Siren! Siren!' Then we heard the Athenian paean across the square, and voices crying, 'Paralos!'

The seaman came racing up the square to us, and the oligarchs made off. A few timid citizens had run indoors, but most joined up with us, cheering Lysis and me as leaders, because they saw us on the steps. It was just like a happy ending to my dream. People were still taking up the cry of 'Death to the tyrants!' But now I heard a different note in it. There was a huddle of men in the corner of the square; and as I looked, a face rose up from the midst, with blood on it, and the eyes wide, staring about. Someone was being mobbed there. This is a thing that you do not see in war; it was like filth flung on my exultation.

I pulled at Lysis' arm, and pointed. He saw, and calling for silence, spoke to the crowd. He said this was a great day for Samos, for her enemies had declared themselves. But the work was hardly begun; we must go forward with proper discipline, and seize the armoury. All traitors would be tried when the city was secure, and meanwhile we must attack only those who resisted us, for we could not put injustice down by doing it ourselves. Then he said that Samians and Athenians, as long as they loved justice, would be friends together; and this got them cheering. It was a very good speech for someone who had only just got his breath back after such a fight. The Samians picked him up and carried him some way shoulder-high; and for no reason, in the way of crowds, they did the same with me. Being now high enough to look, I craned over to see if the man they had been mobbing was on his feet again. But he was still lying there.

That was the start, as we saw it, of the fight in Samos. There were, however, other beginnings; for the oligarchs had struck all over the town, choosing for their first victims such people as Hyperbolos, who were generally disliked or despised, and whom they thought no one would strike a blow for, so that they might get off to a good start under the pretext of cleaning up the city. In some places this succeeded; but in others people knew what it meant; so already battle was flaring up all over, like fire in thatch with a high wind blowing.

As everyone knows, the oligarchs were beaten everywhere, and the democrats left masters of the town.

That night, when we had left our comrades, Lysis and I sat together in his little reed hut near the shore. We were weary with battle, but still too stirred to rest; we dressed our wounds, which were nothing much, and ate, for we were hungry, having had no time before. On stools at the scrubbed wooden table we sat over our wine. The sea sounded on the shore; outside the stars twinkled above, the watch-fires and harbour lights below; on the table between us stood a shallow clay lamp which had just been lit. Lysis sat chin on fist, looking at the flame. Presently he said, 'Why are you a democrat, Alexias?'

If I had now to answer truly for the youth who sat at the table, I might say perhaps, 'Because of my father, or of the Rhodian woman. Because I love you.' But of course I replied that I thought democracy more just.

He said, 'Undeceive yourself, my dear; it can be as unjust as anything else. Take Alkibiades, who by the way, I suppose will soon be commanding us.' I stared, the thought coming home to me for the first time. 'Get used to it,' he said. 'He may seem shop-soiled; so he is; but it is arguable how much loyalty a man owes to a City which has outlawed him unjustly. Whatever else he had done in his time, he no more broke the Herms than you and I did . . . Tell me, is it better for all the citizens to be unjust, or only a few?' – 'A few surely, Lysis.' – 'Is it better to suffer evil, or to do it?' – 'Sokrates says to do it is worse.' – 'Then an unjust democracy must be worse than an unjust oligarchy, mustn't it?' I thought it over. 'What *is* democracy, Lysis?' – 'It is what it says, the rule of the people. It is as good as the people are, or as bad.'

He turned the wine-cup in his hand. The black of his eyes, which had been wide open, grew small from looking at the flame, and the iris pleated, like grey and brown silk catching the light.

'They held an Epitaphion at Athens,' he said, 'in the first year of the war, in honour of the fallen. The ashes and the offerings were carried in state along the Sacred Way, with an empty bier for the bodies that were lost. It was only a few months before your birth; perhaps your mother carried you in the procession. I was seven years old. I stood with my father in the Street of Tombs; it was cold, and I wanted to run off and play. I stared at the high wooden rostrum they had built for Perikles, waiting for him to climb it, as children wait for a show. When he appeared, I admired his dignity and his fine helmet; and the first sound of his voice struck a kind of thrill upon my ear. But soon I grew tired of standing with cold hands and feet, and doing nothing; I thought it would never end; the weeping of the women had disturbed me, and now the people listened in so deep a silence that I was oppressed by it. I stood staring at the gravestone of a lad carved with his horse; I can see it to this day. I was glad when it was over, and if you had asked me a year later to quote the speech of Perikles, I doubt if I could have fished you up a dozen words. So before I left, I looked it up in the archives. And there were the thoughts that I had supposed I owed to no one. While I read, I still could not remember hearing Perikles say these things. My soul seemed to remember them, as Sokrates says we remember music and mathematics, from the days when we were unborn and pure.'

I told him I had heard of the speech but never read it; and he quoted me as much of it as he could remember. Since then I have read it many times. But since I never knew Perikles, to me it is always Lysis who is speaking; I see not the tomb and the rostrum, but the lamps of Samos through a doorway, his shadow thrown big upon the wall, the piled armour shining beside the pallet, the black glossy wine-cup, and his hand, with an old ring of plaited gold on it, touching the stem.

'Men are not born equal in themselves,' he said to me after, 'so I think it beneath a man to postulate that they are. If I thought myself as good as Sokrates I should be a fool; and if, not really believing it, I asked you to make me happy by assuring me of it, you would rightly despise me. So why should I insult my fellow-citizens by treating them as fools and cowards? A man who thinks himself as good as everyone else will be at no pains to grow better. On the other hand, I might think myself as good as Sokrates, and even persuade other fools to agree with me; but under a democracy, Sokrates is there in the Agora to prove me wrong. I want a City where I can find my equals and respect my betters, whoever they are; and where no one can tell me to swallow a lie because it is expedient, or some other man's will.'

Then the day's weariness came down on us, and we slept. And the next day, the *Paralos* set out to bring the good news to Athens, her prow garlanded, the rowers singing at the oar. When we had cheered them away, I went to the temple and offered a kid to Zeus, for saving my father in his own despite.

We had no more trouble with the oligarchs, whose only care now was to hide their traces and save their skins. After the *Paralos* sailed, we spent a very peaceful week; I mean to say that it was peaceful in Samos. I cannot say quite the same for myself; for within the next two days Lysis remarked to me, in the easy way he had at such times, that he had met a girl in the town who had taken his fancy, and was going that night to visit her. This was the first time it had happened, that I knew of, since things had changed between us; and I was surprised to find how much I minded it. You might almost have thought, from my vexation, that he had been caught by some youth who could seriously engage him. It was absurd, considering his fidelity.

I was oiling the straps of his armour and mine (leather perishes quickly in sea air) and I kept busy at it, to hide my thoughts. But he noticed I had got rather quiet, and asked whether I would like to come too, for he was sure his girl could find another one for me. I thanked him, and said I would come another night. He stood combing his hair into curl, and whistling to himself; then he looked round, and sitting down by me, urged me very kindly to come. He said among other things that I was my father's only son, and should have one day to marry; and I should not know whom to choose, or how to make the best of her, if I had not got myself used to women first. I told him I liked them well enough, but not tonight. The truth was that his encouragement had rather missed its mark, reminding me that it would be he, in the natural course of things, who would get married first. People I knew seemed to take this lightly enough; I had seen them acting groomsman to their friends with perfect cheerfulness; it distressed me to think myself more given to extremes, and less capable of reason, than other men. Indeed, when I look back, I cannot understand myself at this time of my life.

When he had gone, I went out walking; for the god, having marked me down for punishment, spared neither my mind nor body, and I could not stay in bed. There was a young moon in the sky; I went up by the footpath to Polykrates' castle, and sat looking out to sea. The place smelled of sheep, for the flock was in the fold; there was a smell too of thyme, and of green things in spring. I complained to the god that he was unjust to me, who had never insulted nor defied him; but with face averted he accused me, reminding me of my former unkindness to Lysis, who had shown nothing but kindness to me; and of how, long before that, I had cared nothing for Polymedes, or for a dozen others whose names, even, I had not kept in mind. He said too that by my own will I had become his bondsman; and that since he was the giver of more joy to men than any other deity, it was natural his chastisements should give more pain. So I acknowledged his justice, and at last went home; and when Lysis came back, I pretended to be sleeping.

As it turned out, he found the girl more pleasing than he had expected, and went back to her several nights running. I suffered at the time. Yet it has left less mark upon my mind than wounds which seemed slighter at first, where someone of small consequence has failed me in loyalty or honour. As the mould is broken and falls to dust, while the statue of bronze endures, I cannot call the pain to life again; yet remember like yesterday the scents of night, the Galaxy hanging like spray in the deep sky, the cresset burning on an anchored ship, and the cry of a waking lamb answered by the night-jar.

I don't know how long all this would have gone on. The thing was getting a hold on me that was past all sense, and Lysis had even asked me whether I was ill. But serious matters broke in on us, and blew such follies away.

The trierarch of the *Paralos* arrived alone, in a trader from Aegina. The ship had reached Athens to find the oligarchs already in control. Made desperate by the loss of Alkibiades, they had not dared to await results in Samos, but moved at once. They had falsely reported the coup successful and Alkibiades on the way; and getting power on the strength of this, had stopped all payment for public office and dismissed the Senate. Between hired bullies and informers they were keeping the people down, and their own moderates quiet by promising an electoral roll of gentlemen, which was to come out shortly.

When they knew what news the *Paralos* brought, they dared not let the City hear it. They turned the whole crew off the ship of honour, where it was their right to serve, transferred them to a troopship just leaving port, and imprisoned those who refused to go. The trierarch, by luck, had seen what was happening from the dock, and slipping off among the shipping had escaped to bring back word. He added that any soldier had only to look at the new fort they were building on the harbour, to see what it was for: to hold the grainstore against the citizens, and make a bridgehead for the Spartans to land.

You might have supposed this news would have flung all Samos from triumph to despair. But our blood still glowed with victory, our souls with our just cause; we were like the men of Marathon when they marched straight off the field to take their stand before the City, knowing the gods were with them.

The day after we got the news, Athenians and Samians together, soldiers and seamen and citizens, trooped up together to their hilltop acropolis. There we took an oath of fellowship, to defend each other's liberties, pursue the war, and make no terms with our enemies, at home or abroad. It is a great open field up there, girt with an ancient wall; larks flew up singing when we raised the hymn to Zeus, and the smoke of the offering rose straight to heaven.

I have never felt less like an exile. It was we who were the City now, a free Athens beyond the sea. We carried her sword too and her armour; it was the Navy, not the government at home, which levied the island tribute to finance the war. The sun shone; the sea like hammered silver flashed below us; we felt we were making a new thing on the earth.

Afterwards, down in the city, every Athenian found himself pulled into a Samian house and set in the guest's chair, while they brought out the best wine and spiced figs and anything they had. I told the story of my life, or a good part of it, at three Samian hearths that evening; and when Lysis and I met in camp we were neither of us quite sober. But we were happy, and full of faith. He had forgotten all about the girl; and, what was more remarkable, so had I.

It was a warm spring evening; one smelt the sea, and supper cooking on pinewood fires, and the scent of flowers upon the hillside; we sat in the doorway of our hut in the late sun, greeting friends as they passed. And we opened a wine-jar, to drink to our enterprise, 'For,' said Lysis, 'half sober is neither here nor there.' But our minds only sparked brighter with the wine; we settled the affairs of all Athens and Samos between us, and went on to win the war.

Presently the trierarch of the *Paralos* came by, and stopped to drink with us; and Lysis offered him some courtesy on the loss of his ship. He laughed and said, 'Don't pity me, but the trierarch who's commanding her now. I know those lads. The net won't hold the dolphin. I'll lay you five to one that the first chance they get in open water, they clap him in irons and run for Samos.' (I may add that he won his bet.)

It still put him in a rage, he said, to remember what he had seen in Athens. But now the dark tale was lightened by our hopes. 'When Alkibiades takes command here,' he said, 'they can't last long. They have lost the moderates, you know already. Theramenes and his party are only biding their time. They came in on the promise of a limited franchise, a principle I don't hold with but still a principle. Now they know they have got a tyranny, they won't bear it longer than they need.'

I listened silent, ashamed that this stranger should do my father more justice than I had done. Many things came back to me, from my first years. When I came back from the mountains, I had found in my room the silver I had put down for Sostias, wrapped in a cloth.

'But,' said the trierarch, 'I almost forgot what I came here first to tell you, that an Army Assembly is fixed for tomorrow; you will hear the herald very soon. Half the ships in the fleet are in the same state as yours, the trierarch fled to Miletos, and the First Officer carrying on. The new promotions are going by vote. If I were as sure of a ship as you are, Lysis, I'd sleep well tonight.'

I looked at Lysis, my contentment crowned. He put it aside, from modesty; but the trierarch said, 'Your pilot was heard to say of you, "He knows a ship's not steered from the same end as a horse." And that's a paean, from a pilot.' Which was true enough; for between the soldier who fights a ship, and the seaman who sails her, is a contention as old as Troy.

He went away, and we heard the herald; then we filled and drank, not naming the good news for fear of tempting the gods. The evening sun glowed like bronze upon the reed thatch of the roofs; here and there men were singing about the fires. I said in my heart, 'Such things as these are the pleasures of manhood. We must do the work of the season, as Hesiod says.'

Lysis caught my eye above the wine-cup. 'To beautiful Alexias,' he said, and jerked the lees out of the doorway. They made an alpha in the dust; he could do it, from practice, three times out of four. He yawned, and smiled, and said, 'It is getting late.'

But we sat a little longer; for as the sun sank, the moon had risen. Her light had mixed with the afterglow, and the hill behind the city was the colour of the skins of lions. I thought, 'Change is the sum of the universe, and what is of nature ought not to be feared. But one gives it hostages, and lays one's grief upon the gods. Sokrates is free, and would have taught me freedom. But I have yoked the immortal horse that draws the chariot with a horse of earth; and when the one falls, both are entangled in the traces.' And I thought of Sokrates, and saw the logic of my case.

Lysis said to me, 'Those are long thoughts to keep unshared.'

'I was thinking,' I said, 'of time, and change, and that a man must go with them as with a river, conforming to what is. And yet at last, if we are never so obedient, or if we call defiance, the last change is still to death.' – 'That last?' he said, and smiled. 'Never state an opinion like something proved. Today we have lived as if it were not so; and we have felt that it was good.' His face was calm in the brightening moonlight; it came to me that in the use of his courage, and the faith of his cause, and in the exaltation of our vow upon the hilltop, he had found himself again.

We sat in thought. I turned my eyes from the mountains, to find his turned to me. He laid his hand on mine. 'Nothing will change, Alexias. No, that is false; there is change wherever there is life, and already we are not the two who met in Taureas' palaestra. But what kind of fool would plant an apple-slip, to cut it down at the season when the fruit is setting? Flowers you can get every year, but only with time the tree that shades your doorway and grows into the house with each year's sun and rain.'

Indeed he was too good for me. Often it has seemed to me that it was only he who made me a man.

Helios had plunged his red hair in the waves of the sea,

and the songs were dying round the watch-fires. It was growing cold, and we went within; for, as the men of Homer said when a long day was behind them, it is well to yield to the night.

21

'Welcome home, Alexias,' said a young man in the Agora, who was quite strange to me. 'Do you know you are staring about you like a colonist? Indeed you have been away too long, and it is good to see you.'

'Three years,' I said. 'I know your face well, but . . .' – 'My name,' he said smiling, 'is what you may know better, for I've grown my beard since last we met. Euthydemos.'

We exclaimed, and laughed, and sat to talk on a bench outside a shop. He had grown into an excellent fellow, sound without his old solemnity; Sokrates always knew where to dig for gold. 'I am keeping you,' he said, 'from all your friends, but I must hear your news before the crowd sweeps you away. Alkibiades' men all walk the City dusted with his glory; and so they should. How does it feel, to be hung so thick with crowns of victory?' – 'It feels,' I said, 'like having a good commander.'

He raised his brows, half smiling. 'What, Alexias! Even you! You who distrusted vulgar idolatries, and disapproved of him, as I remember?' I laughed, and shrugged. The truth was, there was not a man of us in Samos but thought the sun rose in his eyes.

'No one knows him,' I said, 'who hasn't fought under him in war. He puts a shine on it. Here in the City they didn't understand him as we in Samos do. He trusts us and we trust him, and that's the secret of it.' At this Euthydemos laughed aloud, and said, 'Great Zeus! He must have given you a philtre.'

I felt myself getting angry, which was absurd. 'I'm not a politician, only a lieutenant of marines. I speak as I find. I've never seen him leave ship or man in the lurch in any action. Men who fight for him don't die for nothing. He sees what each man is good for, and lets him know he has put a stake on it. There was a black squall, and night coming on, when he led out the fleet to take Byzantium; but we all set off singing against the thunder. No one stops to ask questions when he gives an order. He thinks fast. I was with him when he took Selymbria with thirty men.'

I told him the story. It is on the Propontis, and lies on low hills near the sea. We had sat down before it, and beached the ships, and at the time of lamp-lighting were at supper round the fires. The marines of the *Siren*, and of another ship, thirty all told, were on outpost between the camp and the town to guard against surprise; so we were eating with our armour on, and weapons beside us. We had just begun when Alkibiades came out through the tamarisks with his long light stride. 'Good evening, Lysis. Can you spare me a place at the fire? Here's something towards supper.' His slave put down a Chian wine-jar, and he settled himself among us. He was the best of company at such times; any troop he visited would be quoting him all next day; but tonight he was brisk, and told us no one was to turn in, but we must be ready to advance at midnight. He had got in touch with some democrats in the town, who had agreed to open the gates to him. The army was to steal up in the dark, ready to rush in, the signal being a torch held up on the wall.

'I've posted the Thracians over the hill,' he said. 'We can do this business without them. Neither god nor man can hold a Thracian in a taken town; and I passed my word, if the City paid tribute, to shed no blood.' In necessity he killed without softness; but he killed without lust, and seemed always well pleased to get what he wanted without it. Whatever had moved him against Melos (I suppose he saw what the Athenians wanted) that one day, it seems, lasted him a lifetime.

We finished supper, and were mixing the last round of wine. Below us the fires twinkled on the shore; a stade or so away, just out of bowshot, were the dark walls of the town. Night was falling. Of a sudden Lysis pointed and said, 'Did you say midnight, Alkibiades? What's that?'

The torch burned red above the gate-tower. We leaped to our feet dismayed. The army was half a mile away; most of them naked by this time, oiling and scraping-down, or mending their armour before the action. Our eyes all turned to Alkibiades. The prize was dangling, while he watched helpless with only thirty men in arms. I for one was simply waiting to hear him curse. I had heard great accounts of it.

He stood with his large blue eyes fixed upon the torch, and his brows lifted. 'These colonials,' he said. 'People who turn up to a party while one is still dressing. Someone has gone white-livered, I suppose, and rest daren't wait. Pollis, run back to camp, fall in the men, and bring them up at the double. Company, stand to arms. Well, friends, there's the signal, and here we go. Forward!'

He ran into the darkness towards the town, and we ran with him, as if it were the most reasonable thing in life. As we got to the gates they swung open; we went through into a street where the leader of the plot ran breathless by Alkibiades, explaining the untimely call. I could just see the man bobbing up and down, and Alkibiades looking about, not listening. Just as we got to the Agora, with a great noise and clatter and calling to arms, the Selymbrians came tumbling out around us.

Lysis moved up to me and set his shield against my side. I wondered if the gates were shut behind us, and thought, 'If we fall, Alkibiades will see we are buried together'; for he was not forgetful of such things. But I prickled with life, as a cat sparks in thunder; it is the man half dead who fears death. Then Alkibiades' voice, as cool as if we were at exercise, said, 'Herald, sound for a proclamation.' Our herald sounded the call. There was a pause in the dark streets, with much buzzing and muttering. 'Give this out, Herald. "The people of Selymbria must not resist the Athenians. I will spare them on that condition."'

He stood forth and proclaimed it. Silence followed. We did not breathe. Then a voice, shaken but still consequential, said, 'So you say, General; but let us hear your terms first.' Alkibiades said, 'Then show me your spokesmen.'

His impudence had succeeded. They supposed us masters of the town already; and he held them in talk long enough to make it true. We used to say of him, in Samos, that he was a young man's general.

At the end of the story, Euthydemos said, 'So you and Lysis are still together?' – 'How not? I left him at the dock, seeing the fitters.

There's no better trierarch in the fleet; if you think me partial, ask some of the others.' — 'Indeed, you never praised him, Alexias, beyond his desert. I looked for you both when the squadron came into Piraeus; but the crowds were so thick to greet Alkibiades, that I saw nothing myself but garlands and myrtle-sprays flying through the air towards the crest of his helmet.' — 'It's a pity,' I said, 'that some of this fortune that's gone on festoons and choruses wasn't handed him for ship-money instead. He's been kept short for years. If he didn't work a miracle every month, you'd have no Navy at all. Half our battles are fought for tribute; we've had to squeeze it out where it hurt sometimes, but what could we do?' — 'Well,' he said, 'I think the City is taxed to the limit as it is; let's speak of something pleasanter. I see you have lost no time in getting to the bookshops, and have bought Agathon's latest play.'

'He came into the shop,' I said, 'and I got him to sign it. Not that I set much store myself by such trimmings; it's to take back to Samos, as a present for my girl.'

Out of affection for her, I called her a girl even when she was not there. Euphro never made any great secret of her age, or of having been the mother of a son who had turned sixteen when he died. Indeed, I had met her first in the graveyard outside the city, where she had come with an offering-basket to set upon his tomb. She drew her veil on seeing me near her, out of a sense of fitness for the occasion; and this making her tread carelessly, as she leaned forward her foot slipped, and the basket spilled at my feet.

Like any man who goes much to sea, I was observant of omens; I did not care to have flung to me, in a manner of speaking, a gift meant for the dead. But when she begged my pardon, it seemed to me that her voice had a gentleness beyond the art of her calling; her dark eyes looked clear above her veil, and her brow was fair and white. I bent to pick up the oil-vase for her, and found that it had broken. It came into my mind to buy her another; so I followed her some way off, and learned where she lived. When I brought my gift, she came to the door unveiled and greeted me; not boldly, but as with an expected friend. I had never made love before with a woman who knew, or cared, what manner of man I was. I saw I had been like a man who dispraises wine, never having tasted anything but the lees.

Lysis was glad for my sake, when I told him I had found a woman to please me. When later he saw how often I went back, and how much I conversed with her, I don't think it was quite so welcome to him. His own girl was pretty, but without any accomplishments save one; when he had thoughts to share, he came to me. He was much too generous to show any jealousy; but when I quoted any opinion of Euphro's on tragedy or music he would often find occasion to disagree. With his usual goodness, he agreed to my proposal that we should entertain both our companions at a supper-room in the city; but I can't pretend this party was a great success. Lysis, though Euphro was older than he cared for himself, was pleased with her mind, and quite ready to talk politics and poetry with her, if inclined, I felt, to be a little severe. But the girl cared nothing for such things, and being besotted on him saw rivals everywhere. Upon her interrupting a story of Euphro's and saying those were days she was too young to remember, I could not forbear remarking that I, who was younger, could recall them very well. When Lysis and I met again after taking home the women, we were a little constrained at first and sat thinking it over; till suddenly we caught each other's eyes, and started to laugh.

Now, back in Athens, while the City fêted Alkibiades, we had time to meet friends, and see our homes again.

My father I found looking younger and better than when I left; and pleased, in the way of fathers, that I had got myself attached to a not inglorious corps. He for his part, having come forth boldly with Theramenes against the tyrants, and helped with his own hands to tear the traitor's gatehouse down, was enjoying some deserved consequence in the City. My mother, on the other hand, had aged more than I expected. She had miscarried of a child not long before. But since it was another girl, one could not but feel it was for the best.

Sokrates I found in the Agora, standing in Zeus' porch. His beard had more white in it, for he was past sixty now; but except that he wanted to know all that had happened to me, I might never have been away. Within a few minutes, I was neck-deep in the argument that had been going on before I got there: whether the holy is whatever the gods love, or if they love it because it is holy; whether a thing can be holy that is sacred to one god and hateful to another, or only if all the gods love it alike; what things they all love, and why. Before the end some orthodox person, who had inspired the conversation, went away scandalised, muttering to himself; which was a relief to everyone, for he was one of those who only want to prove themselves right. As for me, it was wonderful to hear again Sokrates saying, 'Either we shall find what we are seeking, or at least we shall free ourselves from the persuasion that we know what we do not know.'

I found, as you might expect after so long, some new faces about him, and one half-familiar one that puzzled me at first. It belonged to a young man of, I thought, about my age, broad and strong-looking, with intent deep-set eyes in a powerful face. I was sure he was strange to me, yet something stirred my memory; I wondered if I could have met some kinsman who resembled him. As soon as he saw me looking, he smiled at me; I returned it, but still could not place him. In stillness he had a somewhat chilling dignity; his smile however was modest, almost shy. He did not often intervene in the debate, but whenever he did, he changed the course of it; and I was struck with Sokrates' manner at such times. Not that he seemed to make much of the young man, nor treated him with that tenderness he used to show Phaedo; but he seemed to grow more than ever himself. Perhaps it was because he found his thought so quickly followed; they had to go back sometimes to let others catch up with them. While I was still puzzling my memory, he said, 'Yes, I know, Plato; but if you always take the steps in threes, one day you will miss a cracked one.'

As soon as Sokrates had gone, he strode over and grasped my hand, asking how I was and if Lysis was with me. 'I've scarcely seen you, Plato,' I said, 'since the Games. But I can see I ought to say Aristokles now.' — 'None of my friends do. If you were not still one, Alexias, I should be very sorry.'

We walked off together talking. The old-time formality which had sat on him oddly as a boy, now fitted him like good armour. I use the comparison purposely; he is a man, I think, easily wounded, but very unwilling to have it known. People meeting him first in manhood seldom suspect it, for he is very well able now to give blow for blow. You would have taken him for at least as old as I; I had seen that most of the young men about Sokrates were afraid of him.

I asked if he was still wrestling. He said, 'No, except for a friendly bout. The Isthmus cured me of that ambition. One exercises to be a whole man, not a creature bred like a plough-horse to do one thing.' He had grown much taller, and this with the change of exercise had greatly improved him; he was big, but not out of balance for his build. It was one reason for my not having known him. 'In any case,' he said, 'the Twins claim one now oftener than the palaestra.' On his arm was a spear-thrust hardly healed; since Euboea fell, the raids had got worse again.

I did not ask him how he came to Sokrates: it seemed as silly as asking an eagle how it came to fly. It was he who opened the matter to me. 'At Corinth,' he said, 'you listened so kindly to my youthful nonsense, that I probably told you I had notions of myself as a poet, and was writing a tragedy.' – 'Yes, of course; upon Hippolytos. Did you finish it?' – 'Indeed I did, and revised it again last year. I showed it to my uncle, who has often been generous in putting his good judgement at my service; he approved of it, and other friends were kind, so on their advice I decided to enter it for the Dionysia. I was so zealous about it that I got there before the bureau was opened for competitors, and stood waiting in the portico of the theatre, with my roll in my hand. Sokrates was standing there too; not in impatience, as I was, but lost in thought. I had heard of him from my uncle, who saw him often at one time, but parted company with him, I understand, upon a point of philosophy. I am speaking of course of my uncle Kritias.'

Recollecting myself, I said, 'Of course. But what about Sokrates?'

'Seeing him there, oblivious of my presence, I took the occasion to look at him. What he was meditating on, I have never asked him. But as I gazed on his face, a strange, indeed a painful quickening seized me, like a child before the birth-cry. While I was still trying to understand myself, he came out of his meditation, and looked straight at me. He walked over, and asked me if I was entering a

tragedy, and what the subject was. Then he asked me to read him
some. You may be sure I obliged him very willingly. At the end
I paused for praise, which I had not so far been disappointed in;
and, indeed, he praised it highly. Then he asked me the meaning
of a simile. I had thought it clear to any lettered person, for one
does not write for fools; but as I began to explain, I became aware
all at once that I had meant very little by it, and the little was not
very true. He asked, in the gentlest way, to hear some more; this
time he said he was in full agreement, and told me why. But much
more than his irony, his praise revealed me to myself; he had seen
in the passage something so much beyond my own conception,
that the whole work, thus regarded, fell to pieces in my hands.
I had not the shamelessness to accept his praise. I told him he
had opened my eyes; that I could not be satisfied with the work
as it was, but should take it home and re-write it. We had now
gone down from the portico and were walking together, and had
come to the central meaning round which the play was framed: the
dealing, I mean, of Theseus and Hippolytos with the gods, and the
gods with one another. All morning we talked, and at the time of
the noonday meal I went home. In the afternoon I read my tragedy
again, and my other verse. Some of the lines were not unhappy, and
the choruses did not limp in the foot. What would you say, Alexias,
of an embroidered mantle made to clothe a god, whose image was
still unshaped in the marble, scarcely the drill-holes made? I saw
that to take pleasure in this stuff was to load my soul with chains,
when wings had been offered me. So I called for a brazier, and
burned it all.'

Whatever it was I said to him, he did not seem put out by it;
so I suppose it was without offence. There met and wrestled in me
love and envy of an excellence beyond my reach. For a moment, I
think, I was a child at the music-class again, and jealous as a child.
But presently I remembered some of the lessons Sokrates had taught
me, and that I was a man. So I asked Plato if he remembered any of
his play.

I saw him hesitate. He was a poet after all, and not much above
twenty. At last he said, 'Well, there was one passage he seemed
not to think unsound. You must suppose Hippolytos has just

died; the young men's chorus invokes Aphrodite, the author of his fate.'

He repeated it. I was long silent, my soul freed of its folly, humble before the Immortals. At last, afraid I had seemed uncivil, I spoke, but could only say, 'You burned this, and you kept no copy?'

'When one offers to the gods, one brings a whole beast to the altar. If it was an image of what is not, then it was false and ought to be destroyed; and if of what is, then a little fire will not destroy it. It is nearly noon; won't you come home and eat with me?'

I was about to accept, when just as in old days the trumpet-call shuddered across the City. 'They are getting insolent,' he said. 'Forgive me, Alexias; I shall look forward to it another day.' He went off to arm himself, but not without pausing to say that the troops in Ionia had long taken the brunt of the war. His manners were always good, and I suppose he knew I had no horse now.

I had other friends to see about the City. Phaedo, when I called on him, ran up and embraced me. I was glad of this not for my sake alone. Ever since he left Gurgos', I had never known him touch anyone of his own accord; I inferred some later happiness to have been his physician. But his chief love, I found, was still philosophy. It was evident his mind had increased in power and keenness; and, after a little talk, I learned that its whetstone had been Plato. Antagonism of ideas, mixed with respect, had drawn these two together. Perhaps in the real substance of their souls, they were not so very unlike. The higher the dream betrayed, the deeper the bitterness; if the man survives, he will be on guard against dreams as a shepherd watches for wolves. Phaedo said, 'He tells me that if I don't take care, I shall spend my life clearing the ground, and never come to build. I say, of course, that he's one to start building before the foundations have settled. He's certainly nimble at meeting an objection; still, I think he'll admit to you that I've cracked his logic here and there.'

My next visit was to Xenophon. He was as much changed as anyone, yet more than ever the same. It was as if I had been acquainted before with an outline sketch of him, which the artist was now filling in as he had always intended. He was every inch the old-style Athenian knight; soldierly, well-bred, the sort of cavalryman who breeds his own horse, schools and doctors it; who prides himself on being quick in war, and in talk at the supper-table, but says he has no time for politics, meaning that his politics are set and that's the end of it. Not being one to run after new fashions, he had grown his beard. It was a curly chestnut one, as dark as his hair; smartly clipped, with the upper lip shaved after the Spartan manner. He was quite as handsome a man as he had been a boy.

He was pleased to see me, and congratulated me on having seen so much action. He himself was not long back in the City, the poorer for his ransom-money; he had been taken prisoner by the Thebans, and kept some time in chains. When I commiserated him, he said it would have been much worse but for a friend he had made there, a young Theban knight called Proxenos. Learning that they had both studied with Gorgias, this young man visited him in prison, talked philosophy with him, went surety for striking off his fetters, and did everything possible to ease his captivity. Since he had been ransomed, they still exchanged letters when they could. He spoke so warmly of Proxenos, that with almost anyone else I should have thought they were lovers; but you would be very rash to assume such a thing of Xenophon.

Our talk turning to Sokrates and his friends, I soon came naturally to speak of Plato. But I noticed at once a touch of frost upon the air. When I had time to observe and consider, I did not find this very hard to understand.

I am sure it was not mere envy. Man or boy, I have never found in Xenophon anything mean or base. He was always a practical man, honourable, religious, with a set of fixed ethics, not wrong but circumscribed. Point out to such a man a clear and simple good, and he will follow it over the roughest country you like to show him. Sokrates had taken him as he found him, loving his good heart, and not teasing his mind with formal logic beyond what one needs to detect a lie, nor with sublimities he could not soar to. He loved Sokrates: and, loving too to be settled in his mind, he liked to think the Sokrates he knew was all the man. But within Sokrates' soul, I think, was a temple in a solitude, where no one had visited him from youth to age, save his daimon who warned him of evil, and the god he prayed to. Now a foot was on the threshold. Xenophon had decided long since that Sokrates thought divine speculations better let alone; when he found he had deceived himself, it grieved him.

As for Plato, he was the last man to be insensible of dislike, or to turn it off easily. When Xenophon was there, he withdrew into his citadel, which looked like arrogance and partly was. I don't think his friendship with Phaedo went to help matters. Xenophon had always shown Phaedo courtesy, but that was as far as it went. His sense of propriety was strong; he could never quite get Phaedo's past out of his mind, nor feel quite easy in his presence. But Plato swept all this aside with the largeness of his royal blood; he preferred the aristocracy of minds. Moreover, as if these things were not enough, one never saw Xenophon paying court to a youth, nor Plato to a woman; and such extremes of nature tend naturally to discord.

As the days passed, I saw my father was a happier man than before. Here and there I heard hard things said of Theramenes; that he had consented to a good deal of tyranny and violence in the beginning, and broke away to be on the winning side when he felt the turn of the wind. Some malicious person had nicknamed him Old Sock, meaning that he would fit on either foot. I knew from his table-talk that he valued his own shrewdness; but he had been good to me, and I did not believe his detractors. Of course the oligarch leaders had called him a traitor; but since these persons were mostly skulking at Dekeleia, joining the Spartan raids into Attica, their censure was nearly as good as praise.

Lysis got out to his farm whenever he could. It was years since he had seen it, and the bailiff, though fairly honest, had had his own way too much. My father liked to see himself to what was left of ours. So I had time to walk with Sokrates, and to go about the City seeing what was new.

One day I turned into the colonnade at Mikkos' palaestra to see if my old trainer was still there. But as I entered I heard cymbals, flute and lyre, and found the boys instead of exercising were practising a dance in honour of Apollo. It was nearing the time when the sacred ship goes to Delosto to celebrate his birth. Having once danced for him myself, I stayed to watch. The senior boys seemed, as one always finds, much younger than those of my day. They had just come forward to rehearse their part of the dance, some of them carrying baskets, water-pitchers and so forth to represent the sacred objects, others green branches to wave as laurel boughs.

Upon a clash of cymbals the first line fell back, and through it leaped the second line to lead the dance in turn; and in the centre, hidden from me till then, I saw a boy. So one begins, when one means to describe someone: but while I have looked at the paper, making ready to write, the shadow has moved upon the wall. For the sake of saying something, I will note his eyes, which were of a blue more like the night sky than the day, and his clear wide brows. Mention ought also to be made of a defect he had, that his hair was grey, almost to whiteness. Some fever he had suffered had left it so; this I learned later, I forget from whom.

It was, as it seemed, a late rehearsal; for instead of the gymnasium flute-player they had the real musicians who would play for them before the god. As I looked at the face of the boy dancing, I saw it filled with the music. He was, perhaps, himself a player of some instrument, or a singer. One saw the other boys taking their time from him, for he was never off the beat, and when they danced in single file he was set to lead them. He was not, however, given any solo to perform, being perhaps not counted perfect enough in his body to please Apollo, because of his hair. But then, I thought, they should have kept him altogether away; for he being there, what god, or what man, could have eyes for any other?

The small boys next came on and the elder ones stood back; but on the face of this lad I saw the same look, calm yet sparkling, as when he had been dancing himself. I think they had not rehearsed with the music before, and the dance came to him as a picture seen by daylight, after the light of lamps. When one of the others spoke to him, he did not hear at first; then he answered smiling, without moving his eyes, watching the dance.

I stood gazing, leaning upon a column, I do not know how long, time having grown still for me, like a pool deeper than it is wide. Then during a pause for rest, one of the musicians moved as if to go; I awoke to the flux of things, knowing the practice must end soon and the boy be gone. Now for the first time I looked about the colonnade, in search of someone I knew; and, a short way along from me, I saw Plato standing alone. I greeted him, and talked a little about the dance. Then, as easily as I could, I asked him the name of this boy or that, starting with those who had danced the solos. He told me, where he knew; presently I said, 'And the grey-haired lad, the file-leader there, do you know his name?' He answered, 'His name is Aster.'

His voice was quite low; yet the boy, who all this while had not glanced my way, lifted his head upon his name, and turned towards us his sea-dark eyes. Upon this moment my memory hangs transfixed; I do not know if they smiled at one another. As, while the lightning leaps between sky and sea, the shape of cloud or wave is indistinguishable, so with their joy.

Walking away through the City, I saw I had been foolish not to watch the dance through to the end, and have the memory. For one can bear more than one supposes; and in Thrace once, when an arrow broke in me and they cut down for the barb, from having fixed my eyes on a mere bird in a tree I can see every feather still. But I had walked too far to turn back. As the pines that girdle Lykabettos touched me with their shade, I wondered what had brought me there. Then, a little higher up the mountain, where the rock feeds nothing but a few small flowers, a voice in me said, 'Know yourself.' And I perceived the truth, that one does not feel such grief for the loss of what one never had, however excellent; I grieved rather for what had once been mine. So I did not sit down upon the rocks as I had meant to do, but climbed to the peak of the mountain, where the little shrine stands against the sky. There, remembering what is due to the gods and to the soul through whose truth we know them, I lifted my hand to Zeus the Father, and vowed him an offering, because he had given Sokrates in due time his sons.

After a while I thought I would go to the City and find him; he seemed always to know when one was fit to listen and not to speak. Then I saw from the mountain the road to Lysis' farm. He had not asked me for help; yet he was short-handed, and perhaps he had only thought I would rather see friends in the City. There was always the chance, too, of a stray band of Spartans getting through the Guard. I was ashamed that I had let him go alone. So I went down, and borrowed a horse from Xenophon, and rode out to do what he might need.

22

We saw Alkibiades proclaimed upon the Pnyx supreme leader of the Athenians, a place that only Perikles had held before him; we cheered him as he stood on the great stone rostrum, his bright hair crowned with a wreath of golden olive, looking over the City like a charioteer above his team. We saw the curse pronounced against him for impiety thrown on its lead tablet into the sea; and marched with him along the Sacred Way, escorting the Procession of the Mysteries to Eleusis in King Agis' teeth; the first time since Dekeleia fell that the City had dared to send it by land. We saw him received into the great temple, like the Goddess's favourite son.

Even his enemies joined in the paean of praise, lauding his victories so that the people, who never tired of gazing, would send him off to get more. It was said in those days that he need only have whistled, and Athens might have had a king again. Had he not come when we were beaten to our knees, and oppressed with tyrants, and made us the masters of the sea? But he left for Samos again before three months were up; and when people marvelled at his modesty, we who had come with him only laughed.

We thought for our part that we could guess his mind. Nothing would content him now but to win the war. He was not moderate in any of his desires, but above all he liked to excel. It would be a sweet day for him when King Agis came suing for terms of surrender. The war had lasted twenty-three years now; he had been engaged in it, on one side or another, since he was a young ephebe, whom a sturdy hoplite, one Sokrates, had pulled out wounded from under the spears of Potidea, giving him back his life to use as he chose.

So we said goodbye to friends and kindred, and made ready to sail. Once, before I left, I went back to Mikkos' school to watch the boys at exercise. But this time my old trainer was there, and kept me talking; so it was only for a moment that I saw the boy Aster, standing with the javelin poised at his shoulder, aiming at the mark.

We sailed to Samos, and dined out with envious friends upon our news from the City, and settled down to the war again.

But lately, over in the Spartan base at Miletos, we found that there had been a change. We had profited well in the past from their stupid old custom of changing admirals every year. Sometimes the man they sent had never even been to sea before. Just lately the time had come round again. The new man was called Lysander.

It did not do nowadays, we found, to reckon on a Doric wit. He had contrived very soon to meet the young Prince Cyrus, Darius' son, a heart of fire in whom Marathon and Salamis rankled as if they had been yesterday. The Spartans he forgave; no one had lived to boast of Thermopylae. It was the Athenians who had turned the host that drank the rivers dry. So he gave Lysander money enough to raise his rowers' pay.

Neither side owned slaves enough to row a fleet. Each used free aliens mostly, who worked to make a living. Ours, therefore, began at once slipping over to Lysander. He had moved his fleet from Miletos, where we had had it under our eye, north to Ephesos. There, where a deserter from us could reach him in a day, he sat at ease, drilling his men, choosing the best rowers, and spending Cyrus' silver darics on timber and pitch.

We had all been ready to push on to Chios, whose capture would have been decisive. None of us doubted it would fall to Alkibiades; after all, he had taken it before, when it was ours. But now, with Lysander's fleet between, and not enough silver to bid against him for rowers, we must wait for money from Athens, or sail to squeeze tribute out. One does not expect a commander-in-chief to sail on such petty missions, when his mind is fixed on total victory. For the first time on Samos, Alkibiades was bored.

As men make light of the first signs of sickness, so did we of the change we began to find. We were angry with the Athenians at home, for plaguing him with despatches about the delay; the injustice put us on his side. 'Let him be merry sometimes,' we said;

'by Herakles he has earned it.' If when we wanted orders the street of the women had swallowed him up, we laughed, and saw to it for him, and said that when he had work worth while he would be there soon enough. If he was drunk, he was not silly drunk; and we put up with a good deal of insolence from him because he had a way with him even then. But we seldom saw him on the ships. The rowers we had were a rough lot, the remnant when Lysander had picked the market over; if their pay was behind, they would grumble and curse even in his hearing, knowing we dared not pack them off. He would make a joke of it, or would not hear; but I think it burned his soul, even from scum like these. He was in love with being loved, as some people are with loving.

From this cause, I fancy, more than from indolence, he came less and less aboard, and used to send his friend Antiochos instead.

I can't pretend that I disliked this man as much as some did. On the *Siren* Lysis always offered him a drink, saying to me that it was a pleasure to hear anyone talk who knew his work so well. If he was vain of his seamanship, he was a fine seaman, bred to it from childhood; he could both sail a ship and fight it, and the most villainous rowers cringed before his eye. As things were, he was much fitter for the harbour drill than Alkibiades; he had humour too, or you may be sure they would not have been friends so long. But if he got on a ship where the trierarch stood on his dignity at getting his orders through a pilot, or would not be told anything, he lost patience quickly, and was not very careful of his tongue. He had come from the people; if he did not expect to have it thrown at him in a city like Samos, I do not blame him; however, he was very much resented. The more so because Alkibiades, whose fortunes he had shared through all the years of exile, would never hear a word against him.

Presently money got so tight that Alkibiades decided he would sail out himself to collect arrears of tribute. He was taking half the fleet north to the Hellespont, and leaving the rest behind to hold the Spartans. He roused himself to inspect the ships of his squadron; then he went back to his girls again; and the news broke that he was leaving Antiochos at Samos in supreme command.

Our hut was full half the night of men standing about and

swearing, drinking our wine, and saying what they would do, with the heat of men who know they can do nothing. At length some of them decided upon a deputation to Alkibiades, and invited Lysis to lead it. 'Good luck to you,' said he, 'but count me out. I came to Samos as a lieutenant; my men promoted me by vote. I didn't equip my ship, nor fit her, nor do I pay my pilot's wage. Dog doesn't eat dog.' — 'Don't compare yourself with that fellow,' someone said; 'a gentleman is another matter.' — 'Tell Father Poseidon so next time he blows a gale. Old Bluebeard is the first democrat. And if you're calling on Alkibiades, bear in mind that he'll have all the company he needs, by this time of night.'

Some cooled off at this; but the angriest urged one another on, and went. They found him, I believe, with his favourite girl, a new one called Timandra, and in no mood to be disturbed. He told them shortly that he had been appointed to lead a democrat army, and, not having heard of any change, had given command of the fleet to the best seaman in it. This, with the blue open stare that made his insolence bite like a wind off the mountains, sent them home with flattened hackles. He sailed next day.

He called a council of the trierarchs just before he left; not to explain himself, but to tell us we were only to fight defensive actions while he was gone, and none that were any way avoidable. We were only half a fleet; and all of Lysander's was in port.

I was busy just then. The Samians were about to hold the Games of Here, and learning I was a crowned victor, called me in to help train the boys. I found I liked the work; there were some fine youngsters there, whom it was a pleasure to give advice to; so I listened with half an ear when people complained of Antiochos, and of the blunt way he told the trierarchs that they were letting the mastery of the sea slip through their fingers. Now Alkibiades was gone he got us out twice as often on manoeuvre. Lysis, and some other keen young captains who wanted to learn, did not mind it; but some of those who owned their ships were so angry at being run here and there at a pilot's orders, that they could have eaten him raw. Before long he decided that we needed an observation post at Cape Rain, across the strait, in case Lysander should try to slip north and take Alkibiades in the rear. So he took a score or so of ships, and stood across to Ionia.

It seemed to me a folly. Samos has high mountains inland, from whose tops one sees a great space of sea all mixed with sky, and the isles like dolphins swimming in cloud. We kept lookouts up there, who could very well tell us what Ephesos was up to. It was one of these very men, indeed, who rode his mule down into Samos some days later, to say that a sea-fight was going on just outside Ephesos harbour.

It had taken him some hours to get down from the mountain. We stripped for action, and stood by. Then another scout came from the hills to eastward, and reported a great smoke-plume rising from Cape Rain, as if someone were putting a trophy up.

We were not left uncertain long. Hard on this news, south through the straits limped the crippled ships, those that were left, with ragged oar-banks and started timbers, the men bone-tired with baling, the decks full of the hurt and half-drowned, picked up from the sinking wrecks. We helped the wounded to disembark, and sent out for wood to burn the dead.

After three years of victory unbroken, we had forgotten the feel of a defeat. We were the army of Alkibiades, for whom, when we entered a tavern, all other troops made way, or left, if they had lately shown their back in battle; for we were choice about whom we drank with, and made no secret of it.

Ship after ship came in, confirming the tale which at first we had disbelieved. Antiochos had sailed out of port that morning, on patrol as he said, with a couple of ships, dropped sail outside Ephesos harbour, and rowed right into it, across the prows of Lysander's beached warships, shouting insults, till the readiest put out in chase of him. The Athenians at Cape Rain, seeing an engagement going on, sent some ships to help; the Spartans reinforced their own; and this went on till both fleets were fully engaged, all piecemeal and haphazard; with such result as, considering the difference in numbers alone, might have been foreseen.

Already an ugly crowd was gathering on Samos water-front, waiting for Antiochos to come in. If he had been stoned, I don't think some of the trierarchs would have stirred to stop it.

As for Lysis and me, though we had lost good friends in the action, it had got beyond that with us. We saw that this man, who had been loyal to Alkibiades through every change of fortune for five and twenty years, would now be his ruin. After these months of idleness, his credit in Athens would never hold through this. His enemies would get at last all they had needed. So we two waited, a little ashamed perhaps of our curiosity, to see how a man would look who had done such a thing to his friend, and had yet to bring him news of it.

'Did he run mad?' I said. 'He could close-haul anyone; a planned assault, even against odds, would have given him a chance.' – 'How many trierarchs do you think would have followed him, clean against orders, if he had asked them first?' – 'They say,' I answered, 'that he has been at Alkibiades for years to give him a command. For his friend's sake, I suppose, he gave it the look of accident, not to flout his orders openly.' Lysis shook his head. 'Everyone is to blame,' he said. 'Alkibiades for giving in to him, from laziness, or out of softness for the man because he saw him slighted. The trierarchs who goaded him till he flaunted, like a green lad new to arms, to prove himself as good as they. But he himself most of all, for buying his pleasure with what was not his to spend. The trierarchs hated him, yet they stood by him in his folly; the worst of them, in the event, have shown themselves his betters. All these three years it has been our honour to stand together, to obey a sudden order without question, never to leave a hard-pressed ship without support. All this, which he held in trust, he spent in his own quarrel; and that, though I pity him, I can't forgive. For it will be flawed henceforward, as you will see.'

Just then his ship rounded the point, water-logged, dragging on splintered oars. She came in and beached, and the crowd growled and waited. The wounded were helped or carried off, and still Antiochos did not show himself. Then they brought ashore a dead body, lying on a plank. The breeze lifted the sea-cloak and showed the face. I daresay that when he saw what the end would be, he had not been very careful of his life. He had never feared death, or any man living, except Alkibiades.

The fleet was sighted a few days later, returning from the

Hellespont. There was a great crowd round him when he came ashore, and I was far back in it; but he was so tall that one could see his face over other men's heads. I saw him stare, wondering at the silence; and, when he had the news, I could have told you to the moment when he said, 'Send Antiochos to me,' and got his answer.

He stood quite still, with his blue eyes fixed and empty. He had no need to hide his face when he would hide his heart. There came back to my mind the tale of their first meeting, which I had once heard Kritias tell. There was a table, I suppose, set up in the orchestra of the Theatre, with a row of grey bankers sitting at it; the rich stiff citizens were coming up in turn with their gifts for the public chest, making the most of their progress down the aisle; the tallymen counted, the herald announced the sum, the crowd cheered, the donor bowed and went back to the compliments of his friends and sycophants. Then over the dusty grass strolled Alkibiades, and hearing the noise had a whim to see whom they could be cheering when he was not there. He walked through the pine-trees and came out above the benches, and asked what was going on; and his love of emulation quickened. So down the long stairs strode the youth, tall and strong and shining, and everyone applauded the mere sight of his beauty: it was said in those days that if swift-footed Achilles was as perfect of face and form as Homer sang, he must have looked like Alkibiades. He walked up to the board where the bankers were sitting behind their boxes, and planked down the gold he had been taking to buy a pair of matched greys for a chariot; the people yelled, and, frightened by their noise, out of his mantle flew the quail with its clipped wing, and flapped about the assembly. The bankers clicked their tongues, the rich men sulked, the people fell about the seats trying to catch the bird and win a look from its master, till in fright it fluttered out on the hillside and lodged in a fir-tree. And while everyone pointed and did nothing, up ran a young sailor with a black beard and gold earrings, and went aloft like a monkey, and fetched down the bird, and walking up to Alkibiades, gave him a bold bright look with eyes as blue as his own. So golden Achilles held out his hand laughing to Patrokles, and they walked away together through the noise and the longing faces. That was the beginning of it, and this the end.

For a moment or two he stood silent on the water-front, looking before him; then he turned and gave an order. A trumpet brayed over Samos the call to arms; the crowd broke up, seamen ran to the ships, soldiers to the camp to fetch their armour; Alkibiades strode away to his flagship. As I came back with the hoplites I saw him pacing the poop deck, back and forth, or hailing a ship that was delaying and telling them with curses to make haste. Then he gave the word to stand away; the fleet shook itself free of the land, and set sail for Ephesos. I felt my blood run warm again, the poison of defeat gone out of it; we followed him like lost dogs that have found the master and run round him barking, ready to tackle anything they see.

The Spartans were exercising before the harbour when we sighted it. But when we reached it, not one was outside the bar. Lysander had been willing to do business, when he saw victory going cheap; but he knew who was here now to drive the bargain. His ships had their orders; and in Sparta, orders are obeyed.

All day we beat up and down between Ephesos and Cape Rain, while Alkibiades waited for the Spartans to come out and give him battle. When the sun was sinking, we turned for Samos again. The lamps were lit when we got there, beckoning kindly from the harbour taverns. We beached the ship, and I said to Lysis, 'I shall get drunk tonight. Will you come?' He answered, 'I was going to propose it.'

We made a night of it, but in the end we shook off the company we had found and went off together, both feeling, I think, that we could only share with one another what was in our hearts. A grief of loss ran through us, like a tune without words. It was not so much the loss of Alkibiades; for some time past he had been slipping away from us. If you can believe that a lyre may grieve for its own music, when the poet hangs it up and leaves it for boys to play on, that was our grief.

In due course the City censured him, and relieved him of his command. They remembered enough of justice to leave it there; but none of us were surprised when, instead of returning to Athens, he sailed off alone to Thrace. He had built himself a castle there, during his comings and goings; and his enemies said that if he had ever been loyal at heart, he would not have got this bolt-hole ready. On the other hand, he knew the Athenians as a potter knows his clay.

He loved to be loved, but was shrewd enough to guess that if anything went wrong, he would pay at the rate of their expectations. They scarcely believed at home that he was mortal, or that there was anything he could not do. One might have supposed they thought that like King Midas he could make gold stones, for when it came out that on his last foray he had raided one of the subject allies, they were outraged at it; yet they had sent him nothing for months and our affairs were desperate. I for one never blamed him for building his castle; he was justified by the event. He went without saying goodbye to us; in the weeks after the battle he had become impossible; it was a kind of relief to see him go; yet when his sail dropped over the skyline, the sun shone less brightly, and the wine tasted flat.

A whole board of generals was sent out to replace him. We put ourselves in mind of our duty, and said to each other that we were there to fight the war, not to complain of everyone who could not give it the dash of an Olympic chariot-race. That was in the early days.

It was in autumn that the Spartan fleet trapped a flotilla of ours in Mytilene harbour, so that we looked like losing ships and men and Lesbos as well. To avert disaster, they reinforced our fleet with one from Athens, and we all sailed north together. Off the White Isles, on a rough grey morning, we met and beat the Spartans. It had rained and thundered in the night, and a heavy swell was getting up. We cheered when they began to fall back on Chios; none too soon either, for the wind was freshening. But some of their ships were still game; as we found when we saw one coming down on the *Siren*, to ram us on the beam.

She was a big black ship with a dragon figure-head, which opened its red mouth at us. Wind and sea were with her; and though our rowers were breaking their backs to get away, I knew we should never do it. We had rammed twice already, ourselves, in the battle.

I have yet to see a ship do it three times and get safe home, and as it was we were leaking like a basket. We dragged wallowing through the sea, while she swept down on us. I heard Lysis and the pilot shouting to the deckhands to get the spare oars and try to fend off. Then I ran to the arms-rack and took an armful of javelins, issued them to the men, and climbed up myself with the rest to the deckhouse roof, because I saw she was going to strike us on the quarter. As she came on I felt at my javelins to be sure they were sharpened well, picked out the best, twisted the thong round the shaft, and balanced it with my fingers in the loop, ready to get a good spin on it. The *Siren* was a fine ship, and we were all for selling her as dear as we could.

I marked my man, standing on the catwalk, and waited to throw till he started to climb inboard before they rammed. You can often pin a man then by the arm or thigh, and put him out for the rest of the action. He was a Spartan, in a scarlet tunic, a tall man, who had pushed his helmet back to see better. He had a good face, and I was sorry there was no one else so well placed to aim at. The ship came on, very fast, but he stayed where he was, proud and calm with a kind of exaltation in his eyes; till I almost forgot what I was waiting for, and felt like shouting, 'Get in, fool! She's going to strike!' With the heavy swell, their ram was under the water-line, but I could reckon the length. Then I thought, 'Zeus! It's the trierarch!' and brought back my arm and threw. Just as I did it, the ships struck.

There was a great shock and grinding of timbers, shouts from the deck, howls and screams from the rowers' benches below. I was thrown to my knees, and barely held on. As for the Spartan officer, I don't know if I hit him, and it made no difference. The rail of the catwalk, which is flimsy in most ships, split with the shock and over he went. His arm came out, clutching at air; then he met the green sea and sank in his armour like a stone. It may be he was their latest general, Kallikratidas, who was lost overboard in just this way during the battle; Lysander's greatest rival in war, and in honour much his superior; by all accounts, a great-hearted soldier and a thorough gentleman. If he had not been too proud to survive defeat, much might have been altered afterwards.

At all events, he died with his last work done, for the ram had gone right through our side. If it had not been for the ship's great hempen girdle, bound round her stern to stern, I think she would have split in two. As it was, as soon as the Spartans had staved us off, the sea came pouring in.

I sent a last javelin after the Spartan ship, an act of rage as useless as a child's crying; then I leaped down to get some order on deck. Lysis had gone below to deal with the rowers. I whistled up the soldiers and got them into a moving chain, baling. The seamen having the buckets, we had only our helmets to use. We slid and splashed about, while the seamen tried to fish up the ballast for throwing overboard. Our corselets hampered and chafed us; armour was not made for working; but a man who throws away his arms in battle throws away something more, as well as his reputation after. When I saw someone fidgeting with a buckle, I gave him a look that sent him back to work with a red face. It could not be long before the fleet turned back to help us; the Spartans were in flight all along the line; and no one was going to say if I could help it that the men of the *Siren* were picked up in the hour of victory looking like a rabble in flight. From below I heard Lysis' voice encouraging the rowers. I could not see him (I was standing at the hatchway, passing the filled helmets up on deck) but the mere sound of him did me good.

When the crew could not get down to the ballast any more, they started throwing the stores over, and then the spare tackle. When I saw the shields going, I looked the other way. Two or three hurt rowers had been carried up on deck. One, who had been hit by the ram itself, was clearly dying. The others had been caught by the leaded looms of the upper-tier oars, which are counterweighted because of their length, and looked badly knocked about. I caught the eyes of one of them fixed upon me, black eyes with a clear white rim; he looked as if he hated me; but men understand each other at such times for better or worse, and I knew he hated anyone with two good arms, who could save himself in the sea.

Meantime the pilot and some of the hands had got the great sail lowered over-side, and were frapping it over the breach with hawsers run below the keel. It stanched the wound of the ram, and though it was clear she was making water all over her hull, the baling did begin to gain a little. I looked about, as a wave lifted us, in search of help, but all the ships I could see were in trouble themselves. One of them went down as I watched. She settled stern first, her ram rearing up like the horn of a unicorn; then she slid backward, and the water was full of little black heads. I shouted out some nonsense to the men to take their minds off it.

Lysis now came on deck, and split us into shifts, two on and one off, to give us some rest. The men were pleased; but he had gone up first to the deckhouse roof, and I guessed it meant no help in sight yet. The slaves were working along with the rowers. Their benches were under water, but none had been lost; Lysis never kept them shackled at sea. Presently my rest turn came, and I went over to him. 'How goes it, Alexias?' he said, and then, 'You handled the hoplites very well.' He was never too much pressed to think of such things.

'The trierarch went overboard,' I said, 'for what it's worth. Did you see any of our ships?' He did not answer at first; then he said, 'Yes, I saw them. They were hull down, running before the wind.' I stared and said, 'But the enemy will be out of Lesbos the moment he gets this news. Our work's done; why don't they come for us?' – 'I daresay,' he said, 'they want to cut up the Spartans getting away.' But there was a note in his voice which I had not heard since the day at Corinth, when he lay in the temple of Asklepios.

I felt a bitterness beyond speech; presently I said, 'Alkibiades would have come back.' Lysis nodded. I said, 'How many times have we gone to help the lame ducks, and lost a prize by it?' Just then we wallowed into a wave, and shipped enough water to undo a good spell of baling. He said, 'The ship has been stripped; now it is time to lighten the men.' I knew what he meant.

He went over to the hoplites. 'Well, friends, the enemy has run. No Spartan can boast of seeing us throw away our arms. What we would not give up to men, we can offer to Father Poseidon. Gentlemen, unarm.'

I worked away at the wet straps of my armour, trying to be quick with it. He had made me a soldier, and it was his due that I should do it before him. The corselet of Archagoras, with its gold studs and its Gorgon, came away from me. I walked over the wet deck, and dropped it in the sea.

Just then Theras the pilot came up and said, 'You're none too soon, Lysis.' I looked at the weather and saw he was right. 'With your permission,' he said, 'I'll get the deckhouse broken up.' There was no need to say more; one does it at the end, to get spars for the swimmers. Lysis said, 'Very well. Break up the boat too.' We carried a little one, for places where we could not beach, to get water and stores. Theras looked at him; he said, 'How many will she take, in this sea?' – 'Four,' said Theras. 'Five maybe.' – 'She'll give planks for ten or twelve. Break her up.'

I went back to my baling again, and soon heard the crash of the axes. But presently there were other sounds. I told the men to get on without me, and ran on deck. Four of the seamen had turned their backs on the boat and their axes on their fellows. They meant to get away in her, and the riot was spreading. Already there were enough men fighting for the boat, to have swamped her if they had got in, just as Lysis had foreseen. Just then I saw him striding towards the scrimmage, unarmed.

All this was in a moment. But I remember thinking, 'Has he still such faith in men?' Amidships, below the broken deckhouse, there were a few javelins left in the rack. I snatched one up. Lysis was speaking to the men, most of whom had lowered their axes and looked ashamed. But behind him, the man whose eyes I had read beforehand was swinging back an axe-blade over his bare head. I threw, calling on Apollo. The point went deep, just left of the backbone; the weight of the axe swung the man backward, to fall upon the shaft. I think it went through his heart. All the javelins were sharp on the *Siren*. It was one of the things I saw to myself.

When they were back at work again, Lysis came over to me. 'You told me once,' he said, 'that your life was mine. You have taken back your pledge again.' I smiled and said, 'Not for long.' There was a great wave coming for us; when it broke I thought we should founder at once, but we limped on a little longer. I found Lysis' hand in mine; he had caught it to keep me from being washed overboard. He said, 'I wonder what Sokrates is talking about now.'

We looked at one another. After so much action we were short of words, and felt no need of them. I thought, 'It is finished, then: as it is now, will the god receive it.'

Someone came running over the deck to us shouting 'Land!' We stared where he pointed, at a dim grey loom of little islands, beyond the tossing seas. Lysis said to me, 'Where's the water now?' I looked into the hatchway. 'Over the second-tier benches.' He nodded, and blew his whistle to call all hands. He had just told them there was land in sight, and pointed it out to them, when the next sea hit us.

She gave a great sick stagger, heavy and dull; then she foundered, on an almost even keel, quite slowly. I think if Lysis had not shouted to me to jump, I should have stood there, to feel the deck under my feet, till the suck of her sinking pulled me after her.

I don't recall very clearly the time while I was in the water. I remember I had a bit of planking at first, but it was too slight to bear my weight and kept dipping under. I let it go impatiently, then thought, 'It was my life I threw away then; well, it is done.' I did not know east from west; the seas tossed and half choked me; I said to myself that it would be better to sink now and die quickly, but the life in me was stronger than reason and struggled on. All around me in the sea was shouting and crying; I heard someone calling again and again, 'Tell Krates not to sell the land! Not to sell the land!' till his voice was cut off in the middle. My ears roared with water; when I came up there was still shouting, though less than before; something in my head said, 'Listen, attend,' and again I thought, 'How can I? I have enough to do.' Then I listened; and the voice of Lysis was shouting 'Alexias! Alexias! Alexias!' I hailed him back and thought, 'Well, we have spoken to one another.' Then I heard a swimmer gasping near by, and spitting out water, and Lysis was there with one of the stern-oars, pushing it towards me.

I got my hands on it, then, coming to myself a little, said, 'Will it bear two?' – 'You can see it does.' It satisfied me at the time, being half-dazed, and used to believing what he said. I don't think he did more than push it along to help me forward.

We swam a long time, for days and nights it seemed to me. As weariness grew on me, my body forgot its lust to live; there was a heavy pain in my breast; and presently a time came when rest seemed the only thing beautiful and good. I was so dull of mind that I would have let go the oar, and slipped away without a word; yet at the last my soul stirred for a moment, and I said, 'Goodbye, Lysis.' Then I let go. But I felt a great tug at my hair, and rose up again. 'Hold on,' he said, 'you fool, we're close to land.' But I cared only to be still. 'I can't, Lysis. I'm finished. Let me go.' – 'Hold on, curse you,' he said. 'Do you call yourself a man?' I don't remember all he said to me. Afterwards, when I lay in the shepherd's house on the island, coming to myself, I felt my mind all bruises I could not quite account for, as a man might feel his body who had been beaten while half-stunned. I think he called me a coward. At all events, one way or another he convinced me that letting go would be like dying with a wound in the back. Later on at night, while we sat dressed in blankets, drinking black bean soup by a driftwood fire, he began to apologise, but in rather general terms, hoping I had forgotten. So when I saw what he wanted, I said I had.

We two were the only survivors of the *Siren*. Twenty-five Athenian ships were lost in the battle, the greater part of them with all hands.

It was nearly a month before we got back to the City; for the island was a little place, where few but fishermen ever put in. At last we got a Lesbian ship, and made our way back from there. I got home to find the household in mourning for me, and my father with shaven head. He looked old and ill, and was so much moved at seeing me that I was confused by it, and hardly knew what to say. I suppose he may have blamed himself for my leaving home and going to sea. For my own part, time had taught me to see in it only the conjunction of planets and the hand of fate. My mother was much calmer, and said she had dreamed I was not dead. My sister Charis danced about us on her long legs, and complained of the beard I had grown on the island, and would not kiss me till I took it off.

Later, when the house was quieter, and I had told my story, my father said the City was very angry with the generals, and had dismissed them from their command. They had written home various excuses, saying in one breath that the storm was too high for them to turn back for us, and, in the next, that they had told off two junior officers to do it. As one of these was Thrasybulos, and the other Theramenes, whom we had found perfectly reliable in the field, I guessed this must have been an afterthought when the fleet was safe in harbour. Probably half of us had gone down before they started out. Their choosing Thrasybulos as a scapegoat made me angrier then ever. I said, 'When are they going to be tried?'

'As soon,' my father said, 'as they are all back. In the interests of justice, it had better be when the passion of the mob has cooled a little.' I said, 'Let the mob save its pains, Father, and leave them to the men who got off the wrecks alive. We're too few to make a mob. We'll do them justice. I wish I had all their necks in one noose, and my hand on the rope.' – 'You have changed, Alexias,' he said looking at me. 'When you were a child, I thought you too gentle to make a soldier.' – 'I have seen a shipful of brave men betrayed since then. And on a won battlefield I threw away my arms.' And, my anger returning with the memory, I said, 'If Alkibiades had been there, he would have laughed in their faces, and told them to get to the loom with the women; and he would have sailed alone. They can say what they like; but when he led us, we had a man.'

My father sat silent, staring into the bowl of his wine-cup. Then he said, 'Well, Alexias, what you have suffered I cannot make good to you; nor, I daresay, will the gods. But in the matter of armour, if I had been in the City when you enrolled as a citizen, you would have had a suit from me, like anyone else in our position. The estate is not what it was, but I can still take care of that, I am glad to say.' He went to the big press and opened it. There was a suit of armour hanging there, nearly new. 'Take it,' he said, 'to some reliable man, and get it made to fit. It is no good to anyone lying here.'

It was a very good suit. He must have had it made when he felt his strength coming back again. I need not have complained so loudly of throwing away my arms, to a man who had been stripped of his by the enemy. 'No, Father,' I said, 'I can't take this from you. I'll manage some other way.' – 'I daresay I forgot to tell you, Phoenix is dead. Let us admit that the time when we could afford new horseflesh is over; and marching is beyond me nowadays, I find. My shield is over there in the corner. Pick it up, and try it for weight.'

I picked it up, and put my arm through the bands. It balanced well, and was just about the weight I was used to. I said, 'Of course, Father, for me it's on the heavy side. But it's a pity to tamper with a good shield like this. Perhaps, if I exercise, I can manage it as it is.'

23

Soon afterwards, our rabble of generals got back to Athens; all but two who, making use of their skill in avoiding dirty weather, ran away to Ionia and never came home.

Not since the day of the Herm-breaking had I seen such anger in the City. As it happened, the Feast of Families fell just before the trial. Instead of the usual garlands and best clothes, you saw everywhere the drowned men's kindred, dressed in mourning, their heads shorn, reminding friends and neighbours not to forget the dead.

Presently came the day of the trial. I walked to the Assembly with my father; when I had been civil to his friends, I slipped off to find Lysis, but got caught instead in a knot of citizens, kinsmen and friends of the drowned, who begged my account of the battle. I think it was only now, with strangers about me, that I really knew my own bitterness. I told them everything, both what I had seen, and anything I had heard from others.

It was the same all over the Pnyx; people jostled to get near one of the survivors, for we were few. The herald could hardly get quiet when the speeches began.

Nobody felt inclined by now to waste much time on these fellows. When the prosecution proposed that one hearing would do for all six of them, I cheered with the best. I felt warmed with the anger round me; everyone seemed my friend. Then the defence jumped up and made a fuss. It was true there was something in the constitution against collective trails on a capital charge, proper enough, in the ordinary way, to protect decent people; but we all felt this was different. There was a good deal of noise. Just when the defence had made itself heard again, there was a commotion near the rostrum, and a sailor ran up.

You could tell at a glance what his trade was, and there was a pause.

'You'll excuse me, friends,' he said, using a sort of hail, I suppose the only way he knew to make his voice carry, 'for putting myself forward; but I took my oath. I was bosun's mate on the old *Eleutheria*. All I've got to say is, when she went down, I caught hold of a meal-tin, and it kept floating. There was a lot of my mates in the sea all about, and some of the marines, wounded mostly, and knew they couldn't last long. I heard someone shout out, "Antandros," that's my name, "Antandros, if you get home, tell them we did right by the City." And another says, "And tell them what we got for it. Drowned like dogs. You tell them, Antandros." And I took my oath, which a man ought to abide by. So you'll pardon the liberty. Thank you.'

He went running down from the rostrum; there was a moment's silence, then a roar you could have heard at Eleusis. Someone shouted out that anyone who opposed the will of the people ought to be tried himself, along with the generals. We cheered our throats dry. It felt like giving the paean, or being drunk at the Dionysia, or like the last lap of the race when the crowd wants you to win. But not quite like.

So it was put to the presiding senators, whether the trial was in order, and there could not be much doubt of what their verdict would be, if only for their health's sake. But they seemed to be a long time about it; people began to whistle and call; till at length the crier stood up, and gave out that they could not agree.

Where I was, we could not see them; but we made ourselves heard; especially when word was passed along that only one old man was standing out. We were asking only one life each from these cowards, who bore the guilt of hundreds; and they would die in more comfort than our friends in the rough autumn sea. People were asking each other who was this senile quibbler to set himself up a little jack-in-office chosen by lot for the day. 'Has he ever carried a shield?' someone shouted; and I said, 'I suppose he has no sons.' – 'Who is it?' we called to those who were nearer. A voice shouted back, 'Old crackpot Sokrates, son of Sophroniskos the sculptor.'

As the shock of an icy stream to the drunkard stumbling and singing; as the alarm of battle to a man sweating in the bed of lust; so these words came to me. The noise and heat died in me, leaving me naked under the sky. I had been many, but now I was one; and to me, myself, grey-eyed Athene spoke from the High City, saying, 'Alexias, son of Myron, I am justice, whom you have made a whore and a slave.'

When I came back from the silence within me, and heard the noise going on just as before, I could not believe it. I had felt that everyone's eyes must have been opened in the same moment as mine. I looked about me, but the faces were all as before shouting with their mouths open, all alike, like a sounder of hogs.

I turned to the man beside me. He looked like a person of some schooling, a merchant perhaps. 'We are wrong,' I said. 'We ought not to overthrow the law.' He turned round and snapped at me, 'What do you know about it, young man?' – 'I was there,' I said. 'My ship was sunk in the battle.' – 'All the more shame to you,' he said, 'for taking the fellow's part. Have you no feeling for your shipmates?' Soon afterwards, the crier gave out that since only one senator opposed the motion, the others had passed it without him.

I dropped a white pebble in the urn, and, as it left my hand, tried to think that it made me clean.

Lysis overtook me on the slope below the Pnyx. Always my example in courage, it was he who spoke first.

'You know,' he said, 'how the wind comes down in those parts, from the hills of Ionia; blowing a gale, when a mile away it's no more than a capful. It might even be true that the storm prevented them.' I said, 'Alkibiades would have come.' – 'Yes, if he had a pilot. The truth is, Alexias, our navigation's not what it once was. Even in my few years I've seen a change. Alkibiades knew, and Antiochos. These new men are about the common run of captains now. One of them was wrecked himself. We have killed them as a child kicks the bench it bruised its shin on. What has become of us?'

'I have done injustice,' I said. We were shouldered as we walked by men disputing, and justifying themselves; but some were laughing, and betting on a cock-fight. After being a long time silent, he said, 'Madness is sacred to the gods. They give it us at the proper season to purge our souls, as they give us strong herbs to clean out our bodies. At the Dionysia we are a little mad; but it leaves us clean, because we dedicated it to a god. This we offered to ourselves, and it has defiled us.'

'Don't talk so, Lysis. I'm sure you kept your head much better than I did.' He smiled, and quoted a certain phrase, recalling a personal matter between us. Then he said, 'Am I getting old, to find myself always thinking, "Last year was better"?' – 'Sometimes it seems to me, Lysis, that nothing has been the same since the Games.' – 'We think so, my dear, because that was our concern. If you asked that potter over there, or that old soldier, or Kallippides the actor, each would name his own Isthmia, I daresay . . . It has been a long war, Alexias. Twenty-four years now. Even Troy was only ten.'

We were crossing the Agora just then; he pointed to some women at a stall and said, 'When that child was born, it had lasted already as long as Troy, and now she is almost a woman.' His voice must have carried more than he meant, for the maiden looked up, and stared at him. He smiled at her, and she parted her lips in answer, her face lightening for a moment; she was in mourning, and looked peaked and pale. The woman with her, who did not seem like her mother, spoke sharply to her, though one could see she had only thought as a child does. I said to Lysis, 'She must have lost her father in the battle.' He looked after her, over the heads of the crowd, and said, 'Yes, and the last of her brothers too. There were three.' – 'You knew them, then?' – 'Oh, yes. I even know the child herself. She almost spoke to me, till she was reminded she is older now. She is Timasion's daughter, who was trierarch of the *Demokratio*.'

Meanwhile the child was being led away through the market. You could tell from their backs that the woman was scolding her still. Lysis said, 'What will become of her, I wonder? That sour-faced bitch is the eldest son's widow, I suppose. It's a hard time of life to make such a change. She had a slapdash kind of upbringing; the mother, who is dead now, was usually sick, and little Thalia seemed to be always with her father or the young men. Up to last year, even, they no more thought of sending her out when I came than a hand-reared pup; you know how it is sometimes with a late-born child. One son was killed at Byzantium, and one here in Attica in a raid. Then Timasion and the last boy went out just now with the Athenian flotilla. That finished the family, except for this poor little remnant.'

He walked on in thought. When presently I spoke to him he did not hear. 'She was quite pretty,' he said, 'before this happened; at least, she had a good little face. That woman will get her off her hands to the first offer, I suppose, no matter whom . . . They were good stock, Timasion and his sons. I knew them all.'

'Lysis!' I said, staring at him. 'What are you thinking of? She doesn't look more than twelve years old.' He reckoned on his fingers. 'Well, she was born three Olympics ago, the year Alkibiades won the chariot-race; so she must be rising thirteen, at any rate.' Then he laughed and said, 'Why not? One can have patience in a good cause; there are plenty of women meanwhile. Look how much better a horse is, if you have him from a colt.' After a moment I said, 'Well, then, why not, Lysis, if you think so?' I recalled all my anticipations, so different from this; and yet, as soon as one thought, it was exactly like him.

'She will have a small portion, I suppose,' he said, 'so that neither of us will be too much beholden to the other. My sister Niko will teach her the things she has probably not learned at home. I shall take a small house, not scrape to live in the big one. If things improve later, so much the better, it makes a woman respect one more than the other way.' He went running on like this; you would have thought he had had it in mind for weeks. 'What month are we in?' he said. 'I suppose we might as well have the wedding in Gamelion, like everyone else.'

'You don't mean,' I said staring, 'this next Gamelion, do you?' – 'How not? She can have everything ready in three months, surely?' – 'I thought you meant just to get contracted to her now. She's quite a baby.' – 'Oh, I shall have to marry her at once, I can see that. It will be the only way of doing anything with her. As she is whatever defects her upbringing had, she has got its virtues. They taught her good manners, courage, and to speak the truth, if they didn't teach her embroidery. Why turn her over for a year to that pinch-lipped vixen, who will make her sly and prudish and mealy-mouthed, and full of old midwives' nastiness? I wonder if Gamelion is soon enough.'

Recalling the scene in the Agora, I saw what he meant. He said, 'I could tell just how she felt when she saw me, as if she had come on a bit of furniture, or a dog, that brought back her home to her. I told her the story of Perseus when she was six years old.' – 'What are you waiting for?' I said. 'Get your winged boots, and unchain her before the dragon arrives.' He laughed and took my arm and said, 'Bless you, Alexias, I think I will. I suppose today has set me thinking. Since this war began we have spent more than silver; more than blood even; something of our souls. Last time I went up to the High City, I thought even the Maiden herself looked tired. It's time to think of making a son, to start out fresh for the next lap . . . I must get Niko to call.'

Two days later he gave me his sister's report. She had quite taken, he said, to the little Thalia, and did not think her really backward for her age. It was the shock of her loss, and homesickness, Niko said, that had driven her in upon her childhood. Niko reported the sister-in-law not quite such a shrew as Lysis called her; pointing out with some justice that no decent person in charge of a young girl would let her smile at men in the market. But she was a silly woman, set in her ways, and without much feeling, and trying to give the girl three years' training in a month, had made her so nervous she could not pick up a distaff without breaking the thread. 'She thinks the world of you, Lysis, and was going to repeat to me the kind things she had heard her father say of you, only to give me pleasure, for she has a natural sweetness one feels at once. But she was called to order, and shown her own forwardness. I felt so sorry for the poor child; it hadn't crossed her mind till then that my call concerned her, and not one word more could I get from her, you can be sure.'

The head of the household was an ancient grandfather, deaf and so nearly blind that he took Lysis for a youth, because he had no beard. But at last things were settled, the dowry agreed on, and he went with his sister to see the girl.

'At first,' he said, 'I couldn't get her to look at me. Poor little creature, I never saw such a change. One used to hear her from the courtyard, singing about the house. But clever Niko got her sister-in-law upon the iniquities of slaves, which gave me a little time. I told her how well her father did in the battle; she can follow anything you like of that kind. Then I reminded her of our old acquaintance, and said she would find my house a little more like home. She started to look rather less wretched; but I could see that bitch had been at her, putting her in a panic; so I said, "Now you must listen to me, for you've known me longer than any of them. The snatching-up and running at the feast is a game we shall play to amuse the guests, who think it is the best part of a wedding. But the rest can wait," I said, "till we've time to make friends. That's our first secret; now we'll see how you keep it." She looked much better when we left, almost as I remember her.' Niko persuaded him, however, to wait for the turn of the year, and marry in Gamelion, as he had first planned. She said, sensibly enough, that Thalia would be turned fourteen by then, which was really the earliest he could take such a young girl to his house without people talking.

He told me he did not mean to look for another ship; it would be a long time in any case before the fleet was up to strength. He would drill with his tribal regiment (which was mine too), settle down, and farm his land when the Spartans would let him.

I too felt that my place was in the City. My father was not well; a tertian fever he had brought from Sicily often troubled him; when the bout was on he could not do business, or attend to the farm. Not only duty but inclination drew me; for I had been long out of the City; my wits were getting rusty with the sea, and smoked from the watch-fire, and the schoolboys of yesterday were young men, making their voices heard on the colonnades.

So I came back to philosophy, but differently; feeling it in myself and in those I met in talk, a fever of the blood. I had come to it as a boy from wonder at the visible world; to know the causes of things; and to feel the sinews of my mind, as one feels one's muscles in the palaestra. But now we searched the nature of the universe, and our own souls, more like physicians in time of sickness.

It was not that we were in love with the past. We were of an age to feel the present our own, and to suppose it would never outstrip us. In painting and sculpture and verse, the names we grew passionate over looked to us as big as those of Perikles' day, and it still half surprises me when I find them unknown to my sons. But we seldom stood to enjoy good work, as one stands before a fine view or a flower, in simple gladness that it is. As we hailed each new artist we grew angry with the former ones, as with false guides we had caught out; we hastened, though we knew not where. To freedom, we said; the sculptors no longer proportioned their forms by the Golden Number of Pythagoras, as Pheidias and Polykleitos did; and art would do great things, we said, now it had cast off its chains.

Euripides was dead; he would suffer with our doubts no more, nor grieve with our losses. And Agathon had gone to Macedon, as the guest of the rich King, who dreamed of civilising his wild hillmen. For months we used to wonder, laughing, how our sweet singer was getting on up north, and picture him seeking among the rude youth for one whose conversation was not quite confined to women, horses and war. Then one day a traveller brought news that he was dead. It is ill to fall sick among barbarians. After he was gone, even Aristophanes had a kind word for him.

Only Sokrates was unchanged, unless he looked a little younger. His rough-tongued Xanthippe, tamed by kindness or mellowed with time, now that she drew near the end of child-bearing had borne him two more sons. This, if it was more than he had bargained for, he took very cheerfully. He was as ready as the youngest of us to question fixed opinions, and the youths growing up came to him just as we had done, and worried at logic like puppies, tearing things up in the search for truth.

The north had taken Agathon, the gentle singer, but it had given us something back. Kritias had returned from Thessaly to the City.

He had fled there some time after the Four Hundred were overthrown, when some of his doings came to light. In Thessaly the landowners are like little kings, always at petty war. He found good fishing in this muddy water. Presently he learned that there was some discontent among the serfs, for the law in Thessaly does not take much account of poor men. So he intrigued with their leader and got them arms and plotted a rising to suit his plans. It was put down, I believe, with a good deal of bloodshed; but Kritias got safe away. I am sure that in the beginning he was an inspiration to them, and made them feel themselves the darlings of Zeus. Sokrates used to teach us that the human images of the gods contain the shadows of truth, but the lover of philosophy must look through and beyond. From this, I think, Kritias, following his nature, had inferred that religion and law are good for fools, but the superior man is above them. However, I do not pretend that in Kritias' case I am capable of justice.

He passed me about this time in the street, and half-remembering me I suppose in some connection not pleasant to him, gazed, trying to place me. I don't know whether he succeeded; but even the Spartans I had met in battle, seeing only my eyes through my helmet-slits, had looked at me more as man looks at man.

But having pronounced all these opinions, I ought to confess they are worth as much as if a man with fever were to judge of wine. On my last visit to the City, I had caught a sickness I had thought was cured. Now, the cause being near again, I learned it had been sleeping and growing in its sleep.

In this the god was kind to me, that from the start he never tormented me with hope. Nor did he poison his arrows; for what seemed at first sight to be beautiful and good, seems so to me until this day. Being now turned seventeen, he had left Mikkos' school, and was often with Sokrates. There I avoided him, for many reasons; but where music was, he would not be far away. So my memories are set to the kitera, the syrinx, or to a concert of flutes, or clear voices singing; even now sometimes a chord or a descant can make me smell scented oil and bay-leaves, or grass and burning pitch, and torchlight flickers on the stillness of his listening eyes.

Only once I was in danger. In a night of early winter I had walked out on Lykabettos, when the peak stood black against thick-sown stars. Pausing for breath, a little below the summit, I saw on the terrace of the shrine his shape with lifted head, scanning the heaven. For he had the bent towards mathematics and astronomy, that one often finds in musicians. The belt of Orion was above him, and at his shoulder the sword.

I stood on the rocky pathway, between my will and my soul. I had taken the first step, and the second, upon the path, when I saw he was not alone. I was barefoot, so they had not heard me; I was able to get down into the woods again, where a few lamps shine between the pine-boughs, and a few stars. All in all, it is clear that the god took good care of me; and to show I am not ungrateful, on a certain day each year I bring him a pair of doves.

Lysis' marriage was itself a good to me; for nothing could have given me any escape from myself just then, except the serious concerns of someone so dear. I could not intrude a grief he must have put down, if he had noticed it, to a kind of jealousy unworthy of a friend or a man. Being forced to lay it by, I could forget it sometimes and share his happiness. For he was just as happy, it seemed, as a man looking forward to a proper wedding night. I helped him find a little house in the Inner Kerameikos, not far from ours, and furnish it with some of his father's things. He sold a bronze by Alkamenes to buy music and garlands for the feast. 'I should like her to enjoy it,' he said. 'After all, I daresay it's the only wedding she'll have.'

Xenophon confided to me his hearty approval of the match. 'When I marry myself,' he said, 'that is just about the age I shall look for; before they get their heads full of notions, and while there is still time to train them in orderly ways. I can't endure things higgledy-piggledy, and nothing in its place. Order is the first half of a decent life.'

Then it seemed that one moment we were all saying, 'Only a week, Lysis,' and the next it was the wedding morning.

There had been snow in the night. It lay on the roof-tops, under a bright pure sky, thin, hard, and glistening; whiter than marble of Paros, whiter than our wedding robes. The lion-head rain spouts on the temple roofs had beards of crystal a cubit long; the red of baked clay looked dark and warm, and white plaster like curded cream. Helios shone far off and high, giving no heat from the pale heaven, only the flash of his silver hair. When we led the bridegroom to the house of the bride, the lyre-strings snapped with the cold, and the flutes went flat; but we covered it with our singing. Our breath rose in the frosty air in little clouds, in time with the song.

I can't remember ever to have seen Lysis look better. His wedding mantle of white Milesian wool was trimmed with a border two spans deep of pure gold bullion, which his father and grandfather had been married in before him. We had brought him ribbons, of red, blue and gold, and crowned him with myrtle, and with the violets one finds by their scent in new-fallen snow. He strode up to the bride's house, laughing and glowing with the cold. His tunic was pinned at the shoulder with a great brooch of antique goldwork from Mycenae, a gift to some ancestor from Agamemnon, as the story ran. His hair and his garland, and the ribbons on his arm, sparkled with snowdust blown off the roofs. When we came into the guest-room, where the bride was sitting at the old man's side, you could see her little face, framed in its veil of saffron, turn as you watched all into great eyes.

The women swept her up for kisses and whispers. She had good manners, as Lysis had said; but at every pause, as if her eyes had been let out of school they went slipping across. Once he saw it, and smiled straight across at her, and the women all sighed and murmured 'Charming!' Only the sister-in-law leaned forward, to hiss in her ear. She blushed crimson, and shrank up like a rose trying to grow backwards and fold itself away. I think there were tears in her eyes. For a moment I saw in Lysis' face a look of such anger that I thought he was going to make a fool of himself and embarrass everyone. I twitched his mantle, to remind him where he was.

Then the feast was called, and they sat down together between the women and the men. He spoke to her smiling, but she answered in a dying whisper, and pushed her food about her plate. He mixed her wine for her and she drank when he told her to, like a child at the doctor's; and, indeed, the medicine seemed to do her good.

The steward signalled me at the door; I went out and found the bridal car waiting. Everything was in order, the horns of the oxen gilded, the wreaths and ribbons properly put on, and the canopy fixed. It was snowing again; not like meal as before, but like large feathers.

They played us out, and shouted their nonsense; I clambered

aboard, Lysis lifted up the bride to me and got in. We started off, he and I, and the girl between us. She shivered as the cold struck her; he pulled the sheepskins higher, and put his arm with a fold of his cloak about her shoulders. I felt a sudden rush of the past upon me; for a moment grief pierced me like a winter night; yet it came to me like an old grief, I had suffered it long since and now it was behind me. Everything is change; and you cannot step twice into the same river.

The cold was sweet and mild, not like the cold of the morning; it would thaw before dawn. Lysis said, 'Well, Thalia, you were a very good girl, and I was proud of you.' She looked up at him. I could not see her face. He said, 'This is my best friend Alexias.' Instead of murmuring a greeting into her lap in the proper way, she lifted her veil, and smiled. Her eyes and her cheeks were bright in the torchlight. I had wondered before if it was wise of Lysis to give her a second cup of wine. 'Oh, yes, Lysis,' she said, 'you were right, he *is* more beautiful than Kleanor.'

It was the fresh air, I suppose, after the warmth inside. I saw Lysis blink for a moment; then he said cheerfully, 'Yes, I always said so, didn't I?' He caught my eye, asking me to be kind. I laughed and said, 'Between you you'll make me vain.'

She said to me, in the voice I suppose she had heard her mother use to visiting ladies, 'I have heard Lysis speak of you often. Even before he went to sea, while I was still quite young. Whenever he called, my brother Neon would always ask how you were. Lysis would say, "How is Kleanor?" or whoever his best friend was just then. But Neon always said to Lysis, "How is beautiful Alexias?" and Lysis would say, "Still beautiful."'

'Well,' said Lysis, 'now you see him. Here he is. But you must talk to me now, or we shall be falling out.' She turned round, not a moment too soon. It was lucky we had the canopy; hardly anyone had seen. 'Oh, no! You must never quarrel with Alexias, after so long.'

We went jolting on through the wheel-ploughed slush, while in the glow of the torches the snow floated like great flakes of fire. People in the street bawled the age-old jokes about the month of long nights and so forth; and from time to time I stood up in the car and shouted back the age-old answers. When we got near the house he leaned over, and whispered to her not to be afraid. She nodded, and whispered back, 'Melitta said I must scream.' Then she added firmly, 'But I told her no.' – 'I should say not indeed. What a vulgar notion.' – 'And besides, I said to her, I am a soldier's daughter.' – 'And a soldier's wife.' – 'Oh, yes, Lysis. Yes, I know.'

When the time came, and he picked her up at the end of the bride-song, she put up her arms smiling, and caught him round the neck. As I ran after to keep the door for them, I heard a couple of old hens by the wall clicking their tongues, censuring her shamelessness.

Next day I called to see him. There seemed no reason why I should wait till the late hour custom prescribes, so I got there quite early before market-time, to be ahead of the rest. After some delay he came in, half-awake, the perfect picture of a bridegroom next morning. When I apologised for disturbing him, he said, 'Oh, it's time I was up. But I was talking to Thalia till all hours. I had no notion, Alexias, how much sense she has, and grace of mind. She'll make a woman in ten thousand. Don't speak too loud, she's still asleep.'

'Shouldn't she be about her work,' I said, 'at this hour?' Seeing me look at him, he laughed a little shamefacedly. 'Well, she was awake fairly late. She looked such a child, I sat down by her to talk her to sleep, thinking she might be scared alone; but I must have dropped off first in the end, for when I woke, I found she had got a new blanket out of her bridal chest, and laid it over me.'

I said nothing, since it was no business of mine. He said smiling, 'Oh, yes, I can hold my horses till starting-time. With me it takes two to celebrate the rite of Aphrodite; I'd as soon lie with Athene of the Vanguard, shield and all, as a woman I don't please. I know what the child needs of me just now, better than she knows herself. I daresay it won't be for long.'

Certainly as time passed he looked well and happy; and one day later in the year, when he had asked me to sup, as I stood in the little porch I heard from within the sound of a young voice singing in time to some work or other, like water tinkling in the shade. Lysis said, 'You must forgive the child. I know a modest woman shouldn't tell her whereabouts to the guests; but when I see her happy, I can't bear to trouble her with such things. She had enough of that from her brother's wife; I gave her a good present, the bitch, and forbade her the house. There's plenty of time. Her modesty is in her soul. We'll attend to the outside later.'

It was a beautiful golden evening. The small supper-room just held four couches, but looked better with two. There were garlands laid out, of vine-shoots and roses. 'Thalia made them,' he said. 'She sulks if I buy made-up stuff in the market.' It was dressed sword-fish for supper. I was not very hungry, but I did my best because I could see he was proud of it. We talked about the war, which was largely at a standstill. The Spartans had given Lysander another year of command, against their custom, and he was getting money from Cyrus again.

'Don't you care for the fish?' he asked. 'She said I must ask you if the sauce was sharp enough.' – 'I never tasted better. I heard some news on the way that spoiled my hunger. Those two triremes the Samian fleet took the other day; do you know what became of the rowers? They pitched them off a cliff into the sea. That will teach them to work for a side that can afford to pay them.'

He stared at me silent; then said 'Zeus! And when one thinks what was said at the start of the war, when the Spartans did it . . . I suppose you don't remember. We're improving daily; the last proposal was that enemy rowers we caught should have their right hands cut off, or was it both thumbs? I got some black looks in Assembly for voting against it. I'm glad we're out of the Navy, Alexias. Everything one hears from Samos sounds bad.'

The fleet had done nothing for months. The generals did not trust each other, and the men did not trust the generals; rumours were always drifting home that one or other was taking bribes, the kind of talk that had made trouble among the Spartans at Miletos. There was poison in the mere knowledge that the gold was there. 'Konon is sound,' I said. – 'One man in a dozen. I wonder what Alkibiades thinks in that hill-fort of his. They say it looks over half the Hellespont. He must laugh sometimes from the top of his walls.'

'It's Salamis Day,' I said. 'Seventy-five years today since the battle.

Don't you remember how he used to give out a wine-issue? It was on Salamis Day he told that story about the Persian eunuch.' We laughed, and then fell silent together. In the pause I heard again the singing in the house, but softly now; she must have remembered there was company.

'You're not drinking,' he said. The slave-boy had cleared the tables, and gone. – 'No more for a while, Lysis. I'm as merry now as wine will make me.' I found him looking at me. 'It's a deep sadness,' he said, 'that goes in fear of wine.' – 'Are you coming to the race tomorrow? Kallias says the bay will win.' – 'It's the way of the world, it seems. If there's a man one would sooner do a good turn to than any other, that's the man one will see eating his heart out for what one can't give.' – 'Have you known long?' I asked. – 'No matter. No one else knows. Can't you find a woman again, like the one you had in Samos?' – 'I'll look one day soon. Don't think of it, Lysis. It's a madness. It will pass.' – 'You should marry, Alexias. Yes, I know advice is cheap, but don't be angry with me. If a man . . .'. His voice ceased. We both put our wine-cups down, and got up from our couches, and ran to the door. The street was empty. But the noise drew nearer, streaming like smoke, blowing in great gusts upon the wind.

It was not a wail, nor was it a groan, nor the keening women make for the dead. Yet all these had part in it. Zeus gives good and evil things to men, but mostly evil; and the sound of sorrow is nothing new. But this was not the grief of one or two, or of a household. It was the voice of the City, crying despair.

We looked at each other. Lysis said, 'I must speak to the child. Ask someone what it is.' I stood in the porch, but no one passed. Inside the house he was talking quietly. As he left I heard him say, 'Finish your supper, keep busy, and wait for me.' She answered steadily. 'Yes, Lysis. I'll wait.'

A man shouted something far up the street. I said to Lysis, 'I couldn't make sense of it. "Everything lost," he said; and something about Goat's Creek.' – 'Goat's Creek? We beached there once, when we sprang a plank. Half-way up the Hellespont, just north of Sestos. A village of clay huts, and a sandy shore. Goat's Creek? You must have heard wrong. There's nothing there.'

In the streets we saw no one, except a woman sometimes, peering from a door. One, forgetting her decency in her fear, called out to us, 'What is it, oh, what is it?' We shook our heads and went on. The noise was from the Agora, like an army in rout. An echo seemed to go on beyond, into the distance. It was the sound of crying upon the Long Walls, throbbing between the City and Piraeus like a pain along a limb.

A man met us in the street, coming from the Agora. He was beating his breast as he ran. When I caught him by the arm he stared like a trapped beast. 'What is it?' we said. 'What news?' He shook his head, as if we had not spoken Greek. 'I was at Melos,' he said. 'Oh, Zeus, I was at Melos. Now we shall see it here.' He plucked his arm free, and ran on towards his home.

Where the street ran into the Agora, it was plugged at the neck with men trying to shoulder through. As we joined the press, a man coming the other way squeezed out towards us. He stood for a moment, staggered and fell down. 'What news?' we shouted at him. He leaned over and vomited stale wine. Then his head lolled round at us. 'Long life to you, trierarch. Is this the street for the women?' Lysis said, 'This man's a rower off the *Paralos*.' He shouted in the fellow's ear, 'Answer me, curse you,' and shook him to and fro.

The man reeled to his feet, muttering, 'Aye, aye, sir.' – 'What news?' we asked. He wiped his mouth on the back of his hand, and said, 'The Spartans are coming,' and spewed again. When it seemed that all his drink was out of him, we dragged him over to a public water-tap in the street, and drenched his head. He sat on the slab of the fountain, his arms hanging. 'I was drunk,' he said. 'I spent my last obol, and now you've sobered me.' With his face in his hands he wept.

Presently he came partly to himself and said, 'I'm sorry, sir. We've been at the oar three days, with this ahead of us, bringing the news. The fleet's destroyed, sir. Someone sold us to Lysander, by our reckoning. Caught on the beach at Goat's Creek; no help, no cover, nothing. Rubbed out, finished, rolled up like a book.'

'But what were you doing there?' said Lysis. 'It's two good miles from Sestos; there's no harbour and no supplies. Were you driven aground?' – 'No, the fleet made camp there.' – 'At Goat's Creek? Made camp? Are you drunk still?' – 'I wish I was, sir. But it's true.'

He rinsed his face in the fountain, wrung the water from his beard, and said, 'We got word Lysander had taken Lampsakos. We followed him up the Hellespont, past Sestos to the narrows. Then we camped at Goat's Creek. You can see Lampsakos from there.' – 'Great Poseidon!' said Lysis. 'And Lampsakos can see you.'

'We put out in the morning in battle order, to meet Lysander. But the old fox kept to earth. Next day the same. Then rations ran out. We had to walk over to Sestos market, after we'd beached the ships. Four days this went on. The fourth evening we'd just beached again, when we heard a hail. There was a man riding down from the hills; not a country fellow; a good horse, and a night's seat on it. The sun was setting behind him, but I thought, "I've seen you before." There was some young officers looking; all of a sudden they went running as if they were mad, up the road to meet him, shouting out, "It's Alkibiades!"

'They caught on to his feet, his horse, anything they could lay hold of. One or two, I thought they were going to break down and cry. Well, it was always meat and drink to him to be made much of. He asked after this man's father and that man's friend; you know, sir, how he never forgot a face; and then he said, "Who's in command?"

'They told him the generals' names. "Where are they?" he says. "Take me to them. They must get off this beach tonight. Has the fleet run mad? Four days now," he says, "I've watched you stick out your arse for Lysander's toe, and I can't stand it longer. What a station, by the Dog, to take in face of the enemy. What a camp, look at it; not a guard posted, not a ditch. Look at the men, straggled from here to Sestos. You'd think it was Games Week at Olympia."

'Someone took his horse, and he went to the generals' tents. They came out to see what the noise was. They didn't look as pleased as the young men, not by half. Hardly gave him good evening, and didn't as much as offer him a drink. Do you know, sir, what it was that shook me first? It was hearing him so civil to them. He was never a man to bear being made light of; he could always give better than he got. He put the case to them about the camp, very quiet and serious. "Didn't you see today," he says, "the Spartan picket-boats watching your beach? Lysander mans his ships each morning, and keeps them manned till dusk. If he's waited till now it's because he can't believe it. He's afraid of a trap. When he gets word the men don't keep camp at night, do you think he'll wait longer? Not he; I know the man. Every minute you sit here now, you're staking the fleet and the City with it. Come gentlemen, you could be in Sestos tonight."

'They'd kept him standing outside, so there were plenty to listen. I heard General Konon say into his beard, "Just what I told them." Then Tydeus, one of the new generals, steps out. "Thank you kindly, Alkibiades," he said, "for teaching us our business. You're the man to do that, we all know. Perhaps you'd like to take the fleet over; or perhaps there's another of your cup-companions you'd care to leave it to, while you run about Ionia chasing women. What were the Athenians thinking of, I wonder, when they put us in command instead of you? Still, they did it. You've had your kick at the ball. Now it's our turn, so a very good day to you."

'His colour came up then; but for all that, he kept his head. Cool and slow he spoke, with that drawl of his. "I've wasted my time," he said, "and yours too, I can see. Two things I respect Lysander for: he knows how to raise money, and where to spend it." Then he turned his back and walked off, before they found their tongues to answer.

'You could hardly get near for the crowd seeing him off. When they brought up his horse, he said, "There's no more I can do, and if I could, I'd see them to Hades first. They're the losers," he said. "I've still a friend or two across the straits. I could have given Lysander troubles of his own in Lampsakos. I'd only to sound the trumpet on my keep, to have raised three thousand Thracians. They called no man master before, but they fight for me. I'm king in these parts," he said. "King in all but the name."

'He sat on his horse, looking out over the water with those wide-open blue eyes of his; then he wheeled and rode off into the hills, where his castle was.

'That night our Old Man on the *Paralos* stopped all shore leave.

So did General Konon, on his eight ships. But the rest went on the same as they'd done before. And the next night, the Spartans came.'

While our minds limped like spent runners behind the tale, he told us of the battle, or the slaughter rather: Lysander's fleet with its crack rowers racing across at dusk; Konon, keeping alone of the generals his head and his honour, trying to be everywhere at once; ships with half their troops and no rowers; ships with one bank of rowers and no troops. Konon saw the certain end, and got away his little squadron with the *Paralos*; anything from a wreck is gain, the old sea-tag says. The Spartans did not trouble to follow him. They were content with their harvest: one hundred and eighty sail, all the sea-strength of the Athenians, standing on the beach at Goat's Creek as barley stands for the sickle.

At last the tale was done; the man talked on, as men do at such times, but it seemed a silence had fallen. Presently Lysis said, 'I am sorry I drove your wine out of you. Take this and start again.'

Side by side we walked through the streets, silent, between houses that wept and whispered. Night was falling. I raised my eyes to the High City. The temples stood black and lampless, fading into the darkness of the sky. Their sacristans had forgotten them. It was as if the gods themselves were dying.

Lysis touched my shoulder, saying, 'The Medes took it, and wasted it with fire. But next day Athene's olive had sprouted green.' So we joined hands together, in token that we were men, knowing that the time had come to suffer. Then we parted, he to his wife and I to my father, for it is proper for a man to be with his household at such a time. All night in the streets you could see lighted windows, where those who were sleepless had rekindled the lamps: but on the High City night only, and silence, and the slow turning of the stars.

24

When we knew that Athens was alone now, we went up to the High City and took the oath of fellowship. Someone proposed it who remembered the oath on Samos. I remembered too. A lark had sung when we raised the hymn of Zeus, and the smoke rose into the deep blue ether, high as the gods. Today autumn was setting in; the sky was grey over the sun-dried hills; when the priest made the offering, a cold wind blew smoke and ashes into my face.

Night and day we waited for the Spartans, watching the walls. But Athenians came instead to the City.

They were not the captives from Goat's Creek. Those Lysander had put to the sword, three thousand men. They came from the Hellespont cities which had opened their gates to him. Wherever he found a democracy he overthrew it. The worst oligarchs everywhere were already his creatures. They held down the people for him; he gave them the lives of their enemies, and confirmed them in their estates. In a few weeks they slaughtered as many men as the war had killed in years. It seemed to the Spartans at home that Lysander was putting all these lands under the heel of his City, while he was getting into his own hands more power than the Great King.

Wherever on his march he found Athenians, soldiers or traders or colonists, he spared them, and gave them safe-conduct, provided they went nowhere but to Athens. All along the Theban Road, over the passes of Parnes, and down into the plain, they trudged with their wives and children, their bedding and their cooking-pots. All day they walked with dusty feet through the gates of the City, and set down their loads, praising the mercy of Lysander.

Then, when they had rested a little, they went to the market for food.

We had closed the ports of Piraeus as soon as we knew we had no ships to hold them. Only little Munychia was left without a boom, for the corn-ships. At first one or two came in from the Hellespont, which had got through before the battle, and a couple from Cyprus. The corn was stored under armed guard. But the next day as many sacks had to be issued; with all the new mouths, the market was eaten bare. Presently Lysander's fleet was sighted, two hundred sail. They folded their wings on Salamis, and picked it clean. Then they perched there, their eyes upon Piraeus, and waited.

Sparta indeed did us honour; she sent us both her kings. King Pausanias marched his army over the Isthmus and up to the walls. In the Academy gardens he pitched his tents; we could see on the sand-track the Spartans racing, or throwing the disk. They closed the road to Megara; then King Agis came down from Dekeleia, and closed the road to Thebes. Winter came on, first with cold sunlight, then with cold rain. In a little while, even the smallest child could understand Lysander's mercy.

It was not for some weeks that people began to die. At first it was the very poor, the very old, and those who were sick already. As things got scarcer prices got higher; food took all people had; trade dropped, men fell out of work, rents were not paid to those who had lived on them; every day the army of the poor was growing, and when people had been poor for long enough, they died.

The corn was given out by the government, a measure a head. The measure got smaller each day, and last comers got none. The head of the household had to get it. My father used to get up before dawn; many waited all night. People used to take cold when the nights were bad; in this way very many died.

At home, however, we lived pretty well at first. Nowadays the man with a mule was as rich as the man with a horse. Ours was quite young, and salted down almost like venison. When my father killed it, I said, 'We must send Lysis a portion. You know we always do when we sacrifice, and he sends to us.' – 'We are not sacrificing,' my father said. 'A mule is not a proper beast to offer to a god. One cannot keep up every convention now. Your Uncle

Strymon, though he is pretty well off and my own father's brother, sends nothing to me.' – 'Then take it from my share, Father. Often enough in battle Lysis has shed his own blood, to save mine. Now am I to grudge him the flesh of a mule?' – 'There are five thousand men in the City, Alexias, who have shed blood in battle for all of us alike. Shall I send to each of them?' But he sent in the end. A little while after, Lysis sent us a dove. I knew when we met that it distressed him to have sent nothing better, and that he must have gone short for it. It was the same everywhere, except among the rich; but it came hard on those who had said with Pythagoras, 'There is no mine or yours between us.'

When the corn measure was down to half a pint a head, it was determined to send the Spartans envoys, and ask their terms for peace.

The envoys rode out to the Academy; and people watching them recalled how, after Alkibiades took Kyzikos, and again after our sea victory off the White Isles, the Spartans had offered peace, on condition of each side keeping what it had, except for Dekeleia, which they would give back to us if we would take the oligarch exiles in. Because of this last, the democrat leader, Kleophon, had roused up the people to demand nothing but a fight to the finish, promising victory. Now they brought him up on a charge of evading military service, and put him to death. But they say a man ought not to look back, when he comes to the end.

Our envoys were soon home, for the kings would not treat with them. It was a matter, they said, for the Ephors at Sparta. So we sent them off again, on their long ride over the hills and the Isthmus; and they were empowered to offer the Spartans, now, what they had asked, each side to keep what it had. Only now they had everything, except the City itself, and Piraeus, and the Long Walls.

The harbours were over-fished, and the catch grew less each day. When people heard from some courtyard the sound of an octopus being beaten on a stone to make it tender, they would look at each other, as they used to when the frontlet of an ox was hung before the door. A pint of oil sold for two drachmas, if you could find it.

Then the envoys came back again. It was a grey wet day, with great clouds coming in dark from the sea. From the top of the Pnyx you could see the waves capped with white as far as Salamis, and Lysander's ships making for port. The envoys stood up; and one look at their faces made the cold seem colder. The Spartans had turned them back on the frontier, when they heard their offer, and told them to come back with something serious. Let Athens acknowledge the rule of Sparta as subject ally, and pull down the Long Walls for the length of a mile. Then there might be talk of peace.

Out of the silence, a voice cried, 'Slavery!' We looked out towards Piraeus, and saw the great walls of Themistokles thrust out to the harbour, guarding the road, like a man's right arm reaching out from the shoulder to grasp his spear. Only one senator proposed surrender, and he was voted a prison sentence, for dishonouring the City. Then we went down from the hill, each man's mind going back to the matter of his next meal.

I stopped on my way at Simon the Cobbler's to get my sandal patched, and ran into Phaedo at the door. It was a week or so since I had seen him; he was getting rather thin, but having beautiful bones he had changed his looks, rather than lost them. I asked how he was, not liking to ask how he was living. 'Oh, I'm well enough while the paper lasts. People still buy books, to take their minds off their bellies. And I get a little teaching nowadays. They come to me for mathematics, and I make them learn logic as well: Half the world's troubles come from men not being trained to resent a fallacy as much as an insult.'

I looked at the book he held, and at his hand. You could nearly see the writing through it. 'Phaedo, what are you doing here at all? Don't you know the Spartans are repatriating the Melians, and offering them safe-conduct?' He smiled, and looked over his shoulder into the shop. Simon was sitting at his work-bench, a woman's shoe in one hand and his awl in the other, listening to Sokrates, who was talking to Euthydemos with a piece of dressed hide in his hand. Phaedo said, 'We have been defining fortitude. Now having defined it, we can't determine whether it is good absolutely, or conditionally, or in part. But you will find, dear Alexias, if you come in, that Sokrates is comparing it to the process of tanning, and the end will be that, whether it is an absolute good or not, we shall go away with more than we had. Why should I starve in Melos, when the fare here is so good? Come and join us.' And putting his arm in mine, he led me inside.

Meantime the Spartan lines tightened about the City, and it was five drachmas a pint for oil. Everything but corn was on the open market; there was not enough to control. The poor began to expose their new-born infants, when the mothers had no milk. If one walked on the High City, there was always one crying somewhere in the rocks or the long grass below.

The rich had not felt it yet. Such people buy stores in bulk; what they lacked, they could pay for, besides their horses, asses and mules. Many were generous; Xenophon when he killed his favourite charger sent something to all his friends, and wrote us a most gentlemanly letter, making a joke of it, so that it would not shame us to send nothing back; Kriton, I believe, kept Sokrates' whole family alive at one time, and Phaedo at another, as well as the pensioners and dependants he had supported from the first; Autolykos maintained some broken-down wrestler who had taught him as a boy. But none of this could alter the fact; once rich or poor had been a matter of purple or homespun, now it was becoming life or death.

So presently the City chose another envoy, to try again. It was Theramenes. He proposed himself for the mission. He had influence among the Spartans, he said, of a kind he could not disclose. People knew what he meant. He had not been one of the Four Hundred for nothing. However, he had come out on the right side in the end, and done more than most to save the City. If he could get us better terms now, good luck to him. My father was glad of this honour done to so old a friend, who had sent us a good cut of neck off a donkey only a week before.

So he set forth, and was seen upon the Sacred Way, riding with some Spartans towards Eleusis. The City waited. Three days ran into four, and a week into two; and a pint of oil cost eight drachmas.

At the end of the first week I killed the dogs. They had foraged for themselves at first, and had stopped coming to look at us at feeding-time. But now a rat sold for a drachma, and their ribs were showing; and, as my father said, if we left it longer there would be no meat on them at all. When I was whetting my hunting-knife, two of them came up wagging their tails, thinking we were off to get a hare. I meant to begin with the smallest, whom I liked the best, so that being the first he would feel no fear. But he had hidden himself, and from a dark corner looked up at me weeping. There was a little on the biggest to salt away. The others, when I had them skinned, were only good to stew; but we lived three days on them.

Already before this we had sold Kydilla. My father had bought her for my mother when they married; we would have freed her when we could feed her no longer, but it would only have been turning her off to starve. A mantlemaker bought her, for a quarter what she had cost when raw and untaught. She wept not only for herself, but at leaving my mother within a month or two of her time.

All this while there were the walls to man, lest the Spartans grow impatient and try a surprise. At about this time, one of Lysis' men accused another of stealing food, and their swords came out. Lysis running in to part them got a cut in front of the thigh, nearly to the bone. When I called it was always getting better, and did not hurt, and he would walk tomorrow. He was getting no more rent for his father's house, it being outside the walls; now he was losing his army pay, and I thought he looked ill. But he said he had sold the great brooch of Agamennon before the bottom fell out of the market, and that his brother-in-law had sent him something, and that little Thalia was proving a splendid manager, and that they did as well as the next.

The only thing the City was not short of was citizens; we had plenty of spare time between watches. One day I came upon my sister Charis with her dolls about her, giving them a meal of pebbles and beads. 'Be good,' she was saying, 'and eat up your soup, or you shan't have any roast kid, or honey fritters.' Children grow fast at eight years old; there seemed nothing of her but legs and eyes. Next morning I said to my father, 'I am going out to look for work.'

We were having breakfast at the time, a gill or two of wine in four parts of water. He put down his cup and said, 'Work? What work?' – 'Any work. Tanning, or mixing mortar, for all I care.' It was a frosty morning, and the cold made my temper short. 'What do you mean?' he said. 'A Eupatrid, of the seed of Erechtheus and of Ion child of Apollo, touting the tradesmen like a metic, asking for work? Before the day is out, some informer will be saying we are not citizens; it always happens. Let us keep some dignity at least.' – 'Well, Father,' I said, 'if our line is so good, we had better see it doesn't end with us.'

In the end he let me go. Well begun is half done, they say. But at most of the shops I went to, I did not get as far as asking. Each had a waiting knot of men who had been master craftsmen themselves, in Sestos or Byzantium; ready, if they could not get journeyman's work, to sweep the floors. They stood huddled in the cold, stamping their feet and slapping their arms, waiting for the shop to open; looking resentfully at one another, but never at me, because they took me for a customer.

In the Street of the Armourers, every shop with a forge going was full of stray people crowding in for warmth, and to get working-room they were turning them away. Each potter seemed to have a vase-painter mixing his clay for him. The tradesmen who had lost their slaves had all the help they needed, now they were doing no trade.

I passed through the Street of the Herm-makers, and began to grow weary, yet was in no haste to go home. So I walked on into the quarter of the statuaries, hearing, as I passed the workshops, how many were silent. But presently catching the tap of mallet on chisel, I went in to watch, and be out of the cold wind.

It was the shop of Polykleitos the Younger, which used to be full in the mornings. Now there was only Polykleitos himself, and an apprentice carving the inscription on a pedestal. Polykleitos had set up on a wooden block the armature for a standing figure, and was bending it about. I greeted him, and congratulated him on being still able to work in bronze. A man had to be doing well to afford fuel for casting.

He was never talkative at work, and I was surprised that he seemed so pleased to see me. 'Even in these days,' he said, 'people who have vowed something to a god know better than to forget it. This is for a choragic trophy; Hermes inventing the lyre.' He put the armature aside, and reached for his drawing-board and crayon. 'How would you stand to string a lyre, Alexias?' – 'I'd sit to it,' I said, 'like everyone else. But I suppose a god can do anything.' There was a lyre hanging on the wall; I reached for it, and, for something to do, began to put it in tune. 'Won't you sit down?' he said, and threw a blanket upon a block of Paros marble, to take off the chill. 'If you care to play something it's a pleasure.' I played a verse or two of some skolion or other; my fingers were too cold to make much of it. Glancing up I saw him busy with his crayon. One can tell when someone is looking through one's clothes. I laughed and said, 'Oh, no, Polykleitos, I'm not stripping for anyone this weather. Wait for your model, whom you pay to do it.'

He coughed and sharpened his pencil. 'It's difficult just now. A week or two ago, I could have got half a dozen models of the build I need. But today . . .' He shrugged his shoulders. 'Sound anatomy's the tradition in this shop. My father made his name on Olympic victors. It goes against the grain, to work without flesh and bone in front of me. But one finds nothing now by walking about the streets; only hard trained muscle keeps its shape these days; and when a gentleman looks in, well, one's afraid to suggest any arrangement, for fear of giving offence.'

I nearly laughed aloud. I suppose I had usually happened to come and look on with Xenophon or someone well-off. I relieved his fears, trying not to sound too eager. 'The most one can offer,' he said, 'is a little hospitality.' But it was a good deal; he was going to pay me with a meal, which was worth more than money. It would mean that as long as the job lasted, I need take nothing from home. I soon learned that every sculptor still working did this, to make sure the model did not lose flesh too quickly.

Polykleitos treated me very well. He even had a little pan of charcoal brought in to warm me. But I had to stand after all, leaning on one foot with a hip curved outward, for this pose had just come in and was all the rage. I stood holding out in one hand something supposed to be the shell of the lyre, and pointing at it with the other; a simpering pose, as I still think; he was a gentleman for a craftsman, but not the artist his father was.

The pose looked soft, but it was hard work to hold it, especially the first day, for last night's supper had been dogtail soup and a few olives. Once I felt a sinking in the belly, and a web of darkness spun before my eyes; but Polykleitos gave me a rest just then, and I was better. The supper was more than we had at home. I thought I might get a chance to save something but though he conversed very civilly, he kept his eye on me.

I hoped that Sokrates would not turn up to watch the work. Man or god, he liked to see a statue planted firmly on both feet, as they were made when he served his time. My father took my employment very quietly. He himself bore all the hardship without complaint, as one who has known worse. He was not as lean yet as when he got home from Sicily.

Time passed, and no word from Theramenes. When a month was through, we signalled the Spartans and asked if he was dead. But they said the terms were still being debated. One could not buy oil any more, except by barter. The corn was a quarter-pint a head, if you were early. I had arranged to collect Lysis' for him, while he was laid up. It was all I had to give him, to save him from limping out in the black of the winter night; if his wound mortified he would be finished. When my father and I got home, my mother used to make a little fire, and give us our wine in hot water, to warm us up. Then I would stand my watch on the walls, or pose for Polykleitos.

The clay model for the Hermes took him three weeks. Still nothing from Theramenes. When the work was finished and ready for casting, Polykleitos gave me cheese with my supper as an extra, and bade me goodbye. I had half hoped someone might have given him another commission, but of course no one had. At the door he called me back. 'Chremon was asking about you the other day. I think he is still working.' He spoke without looking at me. He knew I had heard the talk of the workshops by this time. I said, 'So I hear. Day and night work. No, thank you, Polykleitos.' – 'I am sorry,' he said. 'But sometimes people are glad to know.'

I went out next morning without telling them at home my work was over. I thought if I searched the City, there must surely be something that would bring a few obols in. The last of our tenants had stopped paying rent now, and the store was nearly bare. There were still a few things to be bought for money; olives, a wild bird, a marten-cat, or even fish if you walked to Piraeus. There was meat too, but it cost a stater a pound. I could go home for once and say I had eaten out, if it came to the worse; but much of that would finish my chance with the sculptors. Polykleitos had been flattering me as it was, towards the end.

I was not attending much to the people around me, and I don't know what made me look up, especially at a woman. It was in one of the streets where the Kerameikos runs into the Agora. At first I was not sure, for she had grown half a span since the wedding; soon she would be tall. Then I thought, 'She is too young to know what she is about. Someone must tell her.' So I overtook her and, speaking gently so as not to alarm her, said, 'Wife of Lysis, are you out alone?'

She caught her breath as if I had stabbed her. Her flesh nearly started from her bones. I said, 'Don't be frightened, wife of Lysis. Have you forgotten Alexias, who was groomsman at your wedding? You know you are safe with me. But you ought not to do this; it would trouble him if he knew.' She did not speak. I heard her teeth knock together, like my father's when the fever took him.

'The streets are not safe,' I said, 'for a woman alone. You need not look like a hetaira, to be accosted these days. There are too many ready to do anything for a handful of barley meal.' – 'We can't afford,' she said, finding her voice, 'to hire a market-girl. And we had to sell the boy. Nobody minds it now.' – 'The woman go two and three together; look and you will see. Since we sold our girl, my mother does always. Another time, you could go with her. But indeed you mustn't go alone, or people will talk. Come, I will walk with you, and see you safe home. If you keep your veil drawn, no one will know.' – 'No,' she said, 'I don't care to walk with men in the City.' I began to speak, then saw her eyes; like a broke gambler, making the last throw.

'Wife of Lysis,' I said, 'what is it? You can tell me; I am his friend.' She looked up at me sullenly, without hope. 'Tell me,'

I said, 'and I will do anything.' And then, feeling my own folly, 'I won't tell him. As a gentleman, I give you my word.'

She pressed her veil with both hands over her face, and started weeping. People were passing, jostling us indeed, but no one took notice. Crying women were not so rare in the City. There was an open space near by, full of rubble. I drew her over, and we sat down on a stone that said, 'Here stood the house of the traitor Archestratos.'

She said, 'If you are his friend, you must let me go. In the name of all the gods, Alexias. If he doesn't eat he will die.' I was silent, looking down at the broken stone, and thinking, 'Why did I speak to her? It was enough before; must I know of this?' Then presently I said, 'Is this the first time?'

She nodded into her cupped hands, sitting cramped upon the stone. 'He has fever, every night now, and his wound doesn't heal. I dress it three times a day, but it's no use without food, and he won't touch anything till he has seen me eat before him. He watches me even, to be sure I swallow it. When I said no, he got up and tried to go out. He thinks he can do anything. He thinks he can live on water.' She wept again. I said, 'I can't take anything from home. My mother is seven months gone. But we'll find some way.' She went on crying. Her tears made great dark patches in her veil.

'An old woman came,' she said, 'selling clay lamps. She said a rich young man had seen me and . . . and fallen in love with me, and if I met him at her house, he would give me anything. I was angry and sent her away, and then . . .'

'It's always a rich young man. Some clapped-out old Syrian sweet-seller. He'll expect you to do it for a supper, and thank him afterwards.' I felt cruel, as the defeated are. 'If you don't go straight back to Lysis, I shall go.' – 'You gave me your word,' she said. As she lifted her head, her veil slipped down. It showed me Timasion's daughter, and the sister of his sons.

'Cover your face. Do you want the City to know you? He will find it out later, and what then?' – 'If he is here,' she said, 'to know of it later, then my life has been long enough.'

'Thalia,' I said. She looked round at me, as a child does when the beating is over. I reached out, and took her hand in mine; it was young and cold, and roughened with work. 'Go home to Lysis, and leave all this to me. Remember, he gave you charge of his honour. Do you think he would sell it for bread? Then nor must you. Go home, and give your word not to think of this again, and I'll send you something tonight. Tonight or first thing tomorrow. Will you give your word for mine?' — 'But how can you, Alexias? You can't take it from your mother.' — 'I shan't do that. There are a dozen things a man can turn his hand to. For a woman it's different. But you must promise me.' She swore with her hand in mine, and I saw her back to the end of their street.

I walked on through the City, along the Street of the Armourers, and of the Coppersmiths, and of the Herm-makers, where each shop had its little crowd of craftsmen lined up for a chance to do the work of slaves. Presently I got to the sculptors' quarter, and found the workshop of Chremon. The door was ajar, and I went in.

He had just finished a marble, and was watching the painter colour it; an Apollo, with long hair dressed in a knot like a woman's, playing with a snake made of enamelled bronze. Chremon had made quite a name for himself among the ultramodern schools. It was the thing to say of him that his marble breathed. I could have sworn that if I pinched Apollo's backside, it would make him jump.

The shelf round the wall was full of sketches in wax or clay; if Chremon had sold as many statues, he had done pretty well. They were all of young men, or youths near manhood; leaning, lounging, crouching, lying, and doing everything but stand on their heads. Just then he half glanced over his shoulder and said, 'Not today.'

'Good,' I said, 'that was all I needed to know.' At that he turned round, and I added, 'I only called because I promised you first.' — 'Wait a moment,' he said. He was a pale squat man, with a bald head, a reddish beard, and great flat ends to his fingers. There was still a good deal of flesh on him. I was glad to see he could afford to eat so well. 'I took you for someone else,' he said. 'Come in.' Then he said to the painter, 'You can finish tomorrow.'

I came in, and he walked round me two or three times. 'Take

off,' he said, 'and let me see.' I stripped, and he walked round again. 'H'm, yes. Take a pose for me. Sitting on your heels, and reaching forward, as if you were putting down a cock to fight. No no, no, my dear. Like this.' He took my waist between his thick hands. I gave him a moment or two, and then said, 'I charge two drachmas a day.'

He stood back from me, crying out, 'You must be mad. Two drachmas! Come, come. A good supper at my own table; no one pays more.' He added, 'I give my models wine.' – 'That's good. But I charge two drachmas.' I looked over my shoulder. 'No one else has complained.'

He shook his head from side to side, clicking his tongue. 'What are young men coming to nowadays? No feeling, no sense of the grace of life . . . Ankles of wing-foot Hermes, face of Hyakinthos, a body for Hylas at the pool; and "I charge two drachmas," like the rap of a mallet. It's a terrible thing, this war; nothing will ever be the same. Well, well, yes. But you must work for that. Here, hold this pot; that's your fighting-cock. The left knee down, touching the floor, and out a little. No, no, like this.'

After a time he got a lump of beeswax off the shelf, and began working it up with his flat fingers. Beside me pink-cheeked Apollo, the Double Talker, smiled down sidelong at his thick green snake.

25

The second month drew into the third, and Theramenes did not come.

Chremon made six studies of me, in wax or clay: holding a fighting-cock; tying my sandal; binding my hair with a ribbon; as Hylas, kneeling at the pool; as Hyakinthos slain by the disk; and as Dionysos sleeping. The Dionysos was a quick one, done without my knowledge. He kept his word about the wine; we had it every evening, half-and-half or stronger. They say any human state has some good in it if you look; and in those days one could be drunk on very little.

I believe he kept me longer than anyone; for I could not count on the shelf more than four sketches from any one model. He fed me better than Polykleitos had, and he paid me my two drachmas every day. I used to meet Thalia at the ruins of the traitor's house, and give her anything I could get for the money, telling her not always to say it came from me, lest Lysis should wonder how I got it. When I came to see him he looked a little better, but strange, with deep eyes and a very clear skin like a boy's. This, I think, came from his drinking much water to kill his hunger; a physician once told me this is good for an unhealed wound, washing the morbid humours from the body; I daresay it was what kept him alive.

It was hard to account to my family for my staying out so late, when, if any man had been seen using oil to burn, his house would have been stoned. If I was gone all night, I said I was on guard duty. Sometimes I saw my father look at me. But there was not much left in the cupboard, and my mother was getting near her time; if he thought it better not to ask questions, I do not blame him.

When she was far gone with child she never looked very well; and she moved slowly now about the house for one whose habit was as brisk as a bird's. Little Charis helped her, and once, getting home at dawn, I found my father sweeping the courtyard, as smartly as if he had done it for years. Then I remembered. I took the broom from him; but we said nothing.

When I had time I used to look about in the open places, getting grass and green stuff to put in the soup. There was a kind of pine that had a kernel good for eating. The Pythagoreans, from their never eating flesh, were very knowing in such matters; anything you saw them pick up you could be sure was safe.

Sometimes Chremon did not feel like work, and had no use for me till evening, and I could not show myself at home. Such days I spent with Phaedo as a rule. I used to lie on the pallet in his room, reading while he wrote, or hearing him teach. He was a good teacher; crisp, sometimes even severe, but always even-tempered. The light from a little window over his shoulder touched his fair hair and fine cheekbone; thinness brought out the breeding in him, but the intellect more. He looked already a philosoper, and as pure as a temple-priest of Apollo. I never told him everything; but once he said, 'It is easier these days to be a man alone.'

Sokrates went about all this while just as usual, barefoot in the cold, in his old mantle, talking and asking questions. Once I found him visiting Lysis. They were discussing Homer. It has always seemed to me that this was when Lysis took a turn for the better; though I daresay the wine and dried figs helped, which Plato sent him next day. Sokrates always knew who could spare a little and who was in most need, and how to bring them together.

But I did not often follow him into the colonnades. Plato would be there with him, and seldom alone. If it is Aphrodite of the Agora who has possessed one, winter and want will cool one soon enough, and the beauty that kept one sleepless is only a little warmth to crowd up to when the wind is blowing. But with this love it was otherwise. He had the innocent eye that looks straight at the soul; and mine seemed written all over with the lessons of Chremon's workshop. So I kept away, and thanked the god who had bestowed him where he could be taken care of. His eyes looked bigger, but bright and clear; his cheek, though it curved in a little, had a touch of fresh colour, from happiness, as I supposed, such as time and change have no power upon; and in his face one could still see music.

Chremon chose the slain Hyakinthos, in the end, to make his statue on. I was glad of this; Hyakinthos lay prone, with an arm flung before the face. At one time Chremon had been very much taken with the Dionysos, who was lying face up.

The third month drew near its end, and on the fig-tree one could see where the buds would be. Then one morning, while my company was on watch upon the wall, a trumpet sounded before the Dipylon Gate, and word ran round that Theramenes was back.

Presently came the call for the Assembly to be convened. The walls had to be guarded, so we could only wait. At last the relief came up. We scanned their faces, and were slow to ask what news. The captain who was taking over from me met my eyes and said, 'Nothing.'

I stared, and said, 'Isn't Theramenes back, then?' – 'Oh, yes, and looking very well. He's been on Salamis, with Lysander.' – 'Well, then, what terms?' – 'Nothing. Lysander sends word he has no power to treat, nor the kings, only the Ephors at Sparta.' – 'After three months? Are you well, Myrtilos?' His only son had died the day before. – 'I suppose, to a man from Athens, even the black broth of Sparta tasted good. He could not get them to better their terms; so he waited.' – 'By Herakles, but for what?' – 'For the City to like the smell of black broth. The oligarchs are rich; they can hold out a little longer. The democrats are dying every day. Soon there will be none; and those who are left, the good and the beautiful, can open the gates to their friends on what terms they choose.'

No man spoke to another, as we went down from the wall. Thinking of the faces at home, I found my courage fail, and went straight to Chremon's. He was cheerful, and offered me a drink though it was not noon. 'Not long now,' he said. He must have looked forward all along to the day of surrender; not because he was an oligarch, but because he liked his comforts, and the rest was all one to him. I took the wine, for I was already cold enough without stripping. The workshop had a little high window, which showed a glimpse of the High City; there was a gleam of light upon Athene's spear. I looked from it to Chremon, rubbing his hands over the charcoal to warm them for work. So much suffered and spent, and this for the end.

Coming home at evening, I found my mother and sister sitting alone. Charis said, 'Father's gone to Sparta.' Being in no mood for games I answered sharply; but it was true. Theramenes had been sent off again as envoy, with full powers to treat. Nine delegates had been sent with him. Since the Spartans would do no business with democrats, and the City did not trust the oligarchs, the nine were chosen from among Theramenes' former moderates, the poorer of them, who had good cause to end the siege quickly. These three months had taught the citizens something.

'Your father had no time,' my mother said, 'to seek you about the City.' I guessed he had not cared to look very far. 'But he sent you his blessing.' – 'You forget, Mother,' Charis said. 'It was "Tell Alexias I commit you to his care." Alexias, will the Spartans give Father some of their dinner?' I looked at my charges, drawn close to a little fire of pine-cones and wood, saved all day against the evening; the child with an old doll on her knees, taken up when her housework was done; my mother sitting in her chair, awkwardly as big-bellied women do, her head small and delicate above her shapeless body, dark lashes lying on a cheek of ivory, all threaded, as I saw in the firelight, with little lines. I passed on Chremon's good cheer, saying, 'Not much longer now.' When they had gone to bed I sat over the warm white embers, thinking, 'What if her time comes at night, and no oil to light the midwife?'

Next day more people than usual dropped in to watch Chremon working. One or two men who knew me. They greeted me, but I thought they looked at one another. There were also some of Chremon's friends, with whom he withdrew to gossip in a corner. I heard one of them say laughing, 'Well, when you have done with him, send him to me.' I knew the man's name; he was not a sculptor. They left, and Chremon came back before I was quite ready for him; my arm partly hiding my face, I did not always watch it as carefully as I should. I knew he was put out by what he saw; he was a man who liked to persuade himself that things were as he wished. If he had been the Great King, he would not have spared the messenger of bad news.

The City granary was empty now; there was no more need to fetch the corn. But a few days later, I woke to find a pigeon limed in the fig-tree; a fat bird too, from beyond the walls. I climbed up for it, and wrung its neck, thinking, 'This day will be fortunate.' As I carried it in, feeling the flesh on it and full of my news, Charis met me in the doorway, saying, 'Oh, Alexias, run quickly. Mother is ill, it's the baby coming.'

I ran to the house of the midwife, who grumbled at going out in the cold, and asked what we had to pay with. I promised a jar of wine, our last, being afraid she would ask for food. She set out complaining; in the porch Charis stood wringing her hands and crying, 'Hurry, hurry.' As I let the woman into the room, I heard my mother groaning, a muffled sound; she had stuffed something into her mouth lest the child should hear.

I sent Charis into the kitchen, and waited before the door. It was time for Chremon, but I did not care. I was pacing about the courtyard when I heard from within a great shriek, and my mother's voice cried out, 'Alexias!' I ran upon the door and flung it open. The midwife called out in anger, but I saw only my mother's face turned towards me, the lips white, and moving without sound. I knelt and took hold of her about the shoulders. But even as I touched her, her eyes set in her head, and her soul went out of her.

I looked upon her, and closed her eyes. She slept. I thought, 'Here is one, then, for whom I need fear no longer.' And then I thought, 'She has borne a child before, and miscarried a child, yet did not die. Famine killed her. If I had brought home what I earned at Chremon's, perhaps she would be alive.' It had seemed to me that, doing what no one is called upon to do, I could dispose the price as I chose; but what is a man, when he sits down to chop logic with Necessity? 'If I had not meddled,' I thought, 'when I saw Thalia in the street, she would have gone on to the house of the bawd, and come back with a little money; Lysis would have eaten, and known nothing, and the food would have kept life in him like any other. What is honour? In Athens it is one thing, in

Sparta another; and among the Medes it is something else again. But go where you will, there is no land where the dead return across the river.'

The midwife had been clacking, and pulling at the clothes. They lay flat now upon the body, which looked as small as a yearling doe. Then hearing another sound I turned, and saw behind me the woman sitting, tying the navel-cord of the new-born child. She said, 'Whom shall I give it to? It is a boy.'

Towards evening, when I had arranged for the burial, I came back to the house. My sister had dried her tears; she had got out her old cradle, and was rocking the child in it. 'Hush,' she said. 'He is sleeping. What a good baby he is! Since I tucked him up here, he has not once cried.'

Her words gave me a hope, and I bent over the cradle. But the child was sleeping, as she had said. He favoured my father's looks; he was fair-haired, and a big child; too big, I suppose, for my mother to bear. 'How shall I feed him, Alexias? If I chew the food first, and make it soft, won't it be as good as milk for him? It is what the birds do.'

'No,' I said. 'He must have milk, Charis. I must take him away tonight, and fine someone to feed him.' – 'I think it's very dear,' the midwife said so. Have we any money?' – 'Not much. So we can't keep him for ourselves. We must find some rich lady, who has been praying to the gods to send her a child. She will be glad to get a fine baby like this. Perhaps she will pretend she is really his mother, and her husband will think he is really his son. They will give him a horse when he is older, and make a knight of him; and some day he will be a general.'

She looked down at the cradle and said, 'I don't want a rich lady to have him. I want to keep him for company, Alexias, when you are out at work.' – 'But he would have no mother here. You must be good, little one.' I feared she would cry again; but her tears were spent. I gathered up the child, and wrapped him in the linen from the cradle. She said, 'That is not warm enough,' and made me take the wool. 'We must give him something,' she said, 'to know him by, when he is a man. Theseus had a sword.' – 'I need my sword. But find him something quickly.' She came back with a branch of red coral which was her own, and hung it round his neck. 'What shall we call him, Alexias? We haven't given him any name.' – 'He must go to his mother,' I said, 'and she will name him.'

I walked across the Agora, with my brother on my arm, and stopped at a potter's stall. As food grew dear, pots had grown cheap, and for two obols I got one big enough, round inside and with a wide mouth. Two obols was more than we could spare; but one must do what one can for one's own flesh and blood, and there were stray dogs running about the City as bold as wolves. At the foot of the High City, in the empty ground where the stones of the tyrants' fort lie scattered, I looked about me. Not very far away I could hear an infant crying among the rocks, but the sound was thin; if any knight's wife was seeking an heir for her husband, my brother would not have a rival long. But if in these three months she had not chosen yet, I thought, she must be hard to please.

He had been quiet, lying in my arm; but now feeling the cold pot about him, he began to cry. It was a strong sound, for so young a baby. I saw him in my mind as a youth, tall like my father, with suitors seeking his favour; bearing a shield in battle, or crowned at the Games; then led with music to his wedding, and seeing his sons. 'Go in peace,' I said to him; bear no ill-will to me, for Necessity yields to no man; and do not complain of me to our mother, for her blood is on your head as well as mine. If the gods had not forbidden it, my brother, I would put you to sleep before I left you, for night comes on; this is an empty place, and the clouds look dark upon the mountains. But the blood of kindred is not to be washed away; and when a man has once felt the breath of the Honoured Ones upon his neck, he will not bid them across the threshold. So forgive me, and suffer what must be. The clouds are heavy; if the gods love you, before morning there will be snow.'

It was dark already. For a long time as I walked away I could hear him crying; then from high on the rocks, about the bastions of the citadel, a dog began howling, and I heard it no more.

We buried my mother in one of the gardens within the City, which had been turned over to this use since the siege began. I did not tell Lysis, thinking him too ill to be distressed with it; but he heard, and sent begging to let them have Charis to care for, and share whatever they had. He said this, though for two days now I had sent nothing, and they were living like the birds themselves. I sent the child, for she was falling into a melancholy. What we had left, I sent along with her; there was only myself left now, and I had my work to go back to.

I went back to Chremon's next morning, feeling the wind cold on my neck, and thinking he would not be pleased to find I had cut off my hair, for, as I remembered, he had not finished the head. But that was no trouble; for when I stood in the doorway, I saw someone else stretched on the wooden dais, in the pose of Hyakinthos. I daresay he had only been waiting to find a model with the same build. Many no doubt who had thought themselves rich when the siege began, were not too proud now to pose for Chremon. I went away before he saw me, and took from him the pleasure of saying 'Not today.'

Two days after this, the envoys returned. I did not myself go out to meet them; though I did not feel as hungry as the day before, everything tired me; when I heard shouting in the street, I went to the door to ask what it was and then lay down again. But as my father told me later, all the City that stood still on its feet came to meet them, and led them straight to the Pnyx to hear their news.

It was this; that the Spartans and their allies' spokesmen had met all together, to vote upon our fate. Then had stood forward the Theban envoy, a man who, as it appeared later, spoke not so much for his own city as out of that pride in public office which makes a man think of himself as god. 'Serve them,' he said, 'as they served the Melians, or the city of Mykalessos when they loosed the Thracians on it. Sell them into slavery, lay waste the City, and give the ground to sheep.' And this being said, the Corinthian supported it.

But if there is not much grace in Sparta, there is reverence for the past. When from time to time they are great, that is the core of their greatness. Curtly and bluntly, after their custom, they answered that Athens was part of Hellas; and they were not for enslaving the City that had turned the Medes. The debate was at a stand, when a man from Phokis stood up, and sang. It was the chorus of Euripides that begins,

Electra, Agamemnon's child, I come
Unto thy desert home . . .

What the Spartans thought of it, no one knows; but after a long silence the allied spokesmen cast the vote for mercy.

So these were the terms they sent us, to lift the siege: Pull down a mile of your Long Walls; receive your exiles back into citizenship; hand over your ships; and as subject ally follow the rule of Sparta, leaving her to lead in peace and in war.

I am told one or two voices were still heard to cry out against surrender. As to the others, I am not the man to despise them. For if, the day before, Chremon had still had work for me, I cannot swear I would not have gone, without any pay, for the sake of a bowl of soup.

Lysander sailed across from Salamis; King Agis came within the gates he had watched so long; but for the first days I kept my bed and my father cared for me as for a little child. He was good to me, setting aside his own grief; and in return, silly with weakness, I forgot he could not know, finding her absent, that Charis was alive. He went a full day thinking her dead, before I perceived his error. Even then he was not angry; but I saw the tears stand in his eyes. Then it seemed to me that at last the Honoured Ones were appeased; and on the thought I slept.

We ate from the first day of surrender; for before the gates were open, people who had a little left were sending to their friends, now they knew their children would not starve. So on the third day, I got on my feet again, and walked out, and saw the ramparts of the High City covered with Spartans, pointing out to each other the mountains of their homes. I thought, 'Thus it is to be the conquered,' but my mind was empty and light and I could feel nothing.

They were throwing down the Walls already. I heard the thud and crash of the falling stonework, mixed with the twitter of flutes. Who began it I don't know; it was not very like the Spartans, and I should guess at the Corinthians; but they had collected all the flute-girls, those who were left, given them wine and a handful of food, and made them play. It was one of the first days of spring, when the light is hard and keen; the girls stood in the road, between the Walls, their faces painted awry, or sometimes, if they were Athenian born, striped red and black with tears, wearing their tawdry finery fit only for the lamplight, piping away; the foreign girls, and some others too, setting themselves to rights after their haste, and making eyes at the victors. And from time to time, as they played, there crashed down one of Thermistokles' great ashlars; and the Spartans cheered. 'This truly,' I said to myself, 'is defeat.' But it was as a dream to me.

So I walked to the house of Sokrates; but outside I met Euthydemos, who said, 'He has gone up to the Temple of Erechtheus, to pray for the City.'

While we stood talking, Plato came up, and greeted us; but when he heard Sokrates was not there, he did not stay. I looked after him, and thought that in the end even the rich had felt it. His eyes were hollow, and the bones of his wide shoulders stood out like knuckles beneath the skin.

I said to Euthydemos, 'It was noble in him to give to others, when he was in such want himself.' He answered, 'No one has filled his belly these last weeks. I don't think Plato starved; when things got tight in his home, Kritias helped them; though I can't endure the man, it seems he has his share of family feeling. Plato was keeping up quite well until a little while ago. But he went downhill in a matter of days after his friend died.'

I put out my hand, and set it upon stone; it was the column of the Herm, that Sokrates had made. It was solid, and upheld me easily. I said, 'Which friend?'

'Why, the same,' said Euthydemos. 'Plato is not one to change lightly. After the youth was left alone (for he had some old father or kinsman who died during the winter) Plato took charge of him entirely. While he had a crust, you may be sure the boy wouldn't starve; he had quite a good colour, and nothing worse than a cough such as half the City suffered from. But one day, as they climbed up to the High City, suddenly he choked and brought forth a flow of blood; he fell down where he was, upon the steps of the Porch, and gave up his spirit. Plato buried him; and now is as you see.'

My soul was alone, neither hearing nor seeing, encompassed by chaos and black night, forgetful of its name. A voice reached me saying 'Drink this, Alexias,' and, my eyes clearing, I saw the face of the Herm above me, and Euthydemos leaning over me with a little wine in an earthen cup. 'I thought, when first I saw you, you had walked too far.' I thanked him, and after resting a little went home. Then I remembered I had not asked where the tomb was.

I sought some days for it, and came on it at last in an old garden at the foot of the Nymphs' Hill, where there were other graves. Places such as this, being within the walls, were emptied later; and I could never learn afterwards where he lay. But the grave, when I saw it, was under an almond tree, which was all in flower, for spring had broken; and there was a brier in bud beside it.

Most of the graves had steles of wood, or an urn of clay to mark the place; but this tomb had a stone. The work was undistinguished; and, remembering Plato's fine taste, I saw the measure of his grief in his not having overseen the sculptor. A branch of the brier had covered the inscription; bending it back, I read the words:

Lightbringing dawn star, kindled for the living;
Bright torch of Hesperos, sinking to the dead.

I looked again at the relief, which showed the youth standing as in thought, and a mourning man with his face hidden. The work was, as we say, sincere, but of so old-fashioned a simplicity that you might have thought the sculptor had scarcely picked up his chisel since Pheidas' day. I stood gazing till, a thought coming to me, I knelt down and found the place where the statuary puts his mark; and I understood, when I saw the name.

26

There are draughts that do not yield their taste with the first sip; but drink them, and their bitterness wrings the mouth.

The stones still crashed from the Long Walls after the flutes were silent, and the victors who had helped for sport had wearied of the game. The Athenians, half-starved, wearied much sooner; but Lysander used to watch the work, a big man, square-jawed and blond, with a mouth of iron.

Meanwhile, in the public places one saw the exiled oligarchs, making themselves at home. Some had entered as soon as the gates were opened; they had been with King Agis' army, sitting before the walls.

Presently the Spartans invited the oligarch clubs of Athens to choose five Ephors, as they called them, to draw up proposals for a government. My father attended these consultations. The upshot was that Theramenes was one of the five, and Kritias another. I believe my father voted for both. But I did not hold it against him. Regarding Theramenes, though he ate while we starved, I daresay it cost us nothing. If he had come back and owned to failure, the people would have been angry with him. It was said that he had employed the time in plotting with Lysander to put his friends in power; but this was gossip and guesswork. Of Kritias my father said to me, 'I can't think what makes you so prejudiced against him. One of our ablest men; a true orator, untainted with demagogy, from whom one can be sure of scholarship and logic. And in his writings, no one sets a higher moral tone.' He had been good to me when I was sick; so I swallowed my answer.

Plato asked me to supper about this time. I went doubtfully, knowing I could not say to him what a friend should. But he singled me out for kindness, even to sharing his supper-couch, though there were others with more claim to the compliment. Whether Euthydemos had gossiped to anyone, no doubt I shall never know.

He was always a graceful host, if rather a formal one; if his mind went wandering, he was quick to cover it. While the rest were talking of events, he said to me, 'I believe this success will be just the thing for my uncle Kritias.'

I had long given up arguing politics with Plato. His mind was the master of mine; and his motives were pure. It was not in him to despise a man for poverty or low birth. But he despised fools wherever he found them, horse or foot; and finding more of them than of the wise and just, he thought that rule by the people must debase the City. Lysis used to say that government was an exercise ennobling to the base, as good soldiering makes cowards brave. Plato, when I quoted this, praised its magnanimity, and disagreed. As for Kritias, the man was his kinsman, and he was my host.

'Till now,' Plato said, 'he has never filled an office worthy of his gifts. Sometimes I have feared it would make him bitter. I can't tell you half his kindness during the siege. I shall not forget it easily; not only on my own behalf, but . . . but that is over.'

I answered, 'It is said, "If Fate were moved by tears, men would offer gold to buy them."'

'". . . Yet grief still puts them forth, as the tree puts forth its leaves." Speaking of my uncle, Charmides and I called to congratulate him; Charmides, you know, takes his career seriously, since Sokrates rebuked his idleness. Kritias urged both of us to come forward in the City's service. Unless, he said, the better sort of people are prepared to do what they can to remedy democracy's abuses, the City will fall into an apathy, or the dissipations of defeat, and lose the memory of her greatness. Though my ambitions till now have lain elsewhere, I confess he moved me.'

I told him, in sincerity, that men of his kind were needed. He had begun, I think, by seeking an escape from his grief, but ambition was stirring in him. I said to myself, 'I am prejudiced. The enmities of youth lack proportion. Perhaps Kritias might have seemed to me a gentleman, if I had met Chremon first.'

One heard Chremon's name everywhere that week. Pasion, the

banker, had just bought for a great price his latest work. Half the City trooped into Pasion's courtyard to see it, and brought back the news that the marble breathed, or at least seemed scarcely to have ceased breathing.

For three days I avoided meeting Lysis. On the third he called. He was walking quite well now, hardly using his stick. We talked a little; but he would fall silent, and look at me. I sought words at random; in my heart I thought, 'I should have fallen on my sword. Once I would not have waited for this.' I could find no more talk, and was silent also. Presently Lysis said, 'I have been to the High City, to sacrifice to Eros.' – 'Yes? Well, he is a powerful god.' – 'And cruel, it is said. But to me, noblest of all the Immortals; "the best soldier, comrade, and saviour" as poor Agathon used to say. It was time to give thanks to him.'

Soon afterwards the new Ephors, having consulted together, called an Assembly, and Kritias addressed it. He spoke as usual very well. His voice was elegantly trained, pitched to carry, without any of those mannerisms that made a man tiresome and human. He had the voice of knowledge advising honest simplicity without despising it. It was a voice to set you at ease, if you liked your thinking done for you.

He proposed a Council of Thirty, to draw up a constitution upon the ancient code, and govern meanwhile. When he read the list, starting with the five Ephors themselves, the people listened at first as children to a teacher. Then there was a murmur; then a roar. The Assembly had awakened, and heard the names. The core of the Four Hundred, the traitors from Dekeleia, every extreme oligarch who hated the people as boar hates dog. The Pnyx echoed with the outcry. Kritias listened, it seemed unmoved; then he turned, and made a gesture, and stepped aside. The shouting died like a gust of wind. Lysander stood on the rostrum, in his armour. His eyes swept slowly over the hill. There was a dead hush.

His speech was short. The breach in the Walls, he said, was two stadia short of the mile; the time-limit was up. If he did not declare the treaty void, and wipe out the City, it was an act of mercy. We had best deserve it.

So the people slunk down from the Pnyx like slaves caught

stealing by the master. Our tongues were getting, now, the taste of defeat.

But the new government was quick to get the public services in order, and people spoke well of it. On the day they appointed a Senate, people met me in the street with congratulations; my father, it appeared, had been named a Senator.

I wished him well. Considering his views, no one could suspect him of time-serving. His work as envoy had brought him into the public eye, and Theramenes had not forgotten him. It was something that they were choosing Senators even as moderate as he.

At first he used to come home full of affairs. You could almost tell in the street which men held office in the new administration, however small. They looked like people who are getting the right food. When men have shared in the City's business since they put on a long mantle, it comes strange to cease. You can watch something wither in them, like a fettered limb. One evening he said over supper, 'Well, I think we shall hand over the City a little cleaner than we found it. In confidence, a rat-hunt is on for tomorrow, and high time too.' – 'Rats, Father?' – 'Those creatures who live off their betters, and bring filth in exchange. How else describe an informer?'

I congratulated him willingly. In the last year, when things were going badly and the people had war-fever, the informers had been a shame to the City. It was only with poor men that they simply laid information and took the reward. If he had a little, they took a bribe to keep quiet, and often informed in the end when he had nothing left. Some worked for themselves, some for rich blackmailers who made a business of it. 'Good hunting, Father,' I said. 'But they're slippery game; they know every crack in the law, they always get away.' – 'Not this time. Since the constitution is still upon the stocks, for once we can cut the law to their measure.'

He laughed as he spoke. I looked up, the sound taking me back to another City; I saw again Hyperbolos falling open-mouthed. 'With the Four Hundred too,' I said, 'that was how it began.'

'Nonsense,' he said; and I saw in his face the annoyance of a man who has been disturbed when he was at ease. 'You will do far better, Alexias, to forget you were mixed up in that Samos affair. I don't say it was any shame to you; too much discretion is unlovely in a youth of good blood; but the rough-and-ready faction fights of an overseas naval base are not understood here in the City. Keep that in mind, or you will do a great deal of harm, both to yourself and me.' – 'Yes, Father. What trial are you giving these men?' – 'A collective one, and too good for them.' – 'Perhaps; but as a precedent?' – 'That we have already, since the trial of the generals who left you to drown.'

The informers were rounded up the next day, and condemned to death, no one dissenting. My father assured me afterwards that he had not seen a man in the dock whose name did not stink throughout the City. The week after, there was another arrest of informers. When I asked him how the trial had gone, he said, 'There will be some delay. One or two cases were more than doubtful. We voted to try them separately.' He cleared his throat and added, 'There was some attempt to influence the Senate against it. But for an interim government, that was going too far.'

There were no more mass trials, and the City was quiet some weeks. Then one morning a Spartan regiment was sighted on the Sacred Way. The Dipylon guard sent a runner to ask what should be done: and the Council sent back word to open.

They marched up to the gate with tread of iron, between the tombs of our fathers. They crossed the Kerameikos, and the Agora, and marched on. People stood in the market, staring upward, while they climbed the ramp to the High City, and marched through the Porch into the precinct of the Maiden. There they stacked arms and pitched their tents. At the feet of Athene of the Vanguard, and about the Great Altar, they lit their campfires and stewed their black broth.

In the courtyard I met my father, looking ill. I fancy he had hoped to avoid me. I said, 'I think sir, you did not know of this.'

'I have come from Theramenes. It appears the Council had word of a conspiracy to seize the citadel, and put the leading citizens to death.' – 'I see, sir. Did he give you any names?' – 'They will be published after the arrests are made.' We looked at each other, as father and son can, needing no words. He meant, 'Don't be troublesome if you want me to keep my temper; I have troubles enough,' and I meant, 'You cannot face me and you know it. I could forgive you if you would own the truth.' I was about to turn from him when he said, 'Theramenes can be trusted to watch events; he has always set his face against extremes. Remember, I expect discretion.' With that he went indoors.

Kallibios, the Spartan general, was undersized for one of his race. His eyes were bitter; you could see in them the beatings of his boyhood, and a black insolence, full of hatred. Beside it one remembered the insolence of Alkibiades like a child's laughter. The Thirty fawned on him, and received him in their homes.

One got used to the sight of Spartans in the streets, staring open-mouthed at the shops, or walking in pairs looking scornfully before them. Some of the younger ones, I admit, seemed modest and mannerly. I saw one such, a fine tall youth, at Pistias' doorway, watching the work, and talking armour with a friend. They looked less dour than most of their fellows; I even heard them laugh. As I passed, the second man turned round and said, 'Good day, Alexias.' I stared, and saw Xenophon.

Turning my face from him I walked away; not so much concerned to affront him, as to believe that my eyes had lied. Next time I met him he was alone. He put out his hand to stop me, with his open smile. 'Why are you angry with me, friend? What ails you?' – 'Only what ails you too,' I said.

He looked at me gravely, like one who has a right to feel hurt, but will set it by. 'See things as they are, Alexias. The City has to be policed: it is a measure against the mob, not people like ourselves. The Spartans respect a soldier and a gentleman, even if he has carried a spear against them. Young Arakos, whom you saw me with, is a splendid fellow. He and I nearly killed each other once in the hills near Phyle. If we don't bear malice, who else should? One must gain by the company of a man of honour, whatever his City. Virtue comes first; hasn't Sokrates always taught us so?' His clear grey eyes looked straight into mine; he spoke from his soul.

I was silent, thinking of schooldays, and the puppy-fights in the washroom. It had seemed hardly more than backing different chariots at the Games. He was looking at me, and I saw the thought in his eyes: 'Do you do well to reproach me? Have

I found a worse friend than Chremon?' But there are things a gentleman does not say. 'There must be order,' he said, 'in the City. Without order, how are men better than the beasts?'

Lysis and I spoke little of events. We knew the rawness in one another's minds, and saw no sense in rubbing salt. We met to talk, or to be quiet, or to hear Sokrates, who was living just as usual, pursuing his enquiries into the nature of man's soul, justice and truth. As always, he took no part in politics, he only followed logic where it led. If some of the statements lately given the people did not stand up to logic, that was by the way.

Plato came less often than he had. When he entered upon politics, Sokrates' only advice to him had been to study law. 'No man expects to throw a clay water-jar without first serving an apprenticeship. Do you think the art of governing men is easier?' When he came to Sokrates, he seldom spoke; he listened, or withdrew into himself. He was like a sick man at a feast, who helps himself only to what he can keep down. I had not the folly to measure his grief by mine, the scar of a meteor's passage, printed on the sky by brightness and the act of flight.

Samos had fallen. Without a fleet they had never had any hope. Lysander had left the democrats their lives, and the clothes on their backs to carry into exile, and given the City to the oligarchs we had overthrown. So his work being done, he sailed home in triumph to Lakonia, with his trophies of war, and a shipload of treasure, of which not a drachma, they say, ever stuck to his fingers. He was a man not greedy of anything but power. But with every Spartan who handled the stuff it was not the same; and there are great changes, I am told, since gold came into Lakonia.

Kallibios' troops stayed on the High City; and every Athenian who wanted to sacrifice had to ask their leave. And now, the Council of Thirty used to make their arrests with a Spartan guard. They began with the metics. I myself saw Polymarchos the Shieldmaker led through the streets. I knew him, a man of culture who entertained philosophers. I turned to a bystander, and asked what was the charge.

'Ah,' said the man, 'they've caught him out at last, it seems.' He was a seedy fellow; the whites of his eyes were like the whites of bad eggs. 'Sold some poor soldier thin bronze with filling, I suppose, and got him killed. That's the way these foreigners make their money, underselling honest men.' – 'Well, we shall see when he's tried if he's guilty or not.' – 'Guilty? Of course he is. He's the brother of Lysias the Speechmaker, who defended these dirty informers, like that Sokrates, who teaches young men to mock the gods and beat their fathers.' I looked at him. You could as well bring logic to a dog scratching for fleas. 'That is a lie,' I said. 'Your mind stinks like your body.' Then I went away and was ashamed. 'It is a sickness,' I thought, 'and I have it like the rest.'

Polymarchos was never tried. It was given out that he had been found guilty of treason, for sufficient reasons, and given hemlock in prison. His brother Lysias slipping out at a back door had got away from Piraeus with his life. Their fortune was confiscated; to the state, the notice said. But the bronzes from their houses were seen in the house of one of the Thirty. Afterwards others of them did much the same. Those who had profited already urged on the rest, so that they should all be in it alike. But Theramenes, it was noticed, refrained. He was looking ill, and when he supped at our house dieted himself, before his stomach troubled him.

Before long, the City got quite used to the sight of people being put away without trial. They were only metics, after all. Then the Thirty began arresting democrats. And from this time on, there began to be two nations in the City. For it was no longer enough that a man, to be safe, should guard his tongue. It was necessary to surrender his soul; and many surrendered it.

One morning my father stopped me as I was going out. After some time beating about the point, at last it came. '. . . So, all things considered, it might be well, while matters are so delicate, not to be seen in public with Lysis son of Demokrates.'

The sunlight grew dark before my eyes. I felt sick. 'Father,' I said, 'in the name of my mother, tell me. Is Lysis in danger?' He looked at me with impatience. 'Tut, not that I know of. But he has no discretion. He gets himself talked about.' I paused to command myself before I spoke. 'For ten years now, sir, when Lysis has been talked about I have had a share of his honour. What shall I sell it for? A bowl of black soup? A kiss from Kritias? How much?'

– 'You are offensive. I speak of common prudence. There are matters which cannot be opened to loose-tongued young men; but we may hope the present state of things will not last to the end of time. Meanwhile, I expect in this house the manners you learned from me, not those Sokrates teaches.'

I saw deep lines about his eyes; lately he often looked tired. 'I was insolent, Father. I am sorry. But would you do yourself what you ask of me?' He said after a moment, 'However, remember I only have one son.'

I set out at once to call on Lysis. On the way, I saw ahead of me a back I knew by its breadth. Autolykos was making his way homeward from the palaestra.

As athletes went nowadays, he was considered notable for good looks and grace. He did not fight at much above the weight he had been at the Isthmus; having held his own against far heavier men, he had now the name of a classic fighter, a type of the golden age. Compared with what one saw now at every Games, I myself had come, little by little, to think him beautiful. At the last Games of Athene he had been crowned again.

I was thinking to overtake him for a word, when I saw at the head of the street Kallibios coming the other way, with two Spartan guards behind him. The middle of the road was mucky, but it was dry by the walls. Kallibios and Autolykos met, and stopped, and looked at one another, neither making way. People in the street about them stopped still where they were.

Kallibios said in his harsh Doric, 'Out of my way, lout.' He need not have shouted to be heard. I saw Autolykos' back, steady as an oak; and then Kallibios' eyes, as his stick flew out.

Autolykos stooped, moving easily, like a grown man playing with boys. As he straightened, above his shoulder appeared the face of Kallibios, rising in the air. His hands beat at Autolykos' shoulders; then he was tossed backward as lightly as a faggot, to land face down in the wet midden. Autolykos, without a glance to see where he had fallen, hitched his mantle and walked on, keeping the wall.

The whole street cheered, except those who were near enough to see Kallibios scraping muck from his face, and they were laughing. At the corner of the street Autolykos before he turned out of sight made the gesture by which a well-bred victor acknowledges applause on his way back to the dressing-room.

The two guards had been rather slow off the mark, getting no orders; now, when they sprinted after, they found their path full of impediments: laden donkeys, scuffling lads, even a group of women. But they soon overtook their man, since they were running and he was not. I think he considered taking them both on, with Kallibios as makeweight; then he saw the crowd following, and smiled, and went quietly. They did not dare to bind him. With every street we passed the crowd swelled, and grew noisier as people took courage from each other. When we reached the road to the High City we must have been near two hundred.

I had started near the front and managed to stay there. As we neared the Porch, I saw a man standing alone between the great pillars of Perikles. Even in that place, he still looked tall. Since the triumph in Sparta, it was Lysander's habit to come and go unheralded. He was a law unto himself.

Autolykos mounted the last few steps, between his guards. Lysander waited, in his scarlet tunic, unarmed, three paces ahead of his men. He was hated for many things, but not for cowardice. He and Autolykos were pretty nearly of a height. Their eyes met, measuring one another; and the voice of Kallibios, spluttering out his charge, grew quick and shrill. Neither of them looked at him.

Spartans do not practise the pankration as we know it. The law of the Games requires the loser to lift his hand in surrender; and no Spartan having done that is expected to show himself in Lakonia alive. So it is an event they do not enter for; but they like watching it as much as anyone. Lysander in particular was very fond of attending the Games, and being acclaimed there.

Autolykos stood in the Porch, calm as marble; I had seen him look so in the temple, waiting to be crowned. Lysander frowned; but could not keep the cold approval out of his hard blue eyes. Kallibios, smeared with mud to the hair, looked at the two big men feeling each other's strength; if he had had the power to turn everyone in sight to stone, he would have begun with Lysander. Everyone saw it, and Lysander, turning, saw it too.

His face told nothing. 'You are Autolykos the wrestler. Is this charge true?' – 'He talks too fast,' said Autolykos. 'I daresay it is.'

Lysander said, 'Let the accused hear the charge, Kallibios. Did you say he assaulted you? What did he do?' Kallibios stammered. Some of us in the crowd gave our evidence unasked. Lysander shouted for silence. 'Well, Kallibios? Repeat the charge.'

So Kallibios related again how he had been tossed in the midden; and the crowd cheered. Lysander said, 'How did he do it, Kallibios? I want a statement. Did he cross-buttock you, or what?' Kallibios stood chewing his lips. Autolykos said, 'No, it was just a thigh-hold, and a straight lift.' Lysander nodded. 'Is it true as these men say, that he took a stick to you?' Autolykos in silence raised his hand to his forehead, where blood was trickling from his short thick curls. 'Charge dismissed,' said Lysander. 'You are not working your farm with your Helots now, Kallibios. You had better learn how to govern free men.'

The city was quiet for a day or two. Then a notice was put up, cut in marble, that Thrasybulos and Alkibiades had been proclaimed exiles.

Thrasybulos had fled to Thebes a week before. It was said to have been Theramenes who had warned him of what was planned for him. His sentence caused anger rather than surprise. But, as always, it was enough to set Alkibiades' name up in the Agora, to make people talk all day. What was he up to, that had scared the Thirty? He had left Thrace, it was said, and crossed to Ionia, and asked for safe-conduct to Artaxerxes the new King. Something was behind it. Some said he would never forgive the City for disgracing him unjustly a second time; others, that what he might not do for love of us, he would do from hatred of King Agis. Even after the battle at Goat's Creek, where he had been driven off with insults by the generals, fugitives came back whom he had sheltered in his hilltop castle, and saved their lives. 'Insolent he may be; but there is no meanness in him. That, from a boy, he never had.' And people said, 'There is hope for the City, while Alkibiades lives.' The news of his banishment seemed a promise of his return. It was said openly in the streets that the Thirty were only in office to frame a new constitution; it was time they presented their draft, and made way for others.

Soon after this, there was a roll-call of the troops; a parade without arms, to re-group the units. On the Academy parade-ground I chatted with some old friends; then, having missed Lysis in the crowd, called to see him. As I got to his house, I heard weeping within, and Lysis saying in the smothered voice of a man distracted, 'Here, dry your eyes. Never mind it. Be quiet now; I must go.'

He came flinging out, nearly knocking me down upon the threshold. He was half dazed, and shaking with anger. Grabbing hold of me, as if I might walk off, he said, 'Alexias. Those sons of whores have taken my armour.' I said, 'What? Who have taken it?' – 'The Thirty. While I was at roll-call. My spear, my shield; even my sword.'

I stared at him like a fool. 'But it can't have been the Thirty. My arms are there; I've just come from home.' – 'Listen.' The street was beginning to roar with angry voices, and men were running from house to house. 'Your father is a Senator,' he said.

There are evils one does not imagine, till one sees them done. As my father had been fond of saying, this was supposed to be a gentlemen's government. A gentleman, and a citizen, was reckoned to be a man who could defend the City in arms.

'Command yourself, Alexias,' Lysis was saying. 'What is this? I have had enough to do already with tears.' – 'I am not weeping. I am angry.' My face burned, and my throat felt bursting. 'Let them take my arms too; what honour is left in bearing them?' – 'Don't be a fool. Arms are for use first, and for honour after. If you have arms, take good care of them. Lock them up.'

Next day we learned that three thousand knights and hoplites had been left their weapons. My father was one, and they had mistaken my arms for his. These only had citizenship, and the right to judicial trial. Over all others, the Thirty claimed power of life and death.

People went about the City like walking dead. There was nowhere to turn. We ourselves had been the source, once, of justice and democracy in Hellas. We were drained by war; ringed with victorious enemies; beyond were the lands of the barbarians, where even men's minds are enslaved. What is there that will season salt?

My father said to me, 'Don't talk so wildly, Alexias. Few or many, a government that does well is good. Kritias is an intelligent man; responsibility will make him careful.' – 'Will you make a drunkard temperate with more wine?' – 'Between ourselves, Theramenes thinks three thousand too few. That is within these walls. But the principle is sound, that of an aristocracy.' – 'Plato believes too in the rule of the best. When he heard Lysis had lost his arms, he could not speak for shame.' – 'Don't quote Plato to me,' my father said, 'as if he were some philosopher. I have heard enough of your scent-shop friends.'

Work had still to go on; I rode out to the farm next day on a hired mule, and stayed overnight. Working stripped in the sun of early autumn, binding the vines, I was happy in spite of myself; the earth, and her fruitful gods, seemed all that was real, the rest as shadows of dreams. Coming home the day after, I went round by way of Dipylon, to return my mule; then, as I walked through the Street of Tombs, I felt a strangeness, and a fear, and knew not why. It seemed colder; the colours had altered on the hills; and looking on the ground, where the sunlight fell in bright rounds through the leaves, I saw that all these had changed their shape, and become as sickles. The heavens seemed turning to lead, and sinking on the earth. And lifting my eyes to the sun, I saw it so altered that I dared look no longer, lest the god strike me blind.

Among the tombs, in the gloom of the eclipse, it was as one supposes the Underworld to be. The hair crept on my neck. Anaxagoras said it is only the dark shape of the moon crossing the sun. I can believe it any bright morning, walking on the colonnade.

Then in the chill, and the livid shadow, I saw a funeral coming on the Sacred Way. It was a long one, as if of some notable person; it came slowly, in the deep silence of people oppressed both with grief and fear. Only behind the bier a young wife, blind with her own weeping, tore at her hair and cried aloud.

I waited for the bier to pass me. It bore a heavy corpse; for six big men carried it, and yet their shoulders bent. Then, as they came nearer, I knew them all. For each was an Olympic victor, a wrestler, a boxer or a pankratiast. And on the bier, upon the brow of the dead, was an olive crown.

I stood and gazed my last on the stern face of Autolykos, whom one seldom saw in life without a smile. Now he looked like some ancient hero, come back to judge us. The gloom thickened, till I could scarcely see his olive wreath and his mouth of stone. Behind him a catafalque was heaped with his trophies and his ribboned crowns. When this too had passed, I joined the mourners, and said to the man who walked next me, 'I have been in the country. How did he die?' In the dusk he peered at me, with eyes of distrust and fear. 'He was walking about yesterday. That's all I know.' He looked aside.

The darkness had reached its deepest. Birds were silent; a dog howled in fear; the woman's weeping seemed to fill the earth and reach to the low heaven. I thought, 'Lysander pardoned him. Nor did Kallibios do it; for Spartans, even where they hate, obey. It was a present to Kallibios, to get his favour. Athenians did this.'

Then I said in my heart, 'Come, then, Lord Apollo, healer and destroyer, in your black anger, as you come to the tents at Troy, striding down from the crags of Olympos like the fall of night. I hear the quiver at your shoulder shake with your footfall, and its arrows rattle with the dry sound of death. Shoot, Lord of the Bow, and do not pause upon your aim; for wherever you strike the City, you will find a man for whom it is better to die than live.'

But the shadow passed from the face of the sun, and when we laid Autolykos in his tomb, already the birds were singing.

It seemed to me then that that soul of Athens lay prone now in the dust, and could fall no lower. But a few days later, I called at the house of Phaedo. He was out; but he had some new books, so I read and waited. At last his shadow fell on the doorway, and I rose to greet him.

He looked at me in passing, as if trying to remember who I was; then he walked on, and back again, up and down the room. His hands were clenched; I saw, for the first time in many years, the halt from his old wound catching his stride. After he had taken two or three turns, he began to speak. On the benches of a war-trireme I have heard nothing liked it. While he was working at Gurgos', I don't remember hearing him use any phrase that would not have passed at a decent supper-party. Now there came pouring out of him the silt and filth of the stews, till I thought he would never stop. After a time I did not listen, not because it offended me, but for fear of the news that was coming when he ceased. At last I put out my hand and stopped him in his walking, and said, 'Who is dead, Phaedo?' – 'The City is,' he said, 'and stinking. But corpse-loving Kritias keeps his mother above ground. They had passed a law forbidding logic to be taught.'

'Logic?' I said. 'Logic?' It made no sense to me; as if he had said there was a law against men. 'Who can forbid logic? Logic is.'

'Look in the Agora. There is a notice in marble, making it a crime to teach the art of words.' He burst out laughing; like a face in a dark wood, as Lysis had once said. 'Oh, yes, it's true. Did I teach you anything new, Alexias, just now? Learn it, write it down, it is the speech of a slave. I am starting a school in Athens; be my first pupil, and I'll take you free ' His laughter cracked, he threw himself down upon his work-bench at the table, and laid his head in his arms among the pens and scrolls.

Presently he sat up and said, 'I am sorry to make a show of myself. In the siege, when one felt one's strength drain out a little every day, one had more fortitude of soul. It seems that want of hope unmans one more than the want of food.'

I half forgot his news in his pain, for he was dear to me. 'Why, Phaedo, should you grieve so much? If the gods have cursed us, what is it to you? We shed the blood of your kindred; and to you we did the greatest of all wrong.' But he answered, 'It was the City of my mind.'

'Go back to Melos,' I said, 'and claim your father's land from the Spartans. You will find more freedom there than here.' – 'Yes,' he said. 'I will go, why not? Not to Melos; nothing would bring me to see it again. To Megara perhaps to study mathematics, and then to some Doric city to teach.' He stood up, and began sweeping his books together on the table. Then he smiled, and said, 'Why do I talk? You know I shall never leave Athens while Sokrates is alive.'

I smiled back at him; and then, in the same moment, the same thought came to both of us, and our smiles stiffened on our lips.

When I called at Sokrates' house, he was out; it was to be expected so late in the morning, yet I was afraid. As I turned away, Xenophon met me, and I saw my own fear in his eyes. We forgot the constraint of our last meeting. He drew me into a porch; even he had learned at last to drop his voice in the street. 'This Government will never be worthy of itself, Alexias, while Kritias is in it. I voted against his election, I may say.' – 'I don't suppose he got many votes from Sokrates' friends.' – 'Except from Plato. One thing is certain, Kritias has never forgiven Sokrates in the matter of Euthydemos. This law is framed against Sokrates, personally. Any fool can see it.'

'Oh, no,' I said. 'It is against the freedom of men's minds, as Phaedo says. No tyranny is safe while men can reason.' – 'Tyranny is not a word I care for,' he said stiffly. 'I would rather say a principle is being misapplied.' And then looking suddenly as I had known him since boyhood, 'If you don't remember Kritias' face that day, I do.'

At first it seemed absurd to me. I had seen the fair Euthydemos only lately; he had been drinking to the birth of his second son. It was natural that where Phaedo saw thought in chains, Xenophon should see one man's revenge; he had the more personal mind; yet there are times when feeling sees more than intellect. I said, 'You may well be right.' We looked at each other, not wanting to say, like fools or women, 'What shall we do?'

'Phaedo tells me,' said I, 'that a saying of Sokrates' is running round the Agora: When hiring a herdsman, do we pay him to increase the flock, or make it fewer every day?' – 'We shall delude ourselves, Alexias, if we expect him to study his safety before his argument.' – 'Do we even desire it? He is Sokrates. And yet . . .' – 'In a word,' said Xenophon, 'we love him, and are only men.' We were silent again. Presently I said, 'I'm sorry I was uncivil last time we met. You have done nothing contrary to your honour.' – 'I don't reproach you, since Autolykos died. I myself . . .' Then we saw Sokrates coming towards us.

In our joy at seeing him alive, we both went running, so that people stared, and he asked us what the matter was. 'Nothing, Sokrates,' said Xenophon, 'except that we are glad to see you well.' He looked just as always, cheerful and composed. 'Why, Xenophon,' he said, 'what a physician we have lost in you! One glance can tell you not only that my flesh and bones and organs are sound, but my immortal part too.' He was smiling, in his usual teasing way; yet my heart sank, and I thought, 'He is preparing us to bear his death.'

Hiding my fear, I asked if he had seen the notice in the Agora. 'No,' he said. 'I have been spared the pains of reading it by a friend, who, lest I should offend through ignorance, was kind enough to send for me, and recite it to me himself. I think I may rely on his memory of it, since he is the man who drew it up.'

A dark flush rose from Xenophon's beard to his brow; from a child he had been made to control his features, but this he had never overcome. 'Are you telling us, Sokrates, that Kritias sent for you to threaten you?' – 'Not everyone is privileged to have a law expounded to him by the lawgiver himself. It gave me the opportunity to ask him whether the art of words was being banned in so far as it produced false statements, or true. For if the latter, we must all refrain from speaking correctly, that is clear.'

His little bulging eyes laughed at us. Often he would recount to us blow by blow a set-to he had in the palaestra or the shops with some opinionated passerby. Now he described to us this colloquy, in which ten to one he had talked his life away, in just the same style. 'By the way, how old are you, Xenophon? And you, Alexias?' – 'Twenty-six,' we both said. – 'By the Dog, what has become of my memory? I must be getting old. For I have only just now been forbidden to converse with anyone under the age of thirty.' This was too much; we burst into wild and angry laughter. 'That, at the end of our conversation, was how Kritias interpreted his new law to me. I am the subject of a special amendment; a singular honour.'

Afterwards, going back through the Agora, we heard one householder say to another, 'One thing we can say for the Government, it has taken some abuses in hand. It is time someone put down these Sophists, who trip a man up and twist him round till he can't tell right from wrong, and give young fellows a back answer to anything you say.' When we had passed, Xenophon said to me, 'Those, Alexias, are the people you want to be governed by.' – 'The many rub off one another's extremes,' I said, 'like pebbles on a beach. Would you rather have Kritias?' But we parted friends. Even today, when we meet, it is much the same with us.

From that time, Sokrates' friends were bound in a conspiracy. Someone would arrive at his house very early each morning, bringing some question for advice. While he talked, and put off going out, others would turn up, and get a full discussion going. We kept an eye on the street; there was a back way out, at need, over the rooftops. Usually we managed to keep him in at least while the Agora was full.

I remember the little whitewashed room was full of people; the first-comer sitting on the foot of Sokrates' bed; the next perched on the window-sill; most of us on the floor; and Xanthippe grumbling loudly inside that she had no chance to sweep house. Plato would come in, silently, and sit down in the darkest corner. For he came now every day; no more was heard of his legal studies. His absent fits were over; you could see him following every word and running ahead; but he seldom spoke. His soul was in strife, and we all pitied him, as far as men can pity a mind much stronger than their own. I except Xenophon: for he knew, I think, that Plato was wrestling with matters he himself did not wish to question; and it made him uneasy.

Those of us who were going used to gather at the shop of Euphronios the Perfumer. It was not so fashionable that everyone went there, so not full of strangers who might be informers for all one knew. We would arrive and go through the civilities a scentmaker expects, sniffing the latest oil he was compounding, pronouncing it too heavy or too light or too musky, or sometimes, to keep him sweet, praising and buying. Sokrates when we got to his house used to wrinkle his snub nose, and tell us a good reputation smelt better.

But one morning, the man who had gone early met us in the doorway (it was Kriton's son, Kritobulos) and said, 'He's not at home.'

In the silence, Euphronios was heard saying, 'Just try this, sir.

Real Persian rose attar. The flask's Egyptian glasswork. For a special gift.' – 'I've been everywhere,' Kritobulos said, 'about the City. Yes, send me two, Euphronios.' – 'Two, sir? That comes to . . .' Kritobulos came over and dropped his voice. 'Someone said he went to the Painted Porch.'

Young people who go now to see the picture gallery will scarcely imagine it as a place where men walked in by daylight and came out at night feet first. The Thirty questioned suspects there. They used it, of course, for other business too; but the graceful columns, the painted capitals and the goldwork, stank of death like the warren of the Minotaur.

'Someone always says that,' said Lysis presently. 'People who would sooner run about with bad news than none. He may have got up early to sacrifice.' – 'Father is trying to find out. If we learn anything, I'll come back.'

Men in a common trouble draw naturally together; yet for a moment, each sat stricken in a grief that seemed all his own. Xenophon, hands upon knees, stared at the wall. He always looked out of place at Euphronios'. If he was offered a free sample, he would say, 'Not for me. Have you something for a girl?' Apollodoros was twisting his big red hands till the knuckles cracked. He had joined us lately, and was something of a trial to us, being so simple that his company had the inconvenience of a child's without its charm; he was ugly too, with a bald brow and wide ears. Some of us had amused ourselves at his expense at first, till Sokrates had taken us aside and made us ashamed. It was true, indeed, that the young man had no false conceit of knowledge, but came with modesty seeking the good he knew not how, as cattle go seeking salt. However, having no self-command, he had now got Euphronios uneasy. Serious gatherings were unwelcome at that time in any shop. Lysis and I, who had had our training in Samos, managed to cover him, pretending he was distraught with some love affair.

Euphronios cheered up, and began setting out his new stock. Presently he looked round. 'Why, Aristokles, sir, you came in so quietly I never heard you. And I've got news for you. The oil of rosemary you used to order last year, at last it's in again.

The very same pressing, sweet and dry, I'm sure you recall it.' He smeared a bit of linen and held it out. Plato after a moment's silence said, 'Thank you, Euphronios, but not today.' – 'I assure you, sir, you'll find it equal to last year's in every way.' – 'No, thank you, Euphronios.' He strode to the door and said, 'Shall we go?' Phaedo came over to him and said quietly, 'Not yet, Plato. Sokrates isn't in.' – 'Not in?' said Plato slowly. He drew his brows together, as a man does whose head is aching, if you ask him to think.

Phaedo was beginning, 'Kritobulos says . . .' when he himself appeared in the doorway, coming in from the colonnade. He was a handsome young man, dressed to make the most of it. His mantle had embroidered borders, his sandals were studded with coral and turquoise, and his face was the colour of bleached hemp. 'They did send for Sokrates. They were making up a posse for an arrest. For Leon of Salamis, people say. They sent for Sokrates to join it.'

We turned towards the door, to hide our faces from Euphronios and his slaves. I saw Xenophon's lips move silently cursing or praying. This was the Thirty's newest method, with anyone known to be critical: to force him into sharing one of their crimes, so that shame might silence him. Those who refused did not live very long.

Kritobulos said, 'Sokrates went to the Porch, when he was summoned, and asked what the charge was. When they wouldn't tell him, he said, "No," and went home.'

The silence was broken by Apollodoros, who gave a loud sob. Xenophon took him by the shoulders, and marched him outside. I turned to Plato. He stood still in the shop doorway, staring straight before him at a hetaira who had come buying scent. She pulled her silk dress tight across her buttocks and smiled over her shoulder; then, as his eyes did not move, went shrugging off. I had been going to speak to him; but there are doors at which one does not knock.

At last he turned, and touched Phaedo's arm, and said, 'Don't wait for me.' Phaedo paused, and looked at his face, and said, 'Go with God.' I was surprised, but too disturbed to feel it much. Just then Apollodoros running forward cried out, 'Oh, Plato, if you are going to Sokrates, do let me come with you.' At this moment his clumsiness was too much; two or three of us exclaimed in anger. But Plato took hold of him and said, gently and clearly, 'Don't go to Sokrates now, Apollodoros. He will be settling his affairs, perhaps, and speaking to his wife and children. I am not going to Sokrates; I am going to Kritias.'

He walked off along the colonnade. Watching him go, I recalled how the old Attic dynasty had ended; when King Kodros rode out alone to challenge the Dorians, because the omens had promised victory if the king were slain. They thought it impious to give him a successor; they set a priest on his throne, and dedicated it to the gods. I thought, 'A man may leave his sons behind him, and yet not live long enough to see his heir.'

What passed that day between Plato and his kinsman, none of us ever knew. If you ask how a man of twenty-four could put shame into one of five-and-forty, when Sokrates himself could not, I have nothing to say, except that Sokrates defied the Thirty, and lived. It was a saying of his, which all his young men knew by heart, that when you assume the show of any virtue, you open a credit account, which one day you will have to meet or go broke. It may be that what Kritias had seemed to his nephew was worth something to him. No man is all of a piece. If I had myself to choose someone who should find me out in a lie, Plato would come very low upon my list.

Nowadays, as in my boyhood, I went much to Piraeus, but for a different cause. One breathed the air of the sea there; and the quiet was not the quiet of the City above. They were quiet like seamen who have got a bad captain, and are all of one mind. One day the yard will fall from the block, or a hawser be stretched ankle-high on a dirty night.

Lysis and I were walking there, to a certain tavern where one could talk freely. As we passed through Spice Street, where some of the women have their houses, we saw one of them come out in a mourning veil, and lock up her door, and walk away with her head bowed, on which two others, who were gossiping in the street, turned and laughed at her. Lysis stopped when he saw it, and said to them, 'Come girls, don't mock at grief. The gods don't like it. Tomorrow it might be our turn.' One of them tossed her head at him. 'May they send me nothing worse that what she suffers! A man who, if he had ever seen her again, wouldn't have known her from a Hyperborean, you may be sure. Such airs and graces. She to mourn for Alkibiades!'

We stared, and stopped in our tracks, and said, 'For whom?' – 'Oh, hasn't the news reached the Upper City? The Chian trader brought it. Dead in Phrygia, so they say; but like as not it's another of his tricks. Never mind him; come in, tall darling, and take some wine with us. My sister will look after your friend.'

We hurried to the tavern, and found pilots and captains vowing and swearing Alkibiades was not dead. He was at Artaxerxes' court, making alliance with him; or raising an army of Thracians to free the City. There was even a rumour that he was in hiding in Piraeus. But in the City, Xenophon said to me, 'Sokrates believes it, and had gone away to meditate. If it were false his daimon would have told him.'

Next day we met some Chians from the ship, and questioned them.

One said, 'He was killed over a woman. How else would Alkibiades die?' And another, 'He had her in his house, and the men of her family came after him. Six to one they were, but it seems no one cared to be first. They threw torches at the thatch while he was sleeping. He woke up, and choked down the fire with the bedding, while he got out with the girl; then he ran at them naked, with only his sword, and his cloak round his arm for a shield. None of them would stand up to him; so they shot him full of arrows at twenty paces, by the light of the fire. And that was the end of him.'

Often, on campaign, he would come and sit at our watch-fire, to scrape and oil. He was vain of his body, fair-haired and glossy brown, clean as good food; the only marks he had were an old white spear-wound, and, sometimes, a love-bite from a woman. I saw his eyes, drowsy and blue, in the light of the crumbling embers. 'Who'll give us a song, before we turn in? You sing, Alexias. "I loved you, Atthis, I loved you long ago." Sing us that.'

Lysis said to the Chian, 'What girl was this?' – 'I don't know her City. A girl called Timandra.' – 'But he had her in Samos. She was a hetaira.' – 'She buried him,' said the Chian, 'whoever she was. Wrapped him in her own dress, and sold her bracelets to put him down in style. Well, fortune's a wheel, sure enough. Brought up by Perikles; raced seven chariots at Olympia; and buried by a whore.'

Afterwards Lysis said to me, 'If that girl had father and brothers, it's long since they went seeking her. And men revenging their honour show a little more spirit, or they stay at home. But hired killers aren't paid to shed their own blood. In Phrygia . . . yes, he must have been going to Artaxerxes. I wonder if King Agis ordered it, or someone nearer home.'

All over Piraeus, and up in the City, you could hear people declaring in the street that Alkibiades was not dead. In some of the poor quarters, more than a year after they were saying it still. But the Thirty went about cheerfully, like men who have shed a fear.

One day I came home from the farm, where we were getting our first small harvest in. The olives had put out strong shoots again; one, which had been only half scorched, was even bearing. I had brought home the crop, and came in calling, 'Father, look here!' His voice from within said, 'What is it?' At the sound, I put down the panier, and came in quietly. He was at his desk, his papers before him. 'Sit down, Alexias. I have things to say to you.' I came and sat down by him, looking at his face.

'These,' he said, 'are the deeds of the farm. Here are the deeds of the Euboean land; waste paper today, but the future no man knows. I have no debts. Hermokrates still owes us a quarter's rent, and can now afford to pay it.'

I looked at the paper on the desk, and saw what it was. 'Father,' I said. – 'Don't interrupt, Alexias. Kydilla, after her long service, ought to have been bequeathed her freedom. I have put nothing in writing, but express to you as my wish that when the estate can run to it, you will find her if you can, and buy her out. The time I leave to your honour and common-sense. Don't give your sister Charis in marriage before she is fifteen years old. Alkiphron of Acharnai has a likely son, and the lands march; but times are uncertain, so that too I must leave in your hands.'

I heard him till he had done. 'You know, Father, I will do all you ask; God keep it far from us. What has happened?' – 'Have you not heard, then, that Theramenes died today?'

'Theramenes?' Even of Alkibiades I could believe it sooner: he was an acrobat, as Kritias once had said; one knew that some day the rope would break, or the sword slip. But Theramenes was shrewd like a mountain fox, who does nothing for show, and digs no earth without a second door. 'Murdered,' my father said, 'by the Council, under the form of law.' He tipped a loose tile in a corner, set so well that I had never seen it, and put the will in the hole. 'If when you come for this you find other papers, burn them, but read them first. I should wish you to know you are the son of a man who did not consent to tyranny.'

'I never supposed it, Father. Through my own fault you do not know me.' And I tried to tell him what I had been doing. But he was displeased to hear I had made connections in Piraeus. 'I had sooner you spent your time with flute-girls. I thought no good would come of your going to sea, and mixing with riff-raff.' – 'Father, we will talk of that later. What happened today?'

'Kritias indicted Theramenes on a charge of treason. In his defence before the Senate, he did not deny that he opposed the Council, as its aims are now. He accused Kritias boldly in turn, of having betrayed the principles of the aristocracy, and set up a tyranny instead. I have no time to give you his speech, but I never heard an abler. The whole of the Senate, except the notorious extremists, acclaimed him at the end. About our verdict there could be no doubt, nor the sequel; he had put Kritias in the dock in his room. But meantime, a rabble of young louts had crowded in upon the public floor. Before the verdict could be voted on, they began shouting, and waving knives: men of no city, metics out of work, soldiers broke for cowardice, such men as take to the trade of hired bully for money or from choice. These, Kritias said, had come to make known to us the people's will. Well, some of us who had faced a Spartan battle-line had seen bigger men. We pressed for a vote. Then Kritias reminded us that only the Three Thousand have right of trial; and holding up the list, he crossed the name of Theramenes off it.'

I marvelled that no one had thought before of something so

simple. My father went on, 'He was condemned out of hand, by order of the Thirty, and was dragged off from the very altar of the Sacred Hearth, crying on gods and men for justice ... He was good to you, Alexias, when you were a boy, so I daresay you will be glad to hear that he died creditably. When they gave him the hemlock, he drank it straight off, all but the lees; those he tossed down, and called, "This for Kritias the Beautiful." Even the guards laughed at it.'

He paused. I said, staring at him, 'But, Father, how do you know that?' – 'I was with him,' my father said. 'He has been my friend these thirty years. When we were lads, we served in the Guard together. There was a notion, in the beginning, that the City was going to be governed by gentlemen. Because Kritias has forgotten it, we need not all do so, I suppose.'

He glanced at the tile where the will was buried, and tapped it down with his foot. 'Over Apollo's sanctuary,' he said, 'at Delphi, the navel of the earth, is written "Nothing too much." Extremes breed one another. I have tried to give you a decent education; yet you, too, instead of learning from the sight of tyranny to fear all extremes, can only fly from one to its opposite. And a man like Theramenes, who had risked his life often, and given it at last, in the cause of moderation, gets nothing for it but a vulgar nickname. There is some reason, I suppose. Well, he is dead. The Council made no difficulty when I asked to attend him in the prison. Kritias said they were glad to know who his friends were.'

I opened my mouth, to say I know not what; but I could see he thought me a fool, and it made my tongue heavy. 'You must be out of the City, Father, before the night. I will go and hire the mule I go to the farm on; no one will notice that. Will you go to Thebes?' – 'I shall go to my land,' he said. 'It will take a better man than Kritias to send me chasing over the border like a slave on the run. A hundred years and more before we owned any house in Athens, the farm was our home. It is a pity we left it. Men are better watching the seasons, and putting good into the earth, than running together in cities, where they listen all day to each other's noises and forget the gods. Acharnai is quite far enough.'

'I doubt it, sir. I beg you to go to Thebes. The Thebans hate

Lysander now more than they ever hated us; they have sworn not to give an Athenian up to him. Some of our best men are there.' I was going to name Thrasybulos, but remembered in time. 'I should have gone myself, if it had not been for the harvest. Leave the farm to me; I will see to that.' At length he said unwillingly that he would go to Thebes. 'Take your sister,' he said, 'to the house of Krokinos. Though only a cousin he has family feeling; he offered to take her of his own accord. I have arranged for her keep.'

At the fall of dusk I led round the mule. As he mounted, I saw he was shivering. 'It's this accursed fever,' he said. 'I knew I was in for a turn. It's nothing; I have taken the draught for it. The air is better in the hills.' – 'Give me your blessing, sir, before you go.' He blessed me, adding immediately after, 'Don't fill the house while I am gone with drunken sailors, or those young nincompoops from the scent-shop. Perform the sacrifices on the proper days, and keep some decency in the place.'

Afterwards I led Charis to our cousin's house. 'Please,' she said, 'can't I stay with Thalia and Lysis? I like being there.' – 'You shall go again, when Father comes home. Just now Lysis might have to go away too, and Thalia would be at his sister's then.' She did not ask where our father had gone, or why. I never knew a child of her age with so few questions. A year or two before, she had been full of them.

Krokinos' house was overflowing with women to the doors. A good fellow, as unlike as possible to his father Strymon, he and his wife had taken in the womenfolk of their remotest kindred, if they were exiled or had to fly. Strymon himself, after getting through the siege without losing any flesh to speak of, had died a month afterwards of a chill on the belly.

Next day early, I packed a bag and set out for the farm, on an ass I had hired outside the walls. On Lysis' advice, I meant to stay there for a week or two. There was plenty to do, and no sense in being about the City when my father was missed. Lysis had promised to come often and bring me news.

It was a beautiful fresh morning when I rode into the hills. Everywhere the wasted farms had started to bear again. In one they were treading the grapes. A little bare boy, driving goats, gave me a smile of milk-teeth and holes. The birds were singing; the cool westward-leaning shadows were the colour of Athene's eyes. I rode up to the farm, humming to myself *The King's Wife of Sparta*. Then I saw that the door stood open.

I thought the place must have been broken into, and ran inside. Nothing seemed disturbed, except one of the beds, which had a blanket on it. But as I walked about, I found my foot was leaving a stain on the floor. Going back to the door, I saw what I had trodden in.

I followed the blood-trail down the path, and across the farmyard. At first there were footsteps, then the marks of hands in the dust, and of a body dragging itself along. Up on the hillside, a mule was cropping the scrub.

I found him at the well, lying on the stone of the well-head, his head hanging over the shaft. I thought he was hours dead; but he said, in a voice like dry grass brushed with foot, 'Draw me some water, Alexias.'

I laid him down, and drew water, and gave it him. He had been stabbed in the back, and again in front when he turned to fight. I don't know how he had lived so long. When he had drunk, I bent to raise him, and carry him to the house; but he said, 'Let me alone. If you move me I shall die; I must speak first.'

I knelt beside him, and dipped my cloak in the water, and cooled his face with it, and waited, 'Kritias,' he said. I answered, 'I shall remember.' He sunk back into himself, being near his death, and his mind lost in shadows. Presently he said, 'Who is it?' I answered, and he came to himself a little.

'Alexias,' he said, 'I gave you life. Twice over I gave it.' I said, 'Yes, Father,' thinking he wandered. Then he said, 'An untimely birth. Sickly and small. One could forsee no credit in you. A man has a right over his own stock. But your mother . . .' He paused; not as before, but with his eyes on me, seeking strength to speak. I said, 'Yes, Father; I owe you a debt.'

He muttered to himself; I heard a few words: 'Sokrates' and 'Sophists' and 'young men today.' His eyes widened, and he pressed his clenched hands back upon the earth; and lifting his voice, as one might lift a heavy stone, he said, 'Avenge my blood.' Then he shut his eyes, and turned his head away, and muttered again.

I took his hand, and grasped it hard, till his eyes turned towards me. 'Father,' I said, 'since I was seventeen I have borne arms for the City. I have not run off any field, though I was fighting strangers only, who had done me no wrong. Am I so base of soul as to forgive my enemies? Believe, Father, that you begot a man.'

His eyes met mine; then his lips parted. I thought he was grimacing in pain, but perceived presently that he was trying to smile. His hands closed on mine, so that his nails pierced my flesh; then it slackened, and I saw that his soul was gone.

Soon after, the hired men, who had fled from the murderers, came back ashamed. I did not reproach them, for they had no arms, but set them to dig a grave for him. At first I had meant to burn his body, and bring back his ashes to the City; but remembering his own words, I buried him in the old plot of our ancestors, which they used long ago before we lived in town. It is a little way up the hill, above the vineyards, where the earth is too poor to farm; but you can see a long way from it, and pick out, when the sun is right, the flash from the High City, when it strikes Athene's spear. I set the offerings on the grave, and poured the libations. As I sheared my hair for him, I recalled that it was the second time; and yet, I thought, the first time too it was not unfitting.

I laid it on the grave; then heard behind me a movement, and turned swiftly, my knife in my hand. But it was Lysis standing there. I perceived he had been some time waiting, in silence, while I finished the rites. He came forward and took the knife from me and cut off a lock of his hair in token of respect, and laid it on the grave. Then he held out his hand to me, and, when I took it, said, 'Come, my dear, get together what you have. We are going to Thebes.'

'No, Lysis. I must go back to the City. I have a matter to settle there.' — 'From Thebes it can be settled better. So Thrasybulos writes. I should have come out tomorrow to talk of it; but I had word they were coming for me tonight.' He smiled and said, 'Two men warned me, neither knowing of the other. Manhood may be sleeping in the City, but it lives. It has slept in me too, Alexias. I should have gone long since, and tried to do what Thrasybulos has been doing. Weakness held me. It is hard to watch over the green shoot, and then when the flower opens to go away.'

We set forth within the hour upon the mountain road, going on foot, for we had sent back our hired mounts to the City. At first we were silent; he because the parting he had come from was a wound that still bled in him, I because I seemed only now to know myself, when what had pressed my soul into its mould was gone. But in a few hours, with the good air and clear light, and the movement of walking, and seeing places all about where we had fought in the Guard, sorrow lifted from us; and Lysis told me about the force Thrasybulos was raising to free the City. The road climbed high; the air grew sweet and thin; we saw the stone fort of Phyle on its steep hill watching the pass, and left the road lest the guard come out to challenge us. We had a hard scramble over the mountain, but made good going after, and were out of Attica by fall of dark.

So we turned aside, and in a sheltered place between rocks we made a little fire, and ate what we had. It was like the days on campaign; we sat recalling old fights and old comrades, till sleep made us heavy. Then we fell to disputing, as we had years back, whether the thicker of our cloaks should be spread to lie on, or above to keep out the cold. When one, which of us I can't remember, had given way grumbling to the other's view, we came to spread them, and found there was not a bit to choose between them for thickness; so we laughed, and lay down to sleep.

We were tired, and slept late. I opened my eyes to find a blush of dawn already on the peaks; then I heard a voice say softly, 'One of them is awake.'

I touched Lysis to rouse him without noise, and felt for my dagger. Then I turned my head; and saw two youths, or boys rather, sitting on their heels and smiling. They were dressed for hunting, in leather tunics and belts and shinguards; one was sturdy and fair, the other long-limbed, and dark. The fair one said, 'Good morning, guests of the land. Can you eat a hunter's breakfast?'

We greeted them, and they led us off to the place where their horses were. There was a fire, and a hare wrapped in clay and leaves baking in the embers. The lads got it out, burning their fingers and swearing and laughing, and cut it up, and handed us choice pieces on the points of their knives.

After they had asked the latest news from the City, 'Tell me pray,' said the dark one, 'how a man can converse with another whom he doesn't see or hear?' Something in the way he put his question told me he studied philosophy; so I said smiling, 'Enlighten my ignorance, best of men.' – 'He can now if he's a Theban; for our new law is that when we meet you Athenians crossing the hills to take up arms against the tyrants, we don't see you or hear you; and quite right too.' – 'However,' the fair one said, 'coming on you asleep, we forgot for a moment you were invisible, and said, "These two like us are old friends, and for friendship's sake we ought to entertain them." Kebes and I took the vow of Iolaos, you see, a year ago today. My name is Simmias.'

We introduced ourselves, with compliments on their long association. You could not have told which was the elder, except that Kebes, the dark one, had his boy's hair still. The sun rose as we ate, round and back above the valley mists. Simmias said, 'Our teacher, Philolaos, the Pythagorean, considers the sun to be a great round mirror, reflecting back the central fire of the universe, like a polished shield. But why the fire grows red at sunrise, and white at noon, we cannot determine to our satisfaction; can we, Kebes? How do the Athenian philosophers explain the sun?' – 'In nearly as many ways,' said Lysis, 'as there are philosophers. But our teacher says that the nature of Helios is a secret of the god; and that a man's first business is to know himself, and seek the source of light in his own soul. We don't eat everything we see, but have to learn what our bodies can turn to good. So with the mind.'

'That is reasonable,' said the dark Kebes. 'Man's intellectual soul is a chord struck from all his parts, as the music of the spheres is the chord of the heavenly bodies. If the intervals have no measure, it can make no more sense of anything than a lyre untuned. So Philolaos taught us.' – 'But,' Simmias said, 'he is soon going back to Italy, and then we shall have no teacher, for we can't be satisfied with any of the others here. But our fathers won't let us go to Athens while the tyrants are in power there; so you see we have our own reasons for wanting them gone. Tell us more about this teacher you go to. Has he anything new to say upon the nature of the soul?'

In the end they put our knapsacks on their horses, and walked with us, talking, all the way to Thebes. That night we slept on supper-couches in the guest-room of Simmias' father. He was putting up two or three Athenians, and the house of Kebes' father was already full. Everywhere one met with friendship; it was hard to believe in the bitterness of former days. They had seen enough, they said, of Lysander's oligarchies, the worst men ruling by the worst means for the worst ends; the friends of liberty were not Thebans and Athenians now, but Hellenes all alike.

Next day the lads wanted to carry us off to hear Philolaos; but we excused ourselves till we had seen Thrasybulos first. It was like old times to go into a plain little wine-shop, and see him pull in his long legs from under the table and come striding over, his brown eyes warm and straight in his lean dark face. 'Samian men!' he said. 'The best news today.'

It was about a week after this that we left Seven-Gated Thebes; but not alone.

We set forth in the red light of sunset, a band of seventy men. Our shields were covered, our armour brazed, and smeared with dark oil. We were all heavy-armed, however we had come from Attica; the Thebans had armed us. Crossing the border we made an altar, and sacrificed victims to Pallas Athene, and to Zeus the King. The omens were good.

The sun sank, but a little moon was up, enough to save our necks on the hills. It would set later, which was well. By its dipping light, we came to the place where the pass hugs the side of the mountain; opposite is a hollow and a rise, and on the rise the stone fort of Phyle, backed against the drop of a great gorge, its face to the Theban road.

We dropped into the valley, going single file by a little path; at the bottom is a stream, from a source in the hill above, very clean and good to drink. There we waited, while a scout stole up under the walls. He had been stationed there, and knew it like his home. He was back within the hour. They were only a peace-time garrison, glad to be easy now the Spartans had gone.

They had given each other the countersign, he said, as loud as a good-day in the Agora.

We crept up to the main gate, just before the guard was due to change again. The moon was down. Someone gave the countersign; when the gate opened, we held it while others thrust in. By good luck, the postern over the gorge, where the rubbish is thrown out, had been left unguarded; the drop is steep, but some of our mountain men climbed in there.

I never saw a garrison so confounded. They hardly resisted, once they understood who and what we were. The officer in charge, thinking of his reputation, put up a fight; but Thrasybulos took him on, and, holding him off without wounding him, asked him across their shields why he was concerned to maintain his honour before rulers who had none themselves, when he might be earning himself a liberator's undying fame. In the end not only he, but half the garrison took the oath with us, and looked, I thought, five years younger and gayer. The rest we held in bonds till it was light, and we could see where they went; then keeping their arms we let them go.

Later Lysis and I, standing the morning watch upon the walls, saw the sunrise. It came red and purple, for winter drew on, and up there one felt already the nip of frost. The gold touched the heights; but below us the great cleft of Phyle, which they call the Swallower of Chariots, was a river of unfathomed mist. Light spread; the mist dispersed; far out through the gorge we saw the Acharnian Plain, threaded with a little road; and at the road's end, dimly shining, the walls and roofs of Athens. In the midst the High City, like an altar, lifted her offerings to the gods. For a long time we gazed in silence; then Lysis said to me, 'I think we are seeing the dawn indeed.'

27

On the second day after, we saw from our walls the army of Athens advancing.

The sky was cloudless, of a thrush-egg blue. Horse and foot they wound along the road, like beads stitched on a ribbon, hardly seeming to move; then the mountains hid them. A little before sunset, we saw them close at hand, upon the pass. We watched the line of men thrown round us, first a thread, then a cord, then a great cable, thick as the girdle of a ship. Five thousand men, I believe, sat down that evening before Phyle. The baggage-train streamed over the bridle-path, bringing their food. When it was finished, more would come. We had only what had been laid in for a force of fifty, and that part-eaten.

They lit their fires, and bivouacked for the night, and pitched tents for the leaders. The Thirty themselves were there. All of us now saw how it was likely to end. But not one, I think, would have exchanged Phyle for Athens. Under our eastern wall, so deep that the pines on its sides looked as small as brush, was the Cleft of the Chariot. There was a door open still to freedom, when the food was gone.

All night the stars shone bright above us, the watch-fires bright below. The dawn was clear. It brought a herald, who bawled at us to surrender to the Council. We laughed, and answered as each man thought good. At the foot of the hill, some of the knights were watching their horses being groomed; rich young men, campaigning like gentlemen. One or two came forward and, with taunts, shouted to us to come down. 'No,' we called, 'you come up. Honour the house. Make us happy.' Suddenly a score or so jumped on their horses, and put them at the hill; perhaps from bravado, perhaps hoping that if they could reach it, they might force the gate.

Phyle was well off for javelins. From the walls I marked down a man who was coming up just below. One or two others would have done as well, but I chose this one to punish his insolence: a well-built fellow, sitting his horse as if he had grown there, showing its paces.

He too was armed with the javelin. He got ready as he rode up the hill; but downward one throws harder. He had seen me; we took aim together; then, in the moment before we both let fly, he checked with a great start, as if I had hit him already. His horse felt it, and reared, spoiling my aim. Struggling with his mount he got his helmet twisted, and thrust it back in order to see. It was Xenophon. For a moment, as he sat the prancing horse with head flung up, we stared into each other's eyes. Then he rode round the side of the wall, and I saw him no more.

The knights were beaten off, and several wounded. There was no more fighting that day. Thrasybulos counted the stores. Then he assembled us, all but the lookouts, and asked us to pray all together to Zeus the Saviour, that, as he loved justice, he would not let it perish out of Hellas along with us. We prayed, and sang a hymn. The evening came down, solemn and red, the air cold, not a breath stirring. And in the night, Zeus the Saviour leaned out to us, and opened his hand.

His hand opened; and, from a sky filled till then with great white stars, came a fall of snow. Cold as the breast of Artemis, and stinging like her arrows, all night it fell, and when day broke it was still falling. The mountain heights stood in the snow-whirl like a world of white marble veined with black. Down below were the thin tents of the besiegers; and the many who had no shelter, huddled round smoking damp fires, beating their bodies, stamping their feet to keep them from freezing, wrapping up the starved horses in blankets they needed themselves. An army of beggars gazed up in envy of our wealth. We called down to them, inviting them to visit us, and we would see that they were warm.

All day it snowed; but by noon they had had enough. The Thirty, used by now to comfort, were the first to go. Then the knights had pity on their shivering horses; then the hoplites marched off; and then, strung out below us, a banquet spread as it were by heaven, the long cumbrous baggage-train, creeping half-foundered in the snow. We flung the gates open. Yelling the paean, as men for whom the gods are fighting, we charged down the hill.

We left red snow that day; and carried up to Phyle food and fuel and blankets to keep us like kings for a year.

We were snowed up for a time. Then volunteers began to come. Most were proscribed exiles: democrats; or gentlemen too touchy in their honour to please the Government; or simply people whose estates one of the Thirty had fancied for himself. But one or two came from the army that had besieged us; even before the snow they had thought it looked better up the hill. Their soothsayer came, a burning silent man; Apollo had warned him, through the aspect of the sacrifice, not to serve men hateful to the gods.

We were a hundred strong; then two; then three. All Attica, and Megara, and Thebes, heard of the Men of Phyle. We were seven hundred. When bad weather drove us all indoors, there was hardly room to sleep.

The Thirty set a guard on the pass, to keep us from the farms; but we had our own way across the mountains. We were never short of stores. Some we were given for love, some we took from necessity. Our best sport was raiding our own estates. There were scores of us who had had land stolen by the tyrants. They looked after it well, as I found when we raided mine. I had never seen it so thriving and well-stocked since I was a child.

When the work was well on, I found a slave hidden in a grain-bin. 'Get out,' I said, 'and tell me who farms this land. Then you can run free, for all I care. This if you lie.' I showed my dagger. 'By the Arrow of Bendis, my lord' (he was a Thracian) 'my master's name is Kritias.'

I let him go, and went up between the vineyards, with a white cock in my hand. On my father's grave I killed it, to comfort his shade, and as an earnest of things to come, and to show Kritias who had called.

Within a short time the Thirty had had many such reminders; and up at Phyle we were a thousand men. Though only a few could bring armour and weapons with them, all the news was that the tyrants hardly trusted Lysander, even, to protect them now.

It was still deep winter; but hope was strong in us, hard and firm as the buds furled up in the armoured trees. We had no slaves, and were all servants of one another, cooking and cleaning and fetching water in. I never tasted such cold sweet water as it is in the spring at Phyle. There was a gladness in us, such as I have seldom known. I remember tramping a windy hill-track, laden with fuel, singing, and talking of the future when the City was free. Lysis said he was going to get a son; 'though if a daughter comes first, no matter; little girls make me laugh.' – 'I shall write,' I said, 'to those Theban lads, Simmias and Kebes. We owe them some hospitality. They are longing to hear Sokrates.' – 'Their famous Philolaos,' Lysis said, 'is rather too mathematical for me.' – 'Yes, but I shall introduce them to Phaedo. I am sure he would enjoy hearing them talk.'

One morning early, we fell on the guard who held the pass, caught them on one leg at getting-up time, and chased them down into the plain. Soon we heard news of panic among the Thirty. Even the Three Thousand, once the core of their support, did not trust them since Theramenes had been struck off the roll. We rejoiced to hear it; but not when we got the proof of how deeply they feared.

After hubris, nemesis; but madness lets her in. They needed a refuge now, to fortify against extremity; and they chose Eleusis, because at the worst they could fly from it by sea. But having deserved good of no one, they did not trust the Eleusinians not to give them up. So on pretence of an Army exercise, they marched them through a narrow gateway, and had each one seized as he passed beyond. Every man and grown youth of Eleusis they murdered; but not with their own hands, taking like men their guilt before the gods. They dragged them to Athens, and charged them before the Senate as perilous to the City, not deigning to offer any further charge. The voting was open; guilty this side, innocent that; and the Senate was packed with Spartans in heavy arms.

The Senate voted death. So low they had gone, it was only one step lower. But it was the last. They were at the bottom of the pit; and some still had eyes to see it. When the news came up to the mountains, we knew that in the sight of gods and men our time had come.

All next morning we made ready. At noon we ate and rested, for we should not sleep that night. When Lysis and I had seen to our arms, he said to me, 'We look rather too much men of Phyle. Let us make ourselves fit to be seen in the City.' We trimmed each other's hair, but were in two minds whether to part with our beards or not; we had good ones by now, and were at home with them. But Lysis said laughing, 'I want my wife to know me again.' We both shaved in the end, and were glad when it was done; it made us feel we were going home.

When the light was changing on the mountains, we sacrificed a ram, and poured libations. The soothsayer told us the signs were good, and we stood and sang our paean. Soon after we fell in, to begin our march, for we had a good way to go across the hills.

Just before the trumpet, Lysis and I stood on the walls, and looked down the Cleft of the Chariot, to see Athens shine, clear gold picked out with shadows, in the slanting winter sun. I turned to him and said, 'You look sad, Lysis. It has been good here, but we are going to better.' He smiled at me and said, 'Amen, and so be it.' Then he was silent for a time, looking out at the High City, and leaning on his spear. 'What is it?' I said; for my mind was full of memories, which I felt he shared. 'I was thinking,' he said, 'of the sacrifice just now, and of how one ought to pray. It is right for men setting out on a just enterprise to commend it to heaven. But for oneself . . . We have entreated many things of the gods, Alexias. Sometimes they gave, and sometimes they saw it otherwise. So today I petitioned them as Sokrates once taught us: "All-Knowing Zeus, give me what is best for me. Avert evil from me, though it be the thing I prayed for; and give me the good which from ignorance I do not ask."'

Before I could reply to him, the trumpet sounded, and we went down to the gate.

The turn of the year was past; the light saw us through the mountains, and when we reached the plain of Eleusis, dusk hid us on the road. No enemy met us. The Thirty were watching the pass, to guard the farms. A little after midnight, skirting the shore, we came into Piraeus.

At first all was silence. Then the town awoke; but not to outcry or confusion. We had come as a good long watched for, in the sullen patience of men born to the sea. The rumour ran along the streets, and the houses opened. Men came out with swords, with knives, with axes or with stones; women came, decent wives rubbing shoulders with hetairas, bringing cakes or figs, and bold with darkness thrust them into our hands. The metics came out: Phrygians and Syrians and Lydians and Thracians, whose kin the Thirty had killed and plucked, with no more pity than the farmer's wife choosing a cockerel for the pot. When the dawn broke, we knew that all Piraeus was ours, as far as feeling went. But feeling does not pierce heavy armour; nor do stones. The stand was taken, but the battle was still to come.

The frosty sun peered over Hymettos; the day grew bright; and from the roofs we saw the enemy coming, the horses first, and then the hoplites, advancing from the shadow of the Long Walls, into the sunlight of Lysander's breach. When it was pretty clear we were outnumbered five to one, and had no hope of holding the outer defences, we fell back upon the old fortress of Munychia, where the ephebes train. On the rocky road that climbs from the market to the citadel, we took our station, those of us who were heavy-armed, to hold the passage. Behind us, swarming on the rocks were the men of Phyle who had light arms or none, and the people of Piraeus with cleavers, knives and stones.

Then, as one finds in war, there was a pause. The Army of the city was sacrificing, and making its dispositions. Behind us the people shouted to each other; over the harbour, the gulls wheeled and called; down below one heard an order, a horse neighing, the rattle of grounded shields. We fell to the idle-sounding talk of soldiers who wait. I remember saying, 'When did you mend your sandal, Lysis? What a botch you have made of it. Why didn't you ask me, for you know I do it better?' And he said, 'Oh, there was no time; it will last the day.' Then came a trumpet, and the march of armour, and the enemy came into the market-place below.

It looked very wide, emptied of its traffic, with bare stalls; there had been no trading in Piraeus that day. The troops marched in, filling it from side to side, and, as line followed line, almost from end to end. I think their shields were fifty deep. I know that ours were ten.

As they deployed, we began to know them. It was no place for horses; the knights were on foot, but you could tell them by the gold on their armour, their crests of worked bronze. One could do no more than pick out a man here and there, yet I thought, 'Xenophon is not with them,' and was glad. Then to the left we saw the standard; and Thrasybulos called in his great voice, 'The Thirty are there.'

He spoke to us, as he used to do in Samos, of our just cause; reminding us of the gods' favour, when they saved us with the snow. 'Fight, each man of you,' he said, 'so that the victory will feel like yours alone. You have everything to win: your country, your homes, your rights, the sight of your lovers and your wives; joy if you live, glory if you die. There stand the tyrants; vengeance is ours. When I strike up the paean, take the note from me, and charge. We wait upon the gods.'

He turned to the soothsayer, who had made the sacrifice, and now came forward, the sacred fillet on his head. He passed through us to the front as if he neither felt nor saw us. I knew by his eyes that Apollo possessed him. 'Be still,' he said. 'That god gives victory; but first a man must fall. Till then stand fast.' Then he called on the name of the god with a loud cry and said, 'It is I.' And on the word he leaped forward, upon the line of shields below. For a moment, in the suddenness, they stood unmoving; then the spears thrust at him, and he fell. And the walls of Munychia echoed back Thrasybulos' voice, shouting the paean.

We ran down the hill. The slope made our feet light, our purpose gave us wings. It was like the last lap of the race, when the Eros of victory lifts one. I know I killed and killed, yet I felt no anger, more than the priest who sheds the blood of the victim. Lysis and I fought side by side, pressing onward, feeling the line of the enemy bend before us, and give, and shatter to sherds. They were many; but their crust was thin, their centre was soft; they were men not at peace with the gods, or with their own souls. In a little while, if a man of them still stood firm, he was one with nothing to lose. It was while the battle hung so that I heard a voice, trying to rally the line; the voice of a speech-maker, not used to the talk of the field where man speaks to man. I knew it; and leaping forth from Lysis' side (for till now we had gone forward step by step together) I made for it through the press.

I came on him by the stall of a potter, which stood empty at the side of the square. In silence I had tracked him down, not calling his name, or any challenge, for I knew that many desired his company as much as I. Like a lover I sought him, keeping my rivals in the dark, feeling my way. Then he was before me, and through his helmet-slits I saw his eyes.

As we leaned shield to shield, I said, 'You courted me once, Kritias. Now am I close enough?' But he only gritted his teeth and panted; for I had been living hard, he softly, and his breath was short. I turned his shield with mine, and thrust at him, and wounded him in the leg. 'Do you know me?' I said to him. 'I am Myron's son.' I waited for his face to alter; but except when it jerked at the spear-thrust, it did not change; and I understood that this one name meant nothing to him, among the many he had sent to death. Upon this I felt a rage at him, so that my strength flared up like a torch; and leaning hard on him till I bore him backward, I hooked his knee with mine, as I had seen Lysis do it in the pankration; and he went back with a clatter of armour against the racks of the potter's stall.

He clutched a shelf, and it came away; he rolled, and fell on his back, and I leaped upon him and pulled his helmet off. Then I saw his hair was streaked with grey; his face being drawn with fear looked shrivelled as with age, and my stomach turned at killing him; till I remembered he had forgotten my father's name, and thought, 'A beast is under my knees, and not a man.' So I drew my sword, and thrust it through his throat, saying, 'Take this for Myron.' He gasped, and died. Whether he heard me I do not know.

When he was certainly dead, I leaped up, and saw the battle swaying all about me. I lifted my voice and shouted, 'Lysis!' For I thought it long till I could tell him what I had done. I heard his voice rising above the dim call, 'Alexias! I am coming!' Then it seemed that a great rock fell on me; I was crushed and flung into darkness; the sounds of the battle reached me without meaning, as a child near sleep hears voices in another room.

I came to myself in a courtyard full of wounded men. In the centre was a fountain, playing into a basin lined with blue tiles, such as the Medes make. My head ached, and I felt very sick. I must have been struck down with a blow on the helmet, and stunned, but my head was not bleeding; the wound was in my hip, just below the corselet-rim. It was deep, and my blood lay all about me. I must have been speared when I fell. The stain was black and dry at the edges, where it had flowed over the marble tiles; so I knew I had been there some time.

I was thirsty, and the sound of the water made my thirst more. Then when I wished to drink, I thought for the first time, 'Am I captive, or free?' And turning my head towards a man lying near me, I said, 'Have we won?' He gave a great sigh, and rolled his head towards me. I saw he was near death. 'We lost,' he said, and closed his eyes. Then I knew him altered as he was; it was Charmides. I had seen him before the battle, down in the market-place among the knights. I called him by name, but he spoke no more.

I began to crawl towards the fountain, the knowledge of victory giving me heart; but a man who could walk, and use one arm, brought me some water in a helmet. I drank, and thanked him, and asked if the battle was long over. 'An hour gone,' he said, 'and they have declared a truce to gather up the dead. I was there myself till lately. The Thirty have fled; and before I left, the people taking up the bodies were talking together, men of both sides.'

He told me more, but I was too weak to heed it. I looked at my blood on the floor, and trailed my hand in it, and thought, 'Well spent.' For a while I rested; an old woman came out and tied a cloth over my wound; then I opened my eyes and felt better, and began to look about me, and to feel impatient for someone to come and carry me to my friends.

I heard the feet of men bearing a burden, and turned to call to them. But they were carrying a dead body on a shield. The head hung back, and the legs dangled from the knees, and a horseman's cloak was thrown over all, so that the face was hidden. I did not know the cloak, and was turning away, when I saw the two men look at me, and then at one another. Then I felt my heart turn to water, and my wounds grow cold. The feet were showing beneath the cloak, and one of the sandals was mended.

I found a voice, and called to the men, who at first pretended not to hear me. But they stopped when I called again. I said, 'Who is it?' Each of them waited for the other to speak; but presently one said, 'I am sorry, Alexias.' And the other said, 'He died very well. Twice after he was struck he got upon his feet, and again after that he tried. We must go on Alexias, for he is heavy.'

I said, 'Do not carry him any further. Leave him here with me.'

They looked about the courtyard, which was crowded by this time, and then at each other again; and I saw what was in their minds, that wounded men do not like to be with the dead. So I said, 'I will go with you, then,' and got up from where I lay, and followed after them. In the porch I found a spear with a broken head, and took it to lean on. We went a little way, and came to a small pavement before an altar. There was a broken wall beside it, and dust upon the stones; but I could not walk any longer, so I said, 'This place will do.'

They put him down, and excusing themselves to me, took away the cloak and the shield, for they had other bodies to fetch. He had been wounded between neck and shoulder; it was the bleeding that had killed him. He was so drained of blood that his flesh was not discoloured as one sees it in the dead, but like a clear yellow marble. There was blood on his armour, and in his hair. His helmet was off; his open eyes looked, as he lay, straight upward at the sky, as if they asked a question. I had to press my hand over them a long time, before they could close.

His body had not stiffened yet, but his skin was growing cold. He lay already as one of the unnumbered dead. Always, from my first remembrance, whether he rode, or walked, or ran, or stood talking in the street, as far as I could see him I knew him apart from all other men; nor was it possible, in the darkest night, to mistake another's hand for his. Now the flies were beginning to come, and I had to drive them away.

I was weak as a young child, in mind and body, and yet I could not weep. That is well, you may say; for when a Hellene dies commendably, even a woman ought to restrain her tears. I too from my first youth had been taught what is proper to be felt on such occasions; nor had I been ignorant that what I loved was mortal. Yet now I was as a stranger to the earth, and to my own soul. For it said to me that if there be any god who concerns himself with the lives of men, the god himself must suffer with me. And when I thought that the Immortals live far off in joy, holding eternal festival, then it seemed to me that the gods were not.

After I do not know how long, the men who had carried him came back to see how I was. I said I was well enough, and asked if they had seen him fall. They said no, but they had heard him praised by those who had; and one said he had been there later, when he died. I asked if he had spoken to anyone.

'Yes,' said the man, 'he spoke to Eukles, whom he knew better than me, and asked about you; he seemed afraid you might be dead. He said you had cried out for help to him; and I think he got his wound trying to reach you. We told him you had been carried off the field, but not hurt mortally, and he seemed content, and rested a little. By that time his mind was growing clouded, and he was beginning to yawn, as I have seen other men do when bleeding to death. Then he said, "He will care for the child." Had he one, then? But I suppose you know what he meant.' I answered, 'Yes. Did he say anything else?'

'Seeing he was nearly gone, Eukles asked if he wished to leave you anything for remembrance. He said nothing, but smiled. I daresay he had not heard. But when Eukles asked again, he said, "Whatever there is." Eukles showed him he had a ring on, and he tried to draw it off, but it had been there a long time and from weakness he could not. Eukles has it for you; he got it off after he was dead.

'At just this time, the troops of the City fell back altogether from the Agora, leaving us masters of the field; and Thrasybulos ordered the trumpet to sound for victory. He opened his eyes and said, "Is that for us?" I told him yes, and he said, "Then all is well, isn't it?" Eukles answered, "Yes, Lysis; all is well"; and with that he died.'

I thanked him, and they went away. When they had gone, I

lifted his hand, and saw how they had bruised it, pulling off the ring for me. Then I wept.

Presently from the walls of Munychia I heard the victors singing a hymn of praise to Zeus. As I listened, my head swam, and my senses melted in darkness; for walking had opened my wound, and it had been bleeding again. The men were lifting me upon a litter, and debating together whether I was alive. I did not speak, for it seemed no matter; but lay with closed eyes, listening to the triumph song.

28

A year later, on a warm day in spring, I went up to the High City, to receive an olive crown.

It was only one of seventy, which the City had voted to Thrasybulos, and the men who went with him to Phyle. The civil war was over, and the tyranny crushed for good; Lysander had over-reached himself in Sparta, intriguing for a kingship; King Pausanias has got wind of it, and moved to set him down. Seeking to sap his power everywhere, and thinking it policy besides, the kings had given us leave to set up a democracy again. So the City gave thanks to Zeus, and pledged itself to a rule of perfect justice between man and man.

It was strange to stand again in the Maiden Temple, and feel the olive-twigs prick my brow. Many times in my youth I had prayed that Lysis and I might be crowned together; and he, I daresay, had prayed it too. Now it was I who received his wreath for him, and brought it home. I accepted it for Thalia, it being now my place to act for her in this and in all other things. But the mother of my sons has deserved better of me, these five and twenty years, than to be talked of at large, and already I have set down more than I ought.

Afterwards there were speeches, praising the liberators, honouring the dead, and hailing the fair prospect before the City; for though we had lost empire, they said, we had found justice, the greatest gift of Zeus to man. Then there was a choral contest, a race in armour for men, and, as evening fell, a torch-race for the boys.

I sat in the stadium, in the pause between the contests, thinking I would go down presently to see the lads I had trained for the race, and encourage those who might need it. But there was time yet.

The water-sellers and the wine-sellers were busy, for the evening was warm and the runners had kicked up the dust. As you find at such times, friends saw each other from their seats (for it was hardly dusk) and came across, and others made room for them to sit together. Xenophon waved to me, and made his way over. We greeted each other warmly. The amnesty had given both of us a welcome excuse to heal our friendship. I said I had missed him lately in the City, and asked where he had been.

'To Delphi,' he said, 'to consult Apollo, how I should sacrifice before a journey I mean to make.' I asked if he was going far. 'A good way,' he said. 'To Persia, to fight for Cyrus.'

I stared at him, too much surprised to speak. He said, 'Proxenos, my Theban friend, has written to me from Sardis. He is in Cyrus' service already, and tells me he has never met a finer soldier and gentleman. And Proxenos is a judge of such things. A force is needed, it seems, to clean some bandits out of the mountains; and Cyrus is open-handed, which is something to a man whose estate is encumbered like mine.'

'It sounds an odd business to me. Hire an army of Hellenes to clean out bandits? You can't trust a Mede's word; you might be in for anything. Didn't you ask the oracle, while you were about it, whether you should go at all?' He laughed rather shamefacedly. 'That's what Sokrates said. Well, I admit I didn't want to change my mind. But I suppose if Apollo had been much against it, he would have given me a hint.'

I felt more concerned for him than I liked to say. Even in peace-time, he would do himself great harm at home by hiring his sword to the patron of Lysander. But he must know it; he was a soldier and no fool. And I thought to ask him why he was leaving the City, just when things were on their feet again; but I did not ask. For though he held himself still like a knight and an officer of horse, yet there had been something dimmed and quenched about him since the amnesty; he had looked like a man without a future. All through the troubles he had gone, as he saw it, step by step with his honour; in the end he had abhorred the tyrants as much as anyone; but his eyes had opened late; and it was true that the City had little use, at present, for men who had ever been loyal to the Thirty.

'Any man,' he said, 'wants to leave his name on record somewhere about the earth. Even a boy feels it, who carves a tree. I have dreamed sometimes of founding a city; but that is with the gods.' The wine-seller came round, and he stood me a cup; the usual rough stuff they sell at the games. 'Besides,' he said, 'I want to study Cyrus. They call him a man born to rule, and I want to know how such a man is made. One hears a great deal from this faction or that, how they are fit to govern, rather than anyone else. As Sokrates always says, a mason, or a smith, can tell you clearly how he qualifies for job; but no one has defined the qualifications of a ruler; or, rather, no two agree on the definition. Trouble always comes of not defining your terms; but more trouble than most, it seems, of not defining this one.'

'Good luck, then,' I said, 'with your definition. But bring it back here, for your friends to share.' I looked at him, tipping down the coarse wine like a man who expects to put up with worse. I felt I was looking my last at the lad I still remembered. I was right. When I saw him again, it was five years later, and not in Athens. He was tanned like the thong of a javelin, and as tough as the shaft, a soldier who looked to have been cradled in a shield; but the oddest change, I think, was to see in one always so mindful of convention that careless outlandishness you find in irregular troops of great renown; men who seem to say, 'Take it or leave it, you who never went where we have been. We are the only judges of one another.'

He went off to some other friends; and I, seeing someone sign to me, stood up, and recognised Phaedo, and went over. Plato was with him, and, a few benches lower, Sokrates in talk with his old friend Chairophon, who was back from his exile with the democrats. They did not see me, coming behind; but Plato made me sit beside him. When we meet in public places, he has never ceased to show me courtesy. But he does not ask me to his house. Though I never came forward as the killer of Kritias (no man will boast of what he has bought too dear) yet it was known to a few; and no doubt it will be a bad day for the City, when men are so lost to piety that they play host to the shedder of a kinsman's blood.

We talked of indifferent things, and watched the juggler who was tossing torches in the Stadium, for twilight was falling. On the bench just below ours, Anytos was talking with some friends. He too had been crowned that day for his work in the resistance, and no one had deserved it better. He had laboured in exile almost as hard as Thrasybulos, and fought well at Piraeus though no longer young. He was a man who had never done anything by halves. Long before, when all the City was in love with Alkibiades, Anytos' passion had been notorious above all the rest, thriving on scorn and even on public insult. He had given a banquet once, it was said, to which the youth had refused to come. But Anytos did not cease his importunities, begging him almost on his knees to come on any terms. Alkibiades went off laughing; when the guests arrived, he was not there; but half-way through he appeared, standing in the doorway. Entreated to come in, he said nothing, but sent his servant to pick up the silver wine-cups on the table, and walked away with them, still without a word. This happened in the days when he was running after Sokrates; who, never asking anything for himself, I daresay had made the youth more contemptuous than before of his groups of slaves.

Nowadays, however, Anytos was being hailed everywhere as a saviour of democracy; and had become the very type and pattern of a democrat. He made it a pride to go about with his right shoulder bared, like a workman, instead of the left; this though he was very well off, and employed in his tannery both freemen and slaves. He was making a name for himself in politics; this evening one saw him interrupted by many greetings, as he conversed with his friends.

'Well,' he was saying, 'we fought for this, and now we see it. Here sit the people, come into their own; the simple folk, met in brotherhood to proclaim their triumph, to honour the old virtues, to share their pride and feel their happiness. A day of scorn for the half-hearted, the triflers and equivocators, and any who did not feel their struggle as his own. Theirs is the future; this is their day.'

His friends applauded. But Plato turned impatiently to Phaedo, saying, 'What does the man mean, with all these booming words? Who are these people? Which persons? Who are the simple –

Phaedo, what about you? Do you feel your happiness, Alexias? . . . Forgive me. You are free to ask me the same.'

I said, 'It's a figure, I suppose.' His voice was always high and clear; I thought, from Anytos' back, that he had overheard.

'A bad one then; for it is a figure of what is not. There is no People here. There are twenty thousand bodies, imprisoning each soul, the centre of a cosmos no other sees. Here they pause, and in each other's company trifle a little time away, before each takes up again the labour of his solitude, by which alone his soul will live or die, his long journey home to God. Who can do good, without knowing what it is? And how will he find it, except in thought, or prayer, or in talk with a few truth-seeking friends, or with the teacher God has sent him? Nor will it come in some catch-phrase that can be shouted in the Agora, meaning the same to all who hear; but by long learning of the self, and of the causes of error, by bridling desire, and breaking it like a hard-mouthed horse, and coming in submission to the truth again, only at last by long labour it will be refined like gold. None of these things will happen in a crowd; but rather bending like a reed before the wind of wrath, or fear, of ignorant prejudice, catching by infection a false conceit of knowledge, or at the best a true opinion, not weighed and sifted out. What is the People, that we should worship it? Shall we worship the beast in man before the god?'

I saw Anytos look round, and almost speak. He was now very clearly angry; but seeing me he held his peace, thinking, no doubt, that I was a proper person to deal with the matter.

'But,' I said, 'men must come together to make laws, and for war, and to honour the gods; they must learn to act for the common good. For such proper purposes, they must feel themselves a Demos, surely, as seamen feel themselves a crew.'

'Yes; but let them beware of the lie in the soul. Men worship such words; and then, feeling themselves a part of what can do no wrong, swell up in hubris, thinking only how much higher they are than another set of men, not how much lower than the gods. What is the Demos but as a wave of the sea, that changes substance a thousand times between shore and shore? What is its archetype? Let us allow that the divine mind may contain, as well as the ideas of justice, holiness, and truth, an idea of Man embodying them all, in every proportion perfectly tuned and true, as Zeus the Creator first conceived us. You may say that a man so made would be nearer to a god; still, there is room in the order of the universe for such a concept. But how can there be an idea of People? Who can conceive it, let alone love? Were you in love with it, Alexias, when you went to Phyle? No. You were in love with liberty, and have logic enough to know that what you love would perish in your sole embrace. May I speak of Lysis, since today we have remembered him? He loved justice, being a true child of Zeus; and wished to share it, as he would have shared any good thing he had. Why should he love the Demos, he who was great enough of heart to love men? Even if Zeus the All-knowing were to put on earth this perfect man we have postulated, would he love the Demos? I think not. He would love knight and commoner, slave and free, Hellene and barbarian, even perhaps the wicked, for they too are the prisons of God-born souls. And the Demos would join with the tyrants, to demand that he be crucified.'

There was a sound of music in the Stadium below, and a troop of lads came in, with helmets and shields, some holding spears in their hands and others torches, to dance for Zeus. Phaedo got up and said, 'Finish the argument between you; but before the race begins, I want a word with Sokrates.'

'Let us all go,' said Plato. But as we were rising, Anytos, who had turned right round this time, said, 'I thought as much!'

'Sir?' said Plato pausing. Anytos said, 'So you are a pupil of Sokrates, are you?' — 'No, sir,' said Plato, lifting his brows and bringing them down hard. 'I am proud to be his friend. Excuse me.' He walked away after Phaedo, who had not heard.

I was following, when Anytos reached out and plucked my mantle. He had a way of grasping, and slapping, and tapping those he conversed with, being an enemy of all aloofness and reserve, which smelt to him of oligarchy. I felt the respect that was due to his record; so out of civility I sat down again.

'I wonder at you, Alexias,' he said, 'you who have been crowned this very day and honoured by the Demos as a friend, that you can listen to this reactionary stuff and keep your temper. I thought you at least would have ceased to be fooled by Sokrates, now you are a man.' – 'Why, Anytos, I have fought as a democrat, here and in Samos, only because Sokrates taught me to think for myself. And Plato forsook the tyrants, though some were his kin, for Sokrates' sake. He sets each man seeking the truth that is in him.'

I could see him waiting for me to cease, to say what he had ready to say, exactly as if I had not spoken. I had felt easy with him, liking the way he treated every man as an equal; but it is strange to speak with someone one's thoughts do not reach. Of a sudden it was as if a great desert surrounded me; I even felt the fear of Pan, driver of herds, as one does in lonely places.

'That man,' said Anytos, 'ever since I remember, has been seen about with rich young idlers, flaunting their privilege of leisure, and frittering away their best years when they might have been mastering an honest trade. Can you deny that Kritias was his pupil? Or perhaps you would rather say his friend? What is more, ever since the democracy was restored, he has mocked at it, and undermined it.'

'I don't think so,' I said. 'Indeed I don't know what you mean, unless that Sokrates thinks it foolish to choose archons and judges by lot. He says no man chooses a doctor by lot, when his son is sick. Would you?'

His face darkened, and I saw I had stirred some thought that vexed him. 'Take my advice,' he said, 'and don't stay till he corrupts your mind, and leaves you without principle or religion or reverence for anything, as he has other young men.' – 'Corrupts me? Before I talked with Sokrates, I did not know what religion meant. It would be late to leave him now, Anytos. Since I was a child he has been as a father to me, and much more.'

I saw a vein swell in his forehead; and when he spoke again, I perceived he had passed beyond logic, and was delivered up entirely to himself. 'More than a father! You have said it. There is the root of the evil. Who can guide a lad better than his own father, I should like to know?' – 'It depends,' I said. 'A pilot might, don't you think, if he were at sea? Or a physician, if he had fever? The City seems to think even I can do it better, when the boy is learning to run.' And I began to speak of those who were competing in the torch-race, thinking to calm him. But he was angrier than before.

'Quibbles!' he said. 'Everlasting quibbling, eating away the decent principles every man's instinct should tell him are true. How does he get this hold over young men? By flattering them, of course; making them think they have a mission in life to be something out of the way, like that head-in-air young fellow who was sneering at the Demos just now; teaching them that to work at a good trade, where they could learn the meaning of true democracy in give-and-take with their mates, is a waste of their precious souls; that unless they can dawdle about with him all day in the colonnades, talking away everything sacred, they will turn to clods – just like their poor fathers, who have only sweated blood that they might live as citizens and not as slaves.' – 'He was brought up to a trade himself, and is proud of it. All the City knows that.' – 'Don't speak to me of Sokrates. If young men don't pay for his lessons, by the Dog, their fathers pay.'

I followed his eyes, knowing beforehand, now, what I should see. His son, Anthemion, a youth of about eighteen, was sitting a little way further on, in a group of tradesmen's sons, who were gazing at him admiringly. From the sound of their laughter, he had just told a very dirty tale; and as I looked, he beckoned back the wine-seller, as I had seen him do already two or three times. Crude as the stuff was, he was drinking it unmixed, as men do who cannot be without it, a youth with pale hair and brows, a flushed quick-moving face, and desperate eyes.

'He is taking more than is good for him,' I said. 'All his friends are sorry for it. In the days when he was coming to Sokrates, I never saw him drink at all. I don't think he is happy. Not, I am sure, from thinking himself too good to work in your tanyard, but perhaps because it keeps him from using something in himself, as it might be with a bird, if you caged it when its wings were growing.' – 'Twaddle!' he said. 'What does he think he is? He will serve his apprenticeship like anyone else. I fought for equality between man and man. No one shall say of me that I brought up my son to be better than his fellow citizens.'

'Must we forsake the love of excellence, then, till every citizen feels it alike? I did not fight, Anytos, to be crowned where I have not run; but for a City where I can know who my equals really are, and my betters, to do them honour; where a man's daily life is his own business; and where no one will force a lie on me because it is expedient, or some other man's will.'

The words seemed, as I spoke, to be my own thoughts that I owed to no one, only to some memory in my soul; but when I looked beyond the Stadium, to where they were kindling the lights on the High City in the falling dark, I saw the lamps of Samos shine through a doorway, and the wine-cup standing on the table of scoured wood. Then the pain of loss leaped out on me, like a knife in the night when one has been on one's guard all day. The world grew hollow, a place of shadows; yet none would hold out the cup of Lethe to let me drink.

'No,' I thought, 'I would not drink it. For here he lives in the thing we made: the boys down there, dancing for Zeus; people watching in freedom, their thoughts upon their faces; this silly old man speaking his mind, such as it is, with none to threaten him; and Sokrates saying among his friends, "We shall either find what we are seeking, or free ourselves from the persuasion that we know what we do not know."'

I looked down the benches, and saw him in conversation with the wine-seller, from whom Chairophon was buying a round. The flambeaux had been kindled ready for the race, showing me his old Silenos mask, and Plato and Phaedo laughing. I touched the ring on my finger, saying within me, 'Sleep quietly, Lysis. All is well.'

The voice of Anytos, some while unheeded, came back into my ear. 'He taught you a new religion, too, you say. I can believe it. Even the holy Olympians are not good enough for him. He must have his own deity to give him oracles, and sets it above the gods of the City. He is impious; he is anti-democratic; in a word, he is un-Athenian. I am not the only one who has had enough of it. Only influence in high places has kept him from getting his deserts long since. But this is a democracy.'

I turned to look at him, and saw his eyes. Then I knew what it was in his voice that had caught my ear. It was the feel of power. A cold wind blew up the stream of the Ilissos, and swept along the

Stadium. It flattened the flame of the torches, and the black night leaned down.

Someone reached from above and touched my shoulder. 'Aren't you coming, Alexias? Your boys are looking for you. It is getting near starting-time; the dance is over already, and they are going to sing the hymn.'

As he spoke, the choregos raised his wand, and the young boys' chorus rose into the fading sky, like a flight of bright birds, invoking Zeus, the King, the All-Knowing, giver of wisdom, and of justice between man and man. I rose to my feet, the voice of Anytos running on beside me; and before me in the torchlight Sokrates talking to Phaedo, with the cup in his hand.

This book I found among the papers of my father Myron, which came to me at his death. It must be, as I suppose, the work of my grandfather Alexias, who died suddenly in the hunting-field, I being then a young child, and he about fifty-five years old. I have bound it up as it was, being able to find no more of it. Whether my grandfather had finished the book, I do not know.

ALEXIAS, son of Myron, Phylarch of the Athenian horse to the divine Alexander, King of Macedon, Leader Supreme of all the Hellenes.

Also by Mary Renault in Arrow:
The Alexander Trilogy

Fire From Heaven

The boy Alexander, and his rise to power

At twenty, when his reign began, Alexander The Great was already a seasoned soldier and a complex, passionate man, but although resolute, fearless and inheriting a striking beauty, he still needed much to make him The Great. He must survive the dark furies of his Dionysiac mother, who kept him uncertain even of his own paternity; respect his father's talent for war and kingcraft, though sickened by his sexual grossness; and come to terms with his heritage from both.

The Persian Boy

Alexander The Great through
the eyes of his lover and servant

The Persian Boy tells the story of the last seven years of Alexander's life through the eyes of his lover, Bagoas. Abducted and gelded as a boy, Bagoas found freedom with Alexander and was taken into Alexander's household. The beautiful young eunuch becomes the great general's lover and their relationship sustains Alexander as he survives assassination plots, the demands of two foreign wives, a mutinous army, and his own ferocious temper.

Funeral Games

The death of Alexander The Great

As *Funeral Games* opens, Alexander The Great lies dying. Around his body gather the generals, the provincial satraps and the royal wives, already competing for the prizes of power and land. Only Bagoas, the Persian boy mourning in the shadows, wants nothing. Tracing the fifteen years following Alexander's death, *Funeral Games* sees his mighty empire disintegrate, and brings Mary Renault's Alexander trilogy to a dramatic close.

arrow books

The King Must Die

Mary Renault

Bringing Greek mythology vividly to life, *The King Must Die* and its sequel, *The Bull from the Sea*, tell the amazing adventures of Theseus, famous for slaying the Minotaur, defeating the Amazons and rescuing Persephone from the Underworld.

Theseus, the boy-king of Eleuisis, is ritually preordained to die after one year of marriage to the sacred Queen, but he defies the Gods' decree and claims his inheritance – the throne of Athens. His friends are the young men and maidens, slaves of the Gods, chosen for death in the Bull Dance. His fabled enemy is the monstrous, half-man, half-bull Minotaur, devourer of sacrificial human flesh.

In her classic re-creation of a myth so powerful that its impact has survived down the centuries, Mary Renault has brought to life the world of ancient Greece. For here is the true Atlantis legend, with its culmination in the terrible, fateful destruction of the great Labyrinth, the palace of the house of Minos.

arrow books

The Bull from the Sea

Mary Renault

This second book in the story of the legendary hero begins with Theseus' triumphant return from Crete after slaying the Minotaur. Having freed the city of Athens from the onerous tribute demanded by the ruler of Knossos – the sacrifice of noble youths and maidens to the appetite of the Labyrinth's monster – Theseus has returned home to find his father dead and himself the new king. But his adventures have only just begun: he still must confront the Amazons, capture their queen, Hippolyta, and face the tragic results of Phaedra's jealous rage.

Piecing together the fragments of myth and using her deep understanding of the cultures reflected in these legends, Mary Renault has constructed an enthralling narrative of a time when heroes battled monsters and gods strode the earth.

'Takes the raw material of myth and makes it credible . . . I am spellbound by Miss Renault's art.' – *The Observer*

arrow books